We're flying now, and it's a wonder to me that we touch the ground at all, because clearly we don't need to. We are at the spread—on and past, to the water, and I'm letting him now, trusting him, and we're flying. Let me, he says, and I say, Yes, because how can I not . . .

RIDING LESSONS

"Romance and horses go hand-in-hand. . . .
An intriguing and courageous heroine—
and a great horse."

Michael Korda, *New York Times*
bestselling author of *Horse People*

"Sara Gruen writes with passionate precision about horses and their humans and the healing power of love. Annemarie Zimmer is the best kind of character—just like ourselves, with a lot to learn and even more to give."

Maryanne Stahl, author of *Forgive the Moon*
and *The Opposite Shore*

By Sara Gruen

Water for Elephants
Flying Changes
Riding Lessons

SARA GRUEN

RIDING LESSONS

HARPER

An Imprint of HarperCollins*Publishers*

HARPER

An Imprint of Harper Collins*Publishers*
10 East 53rd Street
New York, New York 10022-5299

ISBN 978-0-06-058027-8

First Harper trade paperback printing: April 2007
First Harper paperback printing: April 2004

Printed in the United States of America

Visit Harper paperbacks on the World Wide Web at
www.harpercollins.com

20 19 18 17 16 15 14 13 12 11

Acknowledgments

Writing a novel is an arduous process, and during it I became indebted to a number of people:

To my critique partner and friend, Kristy Kiernan, who was there from conception to birth.

To Erin Narey and Lori Coale for their time, input, and encouragement.

To my mother, Kathryn Puffett, both for valuable criticism and for believing I could do this.

To Brian Porter, Robert Farmer (you old goat, you), and Carolyn Flasch, all of whom helped shape the book.

To Michael S. Beeson, M.D., of Summa Health System in Akron, for providing information about spinal cord injury.

To Susan Laidlaw, a student of 1996 Olympic Dressage Team Bronze Medalist Michelle Gibson and a fine rider in her own right, for answering my questions about the eventing world.

To my agent, Emma Sweeney, for her belief in me.

And most importantly, to my husband, Bob, without whom this simply would not have happened.

Horse • pow • er ('hôrs-pau (-&)r)

1. (*Noun*) A standard measure of power defined as the energy required to lift 33,000 pounds at the rate of one foot per minute, or 55 pounds at the rate of ten feet per second.

2. (*Informal*) The extraordinary capacity of a horse to elevate the human spirit.

Chapter 1

"Are you ready?" says Roger as he gives me a leg up, and I laugh, because I've never been so ready in all my life.

And Harry is, too, with his red neck flexed and his ears swiveling like antennae, but never together—if one is forward the other is back, although sometimes they land impossibly out to the side, like a lop-eared goat's. He stamps and snorts as I lower myself into the saddle and gather the reins, and I forgive him, this time, for not standing still while I mount because while it's terrible manners there are extenuating circumstances and I, too, cannot be still. I run the reins across the black gloves that cover my wet palms and icy fingers and look back at my father, whose face is lined and stern, and then at Roger, who smiles up at me with his face a perfect composite of tension, pride, and joy.

He lays a hand on my booted calf and says, "Give 'em hell, babe," and I laugh again, because I have every intention of doing just that.

And then Marjory is leading us to the gate—

actually holding the reins, as though I can be trusted to take fences of almost five feet but not to steer Harry into the arena.

"Watch your pace going into the combination," she says, "and don't let him rush you. Collect him sharply coming around the turn after the water jump, and if you get past the oxer and you're still clear, hold him back and take it easy because you've already got it even if you take a time fault."

I nod and look across the arena at the judges because I know that already. We can take eight faults and still tie for first, and if we get none or four we've done it, and nobody else has a hope. Marjory is still talking and I nod impatiently and just want to start because Harry and I are going to explode with the excitement of it all, and we're ready, we're ready, oh, we're ready. But I know it's not Marjory who gets to decide so I try to remember to breathe and ignore her and suddenly it's easy, as though I'm in a wind tunnel and all of everything beyond Harry and me is on the outside.

Then I get the signal and I think that it's time to go—think it, that's all—and Harry goes, walking forward so deep on the bit his nose is pressed to his chest, and as we step into the arena I can see our shadow on the ground and his tail on end like a flag. The man on the PA introduces us—Annemarie Zimmer on Highland Harry, with a commanding lead and yadda yadda yadda—but no one's paying attention because they're staring at Harry. No gasps or murmurs this time, not on day three, but then someone goes and wrecks it because I hear some bastard man say, "Now there goes a horse of a different color," and I know from that one remark that he's missed days one and two and I hate him because I know he feels clever for the remark. But I suppose I'd say it too, since you don't see many or any striped horses out there, and before Harry I never knew such a thing existed, but here he is, and there's no denying that. Not today. Not here.

I hear the whistle and press my calves against him and we're off. Harry shoots forward like a coiled spring, so compressed his haunches feel like they're right under me.

I tighten my fingers, No, no, no Harry, not yet, I'll let you, but not yet, and his ears prick forward, together this time, and he says, All right, and gives me a collected canter that feels like a rocking horse, so high on the up and so low on the down. And we rock around the corner and approach the first jump and he asks me, Now? And I say, No, and he says, Now? And I say No, and then a stride later I can tell he's about to ask again, but before he can I say Yes, and he's off and I don't have to do anything else—won't have to until we're over and on the other side, and then I'll just have to ask him again, and he'll do it because he loves me and we're one.

There's the *flap-flap-flap* of leather on leather, the heavy incalzando of hoofbeats, *da-da-DA*, *da-da-DA*, *da-da-DA*, and then a massive push, a hundred thousand compressed pounds exploding forth before—

Silence. As we arc over the fence, the only parts of me in contact with anything are my calves and hands and the balls of my feet although it looks like I'm lying on him, so forward am I and curved around his neck with my face alongside where his mane would be if it weren't braided into a row of nubby topknots. And then *bang*! We've landed, and as soon as his front hooves make contact with the ground I'm back in the saddle and we're headed toward the brick wall and it's perfect. I can tell we're going to be clear because that's just the way it is.

We're flying now, and it's a wonder to me that we touch the ground at all because clearly we don't need to over one, two, three more fences. I lose remembrance of the order of it but don't need to remember because I feel it, looked at it until it became a part of my being, and here we are at the spread now, where White Night and Frito Misto both refused, but not Harry—on and past, to the water, and I'm letting him now, trusting him, and we're flying. I bring him in on the turn, just like Marjory said, and now we're headed for the double oxer, only the combination left between us and the finish, and if we clear just one more, the ribbon is in the bag and we're off to the Rolex-Kentucky, and who knows, maybe the Olympics, because why not? Because anything and everything is possible.

Let me, he says, and I say Yes, because how can I not, and I feel the energy gather in his haunches and then *pow*! He shoots us off the ground and the crest of his neck rises toward me and I thrust my hands forward to keep the reins light and it's beautiful. I catch a glimpse of a few faces over the boards in the spectator stands and I know they're rooting for us, holding their breath—even Dan, who is out there although he's still mad about Roger—and the moment I feel Harry's hind hocks clear the top I know we've done it. We've taken first place, and although we're still airborne I'm rejoicing because we've done it, and it can't be taken away.

His front hooves come down and his neck stretches out, and I allow my fingers to graze his coat in a secret caress as I move my hands back in anticipation of his mouth returning toward me. But it doesn't. Something's not right, although I can't process this because the ground is coming at me as though his legs were sinking right through it. I am confused, because we cleared the jump and I was paying attention to how his legs came down and I'm irked, not scared, and then I'm not feeling anything, because there's an explosion as the ground smashes into me. And then blackness.

The blackness is broken by occasional windows of light and gyrating color, snapping open like the shutter of a syncopated camera. Voices are swirling Oh my God, oh my God, can you hear me, don't try to move her, let us past. Then blackness again before another white light and the rhythmic *thud-thud-thud-thud* of helicopter blades, and someone saying, "Annemarie can you hear me? Stay with me Annemarie. Annemarie, stay with me," and I really wish she'd stop because all I want to do is sink into the blackness. And then I do and it feels good and I wonder if Harry is there.

Chapter 2

Harry was gone, although I didn't find out for almost three weeks. When we came down over the double oxer, Harry's long pastern—the largest of the three bones between his hoof and his foreleg—shattered into nine pieces. His scapula, sternum, and pelvis were broken as well, but it was the pastern that clinched it. There was nothing to be done with those nine bits of bone, so they shot him where he lay.

I was even more broken than Harry, but they didn't shoot me. I was airlifted to the Sonoma Valley Trauma Center, where it was discovered that my neck was broken. Also my collarbone, left arm, eight ribs, nose, and jaw; but it was the neck that really counted.

Because of large doses of methylprednisolone, I floated in and out of euphoria for two weeks, blissfully unaware of the fact that I could no longer move any part of my body. When I finally fought my way to the surface, I was assaulted with questions: What's your name? Where do you live? Can you tell me what year it is? And I was tired—so very tired—

and wondered why people were bothering me with questions that seemed so obvious, and also why the answers remained inexplicably beyond my grasp.

Can you wiggle your toes, can you squeeze my hand, can you feel this, they continued, and of course, I could not. My body felt like a sack of sand with a head attached—I had lost all knowledge of my limbs, that sense of knowing where your pieces are even when you're not moving them. The awareness of pressure from clothes, a whoosh of air across bared skin, a sudden reminder from your finger that it's still attached. All that was gone. There was nothing, there was deadness. It was as if someone had lopped my head off and put it on a plate, and somehow attached the necessary mechanics to keep it alive. And of course, once I became aware of this, I wished they hadn't bothered.

Some time later, through the haze of morphine that was necessary because my face had just been reconstructed, I heard my father speaking with a doctor.

"Will she ever ride again?" he asked.

His voice was muffled, and I had to strain to hear above the equipment that surrounded me: the hiss and release of the ventilator, the machine that chirped in time with my heart, the blood-pressure cuff that wheezed to life at regular intervals.

I think they were behind a curtain, but they could have been at my feet. I don't know, because my head was screwed into a halo, and I couldn't turn to look. The doctor took so long to respond I was afraid I'd missed his answer, but there wasn't a thing I could do to make it easier for his voice to reach me—I couldn't cup a hand behind my ear, I couldn't watch his lips. I couldn't even hold my breath to make it quieter.

When he finally spoke, his words were drawn out and raspy. "Well, it would be premature to make a projection on how much function she's likely to regain," he said. "Our first goal is to get her breathing on her own."

Pappa mumbled something desperate, and then the blood-pressure cuff began to inflate. Over its steady inhalation, the phrases "world-class athlete," "Grand Prix rider," and "Olympic contender" floated around like birds; Pappa, agitated, speaking as though he was sure the doctor was holding back. Negotiating, wheedling, and bullying, as though the doctor would do more if he could only be made to understand how important it was that I get back on a horse.

Again, a pause, and the cuff began its jerky deflation. More fragments of conversation: "spinal shock," "vibratory sense," and "central cord syndrome." And then the cuff fell silent and against the relative quiet of the respirator, I heard my injury explained to my father: how my neck had been broken at the C2 and C3 vertebrae, which usually resulted in catastrophic injury; how extremely fortunate it was that everyone had followed the correct protocol at the scene and immobilized my spine; that the steroid injection I'd been given aboard the LifeFlight would also work in my favor; and finally, that it was possible—and there were no guarantees here, it was important to remember that—but it was possible that when the swelling of the soft tissues went down, I might recover some movement.

As I slipped back into my opium dreams, those words echoed endlessly through my head, only unlike an echo, they refused to fade: *might recover some movement, might recover some movement, might recover some movement.*

If I could have willed the ventilator plug out of the wall, I would have done it.

• • •

Flash forward now. Skip over the nine weeks in ICU and the hell that was mine when I heard that Harry was dead. Past the tortured nights I spent trapped inside my lump of a body and imagining his rotting out there somewhere until someone, mercifully, told me that Pappa had had him cremated. Past the mousy intern with a lazy eye, that incredible individual who first thought to bang a tuning fork against her knee and then press it, humming, against the soles of my feet; past the joy and trepidation I felt when the reverberations of that note—the A below middle C—made it to my brain, indicating that maybe all was not lost. Past the halo traction and titanium skull screws that same intern drilled into my head so that sixteen pounds of weight could be strung from a series of pulleys, stretching my neck and allowing the vertebrae to heal. Past the rehabilitation, the surgeries, the body braces, the parallel bars, the crutches; past the monumental effort and incredible dedication from a retinue of professionals to where I emerged on the other side, a mere fifteen months later, whole and miraculously uncompromised except for an almost imperceptible decrease in sensation at the very tips of my fingers. And finally, past that glorious day the following July when I walked unassisted down the aisle at my wedding, hips swaying under my beaded gown, swishing satin and grace, and breathless with the victory of it all.

I never rode again, although in the end there was nothing physically wrong with me that would have prevented it. My parents have always believed that I never rode again because I married Roger, but they've got it ass-backward. I married Roger so I could move to Minnesota and no one would ever ask me to get on another horse, because no one seemed to understand that it would be exactly that. Another horse.

I tend to think about my accident in terms of metaphors, partly because I think too much and partly because when I finally went to college, I studied English literature. I usually compare it to the first domino to fall, one moment standing solid like a punctuation mark, and then the next setting off a chain of events so inevitable, so unstoppable, that all you can do is stand back and watch.

It's not until twenty years later that the final three fall.

One. Two. Three.

Chapter 3

One.

It's an ordinary afternoon, brutally so, and I'm editing a help file, staring at my screen as though it will yield inspiration. The phone rings, and I reach for it without removing my gaze from the liquid crystal screen.

"Annemarie Aldrich," I say.

"It's me," says Roger. "I was wondering when you'll be home tonight."

"Mmmm. Probably later," I say, my mind still on the file in front of me. There's something about the way it's organized, something that wants changing.

"Do you know what time?"

"Hmmm?" I say. I've almost got it, I'm almost there: it's the first and third paragraphs, they're—

"What time will you be home?"

My concentration is broken and my vision of the topic recedes. I lean back in my chair, aware once again of the world around me.

Beyond my screen, outside the door of my office, people whiz past. There are telephones ringing, keyboards clattering, the sounds of conversation, a stifled guffaw.

"Not sure," I say.

"I'd like to see you," he says.

"Uh, yeah, me too," I say, leaning forward again. An incoming email has caught my attention. "Yeah, all right. I'll try to be home at a decent hour."

"I'll wait up," he says.

"Uh-huh," I say, scanning the message. Damn. The lead writer for InteroFlo wants to submit material for edit this week, is trying to present it as something I've agreed to. Absolutely not, I'm afraid. Not with the SnapShot release. I prop the phone between my ear and shoulder and begin typing a response.

"It sounds like you're busy," says Roger.

"I am, darling. You know how it is around release."

"Well, I guess I'll see you later then."

"Right, Love," I say, making an effort to sound more animated now that it's clear he's releasing me. "Bye."

I hang up.

"Annemarie?"

Another interruption. This time it's my supervisor, whose head and neck are curled around my doorframe.

"Oh, Evelyn," I say. "I'm glad you stopped by. I need you to run interference with Dennis. He just sent a note saying he was going to hand off the InteroFlo files this week. He can't. They're not on the schedule, and I'm eyeball-deep in SnapShot."

Evelyn nods. "I'll speak to him."

"Because that's exactly why I put the spreadsheet on the Intranet, and everybody else has been keeping it up to date, so I'm afraid their projects get priority, regardless of size—"

"Uh-huh," says Evelyn, nodding. She steps inside my office and stands looking at her feet.

"—and I simply can't dredge up a contractor that quickly, or at least not someone familiar with our style guide. I probably won't be able to fit him in for another three weeks, and even then, he's got to get his stuff on the schedule or it's going to fill up again. I cannot—"

"I'll speak to him," says Evelyn, cutting me off. "Look, Annemarie, there's something I need to talk to you about. Do you think you could stop by my office in about five minutes?"

I pause. I'm busy. But she is my boss. "Sure, yeah. I'll be right over," I say.

When I get there, it's immediately apparent that something is going on. Evelyn is standing by her desk. Someone in a suit is sitting at her table.

"What's up?" I ask, eyeing them warily.

"Hi, Annemarie," says Evelyn, coming up behind me and closing the door. "Thanks for being so prompt. Please have a seat."

She reaches behind her and takes a box of tissue from her desk. When I sit down, she places it on the table in front of me.

"What's going on?"

She sits and looks me straight in the eye. "I'm sure you're aware that the company hasn't made its numbers over the last two quarters—"

Good God. I'm being fired.

"—and we were hoping things would get better, but upper management has told us that we need to cut our staff, and I'm really sorry, but you're one of the ones I won't be able to keep."

"What?" I say, although I heard perfectly well. It's more of a statement. I feel my lip curl. If she was expecting tears, she's going to be sorely disappointed.

"This is not a reflection on your performance. Believe me, I'm well aware that your contributions have added greatly to the quality of our documentation—"

She's bloody right they have. Nineteen products, twenty-two writers, and my department—me and three editors. Because of us—*me,* really—it all got edited, top to bottom. Substantively, copyedited, and proofed. I personally took home all the blues.

"Unfortunately, in software, documentation almost never gets the emphasis it deserves . . ."

And blah blah blah. My record will reflect that I was laid off, not fired. I can count on her for a reference, of course. No rush to get out of the building, but here's your crate. Omar will help you get everything to your car, or you can have computing services pack your office instead. Extension of my benefits to carry me over, severance pay based on length of time with the company, counseling should I need it, and all sorts of other crap that I don't hear because I've stopped listening.

• • •

Two.

When I open the front door of our house, Eva is in the foyer. She jumps a little when she sees me, perhaps because she has even more than the usual amount of midriff exposed.

"Oh, hi Mom," she says. She recovers her cool and grabs a jacket from a hook. "You're home early."

I set my purse on the floor and close the door. "Change of plans. Where are you off to?"

"Lacey's."

Lacey? What in God's name were her parents thinking?

"Will you be home for dinner?" I say, stepping out of my Amalfi loafers. I lift them to the shoe tray one at a time, dangling them on extended toes.

"Nope. I'm spending the night," says Eva. She slips past me, her pink backpack slung over a shoulder. I smell cigarette smoke, but let it go. Fifteen has been a tough year, and I have to choose my battles. Our most recent, for which she still has to forgive me, involved a cobalt blue tongue stud that I made her remove. I was absolutely firm—no more riding until it was gone. She called it blackmail, but at least it disappeared.

"Bye then," I say, as the door starts to close.

The door opens again. "Yup, bye Mom," Eva calls through the crack.

When I reach the kitchen, I find a sealed manila envelope on the counter. I have a bad feeling the second I lay eyes on it.

It's a report card. I scan it top to bottom, and then flip it over with an increasing sense of disbelief. I don't know who I'm angrier with—Eva, or the school. Her attendance has been perfectly abysmal, and as a result she's flunking spectacularly.

I pick the envelope up again, and then realize there's something else at the bottom of it. I turn it upside down and shake. A smaller, white envelope falls to the floor.

Inside is a personal note from the principal, signed in a crabbed, back-slanted hand. Dr. Harold Stoddard, Ph.D., wishes to inform me that if Eva is absent once more without explanation, she'll be permanently expelled. At the bottom is a place for me to sign.

I hold it, blinking stupidly for lack of a better response.

I'm so upset I'm shaking. Why in God's name didn't they tell me sooner, when I could still have done something? At this point, even if I manage to keep her from getting expelled, the best I can hope for is that she'll come away with a third of her credits.

I stuff the letter back into the envelope, crumpling it in angry haste. I have no intention of signing it. It's like those infuriating error messages you get right before your computer crashes: Such-and-such has encountered a fatal error—sorry, no way to save your work, be a good girl now and click OK. Okay? No, it's bloody well not okay.

I consider calling Roger at the office, but decide to wait until he gets home. Then we can play rock-paper-scissors to see who gets to call Eva and tell her to get her can home because she's been busted.

I pour a glass of wine and go soak in the bath. I'm at loose ends, and I hate it. The house is clean, and for obvious reasons I have no work to do. I don't have a newspaper, so I can't even look for a new job until tomorrow.

By the time Roger gets home, I'm sitting with my feet curled under me in the living room. I'm trying to make a dent in a year's worth of unread *New Yorker*s, and have graduated to coffee after two rather generous glasses of gewürztraminer.

"God, am I glad to see you," I say when he comes through from the foyer. And I am. Our paths haven't crossed much recently, and I'm looking forward to a bit of company and support. "Get yourself a drink. You're going to need it."

A moment later, he sits beside me on the couch, drinkless, still wearing his jacket.

Something's wrong. Never mind the continued presence of the jacket or the lack of drink, he never sits beside me. He always sits opposite. I look up from my *New Yorker*, seized with foreboding. Somebody has died. I can tell.

He takes my right hand between both of his. They're cold and clammy. I resist the urge to remove my hand and wipe it on my thigh because he's obviously distraught.

"Annemarie . . ." he says. His voice is strangled, as though his tongue were twisted at the back of his throat.

Oh God, it's true then. Who could it be? I don't remember anyone being sick. Maybe it was an accident?

"What is it? What's wrong?" I ask.

He looks down at our joined hands and then back at my face.

"I don't know how to tell you this."

"Tell me what?"

His mouth moves slightly, but nothing comes out.

"For God's sake, Roger spit it out!" I say, setting the *New Yorker* down and adding my left hand to our tangled mess of fingers.

He looks down yet again, and once more I'm left staring at his bald spot. The next time he lifts his face, it's full of painful resolve.

"I'm leaving."

My eyes narrow. "What do you mean, leaving?"

"I'm going to live with Sonja."

I blink at him. The words are out there, swirling around my head, but my ears seem to have repelled their entry. Sort of. I yank my hands away.

"I'm so sorry," he continues. He pulls his hands back into his lap, and then looks down at them, as though surprised to find them there. "I never meant to hurt you. Neither one of us expected this to happen."

"Sonja?" I say. "The intern?"

He nods.

I stare, wide-eyed. Now he's speaking again, droning on about how sorry he is and all sorts of other nonsense that's meant to temper my reaction, but I've gone off on a parallel track. My mind races back to the Christmas party—the only time I've ever laid eyes on Sonja—to her hair, glossy and chestnut; and inevitably to her body, both voluptuous and thin, and encased in a sheath of red sequins.

I interrupt his monologue. "She can't be more than—what, twenty-eight?"

"She's twenty-three."

I continue to stare, aware that my jaw has dropped.

"It's not like that," he says, reading my face. "She's been through a lot in her life. She's very mature."

After everything we've been through—my God, we raised a child together, we practically raised each other—and now he's going to leave me for a woman who's fifteen years my junior? Just eight years older than our daughter?

At first it doesn't compute, and then when it does, I am flooded with anger. And while the rage is gathering, there's a strange split, a part of me that sidles off and starts to analyze, and what it finds is an absurd irony in the fact that *he's* rejecting *me*. After all the years I've put up with his faults, the crap, the almost-but-not-quite-there-edness that's been the very cornerstone of our relationship, and *he's* rejecting *me*?

I suddenly realize I haven't reacted. He waits, staring at me with disingenuous concern. He is leaning forward now, his forehead crinkled, his eyes awash with regret. His stupid, stupid tie rests in his lap. I'd like to strangle him with it.

"Get out," I say.

"Annemarie, please—" His voice is quiet and gentle. He's working hard to project the appropriate level of regret. Something in me snaps.

"Get out! Get out! Out! Out! Out! Out!" I shriek.

Then I throw the African violet at his head. Then the coaster. Then a *New Yorker*, and then another, and then another, and when I run out of magazines, I throw a CD, and my address book, and by the time I reach for my half-filled cup of coffee he's ducking out of the room. It hits the wall with a gratifying crash and explosion of coffee but somehow, disappointingly, remains intact.

• • •

Fifteen minutes later, he comes down with a large suitcase. I'm sitting at the kitchen table with my arms crossed. I'm on the very edge of the chair with my legs extended, almost as if I don't bend in the middle.

I refuse to look at him, although he positions himself directly in front of me. I can't help noticing that he's packed the green suitcase with the broken handle. He's leaving me the good one.

"I'll let you know where I'm staying."

He waits for me to respond. I wish that he hadn't placed himself so that I'm staring at his crotch, but to turn my head would be to respond, so I look through him, past him, and let the tan of his chinos blur until they mean no more to me than the insides of my eyelids. After a few minutes of silence, the tan slips away and I am once again looking at the William Morris willow boughs that grace my kitchen walls.

I hear his footsteps retreat through the house, then the front door squeaking on its hinges, and finally, the quiet click of the latch. Quiet, because he's taking pains to close the door gently, is keeping the doorknob turned as far as it will go until the door is completely closed. He leaves with a whimper, not a bang. In the course of a single day, my family has been launched into outer space.

• • •

Three.

Two weeks later, when it occurs to me that he really isn't going to return, I call my mother. She listens, but doesn't say much. She doesn't seem as upset as I was expecting her to be, which surprises me, because she and my father are Roman Catholics. And then I find out why.

She has been meaning to call me, she says. There's something she has to tell me, she says, only she didn't know how.

"What is it?" I ask, and she doesn't answer.

"Mutti, you're scaring me. What's going on?" I say.

There's another silence, frightening and expansive. Then she speaks.

"Your father has ALS."

• • •

Amyotrophic lateral sclerosis. Lou Gehrig's disease. Motor neuron disease. By whatever name, it robs people of the ability to move, speak, swallow, and eventually breathe, while—in the ultimate act of cruelty—leaving their mental capacity intact. A disease that would terrify anyone, but which holds special terror for me, because I know what it is to be a brain trapped in an unresponsive body.

I didn't absorb much from that first conversation with Mutti, other than that he'd been diagnosed a few months earlier. He'd had symptoms for some time—strange tics and muscle twitches, and then weakness in the legs, progressing to stumbling. It was only when his arms also became affected that they'd put him through a battery of additional tests and handed down the diagnosis.

The idea of such a thing happening to my father—a man who had spent his entire life in physical pursuits—was beyond horrifying, and for a while it displaced, or at least equaled, the headspace required by Roger's betrayal. In the end, though, it simply augmented it, sliding in and taking up residence beside it.

• • •

Ten days later, Eva and I are having a rare mother-daughter moment. We're on good terms again, now that her grounding over the principal's note has expired.

She stands at the kitchen table, slicing a tomato for our salad while I stir the gazpacho. She is bent slightly at the waist, and her blonde hair—straightened through force of will, a paddle brush, and 1600 watts of hot air—obscures her face.

"Is your uniform dirty? Do you need me to do laundry tonight?" I ask, noticing that she's not wearing it.

"No," she says. "I don't need it anymore."

"What do you mean?"

"I don't need it. I'm not going to school anymore."

I freeze with my hand on the spoon, mid-stir.

"What?"

She says nothing, simply picks up another tomato and starts slicing.

"What did you say?"

"I'm not going anymore. I don't like it."

I tap the spoon on the edge of the pot with deadly precision—one, two, three times—and then set it on the counter.

"Over my dead body," I say, turning to face her.

"It's too late," she says, pushing the tomato's core aside with the blade of the knife. "They caught me skipping and they wouldn't let me back in even if I wanted them to. Which I don't."

I glance quickly at the telephone. The red message light is blinking. I look back at Eva, furious.

She tries to play it cool, but when the silence grows conspicuous, she stops slicing and looks up. When she sees my face, she drops the knife, poised for flight.

Both of us bolt for the door. I get there first, bracing my hands on either side of the doorway.

"Oh no you don't! Not a chance, missy. You're not going anywhere."

"As if you could stop me," she says, throwing a shoulder between me and the doorway. We scuffle for a bit, with me trying to keep her from passing, and with Eva launching herself at me like a linebacker. It's pointless. She's as big as me now, and certainly heavier.

I step back and she barrels past me and up the stairs. A couple of minutes later, she comes down again, her pink vinyl backpack stuffed with clothes. She flounces through the house and out the door without ever looking back.

If I'm lucky, she will go to the house of a friend who lives at home, although I know for a fact that she will tell the parents I kicked her out. If I'm unlucky, she will go to a grotty little apartment in the wrong part of town and do God knows what with a bunch of teenagers who live on their own.

I look down at Harriet, my dachshund, who is visibly upset. Harriet likes her people happy, Harriet likes harmony. Harriet has had a hard month.

I tuck her under my arm and carry her upstairs, telling her that everything is all right. But it rings hollow in my ears, because I'm not stupid, and neither is Harriet. Absolutely nothing is all right. Not a goddamned thing.

At the top of the stairs, I stop and look down. I can't see much of the main floor—a length of dark hardwood, some white fringe at the edge of a blood-red Bokhara, Harriet's Geoffrey Beene basket beside the antique hall chair—but I'm struck by how strange and impersonal it all looks. I don't give a damn about any of it, not a stick, despite the fact that until a month ago, I'd have ranked the house among my top accomplishments.

I put Harriet on the floor and retreat to my room. It's the same here: the antique rocker in front of the fireplace, the mulberry eiderdown, the rows of antique books that line the shelves. The framed pictures; the candles on the long dresser, dusty from disuse; the skylight above the bed—all of it carefully chosen, and none of it means anything.

Harriet sits on the carpet in front of the fireplace. She's clearly worried. I lean over and scratch her head, muttering placating noises. Slightly mollified, she lies down, resting her head on her front legs. Her eyes, with their funny worried brows, continue to follow me.

I close the curtains and turn on the lights, one by one by one—ceiling light, floor light, both reading lamps, even the can lights aimed at the winter scene above the mantel. Then I stand in front of the full-length mirror and strip.

It feels for all the world like I'm looking at a stranger. How can someone be so unfamiliar with her own person? When was the last time I took stock of myself, or anything else?

Certainly, what I see bears little resemblance to that eighteen-year-old Olympic contender from so long ago. What I see is a woman on the cusp of middle age with a jagged hysterectomy scar. Or is that a caesarian scar? Both, I guess. A hysterarian, a caeserectomy. I finger it lightly, tracing its path up my abdomen. Then I look at my face; a good face, although it tends to sternness if I'm not careful. Freckled, which goes a long way toward preserving youth. I lean toward the mirror, fingering the lines that I know are there. They're hard to see, even with all the lights on, but I know the location of every one.

There are the scars from my reconstructive surgeries, carefully hidden in the creases of my nostrils, behind my ears, and just past my hairline. And then there are the lines I've earned the usual way: the fine ones that run beside my mouth; the single line, tiny but present, that separates my eyes. It's the face of a woman past youth although not yet middle-aged; the face of a woman who should have arrived at where she wants to be.

But it's not. It's the face of a woman with no job and no husband and a house that feels like anything but a home. All I have left is my daughter, and if I don't do something soon, I have the feeling I'm going to lose her, too.

Chapter 4

Two weeks later, we're on a plane to New Hampshire. Poor Harriet has been banished to the cargo hold beneath us because pets are no longer allowed in the cabin, no exceptions. The girl at the check-in desk assured me that it is heated and pressurized, but still, I worry about my cowardly dog down there in her crate.

There is no question about how Eva feels. She slouches in the window seat, scowling like a singed cat. She has earphones on, the better to avoid conversation with me, and her nose buried in a *Cosmopolitan*. I hate that she reads those things—they're practically pornographic and I hope to God that she has no practical use for the advice she reads therein, but I'm simply too tired to argue.

My mother meets us at the airport. She's late, so by the time we see her, we're moving toward the exit with our bags piled high on a cart. I have two others slung over my shoulders, as well as my laptop and purse, and am leading Harriet on a leash. I'm probably not supposed to let her out of her crate until we leave the airport, but I don't care. What are they going to do? Make me leave?

Eva carries nothing but her backpack and magazine—didn't offer and pretended she didn't hear me when I asked her to help. That's the way my mother finds us, with me leading the dog and struggling to keep the straps of four bags over my sloping shoulders. I'm also trying not to run over anyone with the cart, which is impossible to steer because all its wheels swivel independently.

Mutti frowns, and pulls me toward her by my shoulders. Before we make contact, she starts pushing me away again. At some point in this, her right cheek brushes mine. After five years, this is what I get?

"You're too thin," she says, taking a bag from my left shoulder. She stares at Eva, who stares right back.

"Eva, push the cart," she says. Eva's face hardens, and I cringe. Then Eva moves behind the cart and takes its handle.

Mutti marches toward the automatic doors at the human equivalent of an extended trot.

"Where's Pappa?" I ask, jogging a few steps to catch up.

"He's at the house. He was tired," she says without looking back.

• • •

Mutti leads us to the car, which is actually not a car at all, but a van with a hydraulic lift on one side.

This is my first indication of how far things have progressed. The middle of the inside is reserved for a wheelchair, an empty space with parallel tracks and clamps for securing the wheels to the floor. I have a sick recollection of being the person for whom such a space was left, and panic flickers within me.

"Eva, do you want to ride shotgun?" I ask, opening the passenger door.

Instead of answering, she scuttles past and into the back, where she's safely beyond the range of conversation.

We buckle up in silence, and as Mutti negotiates her way out of the parking lot, nobody says a word. At first I think she's just worried about missing the turnoff, but once we're on the highway, I realize she doesn't want to talk.

I turn to look at her. She's staring straight ahead, gripping the steering wheel with bony hands. Then I sneak a glimpse at Eva in the side-view mirror. Her headphones are on again, and she's staring out the window, nodding angrily in time to Green Day.

"How's Pappa?" I ask, looking back at Mutti.

"Not good, Annemarie," she says. "Not good."

I turn my face to the window to absorb this, watching the sun flash through the trees.

I had forgotten how different the terrain is here. In Minnesota, all is flat and wide. Here, the road winds down through valleys and streams before suddenly cutting up the steep pitch of a hill. The trees come right up to the side of the road, broken only by jutting bedrock and the occasional clearing for a weather-beaten building. The buildings are long and flat, mostly wood frame, and sprawling with haphazard additions. I see a hand-painted sign advertising ammunition, and sit forward to follow it with my eyes.

We pass a billboard, the first I've seen: PAMPER YOUR BABY, KEEP THEM HAPPY AND DRY.

Good God. Go out on a limb, folks. Pick a gender.

I take a deep breath.

"How long has Pappa been in a wheelchair?"

"Eight weeks," says Mutti.

"How bad is it?"

Mutti is quiet long enough that I turn from the scenery to study her profile. She looks thinner, tired. Smaller.

"He still has some movement in his arms," she says finally.

I am sickened by her words, and realize I have no idea what I'm going to find at the house.

We drive the rest of the way in silence, even as we pull through the gates of our farm—or rather, the Maple Brook Riding Academy, as my father would insist I call it.

It looks exactly as it did when I left. The wooden fence that runs all around the perimeter and on either side of the long drive is crisp white, as are the stable and attached arena. The pastures and lawns are as manicured as a golf green, and the two dozen or so horses that graze among them are sleek and dappled.

The drive winds past the white-frame house, between the pastures, and dead-ends at the stable. There are cars in the parking lot, and when I see this, hope rises within me like a sprout breaking the earth. Timid hope, cautious hope. If Pappa can still teach, things can't be that bad. He may be in a wheelchair, but life still has some semblance of normalcy.

Mutti pulls behind the house. The only hint that anything has changed is the ramp leading to the back porch. It could be the same one they had for me, but I don't ask. I'm already nauseated.

"Is that a new car?" I ask as Mutti parks next to a blue Passat.

"No. It's Brian's." She unfastens her seat belt and opens the door. Behind me, the sliding door rattles open along its track.

"Brian?"

"The nurse." Mutti disappears, and I'm left staring at her empty seat.

Flustered, I scramble out. I set Harriet on the ground and then close the seat belt in the door.

"But I thought . . ." I say, opening the door and trying again. "But it looks like someone's teaching a lesson."

"We have a new trainer."

Mutti is wrestling bags from the back of the van and setting them on the gravel. Eva loiters behind her, staring at the trees beyond the stable.

I am frozen to the spot, watching Mutti and hoping that she will eventually look at me. I need her to, need her to impart some kind of knowledge or understanding or even comfort, but she doesn't. She's working out how to carry as many bags as possible, piling them onto her tiny, lithe frame like a mountain-bound burro. Then she hands Eva a suitcase and leads the way to the house.

I follow behind with the rest of the bags and Harriet, straining on her red nylon leash.

The back door leads to the kitchen. By the time I get there, Eva and Mutti have disappeared.

There's a man—Brian, I assume—reading a magazine at the table. He's large and doughy, with soft-looking hands and a sprawling bald spot fringed with short, brown hair.

"Hi," I say, looking around. A baby monitor on the counter catches my eye. A red light shoots across its display, apparently in response to random static.

"Hi," says Brian. He barely looks up from his magazine.

"Is my father around?"

"He's asleep. He's tired," says Brian. This time, he pays attention, staring first at me and then Harriet, as though she were some kind of rodent.

I despise him instantly and not only because of Harriet. Any decent man would have offered to help Mutti with the bags.

I head for the hallway. As I pass the dining room, I see glass doors in what used to be open doorframes. The doors have curtains. There is a metal track in the ceiling and I pause for a moment, following its line with my eyes. Then I continue to the staircase.

• • •

Eva and my mother are standing in the master bedroom next to the pile of suitcases. The room looks the same as it has for more than thirty years, except that there are different lamp shades and the framed pictures are gone.

Eva appears to be looking out the window, but I think she's just avoiding eye contact. She stands with her arms crossed in front of her and her feet planted squarely on the ground. Her toes point slightly inward, and her back is arched so that her belly sticks out in a way that reminds me of a toddler's, or a pregnant woman's. She'd be horrified if she knew that; might even give up the low-rise jeans that have become a sort of uniform. It would be an easy victory, but a cheap one. While I hate that her belly is perpetually bared, I won't intentionally hurt her.

"Now which of these is yours, Eva?" asks Mutti. She leans over and checks the luggage tags. They probably all have Roger's name on them, something I mean to rectify. I probably can't completely obliterate him from my life, but I can sure try.

"These." Eva points first at one and then another, and then waits, expecting Mutti to extract them for her.

"Right," says Mutti, straightening up. "Take them to the room across the hall. You're staying in your mother's old room."

Eva glares at her and once again I brace myself. But then she glazes over: her jaw goes slack, and her thin eyebrows, plucked into curved arches, assume a look of boredom. She slides her arms through the straps of her pink vinyl backpack, and then makes a great show of dragging her suitcases from the room. Harriet trots out after her, and Mutti stands watching, her hands on her hips. When the door across the hall shuts, she turns to me.

"Looks like you have your hands full with that one."

"Is this where you want me to sleep?" I ask.

"Yes." She moves to the bed and fusses needlessly with the sheets. "Pappa and I sleep downstairs now, so there's no reason not to let you have the large room."

"Will you have a room added onto the main floor?"

"No," she says, fluffing a pillow and then smoothing it noisily with the flat of both hands. "There's no time for that."

I nod as a lump rises in the back of my throat.

• • •

I don't know why I thought I'd feel better when we arrived. In fact, now that I'm here, I don't have a clue what to do with myself.

I lie on the bed for less than a minute, and then get up again to pace. There's unease in my soul, a vein of disturbance running through to my core. I was stupid to think coming here would change that. I can't imagine what I was thinking.

So it gets me away from the scene of my defunct marriage. So what? It doesn't change what's happened. It doesn't mean I don't still have a divorce to get through. As for Eva—she hasn't said a civil word since I told her we were going to New Hampshire. As far as she's concerned, I've ruined her life.

I pull a few drawers open to see if they're empty. They are, of course, because Mutti is nothing if not organized. I close the drawers again without putting anything in them.

Just for the hell of it, I give the dresser a little shove. I am surprised at how easily it moves, but then I remember that its drawers are empty. I brush the dust from my hands. Then I brace them on either side of a corner, and push the dresser into the center of the room. It leaves behind a rectangle of dust and lint, a clear outline of where it used to be. I feel uncharitably smug at the discovery, and an instant later am filled with shame.

I move to the corner of the bed. It's heavy and

oak, an old four-poster. I yank half-heartedly at one of its posts. It bends a little, but the bed is resolute. I won't be beaten by a bed, so I squeeze myself between the headboard and the wall, put one foot up on the wall behind me, and push with everything I've got.

The old headboard bends forward as though it might break, but I persist until the frame finally moves with a shudder and a screech. It's slow at first, but once it's in motion, I keep pushing until it slides against the wall where the dresser was. It's as though, having parted grudgingly with the position it occupied for the last three decades, the bed finally decided it didn't mind moving after all.

I move the tall dresser that used to be my father's into the place left by the bed, and then the long dresser over to the space where the tall one had been. Finally, I pick up a small table with scalloped edges and place it by the window. The proximity to the window is coincidence, because the main thing is to get it close to the phone jack so I can set up my laptop.

I hesitate before dialing in, because my mother could be expecting a phone call, but then I do it anyway. I forget to mute the volume, so my ISP says "Good afternoon, Annemarie," in its cloying, fake-cozy, fake-female voice, and in an instant the brief victory I'd felt over the furniture is replaced by irritation.

There are a few emails from Roger, which I don't read, an email from the placement company that my ex-employer has apparently decided I need, and one from my lawyer, with yet another draft of the marriage settlement. Disgusted, I log off.

• • •

Downstairs, Mutti is peeling potatoes in the sink. She looks over her shoulder when I come into the kitchen, and then returns to her task. Harriet is lying under the table, a sausage with legs. Brian is nowhere to be seen.

"What was going on up there? It sounded like you were moving furniture."

"I was."

"What was wrong with the way the room was set up?" she says.

"I wanted to see the stable from the bed. Also, the phone cord wouldn't reach the table," I say. All of which is true, but not the reason I rearranged the room. I don't know why I rearranged the room.

"What was wrong with where the phone was?" my mother asks, persisting.

"I need it to reach the computer."

"Oh." She peels another potato in silence. "Are you all settled in?"

"Not really. I still need to unpack."

"Sit. I'll make coffee," she says. With her Austrian accent, it sounds less like an offer than an order.

"No. I'm fine." What I'd really like is a drink, but she'll think it's too early for that. I could just go and get one, but I don't feel up to my first round with Mutti just yet.

I wander over to the sink. "Can I do anything?" I ask, peering in.

"You can help bring the horses in," she says. She rinses the peeler and sets it on the counter. "Two of the hands called in sick today."

"Sure. Of course," I say, surprised at how relieved I am for an excuse to leave the house. "Is Pappa still in bed?"

"He's getting up now," she says. She extracts a large soup pot from under the counter and sets it in the sink.

"He can do that?"

"Brian's helping him," she says, running water into the pot.

"Ah," I say. "Of course."

And then I close my eyes, because I'm starting to get the picture.

• • •

As I pass the dining room, I hear the sound of a winch cranking. An involuntary shudder runs through me. I hurry past and climb the stairs, rubbing my forearms to smooth the goose bumps.

I stand in front of Eva's door for a moment, gathering strength.

"Eva, honey," I say, knocking politely.

Silence.

I knock again.

"Eva," I say, putting my mouth near the crack. "Can I come in?"

There's a muffled response.

"I can't hear you, honey. Can I come in?"

"I *said*, I don't care."

I push the door open. She's sitting on the edge of the bed, slumped and forlorn. Her backpack is at her feet. Her cheeks are moist with recent tears, and when she sees me, she sniffs angrily.

I sit next to her on the bed, and because the mattress sags, end up closer than I'd intended. My shoulder brushes against hers, and as it does, she shrinks away.

"What do you think of your room?" I ask.

She shrugs.

"You can see the pastures from the window," I continue. "It's nice when the horses are out."

Silence.

"In a minute I'm going to bring them in. Do you want to help me?"

"No," she says furiously, turning to face me. "I want to go home."

"I know that, honey. But Oma and Opa need us here."

"For how long?"

"I don't know," I say. I wish I could put my arm around her. I know this is hard on her.

"Is Opa dying?"

I hesitate for just a moment. "Yes, honey. I'm afraid he is."

She doesn't miss a beat. "We'll go home afterward, right?" she says.

I close my eyes in a sudden, visceral reaction to her selfishness. "Maybe," I say carefully. "I'm not sure yet."

"Well, I am even if you're not," she says. "I'm leaving when I'm sixteen."

I nod slowly, puffing my cheeks full of air. And then, because there's nothing left to say, I pat my knees for punctuation and leave.

• • •

A couple of minutes later, I'm heading down the drive. On either side of me, horses are gathering near the gates of the pastures, milling around in anticipation of their evening grain.

The stable is at the end of the drive, looming like Notre Dame. It's huge, made of stone at the bottom and whitewashed wood at the top. It's shaped in a cruciform, like the cathedral itself, except that there's an Olympic-size indoor arena at the end where the altar should be. It looks deserted, although I know from the parking lot that it is not.

There are two outdoor arenas behind the stable, one with jumps, and one without. Beyond these are forested hills that follow the entire perimeter of the property. In the fall, the hills are spectacular—aflame with red, orange, and yellow—but right now the crowded trees have just the promise of spring on their branches.

I haven't been outside five minutes, but my fingers and nose are already icy. I should have brought my jacket, but I left it in the kitchen, and when I went to retrieve it, I caught a glimpse of the back of my father's electric wheelchair from the doorway. So I backtracked through the house and slipped out by the front door instead.

As I approach the entrance to the stable, one of the hands emerges, trailing a lead rope on the ground. He doesn't greet me, and I don't greet him.

The main part of the building contains two aisles of box stalls. They are separated by a dark, narrow corridor filled with tack boxes, saddle racks, and bridles hanging from hooks. The transepts, the arms of the cross, contain slightly smaller box stalls, which are mostly reserved for school horses. These tend to get hotter in the summer because the ceiling is lower. There is a definite hierarchy involved: the smaller stalls cost less per month, but all have windows. For a little more, you can get into one of the larger stalls in the main part of the building. For a little more still, you can have a larger stall with a window. The prime stalls, the ones that cost the most, are right at the middle of the cross. They have windows on the outside walls, and face the wash racks and arena on the inside, providing plenty of entertainment for a captive horse.

Most of the stalls are empty, although I pass a few whose occupants don't get turned out at all. They are the show horses, the boarders whose owners have visions of making it in breed shows, and the perfection of their coats is evidence of their isolation. Even the possibility of a bite or a kick or a good roll in the mud has been removed.

I pass by Harry's old stall, or rather, reach it and find myself unable to continue. I haven't turned my head yet, am still facing the aisle that leads to the arena, but I can tell that Harry is there. His presence is large and voluminous, an electrical cloud that swirls and draws me toward it like a vortex.

When I finally turn my head, I find the stall occupied by a white Andalusian. CAUTION! says a sign tacked to his stall door. STALLION! DO NOT TURN OUT!

He looks at me curiously with glossy black eyes, and sticks his black-skinned nose out through the space above his feed bucket. His forelock is wavy and impressively long.

I bring my hand up as though to cup his chin, but drop it again before making contact. He waits for a moment to see if I'll change my mind, and then grows bored. He snorts and swings his head around to his hay net. I walk on.

As I get closer to the arena, I hear a voice coming through the sound system.

"Look, you have to find a way of making him canter without staring him down . . . He knows how to do it—now, make him give it to you . . . Come on, he's lazy, that is all . . ."

I detect a French accent, and am perplexed. My father would never hire a French instructor. My father believes in German dressage almost to the point of religion; precision in all things, regimented training, repetition until perfection. Six strides in each quarter of the twenty-meter circle, eight strides in a full canter pirouette; no more, no less.

But it is a French accent, and more to the point, it's French classical dressage that's being taught out there. I slide through the door into the lounge and take a seat facing the window that looks into the arena.

There are a number of parents watching the lesson, waiting for it to end. They turn as one to look at me, but no one offers a greeting, for which I am grateful. I glance quickly at the walls, which are lined with framed pictures of me, and then get up again. I move behind the couch, trying to be invisible.

Six horses are lined up against the far side of the arena with their riders standing by their heads. There is another horse in the center, being lunged by a student while the instructor watches.

The horse is a dark bay, a tall gelding that looks like a thoroughbred, although he may have something heavier in him as well. He wears a double bridle, with the reins twisted and then wrapped around his neck, secured by the throat latch. A lunge line runs through the ring of the snaffle to the far buckle on the girth, and he canters in an easy circle around the student, who holds the lunge line in one hand and a long whip in the other.

"Okay, now put your side rein on," says the instructor. He stands with his back to the window, facing the student and her horse. His hair is light brown, long and thick, and pulled into a ponytail at the back. He is clearly not tall, but like my father, makes up for it with a strong athletic build. He takes three long steps backward, and then one sideways, but I still can't see his face.

The student tugs the line three times gently, and the horse slows to a trot. She draws the horse toward her, gathering the lunge line into loops, one after another, until finally the horse stops and turns to face her. His head is raised, and his nostrils flared. The student says something to the instructor, but I can't hear her. Only he has a microphone.

"There are no stupid questions," he says. "Stupid answers, perhaps." I'm starting to like this guy.

The student fiddles with the side rein, unhooking it from the saddle and attaching it to the snaffle. The horse immediately arches his neck.

"Now see?" says the instructor, stepping backward so the student can begin lunging again. "He knew what to do all along. He knows where to put his head. You've got to make him do that when you're on top, to remind him of where his head is supposed to be. Now the trot, when you're ready. Trot, please."

The horse begins to trot in a widening circle around the girl, who releases loops of line to accommodate the increasing distance.

"That's good," the instructor says. "Good. Allow the horse to enjoy what he's doing and give it to you. And the canter when you want. Smaller circle, smaller circle. Keep a canter, canter, canter . . . Good. Now, larger circle, trot. Okay, now, did you see that? The side rein is a little long. You can see in the transition that the horse pulls his nose up."

The girl stops the horse again to adjust the side rein, and the instructor comes and takes over, gesturing her aside. I can see his face now, first in profile, and then from the front, as he comes around to the other side to remove the side rein. He has strong, regular features and a long moustache, a detail I wasn't expecting.

He unhooks the lunge line and asks the student to hand him a dressage whip. She retrieves one from against the rail, and then waits while he arranges the horse's reins. When he takes the whip, she steps aside.

He stands just in front of the horse's left shoulder, holding the inside rein near the bit, and the outside rein, which crosses the tall gelding's withers, in the same hand as the whip. He stares at a point somewhere on the horse's rib cage, and clicks his tongue. The horse swishes his tail and throws his head. The man clicks again, and touches the end of the whip to the horse's flank. In a flash, the horse kicks a leg out sideways.

I catch my breath. My father would never tolerate such a thing, but this man seems unperturbed. He has no reaction at all. He just continues to stare at the same point on the horse's body, and clicks his tongue softly. The horse kicks out again.

This time, the man stops and approaches the animal's head. He stands motionless beside him for a moment, and then lays a hand on his forehead. The gelding pushes against it, raising his muzzle into the air—one, two, three times—and then slowly drops his head.

Now when the man stands at his shoulder, the horse begins to dance, moving sideways around the man as though he were a pillar. The horse's motion is liquid and collected, his front and back legs crossing with every stride.

Jesus. I don't even want to blink—I'm afraid I'll miss something.

"You've got to do a lot of work-in-hand with this boy," says the instructor, looking back at the student. "The boy doesn't like it, says 'Do I have to?' And the answer is yes, but not until he wants to. To make him want to, that's your job."

It sounds like he's getting ready to hand the horse back to the student. I head for the door, but when I reach it, I look back one last time.

The instructor has mounted the horse, and the animal has taken shape beneath him. His back is raised, his haunches forward, his neck arched—he's perfectly balanced and on the bit, although the reins coming from the double bridle are so light as to be nearly slack. I watch, rapt, as he takes the horse through a *piaffe*—a perfectly cadenced trot on the spot—and then moves forward into an elevated, prolonged *passage*, all without any perceptible motion in his hands or legs. *Descente de main, et descente de jambe.* He's showing off, yes, but why not?

The man and horse are moving in sybaritic union now, floating effortlessly through one maneuver after another: a full canter pirouette followed by a canter half pass with lead change, and then impossibly—brilliantly—a capriole. The horse leaps into the air and hangs there, seemingly suspended. At the apex of his flight, his hind legs shoot out behind him.

I am rooted to the spot. The student is staring as though she's seen God.

"You have to put him on a shoulder in, shoulder in, and again, shoulder in," the instructor says as though nothing unusual has just happened.

"See? He's a faker," he continues, demonstrating perfectly. "He says, 'I can't do it, I can't do it,' but he can. He just doesn't like it."

He stops the gelding, and smiles beatifically down at the student. Then he swings his right leg elegantly over the saddle and disappears from view.

I look at the clock. It's five minutes to the hour, which means the lesson is finishing. And because I'm feeling suddenly shy, I slip out to bring in the horses.

• • •

"Ah, there you are," says Mutti as I come in the back door. She's bustling around the kitchen, gathering cutlery and napkins. "We're almost ready for dinner. Can you call Eva?"

I do, and she appears, silent and brooding. Together we enter the study, which now holds the dining-room set. Even with all its customary furniture removed, it's a tight squeeze.

Pappa is at the head of the table, and at the sight of him, I catch my breath. He has never been a large man—he started his career as a jockey—but his shoulders are broad and he's always been muscular enough to have a commanding physical presence despite his height. Now his limbs are wasted and slack, or at least his arms are—I can't see his legs, because they're hidden beneath the table. There's a strap around his chest that keeps him upright against the back of the wheelchair, and his skin is sallow, his skull clearly visible beneath his face. He looks tiny, birdlike.

"Pappa," I say. Despite my best efforts, my voice cracks. I force myself to walk to him, hoping that what I'm feeling doesn't show on my face. I lean over to hug him, hesitating for just a moment while I figure out how. In the end, I drape my arms around his angular shoulders and press my face to his. His skin is cool and loose, his collarbone prominent.

"It's good to see you, Annemarie," says Pappa. His voice is slower and raspier than it used to be. I can hear the effort involved, both for breathing and articulating. The sound of it causes the muscles in my own throat to constrict.

When I straighten up, little stars explode in my peripheral vision. I close my eyes, waiting for the blood to return.

"Eva, come say hello to your Opa," I say.

She remains frozen, eyes huge, lip twitching. Suddenly I wish we were alone in the room so that we could both express the horror and sadness that we are trying so hard to contain, so that we could mourn the death of this man who is still living without making him miserable with the knowledge of it. But it's stupid to think that he doesn't know what's going on. Pappa always knows what's going on.

"It's okay, Annemarie," says Pappa. "Leave the girl alone."

Mutti enters the room carrying a plate in one hand and a bowl in the other. I spring into action, grabbing them from her hands.

"Here, let me," I say, setting the dishes on the table. "Is this it?"

"No," she says. "There's still the salad, the bread, and the wine."

"Eva, will you help me?" Before I even finish the sentence, Eva is following me from the room.

When we get to the kitchen, I take her in my arms. She wraps her arms around my back and leans into me, whimpering. It's an animal sound that rises from deep within her throat. I'm shocked, almost stricken, by the contact, because I can't remember the last time she tolerated an embrace.

"Oh, Honey," I say, stroking the back of her head. "Oh, Honey. Shh, be quiet now, or he'll hear you."

We stand like this for several minutes. Eventually she pulls away, wiping her eyes. If mine are as red as hers, we don't have a hope of hiding what we've been doing out here. But they know, of course. They know.

We gather the rest of the food in silence, and then return to the study.

For the first time, I notice the extra place setting. "Are we expecting someone?" I ask.

"Jean-Claude usually has supper with us, but he called a few minutes ago. He can't make it tonight."

"Jean-Claude?"

"The instructor."

"He lives here?" I ask. I realize, too late, that there's affront in my voice.

"He's staying in the apartment above the barn," says Pappa. "He had to move for the job, so it seemed logical to offer it."

I look at him when he starts to speak, and then instinctively turn away. I feel terrible instantly, but I can't turn back to face him now. I couldn't make a worse hash of this if I tried.

Mutti picks up a plate and holds it out toward Eva. Eva peers at it, leaving her hands in her lap.

"I don't eat meat," she says.

"Of course you do," says Mutti, continuing to poke the plate at her. "Here."

"No, really. I'm a vegetarian."

"What kind of nonsense is that," says Mutti. "A growing girl like you needs protein."

"I get protein from other sources," says Eva. She is steadfast, remaining polite, but still refusing to touch the plate.

"Nonsense," says Mutti. She stabs a veal cutlet with a fork and slaps it down on Eva's plate. Eva's face clouds.

I step in. "Actually, we support Eva in her decision not to eat meat."

"*We?*" says Mutti, staring at me with one eyebrow raised.

"*I* support Eva," I say loudly. "And if she doesn't want to eat meat, she doesn't have to. Here, sweetheart. I'll trade you."

I pass my plate to Eva, who then hands me hers, holding it by the very edge to indicate her disgust.

"Crazy, the ideas these young people get," mutters my mother, as though to herself. "I suppose next thing you'll be telling me that we shouldn't wear leather, or that we should free all the lab rats. Perhaps we ought not to ride horses, either."

"Of course I think vivisection is wrong," starts Eva, turning the color of beets. "It's monstrous. It's evil."

"Vivi-what?" says Mutti.

Dear God. The woman has no idea what she's getting into.

"Eva has a right to her opinions, just as you have a right to yours," I say loudly.

Mutti turns to me, and just as I feel the wrath of God about to descend, the phone rings. She stares at me for a moment longer, and then leaves the room.

"Here, Eva," I say, handing her the bowl of potatoes.

"Give her the salad too," says Pappa. "And the bread. Put some meat on her bones. Or bread, anyway," he says.

I look over at him, and see that the edges of his mouth are pulled into a terrible grimace. He's trying to smile.

"Thanks, Pappa," I say, hoping I won't burst into tears. I look into my lap, blinking furiously.

"So what do you think of our new instructor?"

I touch my fingers to the corners of my eyes—somehow it seems that if I staunch my tears with fingers instead of a napkin, it won't be so obvious that I'm crying.

"Oh," I sniff. "I think he's very good. I watched him for a while this afternoon. He was riding one of the boarders."

"He's French, you know."

"Yes, Pappa. I noticed."

"Your mother hired him."

"Well, that would explain it," I say, trying to laugh. "How long has he been here?"

"A couple of months," says Pappa. He reaches for his napkin with a drooping hand, and lifts it from the table with great effort. The movement seems to come from his shoulder, to involve his whole arm.

"Do you like him?" I ask, watching the napkin's progress. I can't decide whether to help or pretend I haven't noticed. This new terrain is full of land mines.

"He's not bad," says Pappa, finally dabbing the napkin to the corner of his mouth. "He coddles the horses, though. Into all that New Age stuff."

"Then why did you hire him?"

His shoulders buck. I wonder if he's in pain, and then realize he's trying to shrug. "Your mother liked him. And she's the one who's going to have to live with it."

The wine isn't open yet, so I take the liberty. I am just sitting down again when Mutti returns.

"Who was that?" asks Pappa.

Mutti looks askance at the wineglasses, and then takes her seat beside Pappa. "Dan," she says.

I look up quickly. She's staring straight at me, dripping with self-satisfaction.

No. She couldn't have. "Not Dan Garibaldi," I protest, rising to the bait before I can stop myself.

"Yes, Dan Garibaldi."

"Why is he calling?"

"Why shouldn't he? He's our vet."

I frown. I had assumed Dan was calling because Mutti told him I was back, but to find out that he and my parents have a relationship completely outside of me—well, somehow I was not prepared for this.

"I didn't know that," I say, chastened.

"No, how could you?"

"Enough, Ursula," says Pappa.

He waves a hand in irritation, but then instead of putting it back on his armrest, he reaches for his spoon. I hadn't noticed before, but it's the only implement beside his plate. He wraps his fingers around it, laboriously, and then pauses, gathering strength. Every one of the separate movements involved in getting a single bite of food to his mouth is a struggle. I cannot watch.

When he is finished, Mutti lifts his wine to his mouth. He takes a sip, and she sets it back down again without spilling a drop. Throughout this, neither of them looks at the other or the glass, so synchronized are their movements.

"So why was he calling?" Pappa says.

"He got a horse at auction that he wants you to see. You, too, Annemarie."

"So you *did* tell him I was here," I say.

"Of course I did. You *are* here. Was it supposed to be a secret?"

When I see the way her jaw is set, I regress at the speed of light. These tiny movements, these subtle shifts—a simple hardening of the lips, a nearly imperceptible jutting of the chin—and my maturity strips away like birch bark. I almost say something nasty, but then I see that Eva is watching me, waiting to see what I do. She's slouching again, poking limply at her salad, but beneath her feigned boredom I can see that she's very interested indeed.

"No, of course not," I say. "I don't care who knows I'm here. Anyway, what auction?"

"Dan runs a horse rescue center. They go to the feedlots each year and save as many foals as they can. Then they adopt them out."

I should be impressed, but instead, I'm increasingly grumpy. It's as though Mutti is holding Dan up for inspection, has him grasped firmly between the thumb and forefinger of each hand like a paper cutout. Exhibit A: Dan, the veterinarian. Dan, the patron saint of horses. And what about you, Annemarie? *Hmmmm?* What have you got to say for yourself?

I eat silently, keeping my eyes on my plate, but I doubt very much that Mutti will let it go at that.

And I'm right. A minute later she says, "Aren't you curious?"

"About what?"

"About whether he's married? About what he's been doing for the last nineteen years?"

I slam my fork down and look at her, cocking my head to the side. "Fine, Mutti," I say, crossing my arms in front of me. "Is he married? Tell me, what's he been doing for the last nineteen years?"

She looks at me pointedly—I mean, really pointedly, as though she's somehow managed to make both her nose and chin pointier than they really are—and turns away in disgust.

• • •

I can't believe I let her get to me so quickly. It was not supposed to be like this. Every time I come here—which isn't very often, as she would be the first to tell you—I am determined that *this* time, I will force her to deal with me as an adult. That *this* time, I won't let her drive me into acting like a teenager. And I didn't last a day. If we're like this at thirty-eight and sixty-seven, what possible hope is there for Eva and me?

The rest of the dinner didn't exactly pass in silence, but it certainly passed without any further conversation between Mutti and me. And since Eva's still angry and I couldn't bring myself to look at Pappa, it made for a relatively uncomfortable evening.

I retreated to my room as soon as was humanly possible. Now I'm sitting on the edge of the bed, holding my nightgown loosely in my lap. I look over at the computer on its table by the window, and instantly dismiss the idea of dialing in. In the background, I see the stable. There's a light on in the upstairs apartment and a figure moving behind the curtains. I'm not used to the idea of having someone in the stable apartment. I'm going to have to remember to keep the curtains closed.

I shift my hips so I'm facing the bed, and then stare at it blankly. It's queen size, with four pillows. It seems vast. I can sleep in the middle if I want. I can stretch my arms and legs out into all four corners and sleep spread-eagled. I can scrunch up the eiderdown and use it to buffer my knees, can thrash as much as I like—even take up snoring. I wonder how to arrange the pillows, and then decide that there is no configuration for four pillows that will accommodate a single person sleeping in the middle of a bed. And then I wonder if I'll always sleep alone now, if there will ever be anyone else.

I suppose there's always Harriet.

Chapter 5

When Mutti comes around the corner the next morning, I'm waiting at the kitchen table. I've been here since six-thirty, honing my words.

I'm determined to have it out with her, to let her know how it's going to be. But as soon as she rounds the corner in her quilted turquoise housecoat, I lose my nerve. Something about the way it's zipped up to the base of her throat renders me mute.

"You look tired," she says, passing me on her way to the counter. She turns on the baby monitor, and then fiddles with the volume as it crackles.

"I am. I didn't sleep well."

That's not what I meant to say. I stare desperately at her back, willing myself to continue. But I can't—the whole damned speech is gone.

Finally, I close my useless mouth and stare at my hands.

Mutti grinds the coffee beans, oblivious to my misery. After the coffee starts to gurgle, she comes to the table and sits opposite me.

"So what are your plans, now that you're back?

"What do you mean?"

"Are you going to look for a job?"

"No, of course not."

"Then what will you do?"

I blink at her in surprise. "I thought I'd help out around here. Manage the stable so you could spend time with Pappa."

"Oh, I don't know about that," says Mutti.

"What do you mean? Why not?"

"You've never shown the slightest interest in the stable. Besides, there's more to managing it than you might think."

I am silent for a moment, trying to decide if there's any good way of taking what she just said. Nope—even upon reflection, I'm pretty sure she just accused me of being a bad daughter and stupid all in the same breath.

I shouldn't respond, I shouldn't respond, I shouldn't—

"It's not exactly rocket science, Mutti," I say with undisguised irritation. "I think I'll be able to figure it out. Anyway, that's why I'm here."

"Is it now," she says. Her eyebrows are raised, her expression imperious. She examines her wedding ring, twisting it on her finger.

"What the heck is that supposed to mean?"

"It doesn't mean anything," she says. Her fingers move on to a loose thread on her cuff. I stare hard, willing her to look up.

"Yes of course it does. What do you mean?"

"I'm just surprised, that's all."

"At what?"

"That you want to help at the stable."

"Why?"

She ignores me. She rises from the table and sails to the counter, the very picture of quiet dignity.

"Why?" I ask again.

She still says nothing, just stands with her back to me, pouring two mugs of coffee.

"I asked you a question, Mutti. If you don't think I came back to help, why do you think I came back?"

"I think you lost your job and your husband left you, and you needed somewhere to go. So here you are."

She picks up the mugs and heads for the door and I realize that the second coffee is for Pappa, not me.

I leap from my seat, and reach the doorway before she does.

"Don't walk out on me, Mutti. I want to talk about this."

She regards me coolly. All in all, she seems pretty unperturbed about finding me in her way. I'm starting to feel silly.

"So talk," she says.

"Is this how you want it? Really? Like last night, with you taking potshots at me at every opportunity? Because if it is, forget it. I'll take Eva and go back to Minneapolis."

She looks amused by the threat.

"You know damn well I came back to help," I continue, forcing my voice past the lump that has risen in my throat. "I came back to help and give you more time with Pappa. Jesus Christ, Mutti, why can't you ever take anything I do at face value?"

She stares at me steadily through the steam that rises from the coffee. After an impossibly long silence, she says, "Fine then. Never mind that you've never shown the slightest interest in horses or the stable in all of living memory. You go ahead and run it. You've always done what you wanted anyway."

And then she slips between me and the doorframe, taking the coffee into the dining room to where my father waits. I hear their voices through the baby monitor, and then, because I don't want to hear what she says about me, I leave the house, slamming the door behind me.

• • •

Mutti has nerve, I'll give her that. I don't remember how I phrased it when I told her I was coming back, but I sure as hell didn't tell her I needed a place to stay.

Roger didn't exactly leave me destitute: if I'd wanted to keep the house, I'd have kept the house. I'm the one who spent years massaging it into the perfect home. I'm the one who traveled to Maryland to choose just the right marble for the hearth, who consulted with experts about the right undercoat for the faux finish in the stairwell and had the entire kitchen gutted and redone in quarter-sawn oak when I could no longer stand all-white cabinets.

Despite all that, I found I had no interest in keeping it after Roger left. I suppose it's no great surprise that Sonja also had no interest in living in a house that Roger and I had shared, so we put it on the market. It's about the only thing we have agreed on, and who knows? Maybe if Roger had wanted to keep it, I'd have fought him just to be bloody-minded. Under the circumstances, I think I'm entitled to a bit of bloody-mindedness.

But all this is beside the point, which is that I'm not exactly a homeless wretch coming home to mooch off my parents. I came back for Pappa, for Mutti, and also for Eva—there were all sorts of reasons to come back to New Hampshire, but none of them was self-serving.

I look up and find myself almost at the stable, which surprises me.

There's the clip-clopping of hooves on cement, and a moment later a boy exits, leading two horses, one on each side. Not a safe practice, and one I intend to put an end to as one of my first acts of management.

"Hi," I say, as he passes me. "I'm Annemarie. Zimmer," I add, as he continues to walk. He stops.

"Hi," he says shyly. He's Latino—Mexican, probably, although that opinion is based on nothing more than the fact that almost all the stable hands I've ever known were Mexican. He seems very young, maybe sixteen, although he could be as old as twenty. The further I get from that age, the harder it is to judge.

"What's your name?"

"Jose Luis," he says, squinting into the morning sun. "But you can call me Luis."

"Do you want help with turn-out?"

He shakes his head.

"You sure?"

He shakes his head again, clearly hoping I'll just let him continue on his way.

"Okay then. I'll see you around, Luis."

When I enter the stable, it's clear why he refused my help. There are four other stable hands, all of them in the process of turning out horses.

I stop at one of the stalls just as a gray gelding is led out. There's a laminated sign pinned to his door: PASTURE C, NORTHWEST. It's in Mutti's hand.

So Mutti has the pastures grazed in rotation. I guess I'm not surprised. In her own way, she's as regimented as Pappa ever was.

A few minutes later, I am once again in front of Harry's stall, although this time I don't feel his presence. This time, I'm making the acquaintance of the white stallion, tickling his whiskers. I have just decided that he's a lovely creature indeed when I hear booted footsteps coming up behind me. Then they stop.

"Can I help you?" says a voice with a French accent.

"Annemarie Zimmer," I say, turning and reaching out my hand. This is the second time in ten minutes that I've used my maiden name. I guess I'm reverting to it.

"Ah, the famous Annemarie," says the man in front of me. I bristle.

"Jean-Claude des Saulniers," he continues, taking my hand and bringing it to his lips. This startles me just a little.

"I see you've met Bergeron," he says, stepping backward and placing one hand on the wall. He puts his other hand on his hip, which makes me notice his stance, and then, by proximity, his legs, which are immensely strong. He's wearing breeches, and his thighs are clearly visible through the taut material; thick, with well-defined muscles. Embarrassed, I look away.

"He's lovely," I say, turning back to the horse.

Bergeron swings around, presenting me with his rump. I laugh. "Although you can see what he thinks of me. Is he a boarder or one of ours?"

"Neither. He's my boy," says Jean-Claude with obvious pride. "I brought two with me. Bergeron and Tempeste, the two I couldn't leave behind. The rest were school horses, and I left them with my former partner. Well, sold them to him, of course," he adds with a shrug.

"He's beautiful," I say. "Do you really not turn him out at all?"

"Sure I do," he says. "Every night, after dinner. But only when the other horses are in. Otherwise, he might decide to start jumping fences to get at the girls." He goes to the stall and stands facing it. "Isn't that right, Boo-Boo?" he says. "Only arranged marriages for you."

"Where's your other one?" I ask, glancing quickly at the surrounding stalls.

"The other side. But she's already gone out to play. You'll have to see her later. When is your horse arriving?"

"My horse?" I ask weakly.

"You don't have a horse?"

"I don't ride anymore."

He looks at me in surprise.

"I had an accident," I say, watching his face carefully. "Years ago." His expression is still blank.

It seems unfair for my parents to tell people about my past ("the famous Annemarie," after all) and not tell them about the accident. The accident is everything.

"I'm sorry," he says. "It must have been very bad. But we will get you on again."

Before I can protest, he strides down the aisle and I am left staring at his broad back and narrow waist.

• • •

When I return to the house, I go online. There are more emails from Roger, with increasingly urgent subject lines, and one from my lawyer, which I open first.

She's attached yet another draft of the marriage settlement, which I don't feel like reading, so I send a note back simply telling her that I'm in New Hampshire and that I'll look at it later. Then I send another note asking her not to tell Roger where I am. Then I select all of his messages and delete them.

• • •

By now it's nearly eleven, and high time for Eva to get up. I cross the hall and knock on her door. There's no answer, but I'm not surprised, because like most teenagers, Eva is capable of sleeping through a hurricane.

I knock again, then let myself in. Her bed is empty. Unmade, naturally.

I head for the staircase. I'm almost a third of the way down when Mutti yells up at me. "Wait! Wait! Don't come down!"

I rock back on my heels, startled. I hear the sound of a machine, of an engine running and bearings clacking. My mind goes blank and I retreat upstairs. I don't want to know what's going on down there, although from the sound I'm pretty sure it involves the ceiling track.

I shout down, carefully averting my gaze. "Okay. I won't. But do you know where Eva is? She's not up here."

"No," shouts Mutti. "She's probably at the stable."

Since it seems I'm trapped, I grab a couple of towels from the linen closet and head for the bathroom.

When I open the door, I see Eva lying in the tub. I step back, startled. She has her headphones on. Her eyes are closed, and she's resting her head on the rim.

I haven't seen her naked since she was about ten, and I'm shocked at the sight of her. My God, her body looks like an adult's now, except that her breasts are impossibly firm. And then I realize that above one of them, with a radius of approximately one inch, is a tattoo of a unicorn.

"Eva, oh dear God, what have you done?"

Her eyes spring open in surprise and fright. Then she gets to her feet, sloshing water everywhere.

I step forward, grabbing her arm. She pulls backward, wrenching free and falling into the tub with a huge splash. I turn my back, afraid that if I don't I'll strike her. I can't ever remember being so angry in all my life.

"What were you thinking! You stupid, *stupid* little girl!" I scream, turning back to face her. She's out of the tub now, securing a towel around her body.

There's a scrambling behind me, a commotion as someone runs up the stairs.

"What on earth is going on?" shouts Mutti, coming into the bathroom. "It sounds like someone's being murdered."

"How long have you had it?" I demand, staring at Eva.

She says nothing, just looks down at the red marks my fingers have left on her upper arm. I'll hear about that later, I'm sure.

"*How long*?" I repeat.

"A month," says my daughter, eyeing me warily.

I cross the room. Eva steps backward, but I take her by the shoulders and force her to face the full-length mirror.

"You have no idea what you've done, have you?" I say, yanking at the tucked edge of the towel. It falls to the floor. She kneels instantly to retrieve it, then spins to face me.

The sight of that abomination on her perfect, taut skin makes me want to weep. I stare at her, weighing my options, and I see her doing the same. When she realizes that I've got myself under control again, belligerence slides over her face like a shield. She smells victory.

"You're getting it removed," I say, and then spin on my heels.

"What? Where are you going?" Eva screams after me as I leave the room.

"To look up plastic surgeons," I throw over my shoulder.

• • •

My relationship with Eva has always been fraught with difficulty. Well, not always, I suppose. There was a window when she was a tiny baby, fat and golden, with my blonde hair and Roger's brown eyes, when we were in love with each other in a way that Roger might have found threatening were it not for the fact that he felt the same way. There was probably something significant in the fact that all of our energies converged on this child, and that neither of us had anything left for the other—and, perhaps more significant, that neither of us seemed to notice the lack. Of course, I'm prone to such retrospection now that he's gone. Now that I'm seeing through the prism of our impending divorce, everything seems to foretell of our demise.

But after the initial ecstasy of infancy, things were never quite as they should be. Oh sure, until three years ago, Eva and I could talk. Occasionally we'd even have a good time together, actually enjoy each other's company, but I never felt the closeness that I've always imagined most mothers and daughters share.

I remember one time when Roger and I took her to a petting zoo. I was looking at her wild curly hair framing her face like a lion's golden mane, and the folds on her chubby arms and legs as she approached a goat with outstretched hand. She was pure toddler perfection, and yet somehow I knew I was missing out. The way other mothers fell to their knees when their children cried, the way the fathers knelt down beside them and kept the oats from slipping through their fingers, the ease and happiness that oozed from these people—all of it eluded me. I could never relax into motherhood, could never really enjoy it. There was always something else that demanded my energy, something that kept me from just being in the moment; the kitchen, which fought back. The laundry, which grew organically. The bills, the isolation of staying at home, the stress of feeling as though Roger and I never quite connected. The weight that came on when I was pregnant and then stuck stubbornly to my once-athletic frame.

On the rare occasions that Roger and I would go out without Eva, I would watch the people who'd brought their babies along with jealousy, even though I had my own child waiting for me at home. Somehow, I just knew that their experience was more complete than mine.

I took great pains to hide it, this thing I couldn't put my finger on. I made dresses, I threw parties, I ferried her to lessons—even riding, although the sight of my child on a horse terrified me beyond belief. On each day of every weekend, we had some sort of family activity: hiking, riding our bicycles, going to the children's museum or botanical garden. She grew up loved and knowing it. Even when she got to be a teenager and the landscape changed, I was always paying attention, always vigilant.

I thought that vigilance would act as insurance, and protect us and her from the perils of the teenage years. But how vigilant could I have been if she could get a tattoo?

I close the door to my room, and sit at the little table by the window. With shaking hands, I reconnect to the Internet, determined to find a surgeon who will see us now, today.

It is not the tattoo that frightens me so much—I hate the tattoo, the tattoo is coming off—but that's not what frightens me. What frightens me is that I didn't know about it. And if I didn't know about that, what else don't I know about?

• • •

Twenty minutes later, I descend the stairs clutching a piece of paper. I come down shouting, not even knowing if anyone else is still in the house.

"Eva! Eva, where are you?"

I pause at the bottom of the stairs, listening for signs of life.

"Eva! Get out here!"

At first, I think the house is empty. Then I hear a motor whirring and when I turn around, Pappa appears in the doorway of the living room. Sickness washes over me.

"They've gone out," he says.

"What do you mean?" I ask, staring at my father.

"Your mother took her to the grocery."

I stand with a quivering jaw. Then I explode. "Mutti had no right to take her anywhere. Eva is *my* daughter. We have an appointment with a plastic surgeon in half an hour. I need her here *now*."

I stare at my frail father, waiting for him to defend Mutti. I almost wish he would, because I need the release of an argument. But he doesn't.

I burst into tears.

After a few seconds I hear the motor whirring again, and then Pappa pulls up next to me. With great effort, he raises his hand to mine. When I feel the back of it against my fingers, his skin as fragile as crepe paper, I sink to the floor and lay my head on his knee. It feels like nothing but cloth-covered bone.

"Oh, God, Pappa. Why? Why would anyone with skin as beautiful as that have a goddamned *unicorn* tattooed on it?"

"She was angry about the stud."

"What?" I say, raising my head.

"She was angry about the tongue stud, so she got the tattoo."

I stare at him in horror, and then drop my head back onto his leg. A moment later, his hand is on my head, light as a sparrow. He strokes my hair.

"I know you're upset, Annemarie. It's a shock, I know. But don't get into a state. No, it shouldn't be possible for someone her age to get a tattoo, but it does seem to be the fashion these days."

"But Pappa! It's going to cost a fortune to get it removed. And it will probably leave a scar. I just can't—"

"Hush, Annemarie," says Pappa, continuing to stroke my hair. "Think about it. She got it because of the tongue stud. If you force her to remove the tattoo, who's to say she won't get another one? A bigger one, in a more visible place? Or pierce something else?"

I frown against his leg, but say nothing.

"Better to let her keep it," he continues. "For now. Who knows? Maybe when she matures she'll get sick of it and have it removed. And then you can say, 'I told you so,' *mein Schatzlein*."

I lift my head and look into his face. He hasn't called me that in years.

• • •

I am my parents' greatest disappointment in life, which is made worse by the fact that at one point I was their greatest hope. Oh, I suppose all children are their parents' greatest hope, but this was different. I excelled at the one thing my parents devoted their entire lives to—was doing Grand Prix work by the age of sixteen. When it became apparent that I really was a world-class talent, my father and I traveled all over Germany, France, and Portugal looking for the right horse, although in the end we found him in South Carolina. I knew he was the one the moment I laid eyes on him—hadn't even ridden him yet. I just looked at his powerful red and white limbs and the way he held himself and knew, and Pappa trusted my instinct. Not to mention Harry's pedigree and considerable career to date.

Eight months after he arrived from South Carolina, we packed up again, and this time both of us went off to train with Marjory. From that moment on, we were unstoppable. Until the accident.

I knew from the very beginning that I would never get on another horse, although I never made a declaration. In the early days, there seemed little point.

However, even when my nerves began to get reacquainted and the idea of becoming whole again stopped feeling like a hopeless dream, I still neglected to tell my parents. I stayed silent even as they were making plans for my triumphant return.

They started planting issues of *Eventers Monthly* and *Sport Horse Illustrated* around the house. I'd go into the kitchen and find one on the table, open at an advertisement for a particularly promising eventer, some massively strong Hanoverian or Dutch Warmblood. Next time, it would be on the hall table, or my dresser. I would look at the ad, and then close the magazine, leaving it where it was. It didn't matter how many times I did this. The next day, the next week, there would be another, followed by another, followed by another, until I got to the point where I was closing the magazine without even looking at the horse.

When my parents found out I was leaving New Hampshire and had no immediate plans for doing anything with my life beyond being a wife, it caused a rift so deep that it still hasn't healed. But as upset as Pappa was, it was Mutti who became openly hostile. She believes I broke Pappa's heart, and maybe I did.

There's no question I could have had a career in riding, even if in reduced form. I could have become a trainer. I could have taken my place beside Pappa and made this a family enterprise.

But I didn't. I ended the family dream unilaterally, and although neither parent ever came out and said that, every word they didn't say was designed to remind me of it.

• • •

It seems perfectly natural, then, that Eva, Mutti, and Pappa are watching television in the living room without me. Mutti and Eva are curled up on the couch, and Pappa is parked at the end. The three of them are sharing a bowl of popcorn, thick as thieves.

I stand watching them for a moment, carefully staying out of sight. I'd like to join them, but can't bring myself to do it. My legs don't want to walk into the room.

Instead, I slink off to call Roger.

A woman answers—Sonja, I assume—and I am frozen. I should have expected this, but somehow I didn't. I pause with my mouth open, and then slam the receiver down, holding it there with both hands as though it might otherwise leap up. Then I bring my hands to my face and hyperventilate between my fingers.

A minute later, I call back. This time, Roger answers.

"Goddamn it, Annemarie! Where have you been? I've been trying to get in touch with you for ages. Why haven't you returned my phone calls?"

I am stunned into silence. Roger doesn't get mad. That's one of my complaints about him. There's never been an ounce of passion in him—I never could get a rise out of him, even when I was pitching for a fight.

"I didn't get your messages," I say. "I'm in New Hampshire."

"Oh," he says, sounding perplexed. "Is everything all right?"

"No, actually, it's not. My father has ALS."

"Oh, God, Annemarie. I'm so sorry. I had no idea."

"No, how could you?" I say.

There's an awkward pause as he gropes for something to say. He has never been close to my parents, partly because they never liked him and partly because of my relationship with them, but still, he must be shocked.

"I'm so sorry. I really am. Look, I don't mean to be insensitive, but when will you be back? I need to talk to you," he says.

"I won't be."

"Pardon?" he says.

"We're not coming back. We're staying here."

"What are you talking about?"

"We're staying here. Eva and I are staying here."

For the second time, Roger explodes. "You can't do that! Annemarie, she's my daughter, too—you can't just take her to another state!"

"I have and I did," I say. "And anyway, we agreed to sell the house."

"Yes, but you never said anything about leaving town. Annemarie," he says, shifting gears. "Please be reasonable. Can we please talk about this?"

"What's to talk about? Oh, but I forgot," I say. "Apparently there is something you need to tell me."

"Annemarie—"

"I'm not coming back, and I doubt very much you want to try to force Eva into living with you, so you might as well just tell me whatever it is you want to tell me about and be done with it."

A pause. "I need to see you."

"Why? So you can tell me you're going to marry Sonja? Spare me."

He is silent for so long I wonder if he's gone off the line. Then he speaks. "Please look at the settlement. We can talk when you come back for the hearing."

"Fine," I say, deciding not to tell him that I won't be back for the hearing. Besides, unless his news is that he's leaving Sonja, there's nothing I want to talk to him about.

"Annemarie?"

"What?"

"Could you please put Eva on the phone?"

"Eva," I shout without bothering to cover the mouthpiece. "Do you want to speak to your father?"

I extend my arm, holding the phone toward the doorway.

"No," she shouts back, right on cue.

"You heard her," I say to Roger.

He sighs. "Look Annemarie, I'm not pretending that you don't have a right to be upset with me—and I mean, really, really angry. But please, for Eva's sake, don't foster that in her. It can only hurt her in the long run."

"Whatever. Fine," I say. And then I hang up, because I'm angry with him for being right.

• • •

The day after Roger left me, Eva returned from Lacey's, unaware that against all odds, her father's transgression had eclipsed hers.

When I told her what had transpired, she blamed me, bursting into tears and screaming that if I hadn't been such a bitch all these years he probably wouldn't have left at all. Then she retreated to her room, amidst great stomping and slamming of doors.

When Roger called later that day to give me the address of the place where he was staying, I thanked him and told him I would give it to my lawyer. Of course, I didn't actually have a lawyer, because I still thought he was going to return, but I wanted to make a point. I wanted to let him know he shouldn't wait too long to come to his senses, because there was no guarantee that I'd still be around. Then he asked to speak to Eva.

As I handed her the phone, her face clouded over like that of a baby gathering breath to scream. Before he even had time to say hello, she started shrieking,

"Fuck you! Fuck you! Fuck you! Fuck you!" And then she hung up. She hasn't spoken to him since.

I was horrified, and not for Roger's sake. Eva's been on a slow slide for a while, and I'm beginning to believe her very future is at stake.

Chapter 6

The next morning, the four of us pile into the van and head for the rescue center.

Perhaps "pile into" is not the right phrase. Even though technology has changed considerably over the last twenty years, getting Pappa into the van is a long process: first, Mutti slides the door open and extracts a box with controls. Then she presses a switch that unfolds the hydraulic lift, and then another that lowers it to the ground. At that point Pappa drives onto it, and she reverses the process. After he maneuvers his chair so that he's facing the windshield, she applies clamps to his wheels so that he is secured to the floor. Then, finally, we're on our way.

The whole process has left me sick to my stomach, although I'm not sure whether it's caused by my inability to face what's happening to Pappa or the prospect of seeing Dan again.

I am more nervous than I thought I would be—how will I greet him? Is twenty years enough time to assume that he has forgiven me? Should I hug him?

Shake his hand? Be friendly and effusive, or formal and reserved?

I worry about this until the moment I see him emerge from the doorway of the stable, tall and muscular, the epitome of American masculinity in his jeans and flannel shirt. He stops at the sight of me, and then recovers almost instantly.

"Annemarie," he says warmly. "You look wonderful." He strides forward, takes my right hand in both of his, and kisses me on the cheek. For some reason, I'm suddenly in danger of crying.

"Thank you. So do you," I say. And he does. He looks fantastic. His sandy hair has some gray in it, and his features are a little coarser, but I swear he's as handsome as the day I first clapped eyes on him. I am embarrassed, wishing I'd taken a little more trouble with myself this morning. I also wonder how much he knows about the current state of my life.

"Anton, good to see you," says Dan, turning to Pappa and taking his hand. Then he turns and kisses Mutti on both cheeks. As he takes her hand, I see that her fingers curl around his, that her lips make actual contact with his cheek. I think back to my air hug at the airport.

"And you must be Annemarie's daughter," he says, turning to Eva and smiling broadly. He extends his hand.

"Yes," she says suspiciously. After an embarrassingly long pause, she takes his hand.

"You're as pretty as your mother," he says, and her face hardens perceptibly. It was the wrong thing to say, but he can't have known that. He doesn't know that any comparison to me is an insult of the most enormous proportions.

"So where is this horse, and what's so special that we had to come all the way out to see him?" says Pappa. He sounds curt, and I turn to him, embarrassed by his temper. But Pappa is smiling. Dan laughs immediately—doesn't misread him for an instant—and again, I feel a jolt of jealousy. But why shouldn't they be close to Dan? It's not as if I've been around.

"He's in the quarantine barn. And I think I'd like you to see for yourself."

Dan leads us around the main barn and heads for a concrete building a good distance away.

I follow Pappa, and watching him cross the gravel is almost more than I can take. His head bobs dangerously, as though there's barely any strength left in his neck, and I suppose there isn't.

And then I look over at Mutti, at her wiry little Austrian frame marching purposefully along with my daughter, and I'm angry at her. Angry that she didn't tell me how far the ALS had progressed, for not giving me some warning. For not telling me sooner, although I don't know what I would have done differently. With a husband and a job, I could not have come back—would not have wanted to.

"Oh, damn. Judy's got a horse in the aisle," Dan says, peering into the doorway. "These guys just came from auction and are pretty riled up. I don't want you in the aisle, Anton. It's too dangerous. Why don't you all go around to the right—there's a paddock there. I'll let him out the chute."

I am shocked at how easily Dan refers to my father's helplessness, when I—his daughter—cannot decide whether to acknowledge it or pretend it's not happening at all. I look at Pappa quickly to gauge his reaction, but he is motoring around the side of the building. I follow, jogging a little to catch up, and the four of us line up by the fence.

A minute later, Dan slides the door of the chute open. He's got a rope looped over his arm, and after checking to see that we're all here, advances a couple of steps into the opening, flapping the rope in front of him.

"Hiyah!" he yells. "Hiyah!"

A second later, he leaps onto the second railing of the fence as a horse explodes from the building.

I catch my breath, because I see what he is immediately, even as he's still a whir of motion, a blur of emaciated frame barreling around the edge of the fence.

"*Mein Gott in Himmel*," says Mutti.

The horse comes to a stop across the paddock and stands with his left side to us, flanks heaving, eyeing us warily.

I clap a hand over my mouth, afraid I might cry out.

It is Harry. It is Harry. It is starving, it is mangy, and it is lame, but it is Harry. My knees feel like they're going to buckle.

"Wow, what a weird horse," says my daughter.

"No, Eva," says Dan's voice from behind me. He has come back through the barn, and is standing so close I can feel his breath on my hair as he speaks. "That's a liver chestnut with white brindling. One in a billion. You're lucky if you see one of those in your lifetime. Never mind two."

In coloring, the horse could have been Harry's twin. The same deep red, the color of dried blood, from foot to forelock, run through evenly with white stripes. Absurdly gorgeous, and gorgeously absurd.

"Where on earth did you find him?" asks Pappa.

"In the kill pen."

"What?" says Eva. She turns sharply, her face poised for outrage.

"At the auction," says Dan. "I saw him in the kill pen, and, well, I had to get him. Obviously."

"Where did he come from?" asks Mutti.

"Who knows? He came in with a shipment from Mexico, and before that, we can't trace him. You know what these auctions are like—the horses' histories are the last things on these people's minds. My scanner didn't pick up a chip, either. But there's no real reason to think he's valuable. He's a mess. It's just that with his markings . . ." He looks over at me quickly, apologetically, and then lets the sentence go unfinished.

"Why was he in the kill pen?" I ask. I still can't take my eyes off the horse. His condition is appalling: his hipbones are jutting, and his hooves are long and cracked, forcing his legs to bow at an unnatural angle. The top of his tail has been rubbed to the point of near baldness, and his mane is thin and ratty. He stands with his ears back, watching our every move. Then he paws at the ground, and drops his nose to rub it against his leg.

"Did you see how he came out of the chute? I had to sedate him to get him onto the trailer, and then again to get him out and into the stall."

"He doesn't look crazy now," I say, surprised at how indignant I sound. This is not Harry.

"What's the kill pen?" I hear Eva ask as I move away, following the outside of the fence. The horse keeps his eye on me, and as I round the fence, he turns, inch by inch, so that his left side is always facing me. By the time I get to the far side of the paddock, we're five yards apart.

I lean against the fence, watching his face. There's fear in his expression, although something else, too. I wish I could tell what was going on in that head of his. And what a head—even emaciated, it's lovely. Strong-boned but refined, with a hint of a Roman nose. Hanoverian, I'll bet. In fact, except for the small star, the face could be Harry's.

The horse turns his head, and I have a moment of incomprehension. It's his right eye. It's too dark. Then I realize the socket is empty.

I shriek before I can stop myself, and the horse jerks upright into a rear before shooting off at full gallop. He gets to the mouth of the chute, and then turns so hard I'm sure he's going to fall, and ends up barreling around the perimeter of the fence.

"Oh shit," I hear Dan say. "Annemarie," he says louder now, breaking into a jog and coming around the fence. "Annemarie, I should have told you. Oh, shit. I should have told you first."

• • •

On the way home, Eva alternates between railing against the manufacturers of hormone replacement therapy and mooning ecstatically over the foals. I hear her as a sort of buzz in the background, her fury and outrage acting as a frame for my horror.

I am furious at Dan for blindsiding me like this, for not giving me some warning. It's like presenting someone with their dead grandmother. I could understand it better from someone who didn't know how I felt about Harry, but Dan knows. If anyone in the world knows, it's Dan.

To see Harry like that—I stop myself, shake my head. It's not Harry. It's some poor, decrepit, damaged horse with the same coloring, but it isn't Harry.

"Hey, Ma." Eva's voice carries across the length of the van, interrupting my reverie. "You take that stuff, don't you?"

"What?" I say.

"That stuff made with pregnant mares' urine."

"No. Mine's synthetic."

"Oh." She sounds disappointed.

When we arrive at the house and Mutti begins the process of unloading Pappa, I realize that his paralysis hasn't crossed my mind for the entire trip home.

• • •

That night, I dream of the accident. It's the first time in years, and I wake in a sweat with my heart pounding.

I used to dream of it regularly, and for a long while, took sleeping pills to ward it off. It seemed such an irony—I would have given anything to dream of Harry in any other situation, but I never did. Harry only came to me as we flew over the crest of that oxer. But for almost a decade now, I've hardly dreamt of it at all.

In real life, I lost consciousness on impact, but in my dreams, my imagination supplies all the details. I see the ground coming toward me, and feel the reins go slack as Harry's head hits and snaps backward but my hands continue to move forward. And then I hit, too, first colliding with the immovable Harry, and then sliding around his left shoulder into the ground at almost thirty miles an hour. I feel sandy grit as my teeth disintegrate in my mouth, see white and red patterns as my nose is shattered and my eyes fill with blood. I feel the pain of my helmet digging into the back of my neck, unaware at the time that only the chin harness I was wearing prevented it from snapping my spine completely. I feel—or rather, see somehow, as though I'm outside my body and watching from twelve feet in the air—my arms and legs bouncing back on impact, flapping loose-limbed like a marionette that has been dropped to the floor. And Harry, crumpled and collapsed. Open-eyed and still but for an involuntary twitching of the skin on his shoulder and flank, and one hoof that curls under like a tic, again, and again, and again.

When I wake up, the mattress is bouncing. Although I know that it must be from the violence of my awakening, I could swear that it's from the impact of my hitting it.

• • •

The next morning, I go to the office. It's on the second floor of the stable, directly above the lounge, and like the lounge, it has a window that looks onto the arena.

Jean-Claude is giving a private lesson, supervising

from the ground as a student takes a series of low fences on a gray thoroughbred mare.

I watch for a moment, lulled into a state of meditation by the mare's easy canter.

Mutti's bookkeeping is, of course, impeccable. The operation is larger than I remembered: there are five full-time stable hands, and Jean-Claude, who costs more than I would have thought. When I see his salary on the ledger, I look down at him in the arena, surprised. His résumé must be in here somewhere; I'll have to dig it out and have a look.

There are thirty-two horses; fourteen are school horses, two are Jean-Claude's, and sixteen are full-service boarders. There are regular deliveries of basics, like bedding, hay, pellets, and grain. Additional supplies such as fly spray and monthly meds, veterinary and farrier visits to coordinate, equipment maintenance for the tractors and spreaders. And, of course, a complicated system of pasture management designed to minimize hay use during the summer months and preserve two hay fields for mowing in the fall. Not to mention all the Social Security, tax, health insurance, and other paperwork associated with payroll.

As I riffle through the financial records, I come across a pink legal-size carbon copy of a loan agreement. I pull it out and scan it, a frown forming on my face. It seems that my parents took out an equity loan two years ago to cover the cost of a new roof for the stable. I'm surprised and dismayed—even though they're no longer running an A-circuit barn and it was a large expense, I would have thought they'd be able to cover it. But in fact, they've been running this place on a shoestring.

I suppose it's part of the Austrian psyche, but absolutely everything is in order. And clean, damn it. I think my mother vacuums the insides of the filing cabinet drawers. There's not a hope I can keep things up to her standards. It just isn't in me. My Austrian psyche has been diluted by a lifetime in America.

By the time I've gone through all the files, I've been sitting for nearly three hours. I get up and wander over to the window. I stretch with my arms over my head, and then lean from side to side.

Jean-Claude is teaching a group lesson now, and five adolescent girls are riding at a posting trot around the perimeter. Jean-Claude is walking a small circle at the end of the arena facing one of the girls, and without hearing what he says, I know what's going on, because the girl suddenly sits a beat and starts coming up on the proper diagonal.

I decide to go downstairs for a soft drink. When I get to the bottom of the stairs, I see that the door to the trophy room is ajar. Instead of closing it, I step inside and turn on the light.

No wonder Jean-Claude called me "the famous Annemarie." Even if my parents had never mentioned me, my plaques and ribbons are plastered all over the walls. Not to mention the pictures that line the hallway and lounge.

"Hey there," says a voice, and I turn quickly. It's Dan. I hadn't heard him come in.

"Hey," I say, feeling both fluttery and distressed.

He takes in the contents of the room, and then is quiet. "You had quite a career," he says finally.

"Yup. Peaked at eighteen. Lucky me," I say.

Dan is silent for a moment.

"Look, I, uh, I wanted to apologize about yesterday. I should have known how you'd react, but I guess I got so wrapped up in his coloring I didn't think far enough ahead."

I go over to a tack box and open it. More ribbons, and a binder full of laminated certificates.

"Don't worry about it," I say, trying to sound casual. "How is he, anyway?"

"About the same. Only now he's outside, and we can't get him back in. I don't know what we're going to do if we can't get close to him soon. I'm starting to think maybe it was a mistake to get him."

"It was not," I say fiercely, and then stop, startled by my reaction.

Dan scrutinizes me from across the room. "No, maybe not," he says. "But his feet need work and he won't let anyone near him."

"Do you need to get near him? I mean, right away?"

"You saw his feet."

"What are you going to do?"

"I'll probably end up using a tranquilizer dart."

"Do you have such a thing?"

He nods. "Some pretty freaked-out animals come through the center."

"Yeah, I'll bet."

I'm twisting the bottom of my sweatshirt now, staring at my feet. When I look up, Dan is still studying me.

"It's pretty remarkable, isn't it?" he says, and he doesn't need to say another word. I know he's talking about the horse's coat. I nod slowly.

Another silence. Then he says, "Well, I guess I'll be going then. Is it okay if I pick Eva up at about seven?"

"For what?" I ask.

"For work."

"What are you talking about?"

"Tomorrow. At the center," he says.

"I still don't know what you're talking about."

"Your mother called earlier and asked if Eva could help out with the foals over the summer."

"She did?" I say.

"Is that not okay?"

"I don't know. Nobody bothered to consult me."

Dan is still watching, looking concerned.

"No, it's fine," I say, trying to recover. "If that's what she wants to do, I'd be delighted. At least I'll know where she is and what she's up to."

"Do you want to think about it?"

"No, I just didn't know anything about it. But it's fine. I can drop her off."

"Are you sure? I don't mind picking her up."

"No. I'll bring her."

"All right then." Dan shuffles his feet, and edges in the direction of the door. "I guess I'll be going then. I just wanted to come by and make sure you were okay."

"I'm fine," I say.

He turns to leave, and then stops in the doorway. He drops his head, keeping his hands braced on either side of the doorframe. Then he turns back to face me. "You look good, Annemarie," he says. "It's nice to see you again."

"You too," I say.

And then he's gone.

• • •

I find Mutti in the side garden, pulling weeds. Harriet is lying beside her on the grass, a bloated bratwurst. Et tu, Harriet?

"I just saw Dan," I say, coming to a stop beside her. She looks up at me, squinting because I'm standing between her and the sun. "He tells me that you arranged for Eva to work for him for the summer."

"Yes, this morning," she says, holding a gloved hand above her eyes to shield them from the sun.

"And it never occurred to you to find out what I thought about it?"

"Eva asked me to call. I thought you knew."

"I didn't."

"Okay. Sorry," she says, turning back to the garden and sticking her trowel into the earth.

"No, it's not okay."

She sets the trowel down, and turns to look at me again. "You sound angry."

"I am."

"Why? What harm is there in it? What else do you want her to do for the summer?"

"There's plenty to do around here."

"It's the same kind of work over there," she says.

"That's not the point."

"What is the point?"

I pause long enough to make sure that when I continue, I won't be yelling. "The point is, Mutti, that I am her mother, and that I am the one who gets to make these types of decisions. Not you, not her. You were out of line."

The chin sets, the lips harden, and the face assumes an expression of righteous indignation. "I did nothing wrong," she says in Germanic staccato. "Eva came to me—*she* asked *me* to call Dan and see if he could use her help, and I did, and he said yes. Naturally, I assumed she had spoken to you about it and that you didn't want to call Dan yourself. If that's not true, I'm sorry. But it's not my fault if your daughter doesn't feel she can approach you."

"I'm perfectly capable of talking to Dan. And no matter how my daughter feels about me, you had no right to supersede me."

"Such big words, Annemarie," says Mutti, returning to her weeds.

I am stunned into silence. If I say anything—anything at all—this will deteriorate into something ugly.

So I go in search of my daughter.

• • •

I find her in the aisle of the stable, grooming Bergeron.

The big white horse stands patiently in the crossties while Eva crouches by his left shoulder, massaging his leg with a rubber curry comb. Luis is in the doorway of a stall, shoveling shavings and manure into a neat pile. As I approach, Eva says something to him, and he laughs in response.

When she sees me, she jumps to her feet. "Oh, hey, Ma! Guess what?"

"What?" I say, as animated as a lump of coal.

"Jean-Claude says that if I help him with Bergeron and the school horses, he'll give me lessons."

"He did?"

"Yeah, and guess what else?"

"What?"

"Mutti called that Dan guy this morning, and he said I could help out with the foals over the summer. Isn't that just the coolest?"

I stare at my daughter. She's wearing jeans that come up to her waist, paddock boots that hide her blue toenails, and a sweatshirt that's already streaked with horse slobber. And then I look at her face, which is free of makeup and glowing with an expression I haven't seen in about two years.

"Yeah," I say, starting to nod. "Very cool. Very, very cool."

Chapter 7

At quarter to seven the next morning, there's an ungodly pounding on my door.

"Ma! Come on! I'm going to be late."

I look at the clock, squinting against the harsh morning light.

"Okay, I'm up," I yell, swinging my legs over the side of the bed. Harriet topples grumbling to the floor. "I'll meet you at the car."

I grab yesterday's jeans from the chair and shove myself into them. I stop quickly at the dresser to peer into my puffy eyes, and then run a hairbrush through my hair. When I get to the door, I stop, go back, and apply a little lipstick.

At the rescue center, we find Dan standing on the back of a flatbed truck shoveling shavings into a tractor's wagon. When he sees us, he jumps to the ground and pulls the dust mask up onto his forehead.

"Good morning, ladies," he says, coming across the gravel. "Right on time, I see."

"Wouldn't want to be late for my first day on the job," says Eva.

"Absolutely not," says Dan. "I might have to dock your pay."

"You're paying her?" I say quickly.

"Nope," he says, grinning.

"Oh. I see."

He turns to Eva. "Do you want a coffee before you get started? There's some in the office. End of the aisle in the main barn," he says, pointing a gloved hand. "Then come out and I'll get you started."

"Sure, Boss," says Eva.

I watch her recede into the building.

When I turn back, Dan is looking at me.

"I hope you don't mind her having coffee," he says. "I should have asked first."

"No, that's fine. Eva more or less does what she likes." I'm silent for a moment, thinking two things: that I probably shouldn't have said that, and also that Mutti said much the same thing about me. "Thanks for letting her help out," I continue. "It means a lot to her."

"It means a lot to us, too. We're always short-handed. And short-funded. And short of supplies. Heck, we're always short of everything."

There's an awkward pause.

"So," he says. "I gather you're here for the summer?"

"Yes, at least."

"At least?"

I pause for a moment, wondering how much he already knows. "Roger and I are getting divorced, and with Pappa as sick as he is, I decided to move back."

"I'm sorry," he says. "I hadn't heard. About the divorce, I mean."

"It's all right," I say.

I hear gravel crunching, and turn to see Eva returning with a white foam cup.

"Dan," I say. "Can I have another look at that horse again before I leave?"

"Of course. Anytime."

"Right. Thanks. What time should I pick Eva up, in case I don't see you again?"

"Hey," Eva says, rejoining us with a smile.

"I'll drop her off," Dan says. "I've got to come to your place later today anyway."

"You do?"

"Yes. I'm floating the teeth of some of the school horses."

"Oh, right," I say.

• • •

The horse is standing in the paddock where I last saw him, with his neck stretched out and his ears partway back in an expression of suspicion. Dan has obviously managed to get close to him, because his feet have been trimmed, and he's shod. I look closely—they're corrective shoes, with a bar across the back. Considering what his feet looked like just day before yesterday, I'm surprised they look as good as they do.

Damn, he looks like Harry. And it's not just the white stripes zigzagged evenly across his red coat. His face is incredibly similar. Except for the eye.

I walk around the fence again, this time prepared for what I'm going to find. Again, he turns with me so that I'm always looking at the left side of his face.

When I get close, I approach the fence slowly and lean against it, dropping my chin on my forearms.

"Hey," I say softly. "Hey, Beautiful."

He turns to face me now, and once again, I catch my breath at the sight of that empty socket.

It doesn't appear to be a fresh injury, thank God. It almost looks as though there's skin running behind where the eye should be, hair and everything, although it's hard to tell because it's in deep shadow. There are scars running down his cheek and up over his forehead, long lines where the hair doesn't grow. They look like cracks in the road, repaired with snaking strips of blacktop.

He raises his head and stares at me, his nostrils flaring slightly with each breath. He is sniffing me.

"What happened to you?" I say, without moving.

He snorts and then blows, stretching his neck out to shake. Then he swivels his ears, first one and then the other, but not together, and a fist tightens around my heart.

"Oh God," I say quietly.

One minute later, I stride into the barn, where Dan and Eva are mucking out the foals' pen.

"What are you going to do with him?" I demand.

"What?" says Dan.

"The chestnut," I say impatiently. "The brindled chestnut."

"Uh, well," he says, coming up to speed. "I'll fix him up, and then I'll try to find him a home."

"I want him."

Dan leans on the end of his shovel and stares at me.

"I mean it, I want him."

"You sure about this? He's shaping up to be a handful."

"Absolutely sure. Couldn't be more sure. Sure as anything."

"Well, okay. When we've got him—"

"Now. I want him now."

"No," says Dan, shaking his head. "Absolutely not. For one thing, I can't even get him back in the barn. How are we supposed to get him onto a trailer?"

"You did it before, didn't you? Tranquilizers. Darts. Whatever it takes. All I know is I want him. Now."

"Annemarie, I just don't think—"

"I don't care. I want him, and if you haven't promised him to anybody else, there's no reason for you not to let me have him."

I can see that he's wavering. "I want to be the one to work with him," I continue. "I want to be the one that brings him back. I'll pay for the auction fee. I'll pay you to transport him."

"It's not about the money."

"You bet it's not. I want that horse, Dan."

Behind him, Eva is staring at me with something almost like respect.

Dan continues to search my face, and I lock eyes with him. I feel my chin jut slightly, setting like Mutti's. My lips harden into a thin line.

"Okay," he says, nodding softly. "Okay then. I guess I can't say I'm surprised."

• • •

At dinner, Eva grills me about why I wanted the horse so badly. When I tell her that his markings are almost identical to Harry's, she looks at me blankly. Is it possible that I never told her about Harry? This seems incredible, unbelievable.

"You never heard about Harry? The horse I lost in the accident?"

From the corner of my eye I see Jean-Claude look up quickly.

"He's the one in the pictures at the barn, right?" asks Eva.

"Yes."

"Isn't that why they thought your uterus ruptured?"

I suck in my breath. That is one of the theories, but that's surely not the only context in which she's heard about the accident?

I look at Jean-Claude, who is looking discreetly at his plate.

"Your mother was a world-class rider, Eva," says Mutti, reaching for a plate of pesto gnocchi. She passes it to Eva, and then reaches for the bowl of plum tomatoes and fresh mozzarella.

"Really?" says Eva, looking at me in surprise.

"Olympic bound," says Pappa proudly, pulling the edges of his mouth back into a lopsided smile.

I brace myself for the inevitable inventory of accomplishments, but Pappa stops, because Mutti lifts the wine to his lips. Everyone resumes eating, and for a moment, I think it won't come.

"Olympics, eh?" Jean-Claude finally says, taking a large sip of wine. He leans back to look at me, crossing his arms on his chest.

"She made the Claremont National," says Pappa. "Next stop, the Rolex-Kentucky, and then, who knows?"

"And it was at the Claremont, this accident?" asks Jean-Claude.

"Yes," I say, staring at my plate. I'm dreading the next question.

"And the horse you were riding was striped?" asks Eva.

"Yes," I say.

"So that's what Dan was talking about when you first saw him. You should have seen her today," says Eva, turning to Mutti.

Mutti raises her eyebrows. "I can only imagine," she says.

"Dan said she couldn't have him, and she just kept right on at him. Didn't you, Mom?"

"I guess," I say, embarrassed.

"So he finally gave in. Not like he had a choice," beams Eva. "So what are you going to name him?"

"Uh," I say. "I don't know. I really haven't thought about it."

"Harry?"

"No," I say, offended by the very idea.

"Well, I still think the whole thing is a bad idea," says Mutti, looking imperious. "We have plenty of horses already."

"Not like that, we don't," says Eva. "So are you going to ride again?"

"No!" I say loudly. Then I realize everybody's staring at me. "No, of course not," I say, in as calm a voice as I can muster.

• • •

"Okay Mike, back her up," shouts Dan, waving his arm in a circle. The man in the truck revs the engine and backs it slowly to the gate of the paddock.

"That's not a horse trailer," says Eva.

"No," says Dan. "It's a stock truck. There's no way anyone could lead this guy onto a horse trailer, and there's no way I'd let anyone try." He turns to me and frowns. "You really want to do this?"

I nod.

Mutti and Pappa are thirty yards off, waiting in the van. The plan is to follow the truck back to our place after the horse is loaded.

The brindled chestnut is on the far side of the paddock, against the fence, watching with great suspicion.

"Did you tranquilize him?" I ask.

"You don't see him tearing around, do you?" says Dan.

"Okay," Mike says, climbing out of the truck's cab and crossing the gravel. He claps his leather work gloves together in front of him. "Let's do this."

He and Dan climb the paddock fence and open the gate inward. Then they drop the truck's ramp.

The horse backs into the far corner and stands with his left side toward us, pawing intermittently at the ground.

"Hey Chester . . . Chester!" shouts Dan to a man coming out of the quarantine barn. "Get Judy. I think we're going to need help."

With Chester and Judy standing at either side of the truck's opening, Dan and Mike approach the gelding from opposite sides. He remains absolutely still, with his head raised to the wind. I can see the white of his one eye.

"Come on, baby," I whisper to myself. "Nobody's going to hurt you."

When Dan gets within a dozen feet of him, the horse throws his head into the air and bolts. After he passes Dan, he slows to a fast trot and circles the paddock with his tail on end, throwing his head. Then he comes to an abrupt stop, locking his legs in front of him and disappearing in the resulting cloud of dust.

Dan and Mike approach again, slowly. As they get closer, the horse pins his ears against his head, pivots on his hind legs, and again springs past them.

As he passes the opening of the truck, Mike lunges forward, flipping the lead rope, but the horse simply changes direction, loping back toward Dan.

Dan shakes his head in frustration. A moment later, he and Mike resume their original positions.

Each time they try to round the horse into the trailer, he lets them get within a dozen feet and then bolts. The final time, he barrels past close enough that Mike has to jump onto the fence to get out of the way. It's not the horse's fault—Mike was on the side without the eye.

"This isn't working, Dan," Mike says, dropping to the ground on the other side of the fence. "I'm grabbing a couple of carrot sticks."

"Carrot sticks?" says Eva, turning to me. "If they could get him using carrot sticks, why didn't they just do that in the first place?"

"It's a kind of whip, honey," I say.

"They're not going to hit him, are they?"

"No, of course not."

A few minutes later, Dan and Mike return, carrying short orange whips. They move slowly, silently. When they get into position, they are as still as statues until the horse stops moving. Then Dan gives a curt nod.

They leap the fence and charge. The horse bolts to the far end, near the open truck, and then swivels, ready to dart past. Dan and Mike each hold their arms out, blocking the way with whips. The horse rears and shrieks, and the men lunge forward, shouting, waving the whips in front of them.

Finally, in a series of events that feels like a single, fluid movement, the horse gallops up the ramp with an enormous clatter, Chester slams the wooden gate across the opening, and Judy throws its bolt.

Through the metal slats, I see flashes of red and white as the horse moves around inside, a glimpse of haunch rising and falling, a shoulder disappearing from view as he rears, pawing at the air. There's one long, desperate whinny, and then the sharp crack of horseshoes against the metal side. It starts in a flurry, like popcorn in a microwave, and then drops off to the occasional crash.

Chester and Judy raise and secure the ramp. Dan stands watching, shaking his head.

"Damn, Annemarie. You sure about this?"

I nod my head.

"You don't have any idea what you're getting yourself into, do you?"

"Okay," I say, rubbing my hands in front of me. "Let's get him home."

Eva, excited, runs ahead of me and clambers past

Pappa into the back of the van. As I approach at a walk, I see Mutti in the driver's seat, shaking her head.

• • •

"Waste of a good pasture," mumbles Mutti, as Mike and Dan prepare to release the horse into a small field next to the stable.

"It's not a waste, Mutti," I say irritably. "It means he won't need extra hay."

"But the other horses can't use it, can they? It can't be used in the rotation anymore, can it?"

"No, not right away. But we don't know that he won't get along with the other horses, do we?"

"You are *not* turning that horse out with the herds," says Mutti sharply.

"No, Mutti. I'm not going to do anything right away. But let's not rule out the possibility that he'll eventually settle down and be okay in a herd."

"Huh," sniffs Mutti. "And all this because he's brindled?"

Dan and Mike have the trailer backed through the opening of the pasture now, and are preparing to drop the ramp.

"Oh, I don't know, Mutti. I guess so."

"Perhaps we should have got that other one after all," she says, pivoting on her heel and walking away.

I turn to ask what she meant, but am distracted by the crash of the ramp hitting the ground, and then the volley of kicks from the horse trapped inside.

• • •

But I don't forget. Later on, when Brian is back to put Pappa to bed and Eva is watching television, I step quietly into the kitchen. I stand watching Mutti's back for a while as she finishes the dishes. Her blonde hair is pulled tightly into the same coil it's been in since the beginning of time, and her thin arms jab and jerk as she attacks the last of the dishes. Tonight, she'd made a spinach-and-mushroom soufflé, had watched victoriously as Eva helped herself to thirds. Mutti, the lover of veal, the Schnitzel Queen, has capitulated.

"What other one?" I say, coming up behind her.

"What other one what?" she says without missing a beat. She must have seen my reflection in the window behind the sink.

She turns sideways and pushes the sleeping Harriet aside with one foot so she can open one of the lower cupboards.

"When you asked me if I wanted the horse because he was brindled, you said 'Perhaps we should have got the other one.' What other one?"

Mutti takes a pile of pots from the cupboard, lifts the top three, and inserts the clean one. It reminds me of a baby's stacking baskets.

"It doesn't matter now. It's all in the past."

"What is?"

Mutti puts the pots back in the cupboard and returns to the dish rack with her back to me.

"There's no profit in examining the past," she says.

"That's crazy, Mutti. It doesn't even make sense."

At this moment, Brian emerges from the hallway.

He crosses the kitchen, and takes his jacket from a peg by the door.

"Anton is set for the night," he says, groping behind his back for the second sleeve. "I'll be back at eight in the morning."

"Thank you," says Mutti, stacking plates on the counter.

Brian opens the door and then stares through the screen. "That's some horse you got out there," he says. "A bit skinny, but, well . . . I guess I never knew there was such a thing as a striped horse. You know, other than zebras, of course."

"It's very rare," Mutti answers. I wait for her to point out that zebras aren't horses, but she doesn't.

When Brian closes the door, Mutti switches the baby monitor on.

"Mutti, please," I say as she resumes cleaning. "Please."

She freezes, and then after a long silence says, "Harry had a brother. A full brother, another brindled chestnut."

I gasp as though I've been punched in the chest. "What? When?"

"Seventeen years ago."

"How do you know?"

"Because they called Pappa to see if he wanted him."

I stare at her in shock. Mutti shoots a look over her shoulder, then abandons the dishes and comes to the table to sit down. I sit next to her.

"When you refused to ride again—"

"I did not refuse to ride again," I protest.

"When you refused to ride again," Mutti continues loudly, "your father thought that maybe it wasn't just fear. That maybe it was because of Harry. And so he called the breeder, trying to find another brindled chestnut. He thought that if you knew there was another one coming up that you might start riding again, so that when the horse was ready to be trained, you'd be ready for the horse. And then, three years later, there was another one—a full brother to Harry—and they offered him to your father."

I can feel my eyes widening as she says this, but I've already projected what's coming. By then I was in Minneapolis with Roger. By then, I'd left that part of my life irretrievably behind.

Mutti looks at me victoriously, expecting submission, perhaps even gratitude.

"What happened?" I say quietly.

"Well, obviously you'd made it clear you had no interest in riding again—"

"To the horse, Mutti. To the horse."

"He was an eventer, like Harry. Ian McCullough bought him."

"My God," I say, stunned. Ian McCullough was in the same circuit as I was, had been my most challenging competitor for my final year. He made the Olympic team the year I was hurt. He took my place. "Harry's brother is doing Grand Prix work?"

"Was."

Again, the feeling of being punched in the chest. I search her face for a signal, hoping that she doesn't mean what I think she does.

"He died a few months ago. If you followed eventing at all, you'd already know that. In fact, if you followed eventing at all, you'd already know about the horse."

She stares at me coolly, until I turn my face away in disgust.

I get up quickly, scraping my chair across the floor, and push the screen door open with a straight arm. It crashes shut as I head for the pasture.

When I get there, I climb the fence and walk out toward my horse; my damaged, one-eyed, mangy horse. He lifts his head to look at me, ears flattened in suspicion. I sit down cross-legged in the grass, a good thirty yards away. After he's sure I'm not coming any closer, he returns to grazing.

Suddenly, the loss of Harry's brother, this unseen liver chestnut brindle that I could have had and never met, makes my face contort with grief. Before I know it, I'm sobbing like a four-year-old.

• • •

That night, I search the Internet until almost dawn, desperately seeking information about Harry's brother. I plug one string after another into the search engine—"Highland Farm Hanoverians brindled," "eventers brindled Hanoverian Grand Prix," "brindled chestnut Hanoverian"—until finally I hit pay dirt with "Ian McCullough brindled eventer."

It's an article from an old issue of *Equine World*, lingering on in cyberspace nearly six years after it was written.

"Highland Hurrah takes first at the 1994 Rolex-Kentucky," blares the headline, huge and blue across the top of the page.

Highland Hurrah. I read the name with a rush of

sickness, a feeling of falling. I read it again, and again, and again, staring at those two words until they no longer seem like words but concrete objects that float above my screen.

My connection to the Internet is slow, and the image beneath the headline unrolls in agonizing fits and starts. First, there's a great expanse of blue sky, broken at the edges by trees and pooled into areas of similar color. Then the tips of perked ears; dark, triangular, and pointed. And then, finally, there he is, stretched over the crest of a brick wall with Ian McCullough lying flat against his striped neck, hands thrust forward as his mount takes the massive fence.

I am frozen, blinking at the screen as a lump rises in my throat. This horse looks so much like Harry I don't know how to process it, am almost afraid to try.

Beneath the image, the story has finished loading, and I move on to that because it's easier than looking at Harry's brother. It outlines how astonishingly close the top three contenders were, of how McCullough, in the third Rolex-Kentucky victory of his career, took the $50,000 purse and Rolex timepiece with a lead of only .4 penalty points.

I look at the picture again, and this time I can't get enough of it. I am scanning this brother-of-Harry hungrily, his markings, the shape of his hooves, muzzle, knees, and joints, because I know just how they'd feel under my hands. The sight of him takes me hurtling back, stripping away the layers to where the memory of Harry's body resides intact. The long slope of his shoulder; the warm area—soft as muzzle—between his front legs; the *V* on his chest where the hair changes direction; the swirling cowlick where his rib cage meets his flank. How it used to feel when I ran my hand down his leg, checking for heat. The muscular shoulder leading to long, smooth leg; the gentle, bony swell of knee; the surprisingly delicate fetlock and hard, cool hoof; the soft, warm hollow at the back of his foot, just above his heel. And although it hurts like hell, I linger here in this memory, because it feels real.

Oh, Harry. Oh, Harry. In some ways, I don't think anything has ever felt real since. I think I've been on hold since the day you died.

• • •

When I drag myself out to the office the next morning, I'm heavy limbed and bleary.

Despite having spent much of the night online, the first thing I do is launch Internet Explorer and plug a search string into Google. And then another. And then another.

Forty minutes later, one of the underlined links on the left of the screen says "Brindled Champion Dies in Tragic Accident."

I click the link and hold my breath.

The picture is the same as the first one I found last night, only this time it's a thumbnail version. Highland Hurrah taking a brick wall, exploding with all the energy required to propel fourteen hundred pounds of horse and man over a span of eleven feet that peaks at a height of five.

About halfway through the text, I realize I still haven't breathed.

He died in a trailering accident. He died because someone forgot to put the cab in gear, and the whole thing rolled backward into a propane tank and exploded.

The text is so detached, so very matter-of-fact. As an editor, I usually applaud this, but this article is utterly insufficient. It should describe how terrified he was, tethered into his fiery hell. How his skin and flesh roasted and crackled, peeling from his still-living body as he fought helplessly against his restraints. How after struggling for as long as he could, he finally gave himself to the flames, stretching his long, muscled neck out against the molten aluminum beneath him in the resignation of the dying.

The article ends with "Our sincerest condolences go out to Ian McCullough, whose career with the great Hanoverian was unrivaled, and whose life will never be the same."

I grow murderous as I read this. This was Harry's brother. This was a horse who—had the cosmos not been torn asunder—would have been mine. A horse who ended up dying in the most horrifying circumstances because some mental deficient forgot to put the truck in gear. He died, in other words, because of some idiot who is too stupid to live, and even if it wasn't Ian himself, it was somebody hired by Ian, and that makes him culpable.

I stare at the screen for what seems like forever, my heart pounding with anger and grief. Hating and mourning and wanting to scream, I stare at the tiny pixilated picture as though I might understand better if I looked at it long enough. With my hand on the mouse, I move the cursor idly around the horse's outline, tracing his hooves and ears onscreen, circling the cowlick I know is on his chest. And then, before I know it, I'm leaning forward and typing again, desperately searching cyberspace for another picture, any picture, of Highland Hurrah. In order to mourn his death, I need to reconstruct his life.

Chapter 8

Pappa is deteriorating quickly, falling straight off the edge. Eva and I have only been here for six weeks, but the difference is striking. He is skeletal, so thin it is painful to take it in, skin stretched over bone. His nails are yellow and ridged, his hair white, combed sparsely across his scalp.

He hardly eats anything, at least in front of us. Everything Mutti serves—invariably from one of her new vegetarian cookbooks—can be scooped with a spoon or fork, and when it can't be, she precuts his portion in the kitchen. Even so, it's such an effort, and often the food falls off before it reaches his mouth. When that happens, he rests before trying again. He probably manages half a dozen bites in the course of each meal, and he's literally wasting away. Mutti still helps him with his drink, but never with his food. I'm sure it's because he doesn't want to be spoon-fed in front of the rest of us, as though it's somehow a reflection on him as a person.

That's ridiculous, of course, but I also understand it, having been in the position of not being able to do anything for myself. And like Pappa, I hated asking for help. There were many, many times when I resisted asking someone to scratch my nose, or move my hair so it wasn't tickling my neck, or lift a glass and place the end of the straw in my mouth so I could take a drink. Although it's not the same, of course, because my helplessness came upon me with crashing suddenness, and his is encroaching slowly. His very life is slipping out from under him.

His head now leans against the back of the wheelchair, usually at an angle that suggests he can't hold it upright. Soon there will be wings to the side of the headrest to give him support, or else he'll have to wear a back and neck brace, as I did in the early days of my recovery. His speech is slowing, too, and when he tries to smile, he usually only manages to pull his face into a grimace that is so terrible I try not to look. It's the same with eating, but even though I avert my gaze, I'm aware of every failed attempt, every morsel that tips off the side just as his fork reaches his mouth. I am gripped with sadness, desperation, and anger, too. I don't know where to direct this, although Mutti makes a fine substitute most of the time. And this is grossly unfair, because it is I who am failing, not her.

She spends all of every day with Pappa. Brian comes in the morning and then again at night, but that is only because Mutti can't do the lifting required to get Pappa in and out of bed. Other than that, she is at his side all day. If she works in the garden, he parks beside her in the shade of the patio umbrella. If she's cooking, he reads at the kitchen table. They rent movies, they listen to Wagner, they do jigsaw puzzles—an agonizing pursuit, but unlike with eating, he doesn't seem to mind dropping the pieces and trying again.

There is only one thing Pappa does alone. Every afternoon, just after the horses come in, Mutti opens the back door and Pappa steers out to the porch. Then he drives down the ramp and across the gravel, his head bobbing with each dip in the surface. When he gets to the stable, he stops in front of Razzmatazz's stall.

As soon as he arrives, the nearest stable hand comes and immediately, wordlessly, slides the door open and puts up the stall guard. Then Tazz, an impossibly tall half Percheron, half God-knows-what, with hooves the size of dinner plates, lumbers over and extends his neck into the aisle. He sniffs Pappa's face, his hands, and searches his lap for treats.

Pappa always has carrots for him, never an apple, and I'm sure I know why. Unless a horse takes an apple in one bite, you have to give him something to push against, some counter-pressure while he sinks his teeth into it. And Pappa doesn't have the strength for that anymore. Instead, he comes armed with sections of carrots, which he feeds to Tazz, one by one. Even when the carrots run out, Tazz remains at the stall door, nosing my father and sniffing his chair while Pappa murmurs to him, occasionally bringing a bony hand up to touch the horse's grizzled face.

I find this both fascinating and heartbreaking. The old Pappa would never have shown such softness. The old Pappa would have considered this coddling.

I watch the nightly pilgrimage religiously, but am careful to stay out of sight. Usually, I hang out around the corner, or just inside the wash rack, but always I make sure that he can't see me without turning his chair. And when he does, the sound of the motor gives me ample time to grab a shovel or a pitchfork from the wall and stride past with a jolly "Hi Pappa," as though I'm terribly busy and can't possibly find the time to stop.

It's mean, it's stupid, and it's immature, but I don't know what to say to him. I can't say, "Hi Pappa, how are you feeling today?" because I'm afraid he might tell me. I can't approach him and talk about other things, because that reeks of cowardice. So instead, I pretend that nothing is out of the ordinary, ignoring the physical reminders that are everywhere: the track in the ceiling that leads to the bathroom, the fact that we take all our meals in the study, the terrible, familiar sounds that emerge from the dining room as Brian gets Pappa up for the day.

Eva seems to have accepted Pappa's decline and coming death as a natural part of life, and I admire and despair her attitude in equal parts. Death may be natural, but surely not this death. This death is a theft, an abomination, and too close to a palindrome of my own experience for me to be able to cope with it.

• • •

This is not a good night. I got caught by Pappa in the stable today, and did my usual "no time to talk" routine, and now I feel terrible about it. But short of seeking him out for a conversation, I can't think how to rectify it. So instead, the second dinner is over I make my way outside with Jean-Claude. I climb the fence with a bag of apples, and he goes to the stable to get Bergeron.

His devotion to the white stallion is touching. He spends at least an hour in the field with him every evening, talking to him, grooming him, running a finishing brush over his smooth coat. Sometimes he combs Bergeron's long tail while he grazes, holding it off to the side with one hand and detangling the luxurious white length with the other. He's a man who understands long hair. It makes me wonder about the women he's known.

I go and sit in the grass, as close to my horse as he'll let me come. He's a tough nut to crack. It's been weeks, and I'm still bowling apples across the pasture at him. This amuses Jean-Claude no end, but what else can I do?

It's not as though the relationship is entirely one sided. We're making progress, even if it is slow. When he sees me, he pricks up his ears. He knows who I am. I'm the lady who rolls apples at him.

Tonight, though, he is being particularly standoffish. Our usual routine is that I roll an apple, he goes to get it, and then while he's eating it, I inch a little closer. Tonight, he takes the apple, and then flattens his ears against his head at the first sign of movement.

I turn to go back to the house. From the corner of my eye I see Jean-Claude approach the fence. This is an invitation for me to do the same. I walk dejectedly. I'm not in a mood to talk, but I don't want to be rude.

"Don't let it get you down," he says when I come to a stop. "You know how horses are. Maybe it's something in the wind."

"Or maybe he hates me," I say, leaning against the whitewashed boards.

"No. He will come around."

"You think?" I ask, looking back at my horse. He's munching the last apple fragment, eyes narrowed in suspicion.

"Without question. Already, he lets you get closer, no? You should have seen Bergeron in the early days. A real wild man. Crazy."

"What, him?" I scoff, looking over at the white stallion. "That marshmallow?"

"Yes, that marshmallow," says Jean-Claude.

"When was this?"

"Eight years ago. I was at a barn outside of Montreal looking at a different horse, perhaps to buy, and this guy was chained in a stall at the back. They'd labeled him as vicious—they were going to put him down, but I saw something in him. They didn't want to sell him to me, but I persisted. And now look at my Boo-Boo, my beautiful boy. Eh, Boo-Boo?" he says, raising his voice.

Bergeron lifts his head briefly, his lower jaw moving from side to side. Before long, he returns to grazing, rhythmically ripping grass from the ground and swishing his elegant tail.

"You'd never know," I say. "How did you do it?"

"Love, patience, and time. There is no shortcut, no magic. But it will happen. You will see."

We both look at my horse, who has moved as far away as possible. He is flush with the fence, pretending not to look at us. His ears are plastered back.

"Something has happened to your boy, that is all. You must give him time to trust you, to want to dance."

I've watched Jean-Claude give enough lessons to know his vernacular. "It's not going to happen, Jean-Claude. I'm not going to ride him," I say.

"Well, we shall see," he says. "We shall see. But for sure, you have a nice-looking boy there."

• • •

There's something so charismatic about Jean-Claude's manner that I think he could say anything and I'd believe it. But in this, there's no question. This horse, such a wreck when he came to us, is looking good. Astonishingly good, in fact, and there's a whole lot more to it than just a return to a healthy body weight. With some flesh on his bones, his conformation is beginning to show itself. More and more, he looks Hanoverian. More and more, he looks like Harry.

The similarities in coloring were there in the beginning, as was the shape of the face, but it wasn't until he started to put weight on that the familiar shape began to emerge, like a statue from a hunk of stone.

The change was so gradual that the idea it spawned never hit me in a single moment of recognition. It wormed its way into my head so slowly, so quietly, that I didn't even know what was happening until it was already there. It was probably lurking for weeks, but chose not to reveal itself until it had staked its turf and set up ramparts.

The first time it crossed my mind, I dismissed it as crazy. But as many times as I slammed the lid down, it rose again, seeping around the edges like steam.

Finally, one night, I could ignore it no more. After

I was sure that everybody else in the house was in bed, I snuck down to the study and spent the entire night going through back issues of magazines until I found a photograph of Highland Hurrah. I needed a paper one, one I could take with me.

Then, by the light of the rising sun, I took it out to the pasture and held it at arm's length, comparing it to the horse who stood in front of me, desperately searching first the horse, and then the picture. Then the horse, and then the picture. Picking out a single marking on one, and matching it on the other.

Highland Hurrah is dead. I know this. I also know that he is grazing in my field. I wonder if the wishing of it could make it so, if somehow, mystically, I've caused the lost brindled horse to coalesce, forming him like a diamond by the weight of my heart. I've heard of faith healing, of how concentrated mental energy can cause inoperable cancers to retreat into nothingness—is it really so outrageous to believe that I caused the reincarnation of the lost Hanoverian simply by wanting it so badly?

I know better than to tell anyone about this. They already think I'm crazy. Not Eva, of course, who has thrown herself into her work at the rescue center with a zeal I didn't know was in her, but certainly Mutti does, and Dan. They don't know exactly what's going on, but they suspect I've gone a little off. I can see it in their faces, in the veil of patience that drops across their faces when I'm talking. The sad nods of understanding from Dan, and the hard, sideways glares from Mutti.

It started with the fact that I wouldn't name the horse. At first, this manifested itself with gentle teasing, an amusement at how long it was taking me to get around to it. After several weeks, though, it became obvious that my reluctance was something more, something pathological. Dan, polite and kind to the bone, simply stopped asking. Mutti stopped asking, too, but with a kind of judgmental abruptness.

Of course, I *have* named the horse—or at least, have given him back his old name—but I can't tell them that. They'd think I was nuts. Even I think I'm nuts sometimes. And yet I can't get beyond this belief. It looms as solid as an obelisk.

But eventually even I have to admit that I could not have formed this horse from thin air.

• • •

There's a click and a crackle on the other end of the line as I press the phone to my ear. I know I shouldn't do this, but I'm powerless to stop. When Dan answers, I'm shaking.

"Dan?"

"Yes."

"It's me."

"I know," he says.

Suddenly I am unable to find the words to start.

"Is everything okay?" he asks.

"Yes, fine. It's just . . . I've been . . . Listen, I want to ask you something."

"What?"

"My horse, how old are his injuries?"

"I don't know. It's hard to say exactly."

"Guess."

"Four or five months, maybe. Why?"

"Are they compatible with a trailering accident? And a fire?"

Silence from the other end.

"Dan?"

"I'm here."

"Are they?"

"I guess. They could be. Why are you asking?"

"I think I know who he is."

"You do?"

"I think he's Harry's brother."

"Annemarie—"

"No, I'm serious. I've seen pictures of him—he's a dead ringer."

"Annemarie—"

"I know this sounds nuts, but think about it. How many brindled horses have you come across in your lifetime?"

I pause for him to answer, but he doesn't. There's palpable disbelief in the silence. I think he's trying to decide whether I've gone off the deep end.

"I know this sounds crazy, but it's not. I've downloaded lots of pictures. It's not just the coloring, it's the markings. The markings match. I mean, exactly."

Again, an awkward pause. "Annemarie, I really don't think that's the case."

"I know how it sounds," I say, barreling on, and aware that I'm starting to sound hysterical. "I really do. But you have to see the pictures. It's the same horse."

"Why would someone fake his death?"

"I don't know. Insurance money."

"Why would anyone rather have the money than a world-class eventer?" he says.

"Because Hurrah is seventeen, which puts him at about the end of his eventing career."

Silence.

"You think I'm nuts," I say finally.

"I don't think you're nuts."

"You do. I can tell."

"I think you've been under a hell of a lot of pressure."

"No. You have to look at the pictures."

"Annemarie, he's not Harry's brother."

"But what if he is?"

"If he were, he'd have been microchipped. Not only that, insurance companies insist on a vet identifying the body, especially for a big claim."

I hadn't thought of that. My burgeoning faith sags like a soufflé.

"Look," Dan continues gently. "I understand why you want to believe this. I know—"

"No you don't," I snap. I know it's irrational, but the microchip thing seems like his fault.

"I do. Believe me, I do. I was there, remember? It was always Harry for you. Always. My God, Annemarie—even your dog is named Harry."

"She is not," I sputter in protest. "Her name is Harri—" And then I stop, frozen, stunned by my lack of self-knowledge. "Oh God, I'm nuts. I've actually gone off the deep end."

"Maybe you just need to get out," Dan says. "You know, get your mind off things."

"No, I'm just nuts."

"You have every reason in the world to be stressed

out. You're surrounded by reasons." Another pause. "Look, do you want to do something tonight? After I drop Eva off? I'm not talking about a date. Just a movie and maybe a bite to eat. Just to get you off the farm for a while."

"Um . . . Yeah, okay. Why not."

"Okay then. Good."

I hang up, strangely disappointed that it's not a date.

• • •

Okay, so I'm nuts. On this, everyone seems agreed, and for a few minutes after I hang up, I agree.

I'm not blind to the obvious. I know how irrational this seems. Ian McCullough is a respected sportsman, and what I'm suggesting would make him a felon. But then I return to the pictures, and there's no getting around the fact that this is the same horse. I don't know whether this shows great faith or pitiable delusion.

Standing at the wooden fence, I look from the picture in my hand to the horse in the field and decide that no, it isn't pitiable delusion.

For two decades, I've felt like a lab specimen in a jar. There's been a murkiness over everything, a feeling that I somehow skipped a groove and couldn't get back in. But lately I've been seeing flashes—tantalizing glimpses of what's beneath the veil. I'm starting to feel again in a way that I haven't in twenty years, and I can't let it go.

However irrational it seems, I know the truth, and if it has to be mine alone, partaken in secret like an alcoholic slurping wine in a closet, so be it. I won't let it go.

• • •

Dan picks me up at five, and we go to a movie. It's the most popular of the summer, but I find it distracting because the actors keep taking flight and bounding across the tops of trees. But what I find most distracting is Dan.

True to his word, he is acting entirely platonically toward me. I wonder what he'd do if I just reached out and took his hand. I don't, because it would probably shock him. A woman as recently single as me probably should not be making moves on ex-boyfriends on explicitly declared non-dates. But still, it would be nice to feel the warmth of his hand on mine, or his thigh under my palm.

I look over at his profile, watching as he picks up a few pieces of popcorn.

I remember the first time I ever laid eyes on him—he was in a group of kids bussed over from the local high school to watch me compete. I was accepting my ribbon, and I saw him behind the boards. He was watching intently while the other kids messed around. And then he smiled at me, a huge open grin. It took my breath away.

He is still the most attractive man I've ever seen, with his easy exuberance and clear blue eyes. Even age is looking good on him, which isn't fair, because it isn't looking good on me.

Dan turns to me with a questioning look, flashing a smile. I smile in response, and we both turn back to the screen.

Mutti and Pappa loved Dan instantly. To them, he must have seemed like a gift from God—a nice, respectful Catholic boy who encouraged me in my riding. For the first time in my entire life, my parents encouraged me to have a social life. They let me go out on dates, they invited him to the house, appeared delighted when he showed up unannounced. They even approved of him traveling to Marjory's on weekends, after I went there to train. Dan, it seemed, could do no wrong, and this was the kiss of death.

Could I really have been such an idiot? To pick up with Roger simply because I had seen the disapproval cross Mutti's face when I introduced them? Relishing her discomfort at his Protestantism, her distaste for his flat personality? You might think that a mother would be pleased to have her daughter bring home a third-year law student, but not Mutti, and so I did the only thing that made sense to me. I dumped Dan and started dating Roger.

It's strange how it feels as though if I just reached across the armrest and took Dan's hand we could pick up where we left off. I don't have any reason to believe he's even interested anymore. Indeed, why would he be? The last time we were together, I had a hook. I was special. What am I now?

Dan shifts in his seat as he crosses his legs in the other direction, and I feel the fabric of his sleeve brush against my bare shoulder. I press into him a little, and he does not move away. For the rest of the movie, I concentrate on that little patch of cotton and the soft warmth behind it, hinting of the skin beneath.

• • •

He takes me for dinner at an Italian bistro, and over soft-shell crab linguine laced with tiny cubes of vine-ripened tomatoes, we touch on the subject of our earlier conversation. I laugh it off, trying to give the impression that I've realized how ridiculous it was.

"It just seems so incredible. Just for interest's sake, you should look at the picture and the horse at the same time. I mean, you know the odds of the coloring. Can you imagine the odds of the markings being exact?"

"You'd have a better chance of winning the lottery," he says. He turns his fork over and impales a scallop, slick with butter. A tiny sprig of dill, fernlike, sticks to its side.

"That's why I thought . . . Well, you know."

"I do."

We eat in silence for a few minutes, because we're treading in dangerous territory. Having him think I'm insane would be a definite impediment to resuming our relationship.

"I've been thinking about it all afternoon," he says suddenly, setting his cutlery down and crossing his arms. I look up, unsure what to expect.

"In fact, I did a little research on coat color and genetics, and the odds of two horses having exactly the same brindling are just about nil."

I stare at him.

"Do you still have that picture?" he asks.

"Of course."

"Can I have a look when I drop you off?"

As we walk back to the car after our meal, I slip my hand into the crook of his elbow. He looks down at me, smiles widely, and places his other hand on top of mine.

• • •

"Well, I'll be damned," he says, looking down at the picture and then raising his face to look out at Hurrah.

"See? See?" I say, my enthusiasm getting the better of me.

He shakes his head slowly. "I can sure see why you thought what you did."

I frown. "But look at it! You said yourself that you would have a better chance of winning a lottery."

"You would, if the markings matched exactly. But this picture is from a distance, and you can only see about a quarter of the horse. And look, this whole bit, the area under the saddle and rider, is obscured."

"I know, but look at the shoulder, at the neck. At the star."

To his credit, Dan actually takes the time to do so. His forehead crinkles as he studies the now worn picture. Then he raises his head to look at Hurrah, squinting as his eyes adjust to the distance.

Finally, he hands the picture back to me, nodding slowly. "It's very similar. It really is."

"But you don't believe me."

"It's not a question of believing you."

I purse my lips.

"Think about what you're saying," he continues. "I mean, really think about it."

I stare at the grass, afraid I might cry.

"I don't know how to explain this," Dan continues. "It's an incredible coincidence that they're this similar. Perhaps they're even related—after what I read, I'm willing to believe that these three horses share an ancestor. Maybe even not very far back. But damn, Annemarie . . ."

My eyes fill with tears. Dan steps forward and wraps his arms around me, pressing me against his chest. My face is buried in his shirt, the top of my head under his chin. And oh, he feels good. He smells and feels so good.

• • •

"Have fun?" sneers Eva as I come into the kitchen. She's standing just inside the doorway, leaning against the counter with one arm. She must have been looking out the window.

"I said, *have fun*?" Her voice rises like a siren.

"Eva—"

"You disgust me," she continues. "Dad's been gone, what, ten minutes, and you've already got a boyfriend?"

"No, it's not like that. Dan just—"

"Don't even try to deny it. You're just a horny old woman. You're disgusting! You make me sick!"

Horny? Old? Since when was thirty-eight old? I open my mouth to respond, but Eva is gone, storming into the hallway, leaving a trail of perfumed air behind her.

"Eva!"

"What is going on?" Mutti appears in the doorway, frowning. "Pappa is trying to sleep."

"I don't know. Eva's mad at me."

"Why?"

"Because she misinterpreted something she saw."

"And what did she see?"

I don't really want to tell her, but if I don't, Eva will. "Dan hugged me when he dropped me off."

Mutti continues to stare at me. Then her expression lightens a shade. "I will talk to her," she says.

"No, please," I say quickly, because she's already turning to go. "I'll talk to her. I just . . . I just want to let her calm down first, that's all."

To my surprise, Mutti comes back. She walks to the cupboard, opens it, and removes two small stemmed glasses.

"Would you like a Jägermeister?" she says.

"Please."

She sets the glasses on the counter, and then disappears into the hallway. A moment later she's back, carrying the bottle. She pours a small amount into each glass.

"Do you want it here, or in the living room?"

"Uh, living room," I say.

After we settle into the winged armchairs, we sip our drinks in silence.

"I haven't had this in years," I say finally, holding the little glass up to the light. The lamp shade is rusty orange, the liquid in front of it amber. "It's good."

"Did you have fun with Dan tonight?" says Mutti, and when I look at her to see if her choice of words matches Eva's by choice or chance, I find her staring right at me.

"I did, yes."

"What did you do?"

"We saw a movie and then had dinner."

She nods slowly. "It's good you should get out."

"It wasn't a date," I say.

"So what if it was?" she says. "You need to live your life."

I take another sip of my drink.

"If you really are finished with Roger, that is," she adds.

"He's the one who finished with me, Mutti."

"I know, *Schatzlein*, I know."

This unexpected endearment brings tears to my eyes. I stare at the rim of my glass, trying not to blink.

"Were things bad between you?" Mutti continues.

I sigh, and look out the window. "No," I say, finally. "No, they weren't. But neither were they good. They just kind of . . . were."

"And then this Sonja came along . . ."

"And then this Sonja came along, and I guess Roger decided it wasn't enough."

"Was it enough for you?"

"I don't know. I guess so. It seemed like it at the time."

"Did you try counseling?" she asks.

I look at her to gauge her intent. "No," I say shortly.

"Why not?"

"I don't know. It didn't occur to me," I say.

"Did you want him to stay?"

"I don't think I did, no."

It feels freeing, shocking even, to say this, but Mutti doesn't look surprised.

"Then perhaps it's for the best," she says.

"I doubt Eva would agree with you."

"It is hard for her."

I say nothing.

"You know how it is with fathers and daughters."

"This is totally different," I say quickly.

"Are you so sure, Annemarie?"

I am milliseconds from saying, Yes, because Roger never drove Eva the way Pappa drove me, because Roger has never forced his own ambitions on our daughter. Because Roger actually cares what Eva wants to do, and doesn't bully her, or make her feel like she's ruining his life if she doesn't devote hers to fulfilling his dream.

When I look up, Mutti is watching me. "I know you are having a hard time with this, *Schatzlein*," she says gently, and I know she's talking about Pappa, has read the rant in my face. "But don't wait too long."

I shake my head, my eyes once again filling with tears.

"And I know it wasn't you who started this whole thing, but don't let what's happening between Roger and you get between Roger and Eva."

"He left us, Mutti. We didn't leave him."

Mutti raises her glass and uses it to point at me. "He is divorcing *you*, Annemarie," she says in a voice that is both gentle and firm. "Not your daughter. And besides, you are not blameless. It takes two to get a marriage into this state."

Actually, *I* am divorcing *him*, but I don't feel like arguing. Besides, there's something else I want to ask her.

"So, Mutti," I say, examining the base of my glass and trying to sound casual. "You never told me. What's Dan been up to for the last nineteen years?"

When I look up, there's a smile seeping across my mother's face.

• • •

A quarter of an hour later, I go upstairs and find Eva's room empty. As I turn to leave, I hear the click of a door, and see her slip out of my room.

"Eva?" I say, moving toward her. "What were you doing in there?"

She growls and heads for the stairs.

"Eva!" I call, but she ignores me. I hear her clomping across the main floor, and then the crash of the screen door.

I go into my room and scan it quickly. Everything looks normal. The bed is made, with the usual Harriet-shaped indentation on its cover. My computer is on, but the screensaver is playing.

I move to the window, and see her crossing the yard to the stable, with Harriet close on her heels. Then, without knowing why, I lay a hand on top of the telephone receiver. It's warm.

I pick it up and bring it to my ear. Then I press REDIAL.

There's a flurry of digital tones, and then a pause while the line connects. It rings three times, and then someone answers.

"Hello?"

I freeze. It's Roger.

"Hello?" he says again, after a pause.

I open my mouth, and just as I decide that I'm going to hang up, he says, "Eva? Is that you, honey?"

Damn. He's got Caller ID.

"No. It's me," I say. It never occurred to me that Eva would call Roger. I can only imagine what she told him. I don't think I want to know.

"Oh. Hi," he says.

"Did Eva just call you?"

"Yes," he says.

"Did she sound okay?"

"Why? Is something wrong?"

I feel like I'm digging a hole for myself. "No. Yes. I mean, no, she's just upset with me, that's all. And I didn't think she was talking to you."

"No, she's talking to me. She's been calling me a couple of times a week."

"She has?"

"Yes. Why is she upset with you?"

I parry. "She didn't say anything to you?"

"No."

I shake my head, relieved. "It's not important."

"It's important if she was upset."

"It's just the usual Eva stuff. A mountain from a molehill."

"Well, if you're sure . . ."

An interminable, insufferable silence stretches between us.

"Was there something you wanted?" Roger finally says.

Oh God, of course—he thinks I called him on purpose.

"No," I say. Good grief. Is that really the best I can come up with?

"Is everything okay?"

"Fine, fine," I say irritably.

"I'm glad you called. Are you still checking email? I've been trying to get in touch with you."

"Not really. I've been working at the stable, so I've been using my parents' account."

"Did you know we've got a court date?"

"No," I say, feeling suddenly sick.

"July twenty-sixth."

I sit down, slumped against the little table. That's less than three weeks away, five days after our eighteenth anniversary. "That's awfully fast, isn't it?" I rub my forehead, frowning. "I mean, we haven't actually come to an agreement on the settlement yet."

"I was actually surprised I hadn't heard back from you. Have you read it?"

"No," I say. I'm embarrassed at having to admit this.

"Will you, please?"

"Yes. Yes, I will."

We lapse into another silence, but this one feels deliberate.

"Annemarie?"

"Yes?"

"Are you doing okay?"

"Of course. Why wouldn't I be?" I don't want to have this conversation with Roger. Roger, who probably has Sonja waiting beside him in a silky negligee right now, her smooth, young legs tucked up beside her, a hand resting delicately on his arm.

"I've got to go," I say suddenly.

"Okay. So you'll—"

"Yes, yes. I'll read the settlement."

• • •

Next stop: stable.

It's completely dark now, and as I head across the yard, I am surrounded by mosquitoes. I resist the urge to break into a run, choosing instead to flap my arms uselessly around my head, and hoping that

Jean-Claude is not looking out the window. On some days, there are no bugs at all, and on others, it feels as though they might carry you off into the woods.

The doors to the stable are open, and an enormous black fan, four feet tall, stands at the entrance blasting humid air down the aisles. There are no lights on, but I can see all the way to the arena by the light of the moon.

I love the stable at night. I love the stable during the day, too, but at night, when there's no one here but the horses, it feels like a different world. The sweet scent of hay and shavings, of leather, and manure, and oats. The occasional shuffle and snort, the hissing sound as hay is pulled through nets. And best of all, the scent of horses. Unmistakable, and like nothing else in the world, is the scent of horses. I've been known to go into a stall and press my face up against a horse's neck just to get a snootful. I do that now, before I go looking for Eva.

I check the lounge first, but she isn't there. Then I check the tack room, the trophy room, and the long hallway between the aisles, the one lined with boarders' trunks. She could be anywhere, could have slipped into one of the stalls with a horse, or knelt in the corner of a wash rack, or behind one of the trunks. She could have climbed the ladder into the hayloft, or hidden behind the couch in the lounge. If she really doesn't want to be found, I'm not going to find her.

I slip into Bergeron's stall and run my hand under his mane. Despite the fan, he's sweating. I leave his stall and check a few of the other horses. They're all sweating, and those who have windows are facing them, muzzles pressed to the screen.

I head across the arena to open the doors at the end. As soon as I step out onto the sand, I see light glowing behind me. I stop, and turn around.

The light is on in my office. Eva is sitting at my desk with her feet up. She's facing my monitor, with her hand on my mouse. She hasn't seen me.

I sigh, and cross the arena. At the far end, I slide the massive corrugated doors open, grunting with the effort. The cross-breeze is instant and gratifying, and I stop for a moment, savoring its coolness.

When I turn back, Eva is watching me through the window. She must have heard the doors. We look at each other for a long time, my daughter and I. Then I head back to the house.

• • •

I'm not surprised at Eva's outburst in the kitchen. If anything, I'm surprised it didn't happen sooner. And once again, it seems I've missed the boat.

I knew this was coming, and yet I did nothing. I could have sought her out and given her a chance to talk about it, but I didn't. She's always so angry, approaching her seemed pointless. Perhaps I should have done it anyway, and given her the chance to rebuff me. At least then she'd know that I wish she weren't hurting.

She and Roger were always close, and it's perfectly reasonable for her to miss him. What I don't know how to deal with is her expectation that *I* should too. She seems angry that I've given up on him, although she knows perfectly well that it was he who gave up on me.

I don't know how to make her understand that our

losses are not parallel. The fact that mine doesn't even feel like a loss is something that I don't understand myself, so how can I explain it to Eva?

I should be devastated. I should be trying to win him back, or grow poisonous with rage, or hire a hit man, or something—something! But I'm not, and the absence comes as a shock. I'm angry—yes, of course, make no mistake. But the heartbreak never came.

I expected it—even braced for it—and I thought that the calm that settled was temporary, a way of coping until I could take the hit. But it still hasn't come, and I'm beginning to think it's not going to. I seem to have sloughed Roger off as easily as a snake shedding its skin.

Maybe I shouldn't be surprised. I didn't marry Roger because of an overwhelming need to be with him. I married Roger because Harry was dead and I was paralyzed, and I no longer knew which way was up. Before the accident, it had been so clear, but afterward, it was as if someone had turned the pencil upside down, erased my future, and then casually brushed the crumbled remnants off the page.

We'll still get married, he told me. If we have to, we'll adopt. And while I didn't remember agreeing to get married in the first place, I was so grateful that he wasn't running away from me—me, this hideous head in a fishbowl, this brain on a platter—that I just went along with it.

As horrible as it is to say, in some ways, his leaving feels like a second chance.

Chapter 9

With infallible teenage logic, Eva expects me to drive her to work the next morning, even though she is officially not talking to me.

"Mom, come *on*!" she hollers through the crack in my door, proving that, at the very least, she's still yelling at me.

I sigh, because I'm actually getting a little sick of all this.

I roll out of bed and accidentally send Harriet toppling to the floor. She lies in a bewildered heap. By way of apology, I lean over to scratch her cheek.

As Eva and I climb into the van, Brian's blue Passat crawls around the side of the house. He waves, and I nod curtly. I suppose it's not his fault I associate him with Pappa's illness, but I do. I can barely bring myself to be civil.

Eva looks pointedly out the passenger window for the entire length of the trip. I'm supposed to ask her what's wrong and then ease it out of her against gradually weakening denials, but I'm simply not up for that this morning.

As a result, she is even more foul when we arrive at the center, and jumps out almost before the van has stopped. She slams the door and storms across the yard without so much as a single backward glance.

I park and go looking for Dan. I find him in the main barn, standing beside a big draft horse with a tube of wormer in his hand. The horse is an enormous dark bay with a wide blaze running down his face. He's absolutely huge, probably more than eighteen hands.

Dan breaks into a grin when he sees me. "Annemarie! Hi!"

"Hi there," I say. I put both hands in my pockets and lean against the wall, watching.

Dan sticks a thumb in the gap between the horse's front and rear teeth, and then with his other hand squirts the wormer into the back of the animal's mouth. Instantly, the horse yanks his head up, pulling on the cross-ties and stretching his top and bottom lips as far from his teeth as he can. He looks like a braying donkey.

I burst out laughing. "Oh God, what a face!"

"Not his favorite thing," says Dan, taking a step backward and tossing the empty tube into a garbage can some distance away. He watches to make sure it goes in, and then wipes his hands on his jeans. Then he pats the horse's neck loudly. The big horse continues to flap his lips.

"Ah, poor baby," I say. I approach and reach up to stroke his whiskered face. "What's his name?"

"Ivan. Ivan the Terrible."

"Is he really? Terrible, that is?"

"Not at all. It's his registered name."

"He's registered?" I ask, surprised. I step back, taking a second, closer look at this Ivan.

"You'd be surprised at some of the horses who turn up here. A horse just has to be unlucky, not an old nag."

Dan snaps a lead onto Ivan's halter and then drops the cross-ties back against the wall. They hit—first one, and then the other—with a hollow, metallic clank.

Dan leads Ivan to the door of a stall, and then steps aside. Ivan plods inside, lowering his heavy head and lifting his big, feathered feet carefully over the sliding door track. Then Dan follows him in.

I approach the door of the stall. "Did you get him at an auction?"

"No. He was one of three Clydes we got in about a year ago. He was tied in a standing stall for about fifteen years, as far as we can tell. Never saw the light of day. The neighbors didn't even know there were horses on the property." Dan emerges from the stall and hangs Ivan's rust red halter on a hook by the door. It, like the horse, is enormous.

"Jesus."

"When the owner finally died, the two daughters found Ivan and the others standing in several years' worth of muck and moldy hay, with the worst case of overgrown hooves I've ever seen. To their credit, the daughters called us instead of sending them to slaughter. One of Ivan's hooves was so overgrown it was curled under. We had to cut off about a foot's worth with an electric saw before we could even begin to fix it, and we're still repairing the damage.

Look at the angle of his feet," he says, pointing at one of Ivan's hooves. "Until they get back to normal, if they ever do, he's going to need trimming every two weeks."

I peer in at Ivan's gargantuan feet. They don't look that bad, but now that Dan has pointed it out, I can see that they are a little more perpendicular to the ground than they should be. "That's a lot for a new owner to take on."

"Ivan's not up for adoption. He's what we call a pasture ornament."

I wander over and peer into the next stall. I find myself looking at a palomino rump.

"Who's this?" I ask.

"That's Mayflower."

"She's lovely. What is she? A quarter horse?"

"Yes."

"How did you get her?"

"She was Jill's."

"Oh," I say. I glance over quickly, wondering if I should pursue this. "Mutti told me you were married."

Dan looks grim as he hangs Ivan's halter on the hook beside the door. "She did, did she?"

"Well, actually I asked."

"Oh." Dan says nothing for several seconds. "What did she tell you?"

"She said Jill had ovarian cancer."

Dan has one arm outstretched, and is using it to lean against Ivan's stall. The other is on his hip. He's staring at some faraway point, past and through the stable wall.

"I'm sorry. I shouldn't have brought it up," I say. I'm terrible in these situations. I never know whether people are waiting for me to ask, or wishing I would shut up.

"No, it's just . . . hard," he says. "We were trying for a baby. Had been for a couple of years. We went to a fertility clinic, and it came up through routine testing. There were no symptoms. Nothing. By the time we found it, she was full of it."

"I'm sorry," I say.

"Yeah," he says. "Me too."

Now the silence is conspicuous, broken only by the sound of horses shuffling in their stalls.

"So," I say, with false cheer. "Do you have many pasture ornaments?"

"Sixteen horses and two donkeys."

"Jesus," I say.

"That's aside from the nine horses we have up for adoption. And, of course, the foals. Would you like to meet them?"

I pause for just a second. I'm woefully behind at the office—we're running low on hay and bedding, and of course payroll is coming around again, but when is it not? Payroll is a never-ending horror, the bane of my managerial existence. But there's nothing that can't wait an hour. Especially an hour spent with Dan.

"Sure," I say. "Why not?"

And so begins a tour that is more heartbreaking than I could have ever imagined. Tacked to the door of every stall is a picture of its occupant taken on the day he or she arrived. They are, without exception, beyond belief.

Ivan's front hoof was as long and curled as a ram's horn; his next-door neighbor was a sack of bones, nearly bald from parasites. There is not one horse that I would have looked at and thought could survive, never mind connected with the sleek, contented creature currently residing in the stall.

On to the quarantine barn, where the horses are still recovering from their various traumas.

Eva is standing in the door of a stall, shoveling manure into a muck bucket. When she catches sight of me, she leans her shovel up against the wall and leaves.

"What's up with her?" asks Dan.

"Nothing you need to worry about," I say. "It's a mother-daughter thing."

I meet Caspar, a white Arabian gelding who weighed only four hundred pounds when he arrived. Hannah, an emaciated Appaloosa with deep, unexplained gashes on her flanks, who was saved from slaughter two days before she gave birth to a foal. Miracle, Hannah's filly and a miracle indeed, with her tiny velvet muzzle and inquisitive sweetness. The eight foals from the pee farms, who leap and frolic joyously, occasionally accelerating to full gallop for no apparent reason at all.

"And this is Flicka," Dan says, leading me to the very last paddock. Inside is a slight Arabian mare, all black but for a white strip down her nose that ends in pink. "I'm sure you've heard all about her."

"No, I haven't," I say.

"Really? Eva has never mentioned her?"

"No," I say.

"I'm surprised. Flicka is her special girl. She grooms her every day. Grazes her on her lunch hour."

I say nothing, afraid that the sting of pain will come through in my voice.

"Hey, sweet thing," Dan calls to Flicka. She turns her delicate head, ears perked and inquisitive. She takes a couple of steps toward him, sniffing his outstretched hand with her pink and black nose.

"So what's Flicka's story?" I say, leaning against the fence. She's a tiny thing.

"This beautiful girl was a victim of horse tripping."

"I've never heard of it."

"It's when you take an usually young, usually Arabian horse, do whatever you need to do to get it galloping full tilt, and then lasso its legs out from under it."

"What? Where?!" I demand, outraged.

"Rodeos."

"Surely that's not legal?"

"It is in most states. No legislator wants to touch it."

"Why?"

"Because it only happens at Mexican-style rodeos, and because most other types of rodeo have cattle tripping, so if you allow that and ban horse tripping, it starts to look like discrimination."

"All of it should be banned."

"Of course it should. But it won't be." Dan pauses. "I don't mean to sound defeatist, but I see so many terrible things here. The longer I do this job, the less I like people. The species, of course," he adds grimly. "There are individuals I like just fine."

At the moment, I'm inclined to agree. I run my hand under Flicka's silky mane, feeling her smooth coat ripple under my fingers. She's tiny and slender, almost certainly a yearling. Even her perfect hooves are in miniature.

Dan continues. "Flicka here was lucky. When she

was thrown, she dislocated a stifle, so they sent her off to slaughter and we intercepted her. Most of the horses end up dying in the ring or else grievously injured. And when that happens, they can spend weeks with untreated injuries on their way to slaughter, because why waste money on a vet for a dead horse?"

I've never heard Dan sound so bitter, but I understand completely. By the time I leave, I'm prepared to devote my life to these animals.

• • •

In the afternoon, I'm still so distracted I make a mistake in payroll that might inspire P. J. to leave immediately for Argentina if our bank honored the check. Flustered, I shut the program down and toss the whole stack of time sheets into the basket on my desk. I can do it later. I still have almost three days.

I reach for my mouse, and next thing I know, I'm surfing the Web. I'm spending far too much time at this, but I can't seem to stop. I do it at the house, while waiting for dinner. At night, when I ought to be sleeping. In the morning, as soon as I arrive at the office. It's the promise of finding anything new—a small picture, an old article, a list of scores from some long-ago event.

I've now got fourteen pictures and a slew of articles on my hard drive. Today I find a couple of interesting articles on microchips and equine mortality insurance. I download three pictures, bookmark the sites, and then find myself staring out the window at the arena.

Jean-Claude is giving a private lesson. The student

is an older gentleman, and he's riding Razzmatazz. In a manner of speaking.

Tazz is a consummate professional, going at an easy canter even though the man's legs are too far back, which means his body is too far forward, and he's bouncing out of the saddle with every stride. It almost looks as though he's holding onto Tazz's mane. I dread to think what a horse like Harry would have done with this guy.

"Annemarie?"

"Hmm? What?" I say, startled at the interruption. I minimize Internet Explorer and turn to see who's at the door.

It's P. J. He's blinking at me from under the beak of his dirty red cap, entirely unaware of his close brush with wealth.

P. J. is as grizzled as they come, leathery from years of hard work and hard living. He could be anywhere from thirty-five to sixty-eight. He's a little gnome of a man with a collapsing, sun-darkened face and several missing teeth. But I like P. J. He's good to the horses and he works hard. He's also the self-appointed spokesman of the stable hands.

"Have you ordered the hay and shavings? We're running real low," he says, with his dark face stuck in the crack of my door.

Really low, *really* low. "Uh, no, not yet," I say, suppressing the urge to correct him. "I'll call this afternoon."

"Okay," he says shyly. "I also need you to come look at the outdoor arenas. I dragged them this morning, so I had to take the jumps down. Now I can't remember how they went up."

"Ask Jean-Claude. He'll know."

"He's in lessons until five, and I've got a boarder out there complaining," P. J. says.

"Okay, no problem," I say. I grab my sunglasses and head downstairs.

The irate boarder is immediately apparent. She's middle-aged and stout, with exhausted blonde hair and burgundy Aanstadt Das breeches. She takes one look at me, becomes obviously annoyed, and turns back to P. J.

"I asked for the manager," she booms. Her voice is so adenoidal it causes me to clear my throat.

"I am the manager, actually," I say, placing myself in front of her. P. J., who had opened his mouth, closes it again and steps backward into the shadows.

"Where's Ursula?" she says, turning her attention to me. I can't see her eyes, hidden as they are behind Ferragamo sunglasses.

"I'm her daughter," I say.

"When is she coming back?"

"I don't know. She's taking some time off."

She puts her hands on her hips. "Unbelievable. First, half my lessons get canceled with no explanation. Next thing, I walk in and there's a new trainer. Now there's a new manager. Tell me, what are you planning to change next?"

"Absolutely nothing," I say. "What did you say your name was?"

"See? You don't even know who I am."

I stare at her. She stares back.

"Dr. Jessica Berman," she says eventually.

"All right, Jessica—"

"That's Dr. Berman."

I collect myself and start again. "All right, Dr. Berman, let's see about getting those jumps set up."

I head for the door, with P. J. and Dr. Berman in tow. She's easy to keep track of. She leaks a constant stream of complaints like a dinghy with a hole in it.

"—I suppose that explains why no one told me about Sam's shoulder last week. Also why his salt lick was so filthy. This is supposed to be a full-service barn. I shouldn't have to spend my time rinsing off salt licks and waiting around while somebody sets up jumps."

"The cut on Sam's shoulder was the size of a dime, but I'll make a note in his file that you'd like us to call you next time." At three in the morning. On Christmas Day. "And the jumps are only down because P. J. just finished dragging the arena, which means you'll be the first person to ride, and the footing—"

I stop, distracted. Dan's blue pickup is winding its way down the lane, and then disappears behind the house. I glance at my watch, confused. When the pickup reappears in the backyard, Eva climbs out. She shouts something—I can't hear what, although I can tell she's hysterical. Then she slams the door. She runs into the house, slamming that door, too.

I break into a jog. Behind me, Jessica Berman's complaints continue.

"—then he should have—what's going on? Where are you going?" She shouts this last, her voice achieving a whole new level of grievance.

"I'm sorry. I'll be back in a minute," I shout.

Dan starts to reverse the truck, and then sees me and stops. He waits with the engine running.

I'm almost a third of the way to the house, but I

can still hear her. She's a veritable foghorn: "This is completely intolerable. You'd better think long and hard about how you treat your customers. It's not like you're the only barn in—"

I stop and turn around, ready to explode. "Oh, for Christ's sake, woman, would you just stick a sock in it?"

Her jaw drops. P.J.'s eyes widen.

I have a split second of misgiving, a moment of clarity about what I've just done, and then continue running.

When I reach the truck, Dan rolls the window down.

"What's up?" I say. I lean forward, panting, resting a hand on the open window.

"I had to let Eva go," he says, staring at the windshield.

"What do you mean? What happened?"

"I think you should ask her," he says.

"I'm asking you."

Dan remains motionless.

"Dan, tell me what's going on."

For a moment, I think he's not going to. Then he turns to me. He looks grim. "I caught Eva smoking in the hayloft."

"What?"

"A few minutes ago. With another one of the volunteers. Another teenager."

"You can't be serious." I stare at Dan, willing him to be wrong.

"Where the hell would she get cigarettes?" I continue. "We're twenty-seven miles from nowhere out here. She doesn't even have a bicycle!"

"I'm sorry," he says simply.

"Shit," I say. I take off my sunglasses and run a hand over my face. "Are you absolutely sure?"

He nods.

"All right. Well, thanks for letting me know. And for dropping her off."

He nods, and continues to look at me. It's clear there's something else he wants to say, so I wait.

"Listen, this may not be exactly the right time to say this, but I really enjoyed last night."

I laugh.

"I'm sorry—" Dan says quickly.

"No, please. Don't be. I did too. I really did. It's just . . ." I look hopelessly at the back door of the house.

"I know. I probably should have just called later instead, but . . ." He pauses, watching his hands on the steering wheel. "I'd like to do it again sometime."

"Me too," I say. Our eyes meet and lock.

I sense something mammoth rolling up behind me even before Dan's gaze shifts. When I turn around, an enormous silver Lincoln Navigator is blocking out the sun. The tinted window disappears into the door, revealing furor behind Ferragamo.

"Dr. Berman, I'm so sorry—"

"Save it. My husband will call you as soon as we've made alternative arrangements. Nobody talks to me like that, not even my teenager, and you should hear the way he talks. You should be ashamed of yourself."

"Oh, I am. I really am—"

"I said, save it. I only wonder what your mother would think." She turns her face toward the windshield. The window rolls up, and the Navigator pulls away.

As I stand there wondering just that, I hear Dan behind me, laughing.

• • •

When I reach the top of the stairs, I come face to face with Harriet, who is contemplating a descent. She takes one look at me and scampers into our room, her short brown legs and tiny black toenails skidding out from under her as she takes the corner.

Eva's door is ajar. I stand just outside and rap gently. "Eva?"

After a few moments of silence, I push the door open.

Eva is sitting cross-legged on her bed. Her back is toward me, but she's looking over her shoulder with obvious alarm. Her eyes are bloodshot, her eyelids puffy.

"What?" she says indignantly, as though she has no idea why I'm here.

"Oh, Eva," I say.

She stares at me, her eyelids flickering. Then her chin starts to quiver. A moment later, a large tear rolls off her left cheek. Then it's followed by one on the right. She drops her face into her hands, her fingers splayed. Her nails are short, the blue polish chipped.

I stare at her for a moment, and then cross the room. I drag the wooden desk chair toward the bed and straddle it, resting my arms across its back.

"Do you have any idea how dangerous that was?"

She stops for a moment, searching my face.

"Do you?" I continue. "Do you realize how easily you could have set fire to the whole place? You could have burned down the barn. What do you think would have happened to the horses then?"

"There's a fire alarm! We could have—"

"No you couldn't have. Do you have any idea how quickly hay burns? You wouldn't have had a hope in hell of getting anybody out of there. Most likely you'd have been stuck in the hayloft and burned to death yourself."

She stops crying, and stares at the baseboard behind me. Her expression is one of horrified surprise. Incredibly, I don't think this ever occurred to her.

I get up.

"Mom," she says quickly. She shifts sideways on the bed, looking at me with wild eyes. "Will you please talk to him?"

"Who? Dan?"

She nods.

"And say what, exactly?"

"That I'm sorry. That I'll never do it again."

I shake my head. "Oh, honey. I'm sorry. I can't."

"But the foals, and Flicka! If you don't, I'll never see her again. Please Mom! He'll listen to you!"

I sit on the edge of the bed, and then, when she doesn't move away, tentatively put my arms around her. She leans into me, her body wracked by sobs.

"I know it hurts, honey, but I can't ask Dan to take you back. If I'd found someone smoking in our barn, I'd have done the same thing."

"But Mom—"

"Do you realize what could have happened? Do

you have any idea what happens when a barn full of horses burns?"

We sit in silence for a moment.

"I know it's tough, baby, and I'm really sorry. But you have to use your head. I know it's not exactly the same, but you can help out around here."

"It's not the same at all. There's no Flicka."

I put a hand on the back of her head and pull her closer. "I know, honey. I know."

• • •

Bad move on Dr. Jessica Berman. It turns out she has five horses here—in the main barn, in window stalls—and with the full-service and training options, she represents a sizeable chunk of our incoming funds.

An hour after I return to the office, I vet a call from her husband, who is livid.

"Is this the stable manager?"

"This is she."

"This is Jack Berman," says a deep voice completely bereft of humor. "My wife told me what happened at the stable today, and I'm calling to give you notice that we'll be moving our horses out as soon as we can arrange it."

"Mr. Berman—"

"Dr. Berman."

"Dr. Berman, I'm so sorry about what happened with your wife today, I really am—I have a teenage daughter and we were having a, uh, teenage moment, and I responded to Dr. Berman in a way I shouldn't have. It was totally inappropriate, and I can't tell you how sorry I am. Is there any way I can persuade you to give us another chance?"

"Absolutely not."

"There's nothing I can do?"

"You've done plenty already."

My headache returns. "In that case, while I sincerely hope you will change your mind, the contract clearly states that you must give us sixty days written notice—"

"Unless there's a breach of contract."

"I didn't breach the contract."

"Verbal abuse is definitely a breach of contract. Listen, lady—whoever you are—we didn't bring our horses to this barn lightly. We chose it because we liked the way it was being run. Now suddenly, with no warning and no explanation, the trainer is replaced, and then the manager, and then we find ourselves unable to use the facilities and being abused by the staff."

"Mr.—Dr. Berman. My father—the previous trainer—is very ill, and he had to stop working. My mother is taking some time off to care for him. That's the only reason for any of the changes. I'm here now, and I'm absolutely confident that I can run the barn at the same level you're accustomed to. I know I shouldn't have spoken to your wife the way I did. It was inexcusable, and I can't tell you how sorry I am, but I just snapped. I'd really like the opportunity to make it up to her."

"I'm afraid that won't be possible." His voice is that of someone who will not be swayed. How can someone hear what I just told him and not feel anything?

I sigh. "In that case, will you at least consider

staying until the end of August? If you leave this month, that gives me less than three weeks to fill five stalls."

"That, I'm afraid, is your problem."

And with that, I lose almost a third of our boarders in one fell swoop.

• • •

The next morning, a large eight-horse red-and-chrome trailer comes down the drive. I'm still in bed, floating somewhere wonderful and Dan-related, but when I hear the roar of the truck's engine, I leap out of bed and pull the curtains aside. When I see the trailer pull past the house, I know immediately what's going on.

I throw on yesterday's tee-shirt and shorts, and then thump down the stairs, two at the time. I slide my feet into Mutti's rubber gardening clogs, and set off across the yard at a shuffling jog.

Hurrah is going crazy, throwing his head and trotting back and forth along the fence of his pasture. Each time he reaches the end, he pivots so quickly he disappears into a huge cloud of dust. I haven't seen him so agitated since we brought him here.

"Can I help you?" I shout to the men standing beside the cab. Both of them are staring at Hurrah. The larger one turns.

"Morning," he says. He tips his cap and approaches me, holding out a sheet of paper. "Just moving some horses out."

I grab the sheet and look it over.

"Everything okay?" he asks.

I hand the paper back to him and nod sickly.

Disgusted, I turn and walk to the fence. Hurrah is now cantering along the back of his pasture, covered in a foamy sweat. His head is raised, his ears plastered back. At the end of the pasture, he comes to an abrupt halt, just inches from the fence. Then he swivels and takes off in the other direction.

Before long, I hear the scrinchy-scrunch of hooves on gravel, and turn to watch as Sam I Am, Hello Stranger, Mad Max, Ariel, and Muggins—all beautiful, all expensive—are led one by one onto the trailer. Then the men close it up, tip their caps, and pull away.

I stand watching in desperate silence, following the trailer with my eyes. It winds its way up the drive, stops at the end, and then turns right, its engine roaring with the effort. A moment later, it disappears behind the thick maples.

Gone. Just like that. Four thousand five hundred dollars a month in revenue, and that doesn't even take Jean-Claude's lesson fees into account. I might just throw up.

"What's going on?" says Jean-Claude's voice from behind me. I turn around. He too is rumpled from bed. There's a pillow crease along the left side of his face, and his long hair is free from its customary ponytail.

I'm almost too embarrassed to tell him. "The Bermans."

"Jessica?"

"Yeah, Jessica."

He stares at me in incomprehension.

"They're gone. They took their horses out."

"What?"

"I got into it with her yesterday, and they took their horses out."

"Goddamn," he says. He puts his hands on his hips and stares at the place in the road where the trailer disappeared. "Well, then you'd better keep their deposit money."

Deposit money—of course! I almost cry out with relief.

Perhaps I did cry out, because he turns to look at me. "Are you okay?"

"Uh, yeah," I say, although I'm not so sure. The deposit money will help us get through next month, and I'm thankful for that, but I still have a very bad feeling about all of this. We can't get by without the income from those stalls, not even for a month.

"We'll fill them," he says, reading my mind.

"It's five stalls," I say in despair.

"We'll fill them. My students, they have friends. We'll fill them."

He turns to go back into the stable.

"Jean-Claude," I say quickly. I don't want him to leave just yet.

"Yes?"

"Eva's going to be helping out around here for the rest of the summer."

"She already has been," he points out quite logically.

"I mean, full time."

"She's not working at the center anymore?" His brown eyes stare out at me from under heavy brows.

"Dan caught her smoking in the hayloft."

He says nothing, but his expression shifts slightly.

"She's just at that age," I start to explain.

"Please," he says, holding up a hand. "I have a teenage daughter myself. I know all about it."

Through all our conversations—all the dinners, all our meetings at the fence—he's never mentioned a daughter or an ex-wife. I am simultaneously injured and curious. You'd think he'd have at least mentioned the daughter.

"There is plenty she can help me with," he says. "Plenty. I'll keep her out of trouble, don't you worry. And if I ever find her smoking in our stable," he pauses, and swipes the edge of his hand across his throat. "I'll kill her."

"Be my guest," I say.

He smiles and disappears into the stable.

Alone again, I look into the pasture. Hurrah has stopped pacing. He's standing in the far corner of the field, still looking toward the road. His flanks are heaving, his nostrils flaring.

And then something amazing happens. He turns to me and nickers.

I stare at him in disbelief, not sure whether to move.

And then I go inside and do something stupid.

• • •

"Hello?"

"Hello. I'd like to speak to Ian McCullough please."

"Speaking."

"Ian, I don't know if you'll remember me. My name is Annemarie Zimmer."

I pause, giving him a chance to respond. When he doesn't, I continue.

"We rode in the same circuit for a while, a long time ago."

"Of course I remember. The Claremont," he says.

Those two words make me feel sick, although you'd think by now I'd be past that. I'm only slightly surprised he remembers the accident. I guess it was noteworthy even in his life. I wonder if he was watching. I also wonder if he's aware that he wouldn't have made the Olympic team if I'd still been riding.

"Ah, yes," I continue, and then find myself unsure how to segue gracefully into what I want to talk about. It would help if he'd contribute to the small talk, but that's not going to happen. He's completely silent, waiting. "Well, I've, uh, been out of it for a long time. Out of riding, that is. Complete blackout, you might say."

"Uh-huh," he says, encouraging me to get on with it. I'm suddenly reminded of why I never liked him in the first place. I bet he's wearing a crested jacket right now, with a little pink hankie poofing out of the pocket.

"I just found out that you had Harry's brother. Harry was my horse, the one I was riding at the Claremont."

Silence.

"Anyway, I, uh, I just found out about Hurrah. I mean, that there was another brindled horse at all, and that he got to the level he did. And about the accident."

There is nothing but faint crackling on the other end of the line. For a second, I think I'm talking to dead air. "Hello? Are you there?"

"I'm here," he says. There's no mistaking his

tone—he's stone, stone cold. But I've come too far not to bludgeon on.

"I was wondering if you would mind telling me what happened. With the accident, I mean. When you lost Hurrah."

"Why are you calling me?"

"Because he was Harry's brother, and I just . . . It's just that I know what it is to lose a horse like that."

"I don't have time to talk about this. It was in the trade mags. Look it up." And with that, he hangs up on me.

• • •

Almost immediately after, the phone rings. I leap for it, knocking it off its cradle.

"Hello?" I say, after scrambling to catch the receiver.

"Annemarie? Is that you?" says a female voice.

"Yes," I say, considerably calmer now that I know it's not Ian.

"This is Carole McGee."

Uh-oh. My lawyer. Whom I have been sort of ducking.

She lays into me. I hold the phone slightly away from my ear once I get the gist of her rant. It's hard to believe that the source of all this squawking and yelping is the same demure, comforting brunette who took me into her homey office and told me how the law was set up to protect women like me from faithless men like Roger. She had looked at me with concern and understanding, had pushed a large box of tissue toward me in case I needed it. Which I didn't.

The squawking ebbs into a smoother flow, so I bring the phone back to my ear.

"So you need to think about it, Annemarie. Do you want me to continue to represent you or not?"

"Oh God, yes," I say. The last thing I need is for my lawyer to ditch me this close to the hearing.

"In that case, you need to start being more responsive. I need to know that if I send you something, you'll read it, and if I leave a message, you'll call me back. Especially with the court date looming."

"Yes, of course. I'm sorry," I say. "I really do want you to continue to represent me."

She is silent, and I clench my teeth with suspense. Please oh please oh please . . . "All right then," she says finally. "But if it happens again, you'll have to find another attorney. I simply cannot represent you if you continue to avoid me."

• • •

I haven't been avoiding her. Not really. After all, I did send her an email when we first arrived.

Granted, it didn't include the phone number, but that was simply an omission. And I suppose I did stop reading email after that, but it wasn't just hers—I also stopped looking at Roger's, and the scads of messages I was getting from the job placement firms my ex-employers have apparently sicced on me. It's just that I didn't want to deal with all that just yet. There's too much going on here.

But Carole doesn't know that. All she knows is that she had to call Roger to get my telephone number. I think that's the real reason she's so pissed off, and I don't suppose I blame her.

Chapter 10

When I head for the stable in the morning, I find Eva leading Bergeron to one of the outdoor arenas. She's got him on a lunge line and is dragging a long whip.

"What are you doing?" I ask.

She looks at me as though I were brain-damaged, as well she might.

"Jean-Claude told me to lunge him to get the bucks out," she says grudgingly.

"Wear a helmet."

Her voice rises instantly. "Mom! I'm just lunging him. I'll look like an idiot!"

"He's a stallion. Wear a helmet."

"Geez, Mom," she grumbles. She turns Bergeron around and leads him back into the barn. She doesn't let the fact that gravel is not conducive to stomping prevent her from trying.

When I get to my office, I pull out the Bermans' file and discover there was no deposit money.

My head hurts. Without deposit money, I'm not at all sure we can pay the loan and also cover payroll.

We may be okay for this next round of paychecks, but after that, unless I fill the stalls, we're hosed.

I stare morosely at my empty can of Coke and wonder if there will be any backlash from my phone call to Ian. Am I crazy? Am I losing it? Is this the kind of thing that counts as stalking? What if Mutti finds out?

If she does, she'll go ballistic. Of course, she'll also go ballistic if she finds out what's transpired at the stable, which means I can't let that happen.

I launch Internet Explorer, seeking a few minutes of distraction. An hour later, there's a tentative knock at my door.

"Um, Annemarie?"

I minimize my browser, but remain facing my monitor. "What's up, P. J.?"

"When are the shavings and hay arriving?"

"Not sure exactly," I say, preferring not to admit that I haven't gotten around to ordering them yet.

"Can you find out and let me know?"

"Yeah, whatever."

"When?" he persists.

"Later."

"Because we only have about two days left."

I turn to him, horrified. "What?"

"I've been asking you to get some for weeks," he says, sounding a little horrified himself.

"Oh, Jesus," I say. I spin my chair around so it faces the arena. I am mad, furious—at me, I suppose, for lack of a better candidate, and I don't want him to see my face. "Okay. Okay, I'll call right now."

He disappears, and I lean forward, grabbing a messy stack of papers from my desk. I shuffle through it, searching for the phone numbers that I know I dug out a few days ago. Then I set the whole disheveled heap down again. What I ought to do is read the divorce settlement.

When I'm finished, I call Carole.

"Carole McGee," she says, after the receptionist transfers my call.

"There's something going on. What's going on?" I demand.

There's a pause. "Annemarie?" she asks.

"Yes. This is Annemarie."

"Okay, slow down a minute. Take a deep breath."

"No," I say, shaking my head. I stand up and walk until the phone cord brings me to an abrupt halt. "No, there's something going on."

"What's the matter?"

"I just read the settlement."

"Okay," she says slowly, drawing the word out. "You sound upset."

"I am."

"Which version are you reading?"

"The one you sent yesterday."

"Then I don't understand. He's offering sixty percent. That's a very good settlement."

"Exactly. It's too good. It means there's something going on."

"Like what?"

"I don't know, but I smell a rat."

"What kind of a rat, Annemarie? You need to be specific. Do you think there are hidden assets or something?"

"I'm entirely sure there aren't," I say. I'm pacing the length of the cord now, back and forth, back and forth. The phone is propped between my ear and shoulder, and I'm twisting the cord tightly around the fingers of my left hand.

"Then I'm not sure I understand your objection," she says slowly.

"Don't you see? He's a lawyer. He knows exactly what I'm entitled to. Why would he offer me more?"

"Maybe he feels guilty," says Carole, sounding distinctly exasperated. "If you really don't think he's trying to hide something, my advice would be to sign it before he stops feeling that way."

I drop—kerplunk—into my chair.

"Annemarie?"

"Yeah," I say. I lean forward and open my desk drawer, scrabbling through it for Tylenol.

"Is that a yes?"

"I don't know."

"Listen. I know this is stressful. I know that. But the court date is coming, and if we don't file the petition in time for the judge to read it first, we risk—"

"All right, all right, all right. I'll sign it," I say, slamming the drawer shut. There is no Tylenol.

"Okay. Good. Can you fax it back to me today?"

"I suppose," I say.

"Again, is that a yes?"

"Yes. It's a yes."

"All right then. Don't forget. If you have any questions about it, give me a call. Otherwise, I guess I'll see you in a couple of weeks."

"For what?"

"The hearing."

"I'm not going to the hearing," I say, confused.

Why would she think I'd want to go to the hearing? Isn't that why I hired her?

"You have to. The party who files has to attend."

I drop my head onto my desk. My hair flops forward, covering my face.

"I know this is difficult, Annemarie, but I'll be there with you. You can meet me at the courthouse or come to my office ahead of time so we can go together." Carole has reverted to gentle mode, having brought me back into line. I'm being handled, like Eva, or a horse.

"I'll come to your office," I mumble through my hair.

"Sure. I think that's a good idea. And Annemarie, don't forget to get the signed settlement back to me just as soon as you can. I need to file it."

"Okay. I'll send it today."

"Hang in there. We're almost there."

"Okay," I say meekly.

There's a click as she hangs up. I hang up too, and then sit staring at the phone.

And now, since I don't want to bounce the paychecks, I guess I'd better find out if the bank will let me make the loan payment a little bit late.

• • •

I don't like the manager. Not one bit. I'd like to roast her on a spit.

Okay, I'm no Dr. Seuss, but that woman is completely inhuman. She tells me in no uncertain terms that of course I can make the payment late, but I'll be paying a fee for the privilege. A fee to the tune of several hundred dollars.

I protest, and without anything other than instinct to back me up, rail about how we've never been late for a payment in our entire existence. I must be right, because Attila the Manager doesn't dispute that. But she is entirely immovable: I can pay late, but I will pay more.

But this is just the beginning of my very bad morning. I call the shavings supplier next. He can't make a delivery until next week.

"Next week? No. I'm sorry. That's too late," I say.

"I can't come out any earlier. I'm booked solid until next Saturday," he answers.

"Please," I beg. "I'm going to have horses on bare mats in three days. I'm desperate."

"Sorry. I've only got the one truck."

"What if I get a truck out there and load it myself?"

"I can't let you do that."

"Why?"

"Liability. Look, if you're really desperate, go to a feed store, and get some bagged shavings. I'll come out as early as I can, but I'm booked solid."

I call Kilkenny Feed and Seed. They have bagged shavings, of course they do. For just twelve times the cost of bulk.

There's also a hay shortage. At this point, I'm waiting for locusts to appear.

Our usual supplier, the one Mutti has used for years, is clean out. I wheedle a little, testing to see if he's holding out for more money, but he seems to be telling the truth. But he knows someone else who might have some. When I call that person, he doesn't have hay, but he knows someone else who might. After eleven phone calls, I finally find someone with hay. He wants eight dollars a bale.

"You've got to be kidding!" I blurt.

"Hey, I'm sorry," he says, "there's a shortage."

"We've been paying two dollars a bale. How can you possibly justify charging that much?"

"Like I said, there's a shortage."

"So you're going to make the most of it. Is that it?"

"Do you want the hay or not?"

I pause, and then, because he's holding all the cards and I've got thirty-three—sorry, make that twenty-eight—round-the-clock eating machines downstairs, I place the order. At this price, a single shipment of five hundred bales will just about do us in.

I drop my head on my arms again, and stay there for almost half an hour. When I sit up again, I find the bare skin of my arms has stuck to the desk. They make a ripping sound when I lift them.

As much as I hate the thought, I can't do this anymore. I've got to tell Mutti, before it's too late.

• • •

As I approach the house, I see that the van's gone. I can't face going back to the stable, so I stop where I am and plop down in the middle of the drive. I cross my legs and drop my head in my hands.

The sun settles on my shoulders like a blanket of stinging nettles, and the sharp edges of the gravel poke into the backs of my thighs.

I can't believe it's come to this. I was so offended when Mutti suggested that stable management was beyond me. It's not brain surgery, I said. It's not rocket science.

Actually, it's not, and that makes it even worse. If I had been paying attention, I would have done just fine. But I haven't been paying attention. I've spent the whole summer on the Internet, trolling for information that will confirm my horse is Hurrah.

I pull my knees up suddenly and moan, rocking back and forth on the gravel.

Then I hear a nicker. I stop rocking and listen carefully, continuing to look at the shaded gravel between my legs.

I hear it again.

This time, I lift my head. Hurrah is standing at the fence, only nine yards away. He's looking straight at me, his one eye glistening and fringed with long, gorgeous lashes, his ears forward and curious. And then, while I'm still looking, he nickers again, and I see the soft flesh of his chin and nostrils rumble with the vibration.

I jump up and start walking, without even bothering to dig the gravel out of my thighs. I walk with calm purpose—not slowly, not rushing—but with a sense of inevitability. I climb the fence, and next thing I know, I'm standing at the shoulder of this horse, this creature of my dreams. I raise a trembling hand, poised to touch his neck. I'm afraid to make contact, afraid to break the spell.

He swings his neck around and presses his muzzle up against me, blowing against the cotton of my shirt. And then I touch him, actually feel the warmth of his flesh under my fingers. Before I know it, I'm running my hands over his sun-warmed body, tracing the lightning bolts that zigzag through his blood red coat, memorizing his familiar contours with all the ecstasy of a new lover as he sniffs and blows and bobs his head.

He turns to face me, and I lift my hand up to his damaged face. Gingerly, timidly, I touch his cheek, and despite the lack of an eye, he doesn't flinch when my fingers make contact. I feel the bare skin of black scars, and then swoop back, past the empty socket, until I'm grasping his ear in my fist. I lean up against him so that our legs are almost touching, and run my right hand down between his front legs, over the skin, as velvety and soft as a caterpillar, until my fingers find the cowlick that I already knew was there.

And suddenly, everything, everything, everything is okay.

• • •

When Mutti and Pappa return, I'm sitting at the kitchen table. Harriet is on my lap, having politely asked if I would lift her up. She's never been much of a lap dog, being too short to jump up. She's more of a foot dog, coming over and plonking herself down on your toes. But today, Harriet is needy.

You might think that she's picking something up from me, but she's not. I'm fine. In fact, I'm suffused with something almost like ecstasy. I sit stroking Harriet as though in a dream. My hands are on the dog, but my mind is on the horse.

I'm even beginning to wonder whether I should tell Mutti about the stable. Surely I can find a way to pull us back from the brink.

I'll post advertisements for the stalls. I'll take cash advances on the corporate credit cards to pay for the hay and shavings. I'll use the loan payment to cover payroll, and then, when the new boarders come, I'll ask for security deposits, which I'll use to pay off the credit cards and catch up on the loan.

By the time Mutti and Pappa come in—Mutti clutching a small white pharmacy bag, and Pappa looking almost transparent—I've decided not to say anything. After all, I came here to help, not to add to their stress.

• • •

I return to the office filled with purpose. I am Annemarie, the (ex) Grand Prix rider. Annemarie, winner of the International Association of Software Editors' Award of Excellence two years in a row. I can turn this around. Of course I can.

The first thing I do is call both local papers and place advertisements for the empty stalls. Then, for a small fee, I place online ads at four local dressage-related Web sites, and although I feel a little bit like a fraud for doing it, I mention my own name in the knowledge that it will provide an extra draw for anyone who remembers me. Finally, I call Kilkenny Saddlery to see if they have an advertising board, which they do. I fire up CorelDRAW, and in the space of ten minutes crank out a flyer that offers ten free lessons to people who move their horses to our barn by the beginning of next month. As it prints, I'm waiting with a pair of scissors. Before the roller has even released the sheet of paper, I snatch it out and snip nineteen times, creating a fringe of tear-off phone numbers along the bottom.

Just as I grab my purse to leave, Dan calls. It's as though the day has changed directions, hinged in the middle like a book.

"Hi, it's me," he says, and I feel drunk with the intimacy of his assumed recognition.

"Hey, you."

"Are you free this evening?"

"Uh-huh," I say in what I sincerely hope is a sultry voice.

"Great. I was thinking it was time to have a look at your boy's feet, maybe get those corrective shoes off him. Is it okay if I bring the farrier by at, say, five?"

My heart sinks. "Yes, of course."

"Right. Well, in that case—" he starts, in the kind of rote voice people use right before they wrap up.

I take evasive action. "Dan?"

"Yes?"

"I was wondering if I could cook you dinner."

"I would love that," he says. "When?"

"I don't know. Tonight." I feel brash, brazen. I'm a Cosmo girl, taking control.

"Sure."

"Well, the thing is, can it be at your place? There's always a crowd here."

"Of course. What would you like me to get?"

"Nothing. I'll bring everything."

"Well, okay then. Do you want to just come back with me after we're finished with the farrier?"

"You'd have to drive me home afterward, too."

"I don't mind."

"Okay then," I say in my own wrap-up voice. Except there's nothing rote about it. I'm purring. "I'm looking forward to it."

"So am I," he says.

• • •

Of course, I'm not much of a cook, but I'm not about to let a small detail like that stop me. I never learned—just wasn't interested.

It's not as though I'm completely hopeless—I can make spaghetti, and grilled cheese, and fry a chicken breast, and after Eva swore off meat, I expanded my repertoire to include a few vegetarian items, but they were strictly plebeian. Not what you might expect from the wife of a notably successful patent lawyer, but there you are. I never saw the point. And why should I anyway, when there are perfectly good catering companies around to handle dinner parties?

But suddenly I want to know how. I want to make something rich and scrumptious. Something complicated and impressive and absolutely gorgeous, and I want it to look easy. I want, in other words, to blow Dan away. After all, the last time he was interested in me, I was a prospective Olympian. Now I have to find some other way of impressing him.

I have a vision: We are in his kitchen. It is large, because he lives in an old farmhouse. The countertops are granite, the cabinets maple. The air is suffused with the smell of butter and garlic and seared pan juices. Dan is standing nearby, sipping a glass of wine, and watching in loving admiration as I flit about like a hummingbird. I hover in front of the stove, perfectly coiffed and looking divine in a pale blue sheath dress, giving one pan a shake, poking the contents of another with a wooden spoon, and then changing instruments before pushing something through a wake of butter in a pan on the back burner. Immediately after, I whirl gracefully to scoop a pile of perfectly diced something from a cutting board and plop it, sizzling, into the copper pan on the fourth burner. If possible, I want something in the broiler, too, and the microwave chirping to tell me that it has finished whatever it was doing.

The vision is lovely, but my reverie comes to an abrupt halt when I realize I have less than four hours to prepare. And I don't have a clue what to make, never mind how to make it.

I rush to the house and pull all of Mutti's new cookbooks from the shelf. There are six, but I'm not interested in the paperbacks. I want pictures. I want numbered steps. I want to see how it's going to look at every stage along the way.

I know the minute I see it. Of course, my hand doesn't respond as quickly as my mind, so I have to flip back to find it again. But I do, and there it is, and it is lovely.

A glossy picture, a full-page spread. A gâteau des crêpes—a tower of homemade French pancakes layered with beautiful and colorful fillings, all held together with a light cheese custard. Complicated, impressive, and absolutely perfect. Add to that a light salad of mixed greens, poached pears, and roasted goat cheese, and a bottle of Chianti, and we're in business. And since I'll be making crêpes anyway, I might as well do crêpes suzette for dessert.

I picture the blue-bottomed orange flames leaping

from the copper pan as I swirl its contents with panache. I am already delirious with pride.

I don't have time to copy out the list of ingredients, so instead, I stick the book under my arm and head out the door.

I'm already rolling away from the house when Mutti runs out, flapping her arms. I stop the van and wait for her.

"Where are you going?" she demands, running up to my now open window.

"To the grocery."

"You can't. I need the van to go to the pharmacy."

"You went this morning!"

She stares at me, furious. "And what is your point, Annemarie? Your father is very sick."

"Mutti, please. I won't be long."

"This is ridiculous. You don't even ask before you take the van. How do you know I don't need it? When are you going to bring your own car here, anyway?"

"I'll bring it back after my court date. Please, Mutti."

Her chin sets, and my heart sinks.

"Why do you need to go out so badly?"

"I'm cooking dinner for Dan tonight. At his house. I said I'd bring everything I needed."

She continues to stare at me, and just when I've lost all remaining hope, she says, "Go." Just like that. And then she turns her back to me and crunches across the gravel to the porch.

I'm not entirely sure what happened here, but who cares? I've got the van.

• • •

I make one quick stop at Kilkenny Saddlery to post my flyer, and then head for the grocery. As it turns out, taking the extra time to make a list would have been a good investment, because I could have grouped all the things I needed from each section of the store. Instead, I end up getting things in the order they are listed in the recipes, which means I go to the produce section at least six times. By my third trip to the baking aisle, I've about lost it because time is running short and I can't remember the last time I shaved my legs. I feel like the little kid from that comic strip, whose circuitous route home is marked with a dashed line of loop-de-loops.

When I return to the house, Eva is waiting in the kitchen.

"Hey, let me help you with that," she says as I struggle with the screen door. I grunt and thrust a hand toward her so she can extricate some of the bags, whose thin plastic handles have left purple indentations on my fingers.

"So what's all this for?" she says, putting the bags on the counter and looking into them, one by one. She turns to look at me in surprise. "Are you cooking?"

"Yes, I'm going to Dan's," I say.

Eva freezes—just the slightest hiccup in the flow of her movement, but it's enough for me to see—and then returns to her task. She pulls out a bag of endives, and inspects it carefully.

"Actually, honey, could you just leave everything in the bags? See if there's room for it in the fridge."

"Okay," she says. Now I know she wants something, because otherwise she'd have torn a strip off me for making a date with Dan.

"Hey, Mom," she says casually, and I know it's

coming. She pulls the fridge open and peers in. "Is it okay if I go out tonight?"

"Where?"

"Into town. To Across the Border."

"With whom?"

"Luis."

"Absolutely not."

Her friendly façade crashes to the floor. "Why?" she demands.

"How old is he?"

"Seventeen."

"That's why."

"Mom! I'll be sixteen in October."

"And that's when you'll be allowed to go out on dates."

"It's not a date. All the guys from the stable are going to be there. It's a birthday party for Carlos!"

"All the more reason I don't want you going," I say decisively.

"Why?"

"Because they're older, and they'll probably be drinking."

"No they won't! And anyway, I won't be," she says.

"That's right. Because you won't be going."

Eva explodes. "You are such a hypocrite, do you know that? It's fine for you, isn't it? You can go out with whoever you want whenever you want, and who cares what anybody else thinks? Holy shit, Mother, all I wanted to do was go have dinner with a bunch of people you force me to work with."

"Forget it. You're still grounded for smoking, and, by the way, I'm extending it by a week for that 'shit' you just threw in. And yes, I am an adult, so I do get to go out with whomever I want."

"What about Dad?"

"What about him?"

"How do you think he'd feel about you going over to your boyfriend's for dinner?"

"Who cares? Was he thinking about me when he moved in with Sonja?"

I know instantly that I shouldn't have said that.

Eva stares at me with something like hatred. Then she slams the fridge and leaves.

I stare after her for a moment, wondering if I should go after her. In the end I decide to wait until she's had a chance to calm down.

I spend a few minutes going over the recipes and staring at the pictures. My vision of tonight does not involve referring to cookbooks. I want Dan to think that the magic I concoct comes from my own creative genius, some inspired savant part of my brain.

The instructions for the gâteau involve five different recipes—crêpes, three different fillings, and a cheese custard—so I copy little cheat sheets to stick in my purse. Just a list of ingredients, in the order in which they're used, and the state in which they are supposed to make their appearance. You know, diced, minced, pureed, whatever. Just a little something to jog my memory should I find it needs jogging.

When I emerge from my toilette, Mutti is rinsing spinach in the sink.

"I see you were successful in your quest," she says.

"Yes."

"What are you going to make?"

"Gâteau des crêpes, and crêpes suzette."

Mutti freezes, and then turns to look at me.

"*Schatzlein*, have you ever made either of those before?"

"No," I say, crestfallen at her obvious lack of confidence.

"Don't you think it would be a better idea to try something a little simpler first?"

"No," I say, crossing the kitchen and pulling the cookbook from the shelf to go over it one last time. "I've got the recipes, and there are lots of pictures. I'll be fine," I say.

"Well, you look very nice, anyway," she says, returning to her spinach.

Yes I do. For thirty-eight, I look pretty damn good. It's true that there are lines on my face, but they fall naturally into my smile, and with a bit of lipstick and mascara, I'm feeling almost glamorous.

I spent longer getting ready tonight than I ever have before. I dried my hair with Eva's paddle brush, dragging it through my thick blonde curls until they fell smooth and straight. Blonde is a good color when you're just starting to go gray, and after I pulled it into a knot at the top of my head, I stood admiring the effect in the mirror. My cheeks, which are in fact sunburned, instead look sun-kissed after the slightest dusting of bronzed powder. I even took the extra ten minutes to file the rough spots from my feet. Just in case.

"I think your date is here," says Mutti, looking out the window above the sink.

Dan and the farrier are parked by the pasture. I grab my purse and groceries and walk down the drive to meet them.

When Dan sees me, he comes over and takes the bags. "You look beautiful," he says, kissing me on the cheek. "You didn't need to dress up."

"I didn't," I say, but my cheeks are burning, because it's obvious I did.

"Have you met Francis?" Dan says, returning from the car. He gestures toward the farrier, who is setting up his kit on the flatbed of his truck.

"No."

"He does a lot of work for us at the center. He donates his time there for free, but it would go over really well if you'd pay him for this visit."

"Of course," I say. "It never occurred to me that I wouldn't."

Dan is quiet for a minute, staring out into the pasture at Hurrah, who is halfway across, and staring back at us, sniffing into the wind.

"He looks really good, Annemarie," says Dan. He puts his hands on his hips and turns back to me. "So what do you think? Are we going to need to tranquilize him?"

"I don't think so," I say. "He let me handle him today."

"Do you want to take him into the barn?"

"I don't know about that," I say quickly.

"Will he let you hold his head?"

"I think so."

"Then let's try it out here."

I open the gate and walk across the field. The grass is dry and scratchy, and pokes my sandal-clad feet.

Hurrah's ears are forward as I approach him, and he blows softly in greeting. I take hold of his halter and then run the fingers of my right hand lightly under his mane. When I turn to lead him to the gate, he starts walking before I pull at all.

I hold Hurrah's halter as Francis straddles his left foreleg. Then he lifts the hoof up and back so it's resting on his knee.

"He's got nice feet," Francis says.

And indeed he has: Hurrah's feet are as surprising as the rest of him—pink with black stripes of varying widths. They look like bar codes.

"This is incredible," says Dan, as Hurrah stands patiently. "I can hardly believe this is the same horse."

"It took about a thousand apples," I beam.

Francis works quickly, pulling out the nails and tossing the shoes aside. Then he trims the edges of the gorgeous striped hooves with what looks like a large pair of garden sheers. Finally, he files them until they're smooth.

"Hey Dan, come here for a minute," Francis says, setting down Hurrah's right foreleg.

Dan looks at me, and then moves around to the other side of Hurrah. He crouches down.

I move around to the other side of Hurrah's head so I can hear what they're saying.

"Yup, I think you're right," says Dan, running his hand carefully down Hurrah's leg from knee to fetlock, and then up again, before cupping his knee in his hands.

"Right about what?" I say.

"It looks like he's got some degenerative joint damage. Very mild," he says, noting the look on my face. "Don't worry. It won't cause problems."

"Would it cause problems for an eventer?" I ask.

Dan and I look at each other, because we're both thinking the same thing. Or is he just looking at me like that because he knows what I'm thinking?

Francis, however, is oblivious. "Well, that's it for me," he says. He straightens up and wipes his hands on his leather apron. "I'm really impressed. This horse was a basket case last time I saw him. Skinny as all get-go, too."

A lump of pride rises in my throat.

"It was nice to meet you," Francis says, nodding curtly.

"Likewise. Oh, do you want me to write a check now?" I say, rummaging in my gold purse.

"Nah, I'll send a bill. Maybe I can do some other work for you sometime."

"I'd like that," I say.

As Dan walks Francis to his truck, I look closely at Hurrah's right leg, touching it lightly with my fingers. I can't see anything wrong with it. He looks entirely perfect to me.

I hold the noseband of his halter in both hands and bring his face up to mine so I can kiss it. He obliges, flapping his whiskered lips against my chin.

Then I turn him loose. He walks a few yards away and begins to graze, swishing his tail against imaginary flies. God, he's beautiful. He looks so much like his brother.

Dan comes back and puts an arm around my shoulders, and we stand in silence, watching Hurrah.

"He is really beautiful," he says finally, but I hadn't realized he was going to speak, so I talk over him.

"Dan, you're a vet."

His arm stiffens around my shoulders, and I feel the prickle of embarrassment creeping up my scalp.

"I mean, I know you're a vet. But what I meant was, you've done vet checks for insurance policies, right?"

"Yes, of course."

"So if Hurrah started to show signs of degenerative joint damage, he wouldn't pass the exam, right?"

"Did you just call him Hurrah?"

I look down, realizing my gaffe. I don't want to admit it, but neither do I want to deny it.

Dan's arm drops from my shoulders and he comes around so that he's facing me. "Don't tell me you're still on about that."

I feel like a petulant child, staring at the ground and chewing my lip.

"Oh, honey," says Dan, and the sound of the worry in his voice makes me want to scream. "You know he's not Harry's brother."

"No, I don't know that."

"Annemarie, Harry's dead. Harry's brother is dead."

"It's not about Harry this time. It's really not. It's about Hurrah."

"Annemarie—"

"Look, I know you think I'm nuts, and I'm actually prepared to accept that. But don't write me off just yet. I've been doing some research."

The pity in his eyes is clear, so I pick up the pace, thinking that if I can only keep a few steps ahead of him, I might be able to avoid his coming to the obvious conclusion.

"No, listen, really," I stop, breathe deeply, and then start again, the very picture of self-control. "There are three different kinds of chip technology, three different kinds of scanner."

"There are two, and I have scanners for both back at my place."

"Which ones?"

"What?"

"Which ones? Which types?"

"FDX-B and HDX."

"Aha! But not FDX-A."

"Annemarie, you have to be kidding," Dan's voice is low now, and he's frowning.

"I am most certainly not. The Trovans, Destrons, and AVIDS are all non-ISO, and wouldn't be picked up by your scanner."

"That's because nobody uses them anymore."

"Hurrah's an older horse. Why shouldn't he be microchipped with the older technology?"

Dan stares at me, unblinking, and I stare back.

Then he puts his hands on his waist and turns away from me. After a moment, he walks to the fence.

Hurrah is now upside down, squirming ecstatically in the hard dirt. After a minute, he gets to his feet and shakes off a cloud of dust.

Dan puts his hands in his back pockets, and stands absolutely still for several minutes. Then he returns to where I'm standing.

"Annemarie," he says, lifting his eyes to mine. "I want you to make a deal with me."

"What?"

"I'm going to try to locate an old scanner, but if I

do, and I don't pick anything up, I want you to let this go. It's not healthy."

I nod solemnly, my heart pounding.

"I want you to look at me," he says, putting his hands on either side of my face. He lifts my face to his and looks deep into my eyes. "I'm not going to do this unless we have a deal. If I don't find a chip, you let it go. Whoever he used to be, he's your horse now. So if this really isn't about Harry, it shouldn't matter. Deal?"

I continue nodding, but even as I'm agreeing, my mind is racing to find a back door, just in case there is no chip.

• • •

My plans for the perfect dinner start to go wrong almost immediately. For one thing, the atmosphere in the car is somewhat strained, and for another, the quaint old farmhouse of my vision turns out to be a trailer. A grotty white trailer with its trim peeling off, resting on concrete blocks behind a row of scraggly trees. I am appalled. This does not bode well for the kitchen.

As Dan fiddles with the key, I take a moment to look around. The space between the trailer and the hard, cracked ground is filled with junk and cobwebs, and there's a broken broom handle sticking through one of the cinder blocks.

"Ah, there we go," he says, pushing the door inward. He steps inside and then turns around, holding the screen door open for me. I swallow, and mount the stairs. The wood is rotten, and I'm more than a little worried I might put a foot through it.

The inside is better than the outside, but it's still a trailer. I mean, I suppose you could consider it homey, in a way. A bachelor sort of way. At least it's clean.

The front door opens immediately into the living room. Or actually the dining room, if you can call it that. At any rate, there's a large open area that has a table in it, and off to the right, a couch, chair, and cheesy fake fireplace. To the left, also part of the same open area, is the kitchen.

I stare in horror. So much for the maple cupboards and central island.

"I'll go get your bags," Dan says, pushing past me. The screen slams behind him, devoid of any mitigating spring action. When he returns, I am still standing there.

"You okay?"

"Fine, fine," I say, trying to recover.

I follow him to the counter. There's a loud rustling of plastic as he sets the bags on the counter and starts to unload them.

"Wow," he says, holding the bag of endives in one hand and a Valencia blood orange in the other. He sets them down and picks up the bottle of Grand Marnier. "I can tell I'm in for a treat," he says, holding the brown bottle up to the light.

By now, I've taken an armful of things over to the fridge and opened the door. It's completely empty except for a bottle of wine, three cans of beer, and a jar of mustard. And a box of baking soda.

"Would you like a drink?"

I look back. He's blinking at me innocently. He seems completely oblivious to my horror, which is good. I don't want to insult him. But at the same time, if he lives here, what does he do with all his money? He's a successful vet. I know vets aren't rich, but surely they make enough money to live in . . . well, *houses*. And then it comes to me, and I'm so filled with shame I'm afraid I might cry. Dan lives like this because he has no family. He pours all his money into his horses.

Dan is still staring at me, only now he looks baffled. I realize I haven't answered him.

"I'd love a drink. Thank you."

I close the fridge and walk back to the counter. Instead of unpacking, I finger the edge of the laminate, which is ragged and cracked. I sigh and look back across the living room and dining room, wondering if I'm going to be able to manage the necessary mental adjustment.

Just then, I hear a pleasant *pop*. Dan has uncorked the wine (Thank God! A cork!), and as I hear the *glug-glug-glug* of the glasses filling, I think I may have managed the shift. Everything is going to be okay. If this is what I have to work with, this is what I have to work with.

I line the ingredients up on the counter, and feel the stirrings of pride and excitement return. The glossy, firm endives; the wedge of fragrant, crumbly goat cheese; the wild mushrooms with their earthy, secret scent.

"I didn't know you could cook," says Dan, sliding up behind me and setting a wineglass on the counter. I note from the clink that it's made of real glass. I pick it up gratefully and swirl the pale liquid gently around its bowl, watching the sheer glaze cascade down the sides. Yes, I do believe I'm starting to recover.

"There are a lot of things you don't know about me," I purr. "I'm actually a domestic goddess. Good at all sorts of things."

His eyes widen, locking on mine, and he brings his glass forward slowly until it meets mine with a *clink*.

And this is where I should begin my choreographed dance of the creative genius. I should turn gracefully, and with a naughty, flirtatious look set my glass on the counter and commence chopping, and stirring, and frying, and sending fragrant bursts of delicious steam wafting through the air. I should wield the instruments of my art with grace and speed, should flit between tasks and get my thirteen pots going at once, all while managing to look cool and delicious, pausing once in a while to sip my wine and shoot a suggestive look in Dan's direction.

The problem is, I can't remember where to start, so I have to consult my cheat sheets immediately. But I don't want Dan to know I have them, so instead I retreat to the bathroom. But I have to take my purse, because there aren't any pockets in my dress, and that means he'll think I have my period, which, of course, is impossible, but he doesn't know that I've had a hysterectomy—not that I'm planning to end up in bed with him tonight. Not really *planning* it anyway, but would it really be so terrible if I did?

By the time I get to the bathroom and close the door, I feel like a blathering idiot. I sit on the toilet lid and rummage through my purse for my cheat sheets, my pride and excitement replaced by outright panic. First, I read the crêpe batter recipe, and then close my eyes to see if I can repeat the ingredients from memory. And then I read the ingredients for the fillings. And the salad. And what the hell *are* duxelles, anyway? Are they something you *add* to the mushrooms, or *are* they the mushrooms? And roux? My God, couldn't I have added little hints in the margin, or something? What was I thinking?

Just before I leave, I remember to flush the toilet, and then wash my hands for good measure. I'm beginning to regret not having brought the cookbook. The thing is, I can remember the ingredients for any one thing, but I'm having trouble keeping the ingredients for all of them straight. I mean, I know that half a cup of whipping cream is involved somewhere, but at this particular moment, I can't for the life of me remember where.

Consulting the cookbook wouldn't have been so bad. It wouldn't have been quite as slick as doing it all from memory, but it's a nice-looking cookbook, glossy and colorful. I could have left it open at the right page and stolen occasional glances. It wouldn't necessarily have looked like I was being a slave to it rather than following my culinary instincts.

Back in the kitchen, I take a slug of wine for courage. Then I turn to give Dan my first seductive smile and lean backward into something cold and wet.

"Oh Jesus," I say, leaping forward. I pull the material of my dress as far around as I can to gauge the damage. The spot is immediately above my bottom, an ellipse that's approximately seven inches long and four inches high. And continuing to spread across my beautiful, blue silk.

"Oh, I'm sorry, Annemarie," says Dan, taking a dish towel from a drawer and trying to dab my rear end. I spin violently and snatch the towel from his hand.

He stands looking helpless. "My faucet leaks a little, and it always collects right there. I'm sorry. I should have warned you."

"It's fine, don't worry about it," I snap, twisting like a dog chasing its tail, wiping myself with the towel. Oh God, I'm making it worse.

"Do you want something to change into?"

"No," I say quickly. Wearing one of Dan's teeshirts is not part of my vision. Neither is wearing a stained dress, really, but there you are. I close my eyes and collect myself. Breathe deeply, I tell myself. And again.

I open my eyes, equilibrium restored, and sidle up to Dan. "I'm fine," I say, handing him the towel. "Really."

"You sure?"

"I'm sure."

And then I return to the counter, suck down another mouthful of wine, and get started.

The problem is, Dan couldn't be more in the way. I guess he's just interested in what I'm doing, but it really feels like every time I turn around, he's right there, peering over my shoulder. Which I don't suppose I'd mind if I actually knew what I was doing and thought I was being impressive, but I don't, so all he's doing is frazzling me beyond belief.

When it becomes clear that every single one of my stupid corpse-pale crêpes is going to stick hopelessly to the bottom of the pan and need to be scraped and peeled off with a variety of instruments, I turn around and bark at him.

"Do you think you could wait in the living room?"

Silence, stillness, as though the world has stopped. In the background, a single drop of water falls into the sink.

"Yeah. Sure. Sorry," he says, looking hurt. "I didn't mean to be in the way."

"You're not," I say, utterly miserable. I brush a piece of loose hair away from my face, and then poke tentatively at the rest of my hair to see whether it's all coming down. It's loose, but more or less still up. I resist the urge to go fix it, because I'm starting to despair of ever getting dinner on the table.

Dan retreats to the living room, and I return to the dinner. From there, it all goes downhill.

I poach the pears until they're mushy blobs at the bottom of the pan, and when I try to retrieve them with the shiny slotted spoon I brought along for that purpose, they disintegrate on contact, leaving empty skins swimming in a liquid that is admittedly fragrant, but murky and entirely unusable for my salad. I forget about the roasting goat cheese until it melts into a terrible, smelly black goo that is melded to the bottom and edges of the cookie sheet, and when I throw it into the sink and run water on it to stop it from smoking, it hisses and sputters and releases a violent rush of putrid steam.

"Um, is everything okay in there?" calls Dan, who is sitting obediently on the couch in the living room. Area. Whatever.

"Fine, fine," I chirp.

Right. There has to be some way to save this.

Okay. The gâteau des crêpes is baked, so it doesn't really matter if they're a little bit ripped. Or a complete tattered mess, really. As for the crêpes suzette later, well, I can check if he has ice cream in his freezer and just put the sauce on that instead. That could be quite good. And the salad—so we forego the pears and goat cheese. It will be simple. Elegant. Understated.

I take a deep breath and reach for the wine bottle.

"Are you going to want any more of that?" Dan asks. "I've got another bottle I can put in the freezer."

"Might be a good idea," I say, draining the last of the bottle into my glass. I should really refuse, because I'm already feeling a bit high, but what the hell. I'll just have to be careful. Or else eat something soon.

Out of the corner of my eye, I see Dan rise from the couch.

"Stay there!"

He freezes, startled.

"Tell me where it is and I'll get it," I say quickly, because I can't stand the thought of him seeing the mess I've made.

He looks perplexed. "You sure?"

"I'm sure."

"Okay, it's in the cupboard under the sink. To the left."

And so it is, right by the Drano. I put it in the freezer, noting with dismay the lack of ice cream, and then stand staring at the kitchen. My God, I've absolutely destroyed it, and so far, I haven't successfully completed any part of the dinner.

By the time I set the kitchen on fire, I realize it's hopeless. When Dan figures out what's going on, he rushes in and shoves me aside. I stand coughing and waving my hands in front of my face as he rips one thing after another out of the cupboard until he comes up with a huge, heavy pot lid. He holds it above the flaming frying pan and drops it into place, containing the fire completely.

"You okay?" he says, pausing briefly to look at me. Then he goes to the sink and bangs the window above it, trying to force it open.

I nod miserably, looking at the wall above his stove. From the bottom edge all the way up to where it meets the ceiling, it's streaked with black soot. A spot on the ceiling, almost a foot across, completes the effect. Just then, the smoke detector starts to shriek. So do I.

"Why don't you wait outside until the smoke clears," Dan yells over the din, waving the dish towel up and down. I guess he's trying to coax the smoke toward the window, but he looks absurd, like the matador from Bugs Bunny.

Shaking and on the verge of tears, I go outside and sit on a smelly, wet stump. In the background, the smoke detector continues to shriek its protest.

Chapter 11

There are some men who would let that be the end of the evening. But Dan is not just any man, I reflect as I gaze across at him in the flickering candlelight.

It's two hours later, and we're sitting at a picnic table in Gil's Crab Shack. I'm wearing one of Dan's tee-shirts and a pair of his boxers—fancy ones, they look almost like shorts—and the ambience of the place is such that we fit right in.

The floors are concrete, and dotted with spilt paint. Fishing nets hang from the walls, with plastic crustaceans threaded into them. An enormous orca pool-floatie dangles from the ceiling, more or less inviting a poke from a lit cigarette, and the shorts-clad waitresses wear tee-shirts that say GOT CRABS?

At the end of the patio is a sandy play area, fenced in so that the only exit is past the diners, and squealing, barefoot children fly past like greased piglets.

It is, in other words, perfect.

I breathe deeply as Dan pours the rest of the chardonnay into my glass, watching how far his fingers reach around the bottle. His hands are beautiful, and it occurs to me that I've never noticed them before. They're shapely and strong, with just the right amount of hair. They're perfect—there's not a thing about them that isn't exactly right. Not like Roger's hands. His are lawyer's hands, soft and hairless, with foreshortened, tapered fingers.

Dan sets the bottle down and leans forward, resting his elbows on the table.

"Do you know, Annemarie Zimmer," he says, lifting his glass and leaving his words to dangle languidly.

I smile at my plate of ravaged crab shell, waiting.

"I've never seen you look more beautiful in all my life," he finishes.

I gasp audibly, because someone has stolen all the air. And then I see myself in the glass of the candleholder. It swells out toward me, so my nose is enormous, but the rest is accurate—the wet hair, combed hastily and left to air dry; my face, free of soot but also of makeup; my clothes, a man's extra-large teeshirt that fits like a potato sack, with sleeves that reach to the crook of my elbows. I may look better than I did before my emergency shower, but beautiful?

I laugh so hard wine comes out my nose, and as I grab my napkin off my lap and press it to my face, I catch sight of Dan's expression. And then I stop, because he's staring at me with incredible intensity.

Then it hits me. It hits me like a ton of bricks, or a freight train, or a spotlight in the dark. It hits me like every hackneyed cliché you can think of—

I love this man. I love him, and I have always loved him. The veil has finally lifted, and the colors beneath it are so brilliant I'm not sure I can stand to look. But at the same time, I'm incapable of looking away.

• • •

It's almost midnight before we get back to the farm. As we drive around to the back of the house, I see the curtain in the dining room shift. Unbelievable. I'm thirty-eight, and my mother still waits up for me. I look instinctively at Eva's window, wondering if she's awake too.

Dan pulls in beside Mutti's van. Strange how I've come to think of it as Mutti's van. Pappa is still alive, but I'm already discounting his existence, already writing him off the page.

"So," says Dan. He shuts off the engine, winds down the window, and puts his hands back on the steering wheel.

"So," I say shyly, looking into my lap.

We sit for a moment, listening to the crickets. Then he reaches over and takes my hand.

His hand is warm, and covers mine entirely. There are calluses on his palm and fingertips, and they feel wonderful. For a moment, I forget to breathe.

I can't believe he's here with me. I can't believe I'm here with him. It's as though the last twenty years never happened—someone just lined up the edges and stitched the intervening span into an invisible hem.

In this light, he looks just as he did back then. If anything, he looks even better. Maybe it's because I know what I'm looking at now.

He leans toward me, and I feel giddy. Somewhere over the middle seat belt, our lips touch. Just graze, really, but it's enough to take my breath away. I don't even care about the seat-belt buckle that's digging into my thigh. His lips are warm and full, and they set off a string of electric shocks that run up the back of my neck.

I want those lips back. I want to taste them, to suck them into my mouth, to run my tongue between the smooth hardness of his teeth and the tender flesh of his inner lips. I want to roll them between mine and feel the darting of his tongue. I want. I want. I want.

A moment later, I realize I am frozen there, leaning forward with my eyes closed. I open them. Dan's face is a foot from mine. He looks concerned.

"Are you okay?" he asks.

I nod.

"Because I don't want to rush you . . ."

I close my eyes and shake my head.

"Hey," he says gently, guiding my face so that I'm looking at him. His hand lingers, and then he traces the line of my jaw with his fingertips. "We can take this as slow as you want."

If I were on my feet, my knees would buckle. Part of me wants to scream, No! No! I don't want to take it slowly! Take me to the tack room now! But I don't.

He kisses me again, and then lets his hand slide behind my head until he's cupping the base of my neck. It feels so good I don't know if I can stand it. It's as though a stream of effervescence trails his every movement.

"I guess this means I'm going to have to make up with your daughter," he says.

"I guess it does."

"How should we go about it?"

"I really don't know," I say. I pause for a moment, considering the possibilities. "I guess we could start by all having dinner together. Do you want to come here?"

"I don't know. Are you cooking?"

My eyes snap open. He laughs, and wraps his arms around me. The seat belt digs further into my leg, but I still don't care.

"I'd love to," he says. "Even if you *are* cooking." My face is pressed against his chest, and his voice rumbles through me. Maybe if I'm still, I can hear his heart. I take a deep breath, holding it in.

"Sorry about your house," I mumble.

"Don't give it another thought," he says.

It occurs to me that if I hadn't set his house on fire, we would have ended the evening there. Oh, I would have loved to end the evening there. But that's okay. This is not going to be our last opportunity. Of this, I am sure.

• • •

I enter the house quietly, leaving the light off and trying to close the door gently I know Mutti saw me come home, so I'm guessing she's asleep by now.

I guess wrong. Seconds later, the hall light comes on and Mutti appears in the doorway, her turquoise housecoat zipped up to the soft wattle of her throat. She flicks the kitchen light on, and stands squinting at me.

"Oh, it's you," she says.

"Of course it's me. Who else could it be?" I say, hanging my purse on a hook by the door. And then I freeze.

"Oh no," Mutti says slowly, her eyes hardening. "Oh, don't tell me. She said she'd asked you."

"She did. I said no." I spin on my heels. "Oh God. I'm going to kill her."

"Schatzlein, Schatzlein, Schatzlein."

"I am. I'm going to kill her. I gave her life, and now I'm going to take it back."

Almost on cue, we hear gravel crunching under tires. Mutti and I lock eyes. A second later, a car door slams.

"Do you want me to handle this?" says Mutti.

"Why? You think I can't handle my daughter?"

"Actually, I was offering to be the ogre."

I turn to her, seeing for the first time the gray semicircles beneath both eyes. I stare at her until I hear the door creaking inward on its hinges.

Eva sees us and freezes. Her eyes dart from me to Mutti and back to me, and then land on Dan's boxer shorts.

• • •

Suffice it to say that, once again, Eva is not speaking to me. Actually, I believe the exact phrase was "I hope you drop dead," but that translates roughly into not speaking to me. Of course, this business of not speaking to me didn't begin until she was finished calling me a racist, fascist, bigot, and hypocrite, along with all sorts of other more colorful, if somewhat less inventive, terms.

She's also not speaking to Mutti, who stood physically and figuratively beside me, much to Eva's surprise. After the tattoo, I think she'd come to expect an automatic ally, although how she thought she was going to explain an outright lie is beyond me.

She did her best to play us off against each other—the old "but Oma said" routine—and then stood astounded as Mutti ripped into her. When I sniffed her hair and breath for evidence of cigarettes and alcohol her torpor turned to grievous tears, and then, when I pointed out that I had recent reason not to trust her, she let loose with the string of insults and wished me dead.

When she leaves, stomping and blubbering and utterly convinced of the unfairness of it all, Mutti and I are left standing silently, side by side. Then Mutti turns and looks me up and down.

"What happened to you?"

"It's a long story," I say. A door crashes shut above us, rattling the glass in the painted cabinet against the wall.

"I have time," says Mutti, still staring at me.

"We should get to bed," I say.

"I don't know about you, but I'm going to need something to help me sleep. Come, *Liebchen*," she says. She turns and takes two glasses from the cabinet. Then she turns on the baby monitor, tucks it under her arm, and walks down the hall to the living room. She doesn't look back.

I follow her, although I'm not sure why. It's not that I don't appreciate the thaw, but I'm no fool. I know it's got nothing to do with me and everything to do with Dan. But I follow her anyway. Jägermeister is Jägermeister, after all.

• • •

In the morning, Eva won't answer her door. I know she's in there because it's locked. I decide to leave her alone for now.

I'm halfway to the stable before I realize I didn't brush my hair, but I can't go back, because Brian is already at the house and I don't want to be there when Pappa emerges from the dining room.

It's a beautiful bright day, and even at this early hour, the sun beats down on me in its full raging glory. I'm wearing my usual uniform of shorts and tee-shirt. With the addition of long sport socks and short rubber paddock boots, I'm a real fashion statement.

I pause at Hurrah's pasture and lean up against the fence. He lumbers over and extends his neck, blowing softly onto my hand.

"Sorry, gorgeous. I forgot your apple," I say as he moves from my hands to my pockets.

I hear a car behind me, and turn just as an ancient gold Impala—sixteen if it's a day—passes by, carrying Carlos, Manuel, and Fernando. Following it is an equally ancient metallic green Monte Carlo carrying P. J. and Luis. The windows are open, and the sounds of laughter and Spanish music spill out. P. J. raises a hand in greeting and I wave back.

Eva's words return to me, bothering me more than they should. I'm not racist—of course I'm not—although I'm not at all sure that Luis and the rest of the guys wouldn't find my real reasons for objecting to the match equally offensive. Two years is a big age difference when you're fifteen and seventeen. Seventeen-year-old boys have certain expectations, and I'm sure it's worse now than when I was young.

But the truth is, even if he weren't older than she is, I still wouldn't want her involved with him. It's got nothing to do with his race. It's got to do with his education and prospects, which, considering he's a full-time stable hand at seventeen, equal about nil.

I believe any parent would feel the same way, but the idea of being called on it makes me squeamish. Frankly, I'm glad to have the age difference to hide behind.

I consider whether to say something to the stable hands, but can't find the right opportunity. Luis is omnipresent, but if I'm going to talk to anyone, it will be P.J. But calling P.J. into my office would impart more importance to the conversation than I intend—I'm angry at Eva, not them. So in the end I say nothing.

I'm having trouble concentrating anyway. My brain is occupied by latent thought. It's a mass without form, an ever-changing squall.

I feel like a bumbling anti-Midas, staggering along leaving a trail of disaster in my wake—my marriage, my daughter, the situation at the stable.

There's also Pappa's illness, which refuses to be still even though I've pushed it to the back of my head. I've done more than that—I've bound it hand and foot, shoved it under a tarp, and weighted it down with concrete blocks. But still it bumps insistently forward, like a badly weighted washing machine, until I have to look at it just to wrestle it back to its corner.

I'm also worried about Mutti. This is taking a terrible toll on her, even if I can't pinpoint what. She looks the same, and yet she doesn't. Her hair is pinned into its usual bulletproof coil, but there's something lackluster about it, a dullness that didn't use to be there. Her face, too, is different, in the same indefinable way. It's still lineless—this is a woman, after all, who has spent a lifetime actively avoiding expression—and upon close examination, it appears to be padded in all the same places. But there's something there, a tiredness, almost a resignation, and it frightens me. Mutti is a Valkyrie. Mutti is supposed to be invincible.

All of which makes it even more important that she not find out what's going on at the stable.

• • •

I spend much of the morning plugging rags in the holes of the sinking wreck; or, to be more precise, picking up truckload after truckload of bagged shavings.

Afterward, I help Carlos and P. J. empty them into the stalls. I have something akin to a panic attack when I see how many bags we go through—it's like watching money hemorrhage to the floor in a cloudy burst of dust. Each stall essentially swallows two bags, and at the end of it, the shavings still aren't as thick as I'd like.

I seriously consider leaving the horses in the pastures until the regular shipment arrives, but this just isn't feasible. For one thing, the people coming for lessons would have to truck out to the pasture to retrieve their ride du jour. In this heat, they'd be sure to complain, and my experience with the Bermans has made me nervous about customer relations.

I suppose if I were clever enough, I would keep four or five stalls made up and then rotate the day's school horses, but just the thought of all that organization gives me a headache.

When I tell the guys to pick rather than strip the stalls until I get this sorted out, I catch P. J. shaking his head. Not in defiance, but in a "My God, what have you done" sort of way. I choose to ignore this, and slip up to my office to check the board agreements for people who've specified extra bedding for their horses. Then I go downstairs and empty a third bag into those stalls. What I don't need is more boarders pulling out in a huff.

The hay arrives in the early afternoon in a tall wagon. It's a rickety contraption, taller than it is wide, and threatens to tip when it rounds the corner onto our drive. As it winds past the house, my heart is racing. Please oh please don't look out the window, Mutti. Please be doing something else.

The highway robber is not actually with them, but I growl anyway, particularly as I write and hand over the check. With any luck, his men will go back to him and report how happy his latest customer is. Not that he seems to care.

I care, though. At this rate, we're blowing through money like nobody's business.

• • •

As penance for snapping at the highway robber's men, I help the guys load the hay into the loft.

Loading hay is hard repetitive work. For three

hours we do the same thing, over and over and over: Manuel throws a bale to Fernando, who tosses it to me. I toss it onto the conveyor, and then, at the top, Luis takes it off. He tosses it to P. J., who tosses it to Carlos, who stacks it with the others in the loft.

Again and again I lean over, hook my fingers under twine, straighten up and toss, all in the blazing heat of the sun. Before twenty minutes have passed, there are tiny bits of hay in my hair, my nose, and worst of all, my bra. My arms ache, I itch, and I smell bad.

We work without talking, but that's okay. Writing the check for the hay put me into a bit of a panic, and I'm refining my battle plan in my head.

I'll be careful. I'll be frugal. I'll switch to generic wormer. I'll pull the back shoes off all the school horses. Add that to the deposit money I plan to collect from our new boarders and the credit-card trick I figured out yesterday, and I might be able to make up the money by tax time, which I'm sincerely hoping will be the next time Mutti decides to take a peek at the way things are in the state of Denmark.

• • •

In the afternoon, the horses are inexplicably crazy, galloping around their pastures like a single amorphous cloud, all thundering legs and raised tails. The ground is hard, and soon they're engulfed in a billowing cloud of dust. It's an impressive sight, and everyone who is outside stops to watch.

I have no idea what got them started. It could be the wind; it could be the abrupt change in herd hierarchy set off by the removal of the Berman horses; it could just be that one of them got started and the rest followed suit. Whatever it was, the two herds are pounding across the hard ground in their respective pastures at such a speed that I hold my breath when they approach a fence, picturing shards of board embedded in chests. But they always make it, changing direction at the last moment as one, like a flock of birds.

Hurrah, too, is in full flight, although a fence separates him from the herd of geldings. He gallops from one end of his pasture to the other and then locks his front legs straight ahead of him, coming to such an abrupt stop he almost sits on his haunches. Then he turns and trots back along the fence, whinnying to the galloping herd and holding his tail aloft, the way Harry used to. The resemblance is so striking it takes my breath away. I've seen him panicked, I've seen him fearful, I've seen him rearing and bucking and trying to flee, but I've never seen him move like this. He swings around, strutting and proud, kicking each leg out in front of him like a Saddlebred. His nostrils are so flared I see flashes of red, and his neck is curved in a way that is excruciatingly, achingly familiar. He's simply gorgeous. Gorgeous, and so dirty you can hardly see his stripes.

Ten minutes later, I've got him tied to the outdoor wash rack, blasting him with the hose.

The stream hits Hurrah with such force that much of it splashes back onto me. It's worse when I lift the hose to rinse his back, because the water runs along the back of my arm and inside my shirt.

As I move the hose back and forth, he dances a little in the cross-ties, stamping his striped hooves in the soapy runoff and jerking his head. The water gathers and darkens in the slight depression along his spine, then cascades over his rib cage and flanks. Slowly, the gray stripes give rise to white.

When I turn the stream down to rinse his face, Hurrah flaps his lips, trying to drink from the hose. This strikes me as hilarious, and I obligingly hold it in front of his muzzle while he sucks water from the air.

Jean-Claude appears beside us, leading Bergeron in from the outdoor arena. He's there before I know it, and I almost get him with an errant blast.

"Whoa," he says, ducking.

"Oh, sorry," I say, wiping my forehead with the back of my wrist. A glop of soapy lather falls onto my boot.

"Not a problem," he says, stepping backward. He stands watching for a moment, silent and intent. Then he smiles. "So whose horse is the marshmallow now?"

My eyes tear up instantly. Instead of answering, I turn and slap Hurrah's wet shoulder affectionately.

"From that to this, in just a few days," says Jean-Claude, waving out toward the pasture and then at Hurrah. "Love, patience, and time. Just like I—" He stops. His eyes land on my wet shirt.

I look down hastily. My shirt, while still opaque, is plastered against my front. Ah, so what. Surely Jean-Claude's seen breasts before. I look up again, deciding to ignore the state of my shirt and challenging him to do the same.

"So, you are getting ready to ride, yes?" asks Jean-Claude, eyes locked firmly on my face.

"Of course not," I say.

"Why?"

"I already told you. I don't ride anymore."

Jean-Claude clucks sadly. "Ah, I have upset the lady. Apologies."

Flummoxed, I turn back to Hurrah and scrub the base of his mane with the soapy sponge.

"In that case, you won't mind if I ride him?"

"What?" I freeze, mid-scrub. I look at Jean-Claude, astounded that he would even suggest such a thing. Every fiber of my being screams out against the idea.

"Well *somebody* should," he says, shrugging lightly. "I was watching him earlier, from the outdoor arena. He's a mover, a powerful boy. I would like to see how much he knows."

"I don't think so, Jean-Claude."

"Why not?"

"I don't want to push it. His feet are still recovering," I say, but my face is burning with the lie.

"So, let's lunge him instead."

I search in vain for a response.

Jean-Claude misreads my silence for assent, and breaks into a smile.

"Ah, good," he says, straightening Bergeron's lead rope in his hands. "Bring him into the arena when you are finished. I will wait for you there."

His eyes wander down to my wet shirt for another moment. Then he clicks to Bergeron and leads him into the stable.

After Jean-Claude leaves, I continue in slow motion. I paint hoof conditioner on Hurrah's feet, and then use the clippers to trim his whiskers and the backs of his fetlocks. I spray ShowSheen on his coat, and then rub it in with the palms of my hands. When I run out of all other tasks, I massage Cowboy Magic into his mane and tail and comb it through meticulously.

I'm procrastinating. I know this. What I don't know is why. I should be dying to lunge him, because it will reveal what he knows. But maybe that's the point. Maybe I don't want to know anymore, and I don't understand this, because I've been chasing the truth down like a bloodhound all summer.

In the end, I empty three bags of shavings into one of the stalls left empty by the Bermans, and put Hurrah inside. Then I stand with him, running my hands over his sleek, shiny coat as he munches his gold-plated hay.

I hear footsteps coming down the aisle, and just as I'm wondering how to explain to Jean-Claude that I'm not going to lunge him after all, am never going to allow anyone to lunge him, ever, I hear a voice with a French accent coming over the sound system:

"Okay, now walk down the center line, and ride a right leg yield. No, his haunches are trailing. Feel how his spine is bent? Ride *through* your horse, picture the straight line. Better, better. Okay, when you hit the track, start the trot please . . ."

The footsteps in the aisle belong to Dan. He sees me through the bars of the stall and steps inside.

"Hey, Beautiful," he says. He kisses the back of my neck. "I come bearing gifts."

"Oh, don't," I say, flinching because I'm sure I taste salty. "I'm entirely gross."

"You're gorgeous."

"Oh, give over!"

"You are."

"I'm filthy, soaking wet, and I've got hay stuck in my hair."

Dan stands back and surveys me. "All right then, your horse is gorgeous."

I laugh. "With that I can agree. So what did you bring me?"

"Two things. Flowers, which I dropped off at the house with your mother. She asked me to stay for dinner, by the way. I hope you don't mind."

"I'm delighted," I say, and I am, even though it was Mutti who extended the invitation.

"And I also brought this," he says, holding out a scanner.

My heart lurches. "Jesus."

Dan turns it over in his hands as though it's just another piece of equipment, and then steps forward to Hurrah.

"Dan . . ." I start, but I don't know how to finish. How do I tell him that I've changed my mind? That I don't want to know the truth anymore, not only in case he isn't Harry's brother, but also in case he is? I feel like Pandora, with my hand on the latch.

"I got it from a friend who is in practice with her father. It's kind of a relic, but apparently so is he. He doesn't throw anything away."

As he speaks, he runs the scanner over Hurrah's withers.

I should stop him, but I can't move. My breath is coming fast, and my fingers are tingling. "Dan . . ." I say, as the ceiling of the stall starts to spin. My voice cracks, and I stop to clear my throat. But I can't. There's a lump there now, something I can't swallow past. I think I'm going to suffocate.

Dan is still standing beside Hurrah, oblivious to my distress. He shakes his head, looking at some distant point in the shavings and continuing to wave the scanner over the base of Hurrah's neck.

"Nope," he says finally. He turns to me, shaking his head. "Nope, I'm sorry, honey, but there's nothing there."

He starts to drop his hand, and then it happens. As the scanner passes the top of Hurrah's shoulder blade, it beeps three times.

Dan freezes, looks at the scanner, and then back at me. I stare right back, or think I do, but I can't say for sure because the world is weaving hideously.

"Well, what do you know," he says.

Outside the stall, I hear a clank and a clatter as something hits the concrete. I spin around and see P.J. sprinting toward the exit at full speed. His shovel lies rocking in the middle of the aisle.

Less than a second later, Carlos also runs past, followed closely by Luis.

"What the—?" I stick my head into the aisle and look toward the exit.

It's Pappa. He's two hundred yards from the stable, sitting in the middle of the laneway, absolutely still.

"Oh God. Pappa!" I shout, breaking into a run. Behind me, I hear the stall door slam shut. Then I hear footsteps, and Dan passes me, his long legs swallowing the distance.

He reaches Pappa before I do. By the time I get

there, Dan is leaning over with his hand on Pappa's shoulder, looking into his face. P. J., Carlos, and Luis cluck like hens in the background, peering in and around Pappa's chair for visible signs of a problem and discussing their findings in Spanish.

I come to a stop beside him, gasping. "What's going on? Pappa, are you all right?" Pappa's face is frozen, his mouth slightly open. His lips and tongue look dry.

I turn to Dan. "What's going on? Is he all right?" I search his face for an answer, but he just shakes his head.

I look my father up and down, but don't see anything particularly unusual. There is a bag of carrots on his lap, partially spilled, and his right arm lies on top of them, as though he'd tried to pick them up but couldn't. Pappa's jaw moves.

"Shh, quiet, guys," I say, holding a hand up. "Pappa, what happened? Were you coming to see Tazz?"

He nods twice, a stiff, wooden gesture.

"Is there a problem with your chair?"

The same wooden gesture, but this time from side to side. Then I realize what happened. He was not trying to pick up the carrots that spilled from the bag. His hand fell away from the controls, spilling the carrots, and he didn't have the strength to lift it back up.

I bring a hand to my mouth to choke back the sound that rises in my throat, but it's too late. It's already out.

Dan crouches in front of Pappa. "Did you get stuck out here? Is that what happened?"

I turn away, hastily wiping tears from my eyes.

"Do you want me to take you somewhere?" Dan continues from behind me.

I turn back, sniffing and weepy. "He wants to see Tazz. He comes every night. Do you know where Tazz is?"

Dan nods. "Yes," he says quietly. He rises to his feet. "Anton, is that where you want to go?"

Again, the wooden nod, and then, through the blur of my tears, I see Dan step behind Pappa's wheelchair and flip the switch that lets him control it from behind. And then, amidst the whirring of the motor and the crunching of the gravel, he takes my father in to see his beloved, grizzled half Percheron, half God-knows-what.

• • •

I go back to the house, bursting through the back door in a state of panic. Mutti is standing at the counter, buttering layers of filo.

When I tell her what just happened, she drops her head for a moment. Then she sets her pastry brush down on the cutting board and turns to face me.

I'm still hyperventilating, holding both hands in front of my face and breathing through my fingers.

Mutti stares at me for a moment, and then goes to the corner cabinet. When she opens the door, an avalanche of white pharmacy bags fall onto the counter. She gathers them hastily and shoves them back in, and then reaches past for a small pill bottle.

• • •

Valium is a marvelous thing. I think you could drop an anvil on my foot and I wouldn't care. Actually, that's a terrible misrepresentation. What I'd do is regard the anvil and my injured foot and analyze the situation calmly.

It takes enough of the edge off that, for the first time, I'm able to look at Pappa's illness without being overwhelmed by panic. It doesn't mean I can look it squarely in the eye, but it does mean I can sidle up to the edge and then hesitate for just a moment before shrinking away.

That one moment is long enough for me to see—for the first time, and with blinding clarity—that this is not happening to me. It's happening to Pappa.

• • •

By unspoken agreement, we spend all of dinner pretending nothing happened.

Under the cloak of sedation, I manage to look Pappa in the eye a few times, but each time I do, I find an unbearable weight in the knowledge of his suffering and have to turn away.

But this is just one stratum of the subtle, complex nuances that pass among us. They're hard to keep track of, since they shift and ebb like underwater currents.

Eva is sullen and brooding, because she still hates Dan for firing her. She also hates me for grounding her, and Mutti for backing me up. Jean-Claude she loves, because today he let her ride Bergeron. Jean-Claude seems to have something against Dan, although God knows what, and Mutti—well, against all odds, Mutti seems almost content.

It may all be an act, I just don't know—but she smiles serenely from her place beside Pappa, and reaches over occasionally to squeeze his clawlike hand.

Pappa seems at peace now too, although he doesn't eat a single bite. The stark panic that was on his face this afternoon has been replaced by something almost like tranquility. Perhaps Mutti has crumbled a Valium in his wine, and Jesus—why not? If I can't face what's happening to him, how much worse is it for him?

Jean-Claude needles Dan, and Dan parries politely, glancing at me repeatedly through the bouquet he brought, which Mutti has set on the table in a blue glass jug.

"So I hear you run some kind of shelter," says Jean-Claude. The edge of his lip is curled, as though he smells something distasteful.

"Yes. A horse rescue center."

"And you are a vet too, no?"

"Yes," says Dan, setting his napkin beside his plate and staring at Jean-Claude. I don't know where this is going, and clearly neither does Dan. Jean-Claude knows that Dan is a vet. He's our vet. Even if he's never treated Bergeron and Tempeste, he's been around the stable enough that Jean-Claude must know who he is.

"You are a busy man," continues Jean-Claude.

"You could say that."

"That mustn't leave you with much time for a personal life." Jean-Claude leans back in his chair, his eyes narrowed. He picks up his wineglass and swirls the ruby liquid at the bottom.

"That was certainly true for a long time. But recently things have been picking up," says Dan, smiling in my direction. Mutti beams, and Jean-Claude stiffens visibly.

"And what about you? Do you have a family?" says Dan, fixing Jean-Claude in his stare.

Jean-Claude stops swirling, although the red liquid continues.

"A daughter and ex-wife in Canada. Near Ottawa," he says.

"How old is your daughter?"

"Sixteen."

"That's a nice age."

Jean-Claude and I swing our heads in unison to stare at Dan. I can't say anything because Eva is here, but Jean-Claude does. "It's a hellish age," he sputters. "A terrible age."

"Hey—" says Eva, coming to this unseen daughter's defense.

"Do you see her often?" continues Dan. He presses his knife into the golden filo, spraying flaky crumbs out to the side.

Jean-Claude's eyes narrow further, and then he leans forward, folding his arms in front of him on the table. "Not nearly often enough. You will excuse me," he says, rising to his feet a little too quickly. He nods curtly toward Mutti.

As soon as he leaves the room, Dan leans forward, peering at me through the gladiola stems. "I think he likes you," he says in a stage whisper.

My jaw drops, and Eva's eyes widen. Mutti and Pappa pretend they didn't hear.

"Dan!" I whisper furiously. I hear the back door

close, and then the screen door crack shut against its frame.

"What?" says Dan, as though he has no idea. And then again, looking puzzled, "What?"

• • •

When Brian finally arrives, almost forty minutes late, Mutti, Eva, and I all see Dan to the back door. If I hadn't taken the Valium, I'd probably step outside with him, but at this point, the only thing I'm good for is crawling upstairs and collapsing in bed.

"Dinner was lovely, Ursula," says Dan, squeezing Mutti's hand and kissing her cheek. And then, I assume because Eva is here, he does the same to me.

Said daughter hangs back against the wall, hands shoved into pockets, gaze fixed on the floor.

"Good night, Eva," Dan says. When Eva doesn't respond, he steps out into the night. I lean over and grab Harriet's collar to prevent her from following. Then, almost as an afterthought, Dan steps back inside.

"Oh, Eva. You know, Mike said something to me this morning that got me thinking. He said that Flicka wasn't looking quite right."

My daughter stiffens.

"Not bad, not like there's anything wrong," Dan continues quickly. "Just a little . . . I don't know, dusty. Like maybe she could use a good grooming."

He pauses. "So, Mike and I were thinking—you know, assuming it's all right with your mom, of course—well, we were thinking maybe you'd like to try again. Maybe start coming out to the center again."

Eva looks momentarily stricken, and then screams and heaves herself at him, throwing her arms around his neck. Dan presses his cheek against her hair and lifts her in the air. He's smiling, and staring straight into my eyes.

He sets her down and assumes a stern countenance. "But if I catch wind of a single cigarette being smoked on my property, there won't be any further chances. None. Finito. Do you understand?"

Eva nods deeply and traces an *X* on her chest with her finger. "I swear. I promise. Cross my heart and hope to die," she says, desperate in her attempt to convey sincerity. "Oh Dan," she says standing on tiptoe and hugging him again. "Thank you. Thank you, thank you, thank you, thank you."

I look at the two of them, and am moved almost to tears.

Chapter 12

I wake up fretting in equal parts about Hurrah and whether there are any answers to my ads yet. I won't know anything until I get to the office, but I can't seem to make myself move. It's as though I have a hangover, although I know I don't, because I didn't drink any wine last night. I was too afraid to, what with taking the Valium. But whatever caused it, there are bricks behind my eyes, a potato sack around my brain, lead weights strapped to all my limbs.

Harriet is curled up against me, tucked in like the smaller of two spoons with her wet nose pressed into my chin.

The side of the bed sinks quite suddenly, squeaking hideously.

"Ma, get up."

I open one eye. Eva is dressed and ready. Her hair is pulled into a French braid, and an aura of peppermint and shampoo surrounds her.

"Mmmm," I mumble, and reclose my eye. Harriet sighs and drops her head again. The wet nose lands against a different spot, and I wonder in a vague way whether the moisture is dog sweat, and if so, whether it will make me break out.

"Ma." Eva reaches over and shakes my shoulder. "Come on, I'm going to be late."

I groan and roll onto my back, shielding my eyes with my forearm. "What time is it?"

"Eight. Come on," she says.

"Ten minutes."

"What?"

"Give me ten minutes. Ten minutes. Then I promise I'll get up."

"No! Come on! It's my first day back and I don't want him mad at me."

"He won't be mad at you. Tell him it's my fault. Heck, I'll tell him myself. I need to talk with him anyway."

My daughter sighs grievously, violently even, and I sneak a glance at her from under my arm.

"Oh, all right. Okay. I'm getting up," I say.

I do, but it's hard work. Everything is hard work this morning, from dragging my body out of bed to crossing the kitchen floor, to finding my keys in my purse. It's not until I'm sitting in the van that I wonder where Brian is. He's supposed to be here by now, but there's no sign of his car. He was late last night, too. He'd better tread carefully—Mutti is not one to tolerate tardiness.

When we get to the center, Eva barely waits for the van to stop before she leaps out. She marches straight out to the pasture where Flicka grazes. I get out and stand beside the van, watching.

Flicka is a beautiful little thing, glossy and fine limbed. She's bleaching out in the sun, almost to a grulla, with some dappling on her flanks. The effect is striking.

Eva digs something out of her back pocket. Flicka noses her tee-shirt in anticipation, but Eva is still fumbling. Ah yes, I see now. It's a mint, and Flicka knows exactly what it is. She presses her muzzle insistently against Eva's hands, nibbling the wrapper as Eva struggles to remove it.

My heart tightens when I look at them. They are so oblivious to the outside world that the outer limits of their exclusive universe are almost visible. I know how Eva feels. Oh God, do I know.

• • •

I find Dan in the office, sitting behind a mint green metal desk.

"Annemarie! Hi!" he says, getting up.

I stand just inside his doorway. "Don't do it," I say.

"Don't do what?"

"Don't call the chip in."

He blinks twice, looks confused. "It's too late. I already did."

My throat constricts. "What? When?"

"This morning."

"What did they say?"

"They didn't say anything. All I did was call the hot line."

"Oh," I say, but the word is cracked, like a cry.

"Annemarie, are you okay?"

"Fine."

"You look upset."

"What if it's him? What if they take him away?"

"Oh, baby." He gets up and walks toward me. "He's not Hurrah."

"How can you be so sure?"

"Because Hurrah is dead," he says, putting his arms around me. "I'm sorry if this has upset you. That's the last thing I wanted to do. Believe me, nothing bad is going to happen. Half the time, the contact information registered to the chip isn't valid. Even if it is, you have to remember that this horse ended up at a slaughter house. Whoever is on that chip is not going to want him back."

Dan pulls back and looks me in the eye, keeping his hands on my shoulders. "You do understand that the presence of a chip doesn't prove anything, don't you?"

I nod, but I don't understand anything of the sort. All I understand is that I wasn't thinking far enough ahead, and that I think I may have set something terrible and unstoppable in motion.

• • •

When I get back to our place, I find Mutti kneeling in front of her flower bed, next to a growing pile of amputated limbs. She wields the pruning sheers with dramatic flair, lopping off great lengths of what looks like perfectly good plant to me. Of course, that may be why her garden always looks so wonderful and I always had to rely on a landscaping service.

I stop beside her. "Hey, Mutti. Where's Pappa?"

She looks up at me, shielding her eyes from the sun. "He stayed in bed this morning." She turns back to the garden and resumes snipping.

"Mutti?"

"Yes, *Liebchen*."

"What's his prognosis?"

"You know his prognosis."

"I know, but . . ." God, this is difficult. I can't even form the words. I swallow hard and try again. "How much longer until . . ."

Mutti hesitates for a fraction of a second, and then continues her work. I stare at her thin lithe back and straw saucer of a hat, and wonder what the face beneath it is doing.

"Mutti?"

"That horse of yours," she says, pivoting on her heels and facing me. She braces herself with one hand on the ground. "Jean-Claude tells me that you've made great progress."

"Yes, but—"

"I think he's ready to go out with the herd. Don't you?" She stares at me, her pale eyes steady.

"Yes, Mutti."

"You could try putting him out in D West. Maybe with a small herd to begin with. You could put him in with Domino, Beowulf, and Blueprint."

"Yes, Mutti."

If I don't blink, maybe I can pretend I'm not crying.

• • •

I was anxious about how Hurrah would handle himself, mostly because of the eye, but it's clear from the moment I unhook his lead that I needn't have worried.

Rather than wait for the other horses to come and

investigate him, he trots right over and starts sniffing them.

There's the usual squealing and throwing of heads that comes with horses getting acquainted, but nobody goes after anyone else in a serious way.

I stay close, just in case things get heated. I know better than to throw a new horse into the mix and expect him to slide smoothly in. Any addition means the whole hierarchy needs readjusting—they need to form new alliances, shake out the new pecking order, and the way they do it is with teeth and feet. So I'm surprised and delighted to find Hurrah completely unmarked when I lead him back into the stable in the late afternoon.

Jean-Claude is standing in the aisle talking to the parents of a student I have never seen before. The student, a girl of about twelve, skulks in the background. Her full-seat breeches and Ariat boots speak volumes, as does her father's demeanor.

"If she doesn't want to, then this is not the time," says Jean-Claude as I lead Hurrah into his stall.

The mother mumbles something I cannot hear because at that moment Hurrah's hooves clip the top of the door track.

"Perhaps next year," says Jean-Claude.

"No, that's completely unacceptable," says the father. "That wastes an entire season."

I unhook Hurrah's lead quietly and then stand by his shoulder, straining to hear.

Jean-Claude speaks next. "But the girl just said she doesn't want to jump."

"Of course she wants to jump."

I move to the edge of the stall, lurking just inside.

The father stares, belligerence humming from his body.

Jean-Claude continues. "She does not want to jump. And until that changes, I will not send her over a fence."

The father raises his voice. "I don't care if she wants to or not. Courtney is talented, but she needs guidance. She needs discipline. And if you can't provide it, I'll go elsewhere and find someone who can."

Jean-Claude raises a hand to indicate that he's finished here.

"What's going on?" I say, emerging from the darkness of Hurrah's stall.

The parents, Courtney, and Jean-Claude all turn to stare.

Jean-Claude speaks first. "This gentleman came by to enquire about one of our empty stalls."

"Who are you?" the father demands.

"Annemarie Zimmer," I say, eyes locked on his face. "I'm the manager."

His eyes dart to the wall, to the pictures of Harry and me in our glory days, and then back again. A slight shift in his expression tells it all. He apparently is among those who remember me.

"I'm delighted to meet you, Annemarie," he says, his voice assuming a lower, distinctly more deferential tone. "My name is Charles Mathis. We've known about your barn for a long time, and when we heard that you had a stall available, and that you were back . . . My daughter Courtney is very much like you. She's extraordinarily talented—extraordinarily. But she needs a trainer with a firm hand. She needs discipline, and this guy . . ." He gestures toward Jean-Claude, exhaling in disgust. "Perhaps you can help me."

"I'll do my best. What seems to be the problem?"

"This . . . this . . . *trainer* of yours says he will not work my daughter over fences, when it's imperative that she do so."

"Why?"

"Why what?"

"Why is it imperative that she jump right away?"

"Because without it, she cannot progress."

"How old is she?"

"Eleven."

"Then she has plenty of time to progress. Plenty."

His brows knit, but he doesn't answer. Apparently he expected a different reaction.

"You're welcome to bring your horse here, but Jean-Claude is the trainer, and I stand behind his decisions."

"But surely you understand—"

"I understand all too well, believe me."

"I beg your pardon?"

"Tell me, do you really want Courtney to be like me?"

"Yes, of course."

"No you don't."

Four pairs of eyes stare at me. Nobody moves.

"You do know what my life was like, don't you? I'm not talking about my accomplishments. I'm not even talking about the broken neck, or losing my horse. I'm talking about being forced to spend all my waking hours doing something I didn't want to do. I'm talking about not being allowed to go to school because it would take too much time away from my training. I'm talking about not having any peers because I had virtually no opportunities to meet anybody. I'm talking about being socially stunted and paying for it for the last twenty years."

When I finish speaking, all eyes are glued on me. Even Jean-Claude stares as though I were an oddity. I don't blame him. I am an oddity.

I turn to the girl. "Courtney, do you want to jump or not?"

"No," she says, her small voice as clear as a bell.

"And there you have it," I say to her father.

"She'll jump whether she likes it or not," he says. "She's my daughter, and as long as she's living under my roof—"

"At the moment you're under my roof, and I'm the one who calls the shots. I'm sorry, Mr. Mathis. I wish I could let you come to our barn—you have no idea how much I wish that—but I simply can't. Maybe your daughter will want to jump someday, and maybe she won't. But nobody here is going to force her."

"Obviously I misjudged you."

I wait, because it's clear he wants to continue.

"Maybe you used to be something," he says, one corner of his mouth lifting into a sneer, "but not anymore. Now you're nothing but a sentimental, self-pitying fool."

"And you're an asshole, so I guess that makes us about even."

• • •

Ten minutes later, I'm slumped in the depths of Jean-Claude's couch. My knees are pulled up and I have a hand over my face. My brain is killing me, pounding against my temples.

There's no excuse for what just happened. Yes, he was bullying his daughter and yes, he was unspeakably rude to me, all of which gave me ample reason to refuse to accept him as a boarder, but not to react in the way I did. So why did I?

It's because as I listened to him bitch and carp and insist on his own way, I saw Pappa. The old Pappa, the Pappa of my youth. I haven't seen him in twenty years, but there he was, right in front of me, and all the bitterness, all the resentment—the pent-up frustration of a lifetime—came boiling forth like a volcanic explosion.

Why am I still so angry? Why do I still want to make him understand how much pressure he put on me? Why do I still care? There wouldn't be any point in confronting him now anyway, because the Pappa of today bears no resemblance at all to the man who used to make me get up at five every morning to jog two miles and then ride horse after horse all day. The Pappa of today feeds carrots to ancient ugly horses. The Pappa of today has mellowed beyond recognition, although I have no idea when or how that happened. Maybe it was the illness that changed him. Maybe he's trying to make peace with himself and everybody else before he dies. I can't say for sure, because I've barely spoken with him in twenty years. Our entire relationship revolved around my career, and after my accident, we no longer shared a vocabulary.

"Here," says Jean-Claude. I pull my hand away. My field of vision is filled by a pair of tan breeches and a snifter of cognac. A snifter? The man brought snifters?

"Thanks."

I take it, and swallow more than I should. I know this the second it hits my mouth, but other than spitting it back into the glass, I have no choice but to swallow. It burns its way down and then rises again in a cloud of fiery fumes. My adenoids protest. I breathe in through my nose, which only re-ignites the flames.

"Are you okay?" Jean-Claude asks as I sputter wildly. He sits next to me.

I nod, waving a hand in front of my face.

"You sure?"

I bob my head even faster, and turn so he won't see the color of my face, which feels blue. I sigh and wait for the tears to reabsorb.

After I get a hold of myself, I drop my head onto the back of the couch.

"Oh God. I am such an idiot."

"I wouldn't say an idiot. Perhaps a little . . . tense. But you were right. He *is* an asshole."

"I had to do it. I had to turn him down. It would have been worse if I'd let him come, because I probably would have ended up driving him out or killing him. Does that make sense?" I lift my head and look at Jean-Claude.

He nods solemnly. "*Parfaitement.*"

I look down at my cognac, and in the depths of the rusty liquid, Mutti's face appears. I stare at her for a moment and then swirl her into oblivion. I look up, afraid she might reappear.

"He's going to find someone who will make her jump, isn't he?"

Jean-Claude nods again.

"Asshole," I say.

"I think we've already established that."

Suddenly brave, I take another sip of cognac. I keep this one in my mouth for a while, letting it slide around the sides of my tongue and pressing it to my palate before finally swallowing. This time, I simply relax my throat and let it slip down, anticipating the sensation. Quite nice, when you approach it sensibly. Provides a nice warmth rather than a burn, and ends with a nice tingle. Bolder now, I follow it with another sip. Perhaps cognac is my friend after all.

Mutti appears again, this time in the folds of the green curtain, and I blink rapidly to drive her away.

I turn back to Jean-Claude. "So do you know why she is afraid to jump?"

"Apparently she had a fall. She broke her arm and now she's scared."

"And he still wants to force her to jump? The—" I glance quickly at Jean-Claude and see him brace. Perhaps I've already overused that word today. "—idiot. Idiot! I just don't understand what goes through people's minds. Maybe she's just not a jumper."

"I think she is not. Kids are so different. My Manon, for example, will jump anything. She's a fiend. Completely fearless."

"That's your daughter?"

"Yes."

"Manon," I say wistfully. "That's a lovely name. Does she live with her mother?"

"Yes. In Hull. Québec. Just over the river from Ottawa. Manon trains at the National Equestrian Centre."

"Really!" I look at him with increased interest. The kid must be really good. "It's funny, but I always thought you were French. I mean, from France, not French Canada."

"I am. I'm from Montargis. I went to Canada on a riding scholarship in 1986. My wife, though—my ex—she is *Québecois*, *pur laine*."

"Poor what?"

"*Pur laine.* It means, how do you say—virgin wool. True blood. *Québecois* to the bone. My daughter can trace her history in Québec back for sixteen generations." He emphasizes each syllable of the last two words by stabbing his finger in the air. Then he sighs deeply.

We lapse into silence, nursing our cognac.

"Do you miss her?" I finally ask. It's a stupid question, because I know the answer, but I'm not really asking about him. I'm asking him to make me feel better about taking Eva so far from her father.

"Terribly. Just terribly," he says, staring pensively at the wall.

A fist tightens around my heart. I throw the rest of my cognac against the back of my throat and immediately double over, sputtering violently.

Chapter 13

Other than Courtney, there have been no responses to my attempts at finding new boarders, and the situation is now dire. If I don't take control immediately, I'm going to lose the stable. Not mess it up, not weaken it, not dip into some nonexistent nest egg. I'm talking about actually causing the bank to foreclose.

The first thing I do is call the farrier to find out how soon he can pull the back shoes off the school horses. That will save me fifty dollars per horse every six weeks. It won't make up for the revenue from the lost boarders, but it's a start.

Francis listens politely, and then says, "I can't do that."

"Why not?"

"Because it's a drought year and the ground is rock hard. If you put a bunch of horses out there with nail holes in their hooves, you're just asking for trouble."

"Does that mean I'm stuck with back shoes forever?"

"Not at all. But I'm seeing a lot of bad feet this year because of the ground. I've had to shoe horses that usually go barefoot. To do the opposite would be foolhardy."

When I hang up, I'm just about in tears. My entire battle plan at this point consists of collecting deposits from imaginary boarders and saving three dollars a tube on twenty-seven wormers. That's eighty-one dollars every eight weeks.

I need to get out of here.

• • •

I meet Dan in the middle of the staircase. I had been looking at the tips of my boots, and am startled when I find myself facing the legs and torso of a man. Apparently visibly so, because he takes my elbow to steady me.

"I'm okay," I say reflexively, although I'm just about at the breaking point. I want him to wrap his arms around me. I want to collapse against him, bury my head in his shoulder, and tell him how everything's falling apart.

This does not happen. I look up at him. He's pale.

"What is it? What's wrong?" I say quickly.

His eyebrows knit together, but he doesn't say anything.

"Dan, what is it? You're scaring me."

I hear the fear in my voice, and just as I'm imagining Eva tangled in a thresher, Eva with a hoof lodged in her skull, Eva run over by a tractor, he says, "The registry called."

The wall in front of me starts to swim.

"The chip was registered to Ian McCullough," he says quietly.

I stare at him until the edges of his face lose focus, and then drop down onto one of the stairs. I misjudge it, and jam my tailbone against the edge. Blood whooshes through my ears.

"No," I say.

"Yes."

"No," I say again.

"He's Highland Hurrah. He's Harry's brother, Annemarie."

"No, he can't be," I say sickly. "Highland Hurrah is dead. He died in a fire. It was in all the papers." I wait for Dan to agree with me, but he doesn't. Why doesn't he agree with me? My fingertips start to tingle.

"It's him, Annemaric," he repeats. He sits on the stair and reaches for my hand. I let him take it, but my fingers remain limp as spaghetti. I feel like I'm shutting down.

"Annemarie?" he says gently.

"You told me yourself that the insurance company wouldn't pay out that kind of money without seeing the body."

"I don't know what they saw. I can't explain that. But the horse you have downstairs is Highland Hurrah. There's no mistake."

"Maybe they've reused the chip," I continue. "Or the number. It could just be a typo."

"They can't reuse numbers. Each one is unique."

I pull my hand away.

He watches me for a moment, and then continues.

"I can't explain it. But there's no mix-up with the chip."

The enormity of what's going on hits me, and I moan like a woman in labor, rubbing my forehead with a quaking hand. "Oh God, oh God, oh God, oh God. What now?" My voice is tremulous, barely under control.

Dan shakes his head. "I don't know."

"What are they going to do?"

"I don't know."

I stare at him for a long time. "They're going to take him away from me," I say.

Dan says nothing, eyes locked on mine.

"Why did you do it?"

"Do what?" he asks.

"Call in the chip."

"What?" Dan looks baffled.

"None of this would be happening if you hadn't called in the chip."

Dan stares at me, wide-eyed. "You can't be serious."

"Of course I am. I asked you not to."

"You asked me not to after I'd already done it," he says indignantly. "*And* after you pestered me about the chip reader."

"What pestered?" I continue, my voice rising in irritation. "I asked you about it once."

"You've been obsessed with this all summer."

"I wasn't obsessed!" I hiss.

"Oh really? Then what would you call it?"

"I was just . . . curious."

"Oh really? You had no interest in chip readers, then?"

"That was just research."

"Just research. I see." Dan nods quickly, bitterly.

"I wanted it to be him, but I didn't want it . . ." I struggle for the word, and then sputter stupidly, "*confirmed.* You never asked me whether I wanted you to call in the chip."

"What? Oh, Jesus. This is rich. You're completely nuts, do you know that?"

"No I'm not!" I'm shouting now, as full-bellied and loud as a fishwife. I know this is irrational, but I can't help it.

At the bottom of the stairs, Carlos appears and looks up in alarm.

"What the hell do you want?" I scream at him. He disappears.

"Jesus, Annemarie. It's not his fault."

"That's right," I say bitterly. "It's yours."

He stares at me for a moment, eyebrows knit. "Why are you doing this?"

I can tell from his tone of voice that he's trying to get me to take a step back. But it's too late. It can't be done.

"I'm not doing a *goddamned thing*," I bark.

"I swear to God, Annemarie, you are the most impossible woman I have ever met."

"And you just cost me Harry's brother," I respond.

Dan rises to his feet and stands absolutely still. Then he pivots and rams his fist into the wall. A long crack snakes its way toward the ceiling. I recoil instinctively. Then he walks down the stairs and turns the corner without ever looking back.

I shriek with rage and also punch the wall, both surprised by and welcoming the explosion of pain.

• • •

I'll hide him. I'll deny he's here. Oh, sure, they might be able to get a warrant to scan all my horses, but that won't even occur to them until after they realize I'm not going to cooperate, and I'll make sure they don't figure that out until the last possible moment. By the time they've done the paperwork for a warrant—never mind finding the right kind of scanner—Hurrah will be far, far, away.

I'll claim he was stolen. I'll file a report. I'll move him to . . . Where? To Dan's? Not a chance. If they even *try* to take Hurrah from me, I'll never speak to Dan again. And besides, he won't help me. He's too moral, too good. He won't understand that there is a time and place for everything, including fraud. But it leaves me with a serious problem. Where the hell do you hide a one-eyed striped horse?

• • •

I'm pacing the pasture like a madwoman when the solution comes to me. I stop, press my hands to my mouth to suppress a yelp, and then pat my pockets, checking for keys. I must have left them on the hook by the kitchen door.

A few minutes later, I open the back door to the kitchen. I step inside and lean over, out of breath from my sprint. Eva is sitting at the table, flipping through a magazine. No one else is here, and there's no sign of dinner.

"Where's Oma?" I demand.

"I dunno," says Eva. "The van's here, but I haven't seen her."

I stride through the kitchen, boots and all, and stop in the doorway. "Mutti?" I call loudly into the empty hall. "Mutti?"

A second later, the door to the dining room opens, and Mutti's face appears in the crack.

"Shh," she says, frowning. "Quiet. Pappa's sleeping."

"Is everything okay?" I roll onto the balls of my feet, straining to look around her.

"Fine," she says, closing the door until it and the doorframe flank her ears.

I peer over her head. "You sure?"

"Yes, but can you make dinner?" she whispers.

"Mutti, no!"

She stares at me, gray eyes unblinking.

"Mutti, I can't. There's somewhere I've got to go."

"Annemarie, please."

"Oh, Mutti—" I say. I search her eyes and see that I don't have a hope. "Okay. Fine. I'll do it."

"Thank you, *Liebchen*," she says, before shutting the door with a click.

Liebchen?

I return to the kitchen, desperate. There's no time for making dinner. It's only a matter of time before the insurance company calls or shows up. Maybe I'll take Eva with me and just grab a pizza. Of course, if I do that, I'll have to confide in Eva.

But I've forgotten about Jean-Claude, who chooses this moment to enter by the back door. He surveys the kitchen, clearly as surprised as I was by the lack of evidence of dinner.

"Don't ask, because I don't know," I say preemptively.

"Is everything all right?"

"Yeah, fine. He's just tired," I say.

"Your mother—?"

Jean-Claude is interrupted by the phone. I glare at it, willing it to stop. It doesn't. On the third ring, I answer.

"Hello?" I bark into the mouthpiece.

"Uh, yeah, hi. This is Brian, the home health aide. Is Ursula there?"

"She's busy."

"Is this Annemarie?"

"Yes it is."

"Um . . . Is everything okay over there?"

"Yes, of course it is. Why wouldn't it be?" I say irritably.

"Did you know that your mother canceled my scheduled visits for tonight and tomorrow?"

"No, I didn't."

"Look, this is awkward, but . . . does she have some other help, or is she just planning to manage on her own?"

"I have no idea. You'll have to ask her."

"It's just that she was really upset when I was late the other day—"

"You were forty minutes late. Austrians don't like people to be late."

"I had a flat tire, which I explained to her. But basically . . . Look, all I'm saying is that she's entitled to the help—it's covered by insurance—so if she's canceling because she doesn't want me to come anymore, I can arrange for someone else. She doesn't need to go through this on her own."

I pause. Despite the fact that my skin crawls every

time I think about Brian, I find his concern touching, especially since it appears that Mutti fired him for having a flat tire.

"I'll ask her," I say, trying to sound nicer. "I can't tonight, but I'll find out what's going on tomorrow. Can you call back then?"

"Yeah, sure. Thanks," he says.

I hang up and turn back to the others. Eva is now perched on the edge of the table, sitting on her hands and swinging her tanned legs. Jean-Claude sits in a chair at the head of the table.

"What?" I say, because they're both staring at me.

"Um, dinner?" says Eva, sarcastic to the nth.

"Goddamn it," I say. I turn my back to them and lean up against the counter. Its edges poke into my hipbones.

"What's the matter?" asks Jean-Claude.

"I have to go somewhere."

"Would you like me to make dinner?"

A rush of relief. I turn around, all smiles. "Really? Would you mind?"

"Not at all. Go do whatever you have to do, and come back to the apartment when you're finished. I'll make something there. Eva, would you like to help?"

"Sure," she chirps, sliding off the table.

I grab the keys from the hook and go.

• • •

The color enhancer I thought I saw at Kilkenny Saddlery turns out to be nothing more than a shampoo that promises to "bring out" highlights in specific colors. Bring out? *Pffffft*. Read: waste of money.

There's a hairdresser nearby. I try there next.

"May I help you?" says the pencil-thin woman behind the desk. She is made up till Tuesday, her dark hair cut short. I swear I see purple highlights glimmering in its spiked tips.

"Hi, yes," I say, sidling up to the counter. "Would it be possible to speak with a colorist?"

She looks me over, and then examines her long, eggplant-colored nails. "We don't do walk-ins," she says.

I look down at my hands—at my dirt-encrusted nails and the green slobber on my discolored tee-shirt—and then it dawns on me that I'm being snubbed. Me! Snubbed! By someone who makes a living sweeping up hair clippings!

"I'm not asking for an appointment," I say, enunciating icily. "I just need to talk with a colorist for a moment. And the reason I look like something the cat dragged in is that I just came from a stable."

She crumbles instantly. "Oh God . . . I didn't mean . . . I would never . . ."

A tall heavyset woman sails behind the desk. Her tiny, thin-rimmed glasses perch on the bridge of her hooked nose. Her caramel-colored hair is cemented into place.

"Norah, what's going on?"

"Oh, Lise—do you have a couple of minutes? This lady wants a consultation." Now that her inner cocker spaniel has been revealed, Norah is quaking.

A couple of minutes later, I'm in the back of the shop poring over color swatches with Lise.

"That. That's the color," I say, stabbing the curled sample lock with my finger.

"That? Are you sure?"

"Absolutely."

Lise stands back and crosses her arms over her impressive bosom. Her eyes move between my face and hairline.

"I don't know," she says doubtfully. "I mean, it's up to you, and if you really want me to, I'll do it, but I have to be honest. I don't think it's right for your complexion. You're too pale. You'd look washed out. And I don't normally say this, for obvious reasons, but your natural color is beautiful. Have you considered just getting highlights instead?" She steps forward and plays with the hair on the left side of my face, picking up strands and then letting them slide through her fingers. "I could do foils. Bring it up maybe half a shade. Something more . . . subtle."

"No. This is what I want," I say, pointing once again at the copper red swatch.

Lise continues to look concerned. "All right. But I have to warn you, it's really hard to lift red. If you don't like it, you're going to be stuck with it until the hair grows out."

"Good. Perfect. That's exactly what I want."

She stares at me long and hard. Finally she nods. "Well, okay then," she says. "Let's check with Annette to see when I have an opening."

"Oh no," I say hurriedly. "I just want the dye. I'm going to do it myself."

"I can't sell you the dye," she says, hardening visibly.

"Why not?"

"Because these are professional products."

"Where can I get them?"

Her eyes narrow. "*We* get them from beauty-supply distributors, but you can't. You have to have a license."

• • •

Fortunately, the owner of Helen of Troy Beauty Supplies is not particularly bothered about licenses.

I walk up to the counter and tell him that I need four tubes of Schwarzkopf 0-88, which should be a clue right there that I'm not stocking a shop, but all he does is ask me if I need developer as well.

"What's that?" I say, wantonly handing him clue number two. I'm pretty sure he doesn't care—I've already pegged him as someone who cares more about a sale than some silly legislation.

"It's the catalyst that makes the color stick," he says, proving me right. He turns around and takes three small boxes from the shelf behind him.

"What's it made of?"

"Hydrogen peroxide. It comes in these three strengths," he says, laying the boxes on the counter in front of me. "Here, you'll need these too."

He reaches into an open box and pulls out a handful of rubber gloves. I ignore them, and pick up a box of developer. "Peroxide. Is it irritating?"

"It can be if your skin is sensitive, but it's not a problem for most people."

"What happens if you don't use it?"

"On someone with coloring such as yourself, you'll still get color. On someone with darker hair, you might as well flush your money down the toilet. You've got to lift color before you can add it."

"Good enough. I'll take just the color then."

"You sure? Why don't you take the ten volume. It provides just a bit of lift without drying out your hair."

"No, just these," I say, pushing the tubes of 0-88 toward the cash register.

I've offended him by not taking his advice. I know this because he raises his eyebrows and purses his lips. He also makes a point of not looking me in the eyes again for the rest of the transaction. But what does it matter, as long as I get the color?

• • •

By the time I return to the stable, I'm enjoying a small respite from my initial panic. I can't guarantee that I've stopped the juggernaut, but I've got the ball rolling.

I stop at Hurrah's stall on my way through the stable. He's lying down in the shavings—he's a three-bagger, of course—but clambers to his feet when he sees me.

"Oh, I'm sorry, baby," I say, kissing the velvet muzzle that sniffs and pokes through the feed hole. "You didn't have to get up."

There's a small wooden box screwed to the outside of his stall. I open its lid and drop the plastic bag with the tubes of color inside.

Hey," I say to the still-extended nose. "I got you something tonight." I cup my hand under his chin, squeezing the soft flesh. He flaps his lips. "Sorry, it isn't candy," I whisper, kissing him one last time. "I'll bring you some tomorrow. I promise. If you're a good boy about your special bath, you can have all the mints you want."

• • •

"Ah. You're here," says Jean-Claude, when I let myself into his apartment. I don't know why it didn't occur to me to knock, but it didn't. Fortunately, he does not seem to think this strange.

"Here and hungry," I say, walking to his couch and flopping down. "Where's Eva?" I ask, looking around.

"Finished, gone," he says, waving vaguely. "Kids."

I laugh. After a day like today, a dose of Jean-Claude is exactly what I need.

He is standing by the window, looking over at the house. He has changed from breeches into jeans, and is wearing a burgundy polo shirt, tucked in and cinched with a leather belt at the waist.

"Your chore, it is done?"

"Yup. Yours?"

He looks puzzled.

"Dinner?" I remind him.

"Ah, yes," he says, clapping his hands together in front of him. "Of course. Apologies. First, wine. Then vichyssoise. Your Eva, she helped me. She will be a good cook. She understands food."

"You just happened to have the makings of vichyssoise in your apartment?"

"But of course. You expect me to eat macaroni and cheese for lunch?"

I am charmed beyond belief. "Wait a minute. Did you just say Eva is a good cook?"

"Yes."

"Really?"

Jean-Claude is on his way to the kitchen, but he stops dead and looks at me.

Oops. He probably thinks I'm a bad mother for underestimating her. I go for damage control. "I'm just surprised, that's all. Put it this way. She didn't get it from me."

"You cannot cook?"

"Not very well," I say, deciding, for various reasons, to keep the details of my most recent kitchen disaster to myself.

Jean-Claude stands twiddling the end of his moustache pensively between thumb and forefinger. "Well," he says finally, as though forgiving me, "you are not French."

As he disappears into the kitchen, I laugh out loud.

• • •

The vichyssoise is excellent, as is the *mousseline de poisson a la maréchale*, which Jean-Claude whips together with casual aplomb after we finish the soup.

"Apologies," he says, digging through a bowl of produce on the counter. "I am out of shallots. Ah," he says, extracting an onion and then inspecting it. "I have a Vidalia. That will have to do."

I watch, stunned, as he does exactly what I had hoped to do at Dan's. He starts with about a gazillion ingredients and sets them up on the counter without ever consulting a list. He does other things too, like producing a bowl of cracked ice that screams of competence and glamour. *I* want to make something complicated. *I* want to make something that needs to be whipped over cracked ice.

Instead, I slurp back the beautiful white burgundy that seems to flow so freely, and watch this man who rides and cooks like such an angel. And he really does: when the dinner appears, it is simply spectacular. Sweet seasoned fishcakes, made of nothing but flounder, whipped cream, and nutmeg, sautéed slowly in generous amounts of butter, and served over creamed mushrooms and asparagus tips with *beurre blanc* drizzled over top. It is probably the best thing I have ever eaten.

Now I happen to think that Austrian cuisine is fine. But let's face it: it's a hearty, stick-to-your-ribs kind of fine. But this—well, in many ways, this is better than sex, something I choose not to share with Jean-Claude as the evening ends, in case he wants to test the theory. And I think he might. As I help him clear the table, we reach for the same plate, and his hand rests on mine for a moment. I look up to find him staring at me, his brown eyes smoldering. The air is charged, and I am sorely tempted, because there is one other thing the French are famous for, *n'est ce pas*?

• • •

It's almost eleven before I head back. The moon is high, casting a blue pall over the house and fields, and the wind is heavy and warm, carrying with it the promise of rain.

About halfway to the house, I turn to face the stable.

The floodlights of the parking lot shine down on a single car. A gold Impala.

A moment later, I'm running full tilt toward the stable.

I don't even bother sneaking up to the door of the lounge. I storm right up and throw it open. Before it even hits the wall behind it, I've reached inside and flicked on the light.

Eva and Luis stare at me in horrified unison. They are lying on the couch. Luis is not wearing a shirt.

"Mom! What are you doing here?"

"What am *I* doing here?" I say incredulously.

I step inside and slam the door. A small picture of Harry and me slides down the wall and hits the ground with crash, followed by the tinkle of broken glass.

"Mom! What is it?"

I survey the scene in front of me, and then address Luis. "You," I say. "Go home."

He stares at me for a moment, and then leaps up and grabs his shirt. He pulls it over his head, struggling to find the armholes.

"Mom, don't overreact. We weren't doing anything wrong."

"Like hell you weren't."

"We weren't!"

Luis is now dressed and hovering in the back corner. The only way out is past me, and he's clearly terrified.

Eva turns to him. "She's always like this. Don't worry about it. I'll talk to you tomorrow."

"No you won't," I say.

"What do you mean?" asks Eva.

"He's not welcome here anymore."

Eva looks horrified. "What do you mean? You're not firing him."

"I can't exactly fire you, can I?"

Luis scuttles past, looking sick. From inside the lounge, I hear his footsteps as he runs down the aisle.

"Mom! You're totally overreacting."

"Oh, really. Then why was his shirt off?"

"He was showing me his tattoo."

"With the light off?"

Eva stares at me, arms against her sides. "Please, Mom. You can't fire him. He needs this job."

I lock eyes with her. "Just tell me this. Did I get here in time?"

"In time for what?"

"Did you sleep with him?"

Eva looks horrified. "Mother!"

"Did you sleep with him?"

"No! God, Mom. We were just kissing. Just because you're dying to get into bed with your boyfriend doesn't mean—"

"Trust me, Eva. You don't want to finish that."

She stands silently, eyes filling with tears. After a moment she says, "I love him."

"He's too old for you."

"No, he's not. I'll be sixteen in two months, and he doesn't turn eighteen until April."

"That doesn't matter."

Eva stares at me for a long time. "It's because he's Mexican, isn't it?"

"Of course not," I say.

"Yes it is. You're a goddamned racist, that's what you are."

"And you're grounded for the rest of your life, that's what you are."

I storm out of there, slamming the door behind me. A microsecond later, I hear another picture hit the floor with a crash.

• • •

After I get to bed, I lie awake, listening for the back door. I should have followed her to the house, to make sure she came home, but that didn't occur to me until it was too late.

Eventually, I hear the door open and shut, and then a few minutes later, the click of her bedroom door. I wait about ten more minutes, and then sneak down to the kitchen.

I open the corner cupboard. The paper pharmacy bags are gone, but the Valium bottle is still there. I've been drinking tonight, so I crack one yellow pill carefully in half, and put it on the back of my tongue. Then I turn on the water faucet and lean over, sucking sideways from the running stream. When I did this as a kid, it made Mutti furious. I did it anyway, of course.

I return to my bed to wait. Before long, the Valium kicks in.

This business about Hurrah is terrifying—horrifying, cvcn—but I havc to bclicvc thcrc's a way out. If they think they can just come and take him away, they've got another think coming. I'll fight to the death to keep this horse. I haven't worked out the other details yet, but by tomorrow morning, anyone who comes looking for a horse with white brindling is not going to find one. It's not a permanent solution, but it will let me hide him in the herd until I figure out what to do.

And what am I going to do about Dan? My heart lurches when I remember the sound of his fist hitting the wall. It was a clean sound, a swift *thunk*. The sound of wood reverberating. My own fist hit with a series of crunching pops, and my cartilage continues to protest.

Despite the Valium, an unwelcome surge of adrenaline rushes through me, a terrible longing mixed with sickening regret.

I was out of line, completely unreasonable. I know that. It's just that I was numb with fear—I didn't know how else to react.

I'll call him tomorrow. I'll tell him I'm sorry. I'll tell him that it was the fear talking, and that I didn't mean a word of it. Surely he'll understand that? Surely he'll forgive me?

As I try to convince myself that everything will be all right, I have an increasingly desperate sense that maybe this time I've gone too far.

I shut my eyes, trying to push the panic back down.

Chapter 14

Valium head again. Lead weights behind my eye sockets, cheesecloth around my brain.

When I open my eyes, it's twenty past eight. Even with Valium head, I'm shocked enough to sit up.

Eva usually wakes me up, although I guess I can't blame her for staying out of my way this morning. I look down at Harriet, who's stretched out and snoring at the end of the bed. Other people's dogs wake them up and ask for walks. I think my dog is secretly a cat.

I stop in the kitchen long enough to make some toast, and then duck out the back door.

I pause on the porch, rubbing my upper arms with my hands, still clutching my unbuttered toast. There's a strange feel about the day. The temperature has dropped a good fifteen degrees, and the sky is pea-soup green. It's not raining yet, but it will. I can feel it in my bones. I should go back for a jacket, but that would mean I might be in the kitchen when Pappa gets up.

If Pappa gets up. Can Mutti do it without Brian? Whatever would possess her to cancel the help?

At the entrance to the stable, I hear a nicker, and then catch a flash of muzzle through a stall door. Then I realize that part of what felt strange was the empty pastures. P. J. must have decided to keep the horses in, although I can't see why. Rain won't do them any harm, not in the summer, unless we're expecting lightning. I make a mental note to check in with him.

Still rubbing my upper arms, I go to the lounge, expecting to find Eva. She's not there. I look in all the obvious places, but there's no sign of her. She must have convinced Mutti to drive her to Dan's, knowing that I wouldn't have had a chance to talk to her yet. In many ways, you have to admire the girl.

I go upstairs in search of my polar fleece, which is slung over the back of my chair. As I'm about to leave, the telephone's red message light catches my eye. I pick up the receiver and punch in the code.

"Hello, this is a message for Annemarie Zimmer. Harold Oberweis here. My men delivered some hay recently, and, well, my bank just called and apparently your check bounced. Please call me as soon as possible so we can arrange some other form of payment."

Panic jolts through me.

That check shouldn't have bounced. There should be plenty of money in the account.

I turn on the computer, and a few minutes later am staring at our account balance online.

Oh, shit. Oh, God. They took the loan payment out despite the fact that I told the manager I wanted to make the payment late.

I reach for the phone. Under the desk, my knee

jiggles frenetically. My other hand taps the desktop. *Rat-a-tat, rat-a-tat, rat-a-tat.*

"I need to speak with Sylvia Ramirez," I say when the receptionist answers.

"Please hold," she says.

A click, a few seconds of silence, then a female voice. "This is Sylvia Ramirez."

"Sylvia. Annemarie Zimmer, at Maple Brook Farm."

"Hi Annemarie. How are you?"

"Not so good, I'm afraid. Apparently your bank took out the loan payment, and now I'm bouncing checks."

"Hang on," she says. "Let me take a look."

I hear the clacking of computer keys, then silence.

"I'm sorry," she says. "It was set up as a direct debit, so it came out automatically."

"I told you I wanted to make the payment late."

"Yes, but you didn't tell me it was set up as a direct debit."

It's a good thing she's not here to see my face, that's all I can say. After a moment, I press my lips together Mutti-style and collect myself. "How soon can you put it back?"

"I'm sorry, but I can't."

"What?"

"Once the payment has been made, I can't reverse it. If you'd told me—"

"Why not? You're the manager."

"I'm sorry," she repeats. "I really am. If you want to make the payment late next month, that's fine, but make sure you let me know in advance so I can stop the payment from coming out."

"And you can't put this month's back in," I say.

"No. I'm not even supposed to suspend payments at all, but your parents have been good clients over the years. So I'm willing to do it this time."

This last puts a cork in what I was going to say next. Instead, I thank her kindly and hang up.

• • •

Hurrah stands patiently in the wash rack, probably wondering why I don't just turn on the water. Instead, I dig out a tube of color, reverse the cap, and puncture the seal.

A small line of thick, pearly liquid oozes from the tip. I set it on the concrete floor and reach for a pair of gloves. My fingers are clammy and the gloves are not powdered, and for a moment I'm not sure I'm going to be able to get them on.

My brain is running laps, inner panic belying my outward sense of purpose. It's entirely possible that I could be arrested for this.

Despite the fact that I didn't use developer, I'm worried the mixture will hurt Hurrah's skin. I squeeze a bit onto my gloved finger and bring it to my nose, sniffing tentatively. It's white and opalescent, unlike any other substance I've seen. It certainly doesn't smell noxious. Smells kind of good, even.

And so, taking a deep breath, I squeeze a line of color onto Hurrah's left shoulder and massage it in with my gloved thumb.

Before long, every bit of white on him except the star on his face is covered. I left the star, because developer or no developer, I don't want this stuff getting into his eye. By the time I rub the last little bit into his right rear leg, the mixture has taken on a purple tone, which I take to mean that it's working. I stand up and walk back around to his left shoulder, and then wipe a little bit off with my thumb. Hard to tell exactly what's going on without rinsing it, but it certainly seems darker.

I check my watch, and cross the aisle. Then I turn and sink slowly down the wall until I'm crouching against it. After a moment, I give up and plop down on the floor, being careful to keep my gloved hands away from my clothes.

Okay, so I've dealt with the stripes. That might mean he won't be recognized right away, but it certainly doesn't remove him from danger. He might not be the first horse they scan, but they'll get to him eventually.

Surely it will blow over before too long. Surely they won't spend too much time looking for him. He may have been worth a fortune before, but with one eye and degenerative joint disease?

A crazy thought passes through my head. There's only one other person in the world with as much reason as me to keep Hurrah hidden, and that's Ian McCullough. But I can't call him for help. He's the one who tried to kill Hurrah. I want Hurrah hidden; he wants Hurrah dead.

I moan and let my head drop back against the wall.

"Is everything all right?"

I open my eyes. Jean-Claude is standing in front of me.

"Yeah, fine."

"Where are the guys?"

"What guys?" I say, wondering how to keep him away from Hurrah.

"P. J., Carlos, Manuel. The stable hands."

"What, none of them is here?"

"Nope."

No wonder the stable looked deserted. How could I have missed that? "I don't know. Maybe they had car trouble."

Jean-Claude walks over to Hurrah, and reaches out a hand. Then he stops, sniffing the air. "What is that?" he says, making a face.

"Coat conditioner," I say. "A new kind. Picked it up at Kilkenny Saddlery yesterday."

"Huh," says Jean-Claude, still frowning. He stares at Hurrah for a while, and then walks on. I almost cry with relief.

What the hell am I doing? Did I actually expect to be able to get away with this? As soon as I rinse him off, Jean-Claude's going to know what I'm up to. Or at the very least, he's going to know enough to incriminate me.

It might take a while for someone to notice slight modifications to a bay, or a chestnut, or a black. But we're not talking slight modifications here. We're talking complete transformation. I've got to get Hurrah out of here. Now. Today, before anyone notices what I've done.

I rub a gloved hand over my clammy face, and then realize that I've smeared dye across my forehead. I stumble to my feet and rush to the back of the wash rack to rinse it off. I can guarantee one thing:

my plan won't bloody well work if I dye a piece of my hair and forehead the color of Hurrah's new coat.

I peel off the gloves and thrust my head under the running water, wiping my head and hair furiously in the cold water. I don't have time to adjust the temperature. I'm thinking of Lise's words, about the color being hard to lift. By the time I'm finished, my hair is a matted wet mess, and my teeth are chattering.

Still shaken, I cross the hall and sit back down. I look at my watch. Seven more minutes.

If I want to get Hurrah out of here before anyone notices that I've dyed him, I have to move fast. Finding some old pleasure barn should be easy enough, and without the stripes, Hurrah won't raise any eyebrows. If I don't let on who I am, the stable owner will just think I'm some plain vanilla boarder with a pet horse. If I want to really cover my tracks, I'll show up with a Western saddle. Since it doesn't have to fit, I'll buy the cheapest one I can find. It's just a prop, after all. Something to put on my saddle rack in the tack room.

The more I think about it, the more I like it. It's perfect. It's brilliant. Of course, there's the whole question of getting him onto a trailer, but I'll cross that bridge when I come to it.

• • •

When the time is up, I approach the wash rack again, with trembling hands and heart.

Hurrah stands patiently, with his head low and his eyes at half-mast. He is bored. Hell, he is practically asleep.

I walk past him to the faucet, resisting the urge to run a hand along his side. Then I turn on the water and stare studiously at the hose while I adjust the temperature and pressure. I don't want to look at Hurrah yet, am not sure if I want it to have worked.

Finally, I breathe deeply and turn. The warm stream hits his shoulder, breaking the slick, reddened sludge into blobs that fall to the gray concrete. The residue dilutes easily, rinsing away like blood from a cut.

I rub the area directly under the stream of water with my thumb. It is red, and remains red. As I stare at it, I am seized with a coldness. It has the flavor of fear, but is something more. It's the feeling of conviction, a recognition that I've gone too far to turn back.

I work quickly, rinsing him and rubbing his coat hard to make sure I get all the chemicals off. Then I aim the hose at the floor, chasing the last of the blood red water down the drain. Its color seems portentous. When all trace of the dye is gone, I gather the gloves and empty tubes and stuff them back into the plastic shopping bag. I twist its top, wrapping the slack around it several times. Then I step back and behold my solid chestnut Hanoverian.

The change is remarkable. I suck my breath in through my teeth, and think inexplicably of Macbeth:

I am in blood
Stepped in so far, that should I wade no more,
Returning were as tedious as go o'er

I'm just closing the door of his stall when Jean-Claude reappears.

"This is intolerable. They're still not here. I have a lesson in twenty minutes."

He stands in front of me, directly in front of Hurrah's stall. Don't look in the stall, don't look in the stall, don't look in the—

"Well, have you heard from them?" he continues.

"Er, no." I step away from the stall, hoping that Jean-Claude will turn so that he continues to face me.

"You'd better try to call them," he says, turning. "Do you have their numbers?"

"Probably. Upstairs."

"Well, let's go then," he says, and to my immense relief, leads the way to my office.

When we get there, he stands at the window while I riffle through the filing cabinet.

"This is strange. It looks like they live together," I say, flipping through the pages of the employee files. Three of the hands live at one house, and judging by the address, the other two live next door.

"Yes, of course," says Jean-Claude, flopping down into the couch facing the window. He lies with his head on the arm, one leg bent at the knee. "They're family."

I freeze. "What?"

"Brothers, all of them. Except for Luis. He's a nephew."

"Oh, Jesus."

Jean-Claude sits up, stares at me. "What is it? What's wrong?"

"I fired Luis yesterday. Do you think that has anything to do with this?"

"You what? What for?"

"I found Eva and him messing around in the lounge."

"How messing around?"

I stare at him until he understands.

"Were they . . ."

"No. But they might have if I hadn't showed up."

Jean-Claude looks incredulous. "For this, you fired him?"

"Of course I did!"

Jean-Claude rises to his feet, and continues to stare at me.

Finally I can't help myself. "Why are you looking at me like that?"

"They are teenagers. That's what teenagers do," he says, his exasperation clear.

"Maybe in France. Maybe in Canada. But not here, they don't."

"Oh please," says Jean-Claude, lifting his hand and turning his head dismissively. "You are telling me that you never snuck off and kissed your boyfriend when you were a kid?"

"Never," I say. Before the word is completely out of my mouth, images of Dan and me groping each other silly flash through my head.

Oh dear. I suppose it's possible I overreacted.

Jean-Claude puts a smashing end to all such sympathetic thought. "You are lying," he says simply.

"How dare you—" I start, but peter out immediately. He is staring at me not with malice, but with calm conviction.

"I'm just stating the truth, which you apparently are not."

I groan, and sink back on my chair. "How was I supposed to know they were related? They don't even have the same last name. Two of them are Hernandez, two of them are Santa Cruz, and Luis is a Gutierrez."

"There were two fathers."

"And Luis?"

"Son of their sister."

I get up from my desk, too agitated to be still. "This can't be happening. They can't have quit."

"It appears you are wrong." His tone is coolly impartial. At this moment, I can't believe I've ever found his Frenchness anything other than infuriating.

"That doesn't make any sense. They couldn't all quit. They can't do without the money."

Jean-Claude shrugs. "What else could it be?"

"I don't know. Car trouble."

"Both cars?"

"A family emergency."

He moves his head back and forth, weighing the possibility. "Could be. But the fact remains that all our horses are inside, in dirty stalls, and I am expecting students all day. You must call them to find out."

"How? I don't have their telephone number."

"It's not in the file?"

"No." I stop pacing, but start tapping my foot. I am absolutely desperate. I should be arranging Hurrah's removal from the farm at this very moment.

"Well, you'd better go see them, then."

"I can't. I don't have time," I say. "There's something I need to do this morning. It can't wait."

"If you don't go, you'll have even less time, because you and I will have twenty-seven stalls to muck out. Which, strictly speaking, is not in my contract at all."

I stare at him in horror.

"I'll go," I say finally.

"Good. But first, we turn the horses out. You get started," he says, rising from the couch. He moves behind my desk with elegant ease and sits in my chair. "I will call and cancel the lessons," he says.

Oh dear God. We bring in a hundred and fifty dollars an hour for private lessons, more for groups. We can't possibly afford to cancel our lessons, not even for a day.

I wonder if I should just burn the barn down now, and make a proper job of it.

• • •

When we are finished turning out the horses, I am miserable and dirty and have a taste of what life will be like if the guys don't come back. It's not pretty.

Leading horses out doesn't sound like terribly hard work. But with just the two of us, and with the gates to some of the pastures a good two hundred yards away, taking out thirteen horses apiece starts to feel like work. I end up running beside them, goading them into a trot. I even consider the practice I forced Luis to give up—leading two horses at a time, one on either side.

Afterward, I return to the stable because I have to get the addresses of the Hernandez/Santa Cruz/Gutierrez residences. When I turn the corner, I see Jean-Claude sliding the bolt on Hurrah's stall.

"No! Don't!" I say. He stops and looks at me. I can see that I spoke too quickly, too hard. "I'm leaving him in today," I continue, sliding my hands into my pockets and trying to look casual.

He continues to stare. "Why?"

"I just am, all right?"

So I sound irritable. That's okay. He probably thinks it's because there are twenty-seven dirty stalls to clean. And let's be honest—that's not doing anything to improve my mood.

• • •

On my way to the Hernandez/Santa Cruz/Gutierrez houses, I practice my speech. Which is all very well, except that I've never been very good with directions and I can't find the street.

I'm in the right neighborhood, which makes it all the more frustrating. But I can't seem to pick out the street signs—some of them are obscured by overgrown trees, some of them are actually missing—and none of the streets seems to go in a straight line. Thirty-five minutes later, when I pass one particularly horrible cracked-concrete shoe box of a house for the fourth time, I burst into tears. I pull over to the gravel shoulder, and dig through my purse for my cell phone, which I don't find. When I look up, I see three men approaching the van. All of them are wearing dirty white undershirts. All of them are Mexican.

Next thing I know, I'm peeling out of there as though my life depended on it, shooting gravel behind me and hearing the screech of my tires as they regain the concrete.

When I get back to the stable, Jean-Claude is crossing the parking lot with a wheelbarrow of hay. He sets it down and comes up to the open window of the van. He leans one hand against the door, and puts the other on his hip.

"What happened?" he asks.

"I got lost."

"How?"

"What do you mean, how? The roads are like snakes. Have you ever seen the area?"

"Yes, I have."

I look at my lap, feeling chastised.

"I'll draw you a map," he says.

"I don't want to go back. You go."

"No," he says firmly. "Absolutely not."

"But why?" I plead. "You know the area. You know the guys."

"Yes, and you're the one who fired Luis."

"Exactly!" I leap on this. "So they'd probably have a bad reaction to me. But you, you chum around with them, don't you? You were at that birthday party, weren't you?"

He stares at me accusingly.

"Please, Jean-Claude, please will you go?" I drop my head and look up at him from under heavy-lashed lids, doing my best to look like Princess Diana, although with my earlier emergency hair rinsing, I realize this is probably overly ambitious.

Jean-Claude sighs. "Honestly. Women." He puts his hands on his hips and stares at the outdoor arena.

I wait. Eventually he turns back.

"All right. Fine," he says, opening the door of the van. "I'll go. But you keep mucking out while I'm gone."

I nod gratefully, but as soon as he drives off, I slip back up to my office, because for all I know, this could be my last chance today to find somewhere else to board Hurrah.

Before I start looking at the classifieds, I call Dan. The phone rings a dozen times. Just as I'm about to give up, he finally answers.

"Dan?"

There's a pause. "Annemarie." His voice is cool, distant.

"Do you have a minute?"

"Actually, I'm kind of busy."

"Oh, Dan, please don't be like that. I really need to talk to you."

There's a rustling at the other end of the line followed by silence.

"Dan—"

"I have the farrier here. I'll call you later."

There's a click followed by a dial tone, and I'm left staring stupidly at the receiver.

• • •

An hour later, I hear Jean-Claude's footsteps on the stairs. I refold the classifieds quickly, and rise guiltily from my chair.

"Did you see them?" I blurt.

Jean-Claude leans against the doorway and nods. I can tell from his expression that it's not good.

"So what did they say?"

"They are angry about Luis."

"So they just quit?" I'm on the verge of hysteria.

"There was also the question of their paychecks."

"What about them?"

"Apparently they bounced."

"Oh God." I walk over to the wall and lay my forehead against it. Then I lift my head and drop it against the wall. Then again. And again.

"They will return, but only if Luis can come back too, and not until you come up with their pay."

"I'll find the money. But Luis can't come back."

"They are adamant."

"Why?"

"If he doesn't work next month, he won't be able to go to school in the fall."

"School?"

"New England College."

I blink at him, dumbfounded.

"You are surprised?"

"Yes. Of course. How was I supposed to know he was going to college?"

"Tell me, have you ever actually spoken to the boy?"

I purse my lips.

Jean-Claude continues. "Luis is very sharp, very smart. He's got a scholarship for tuition and books, but the rest he needs to come up with on his own. His parents are still in Mexico. They cannot help him."

I feel the comparison coming and I fight it—I shut my mental eyes and stick my fingers in my ears—but it's no use.

I am such an idiot. More than that—I'm a horrible human being. Luis was never a threat to Eva. Not only is he moving to Henniker in the fall—and surely I could have prevented them from pawing each other too seriously for four more weeks—but all my other objections to him have vaporized, too.

Here is a kid who is making it on his own in a strange country without his parents and has gained a scholarship to go to college. And then there's my kid, who gets everything handed to her, and what does she do? She gets her tongue pierced, gets a tattoo, and drops out of school. And who, exactly, is the bad influence here?

I am strangely close to tears, and think back to my ignominious retreat from Luis's neighborhood a little more than an hour earlier.

I am guilty of exactly what Eva said I was. I judged Luis—and everybody in his neighborhood—entirely on my own expectations.

• • •

As I follow Jean-Claude down the stairs, it occurs to me that unless I can find a way of getting Hurrah out of here without Jean-Claude seeing, the jig's going to be up in just a few minutes.

We muck out one, two, then three stalls, slowly working our way toward Hurrah. By the time we're in the stall next to his, I've chewed my lips raw.

Then, miraculously, Jean-Claude excuses himself to go to the washroom. As soon as I hear the lock click, I rush to Hurrah, throw open his stall, and yank on his halter.

"Come on, come on!" I hiss in a loud whisper, clicking my tongue and fumbling with the lead rope. He lumbers into the aisle. He looks confused, sleepy even. I continue pulling and clicking until he breaks into a grudging trot.

On my way back from the field, I realize how crazy this is. It's conceivable that I've hidden what I've done for this morning, but it's all over as soon as we bring the horses back in. Earlier, if Jean-Claude notices that Hurrah is missing from the herd. Or that there's a new horse, an unidentified one-eyed liver chestnut, running with the geldings.

When I return to the stable, Jean-Claude is standing in the doorway of Hurrah's stall. He dumps a load of manure into a muck bucket, and then leans against the shovel.

"Changed your mind?"

"Yup," I say.

He stares at me with something approaching suspicion.

Cowed, I reach for the other shovel and disappear inside a stall.

It takes almost three hours, and that's with every labor-saving device known to man. We drive the wagon down the aisle so we won't have to haul buckets of dense heavy manure out to the yard. Then we throw the bags of shavings—the damned, damned, bags of shavings!—into the stalls, returning with knives to slash them open and empty their contents. We dump the water buckets into the wheelbarrows so we won't have to carry them outside individually, and then refill them by dragging the hose into the stalls. And then finally, we fill two dry wheelbarrows full of feed—Jean-Claude's with Complete, mine with Senior—and push them up the aisle, scooping the appropriate amount into each horse's feed bucket.

At the end of it, my back, arms, and shoulders are killing me. I am filthy. My hair is matted, because it dried before I could get to a brush. My clothes have manure stains on them, and my shorts are soaking because I sloshed water on them while emptying buckets.

"Well," says Jean-Claude, wiping his hands on his jeans. "Damn."

"Damn indeed," I reply.

He looks at his watch. "In two hours, we have to bring them back in."

"Unless it starts to rain."

"Uh-uh!" he says, shaking his head and waggling his finger. "Do not tempt the fates."

But it is too late. The roof starts to clatter with the sound of rain, a sudden and violent onslaught.

Jean-Claude and I stare at each other in horror. Mine is deeper than his, but only I know that. I am thinking of the dye, and wondering whether it will hold.

"Well," Jean-Claude says, pulling his moustache. "I say we leave them out unless there is lightning."

"Ditto," I say quickly.

He stands staring at me, hands on his hips.

"So," he says.

"So," I say back.

"You will arrange something today, yes?"

A moment of panic; he knows about Hurrah. Then I realize he's talking about the stable hands.

"Yes, absolutely. Today. I'll talk to the bank manager and we can take them cash tomorrow."

"We?"

"Well, you know how to get there and I don't."

He narrows his eyes.

"I have no sense of direction," I continue. "Oh come on, Jean-Claude. You do want them to come back, don't you?" It's a lame attempt at a joke, which he either misses or pretends to.

"Oh, all right," he says, shaking his head. He turns and disappears down the aisle.

Now's my chance. I run out into the rain, sprinting to the field, feeling the water splash up against my calves as my feet land in the puddles that have already formed. My canvas shoes are soaked even before I hit the long grass of the pasture, and my hair is plastered down around my face.

No more than three minutes later, I lead Hurrah into the aisle and come face to face with Jean-Claude.

"I thought we weren't going to bring them in unless—" he starts. And then Hurrah turns his head.

I watch Jean-Claude's eyes. He stares at the empty socket, and then, almost as a double-take, scans the rest of Hurrah.

I catch my breath, and close my eyes so the ceiling will stop spinning.

"*Mon dieu*," he says quietly.

I open my eyes again, searching him for a sign. I could fall on the floor and beg him not to tell anyone. I could cry and plead and hold onto his leg. I could take him to my office and explain the situation, make him understand why I need to do this. If he won't go along with it, I could sleep with him.

Jean-Claude shakes his head, staring at Hurrah with distant eyes. Then he raises his chin, takes a deep breath, and looks at the wall. "I need a drink."

He turns and walks away from me, leaving me standing there with trembling hands and an open mouth. I should say something, should try to explain. I can't just let him—

Just before he rounds the corner, he stops and looks back at me.

"Are you coming?" he says impatiently.

Chapter 15

I love the French. Such a civilized people.

Not only does Jean-Claude not seem to mind that I'm sitting on his leather couch while soaking wet and filthy, he also hands me a snifter of cognac. A very large one. The cognac, not the snifter.

"So then, Madame Zimmer. You want to tell me what is going on?" he says, sinking into the couch beside me. He turns to face me, bringing his left leg up and leaning his arm against the couch's back.

"It's a long story," I say, sucking a fiery stream of cognac down my throat. I brace for its return. Lovely stuff, once you get used to it.

"I can only imagine."

I take another sip of cognac, wondering whether I really want to delve into the whole business. At this point, though, I have nothing to lose. He's already seen what I've done.

"He's the full brother of Harry, the horse I rode in the Claremont."

Jean-Claude's only reaction is a widening of his eyes.

"We didn't know. I didn't know. I mean, I did know—" I'm blathering like an idiot, I know this. But how do I describe what I felt, what I believed? "He was too similar not to be, and so after I brought him here, I started looking up pictures and things. Everything I saw told me it was him."

"He had no tattoo, no chip?"

"He does have a chip, but it's an old technology, so it didn't show up at the auction house or at Dan's place."

"So how . . ."

"I bugged Dan until he found an old scanner, and it picked up a number."

I look quickly at Jean-Claude to see what he thinks. He's staring intently, his cognac resting on his knee.

"So why did you color him?"

"His old owner tried to kill him. I think. At any rate, he reported a trailer accident and that Hurrah was dead. It was in all the trade mags."

"Hurrah? *This* is Highland Hurrah?"

"You know him?"

"Yes, of course. Well, I know *of* him anyway. He was a famous eventer."

I had forgotten that the blackout was mine alone. I sigh gloomily.

"So you think they're going to come for him." Jean-Claude shifts around so he's facing the window.

"I know they will. The insurance policy must have been worth a fortune."

"But why—"

"Degenerative joint disease. And he's seventeen."

Jean-Claude gets up and walks across the room. Moments later he returns with a decanter. He pauses in front of me long enough to refill my glass. Then he fills his own.

"So, I don't understand. If you knew that he was supposed to be dead, why did you want Dan to find the scanner?"

"I don't know," I say irritably.

"It's a reasonable question." Jean-Claude stares at me for a moment before returning to set the decanter down.

"I don't know why I asked him," I continue. "I really don't. It doesn't make sense now, but it did at the time." I pause, trying to figure out how to explain it. "When it occurred to me that it might be Hurrah, the whole thing seemed so unlikely . . . and yet I absolutely felt it in my heart." I pound my chest with my free hand, looking at Jean-Claude to see if he's following my logic. At the very least, he's trying.

"It was very important to me to find out for sure," I continue. "And I guess I got so caught up in it, I didn't think about the consequences of its being true until it was too late."

"And Dan didn't either?"

"Dan didn't ever believe it was Hurrah. He thought I was obsessed with the idea because of Harry. And maybe I was, I don't know. Losing Harry was . . ." I shake my head, unable to continue. "Dan thought that if he proved that this wasn't Harry's brother, I'd be able to let it go."

"And instead, he proves that it is and ends up losing him for you." Jean-Claude sinks back down into the couch. He reaches his arm across its back so that his hand rests perilously close to my shoulder.

"No," I say. "Not on purpose. He thought he was doing me a favor."

"Some favor."

"You don't understand."

We are both silent for a while, and I, at least, am getting tipsy.

"You two, you are involved?" Jean-Claude asks gently.

"I dunno. Maybe. Not anymore." I sigh and look glumly at the wall. "Oh God, I am such a loser! Such a *big fat* idiot!"

"No, you aren't."

"Oh yes, I am." I let my head fall back against the couch, and put a hand over my eyes. "God, everything I touch falls to pieces."

He doesn't ask for a rundown, and I don't offer, although I can't stop it from happening in my head. I'd like to, but my litany of disasters is like an Ohrwurm, to wit: my accident, my failure as a mother, my failure as a wife, my dropped-out, tattooed, belligerent daughter, my blow-up with Dan, my relationship with my parents, my single-handed destruction of the family business, the impending loss of Hurrah—

"What is that?" says Jean-Claude. The cushions shift as he rises.

"What?" I say, removing my hand from my eyes. From outside the window, I can see lights flashing, almost like emergency vehicles.

Almost indeed. When I reach the window, I see an ambulance and two police cars parked in front of the house.

• • •

I don't even rush. I know all I need to by the way they're moving. Slowly, milling around the back door and porch with their hands in their pockets, hunched over against the drizzle.

When the black bag appears on the gurney, I'm not even surprised. I'm not feeling anything at all, although the effects of the cognac have completely vaporized.

I've never pictured this moment, but if I had, I think I'd expect to be hysterical. To scream, and run to the body, trying to throw myself on my father's dead breast.

Instead, I make my way slowly up the lane, stumbling because tears have clouded my vision.

I find myself thinking stupid thoughts—like wondering if Mutti is going to want her bedroom back, and if so, where am I going to sleep?

When I finally reach the house, I walk up the ramp, listening to my footsteps ringing hollow on the wood. The gaggle of uniformed people on the porch turns to look at me. I say nothing. I simply pass them and go into the kitchen.

There's a policeman sitting at the table, filling out a form on a thick pad. He looks up when I enter.

"Where's my mother?" I say.

"In the back," he answers. "The living room."

Afterward, on my way down the hall, I realize that I didn't identify myself.

Mutti is sitting in one of the winged chairs. A woman in a dark blue uniform sits in front of her on an ottoman, which she has pulled up close.

"Mutti," I say.

"*Liebchen*," she says. Her face is drawn, her eyes red. The bags under them are so deep they look painted on.

"Is this your daughter?" the officer says gently, rising to her feet. She's in her early thirties, freckled and pale, with a thick waist.

Mutti nods.

"I think we're about finished. We may need to speak to you again later, after the coroner is finished, but for now . . ." The officer's voice peters out. Then she turns to me. "I'm very sorry for your loss," she says.

"Thank you," I say, staring back into her colorless eyes. Shark's eyes.

"And I'm very sorry we have to do this at all, Mrs. Zimmer. If we had a choice we wouldn't. If you can, try to get some rest. We'll contact you if the coroner decides to pursue it."

What the hell does that mean?

The officer gathers her things. She leans over to push the ottoman back to its original position, and then pauses awkwardly at the doorway. She gives us one last look and disappears, clomping down the hall in her heavy black boots.

Mutti and I stare at the empty doorway. A moment later, there is a buzz of conversation from the kitchen, some shuffling, a chair leg scraping across the floor. The door opens and closes, followed by more footsteps and then voices, hushed and respectful. A jumble of unidentified sounds, then the swishing of windbreaker material, a zipper running up. More thumps and bangs, and then the door opens again. The prolonged screeching of the screen—someone is holding it open, and it moans its dog-yawn squeak every time that person's hand moves—and then the kitchen door closes. I wait for the screen door to snap shut behind it, but it doesn't. Someone has taken the trouble to close it gently.

I turn to Mutti. "Why were the police here?"

She is still sitting in the winged chair, staring into the distance with one arthritic finger held to her lips.

"Mutti?"

"Because I told them what happened," she says after a moment.

My eyelid flickers involuntarily. "What do you mean, you told them what happened?"

She doesn't answer.

"Mutti, what happened?" I say, with increasing urgency.

And then she tells me. The police were here because Pappa killed himself. The ambulance was here because they were not taking Pappa to a funeral home. They were taking him to the morgue for an autopsy—a final indignity I cannot bear to think about.

I listen with increasing horror as Mutti describes how they spent the last six weeks going from doctor to doctor, collecting the phenobarbital elixir prescribed for Pappa's seizing muscles, and hoarding it until they were sure they had enough. Then Mutti mixed it into vodka lemonade, and held the straw to Pappa's lips.

When Mutti tells me this, a vision of the white pharmacy bags exploding from the cupboard flashes in front of my eyes. Brian's phone call, his canceled appointments. Mutti's face in the crack of the door, last night.

"Oh, God," I say, trying to take it all in. "Was it . . . Did he suffer?"

"No, *Liebchen*."

"Was it fast?"

An involuntary spasm wracks Mutti's body.

"Mutti?"

After an excruciating silence, she speaks. "It took eighteen hours."

"Eighteen hours!"

"And then I waited six more." She leans forward, her face contorted with grief. For the first time, I think she might cry. "I had to wait until I knew he was gone, because . . . I couldn't tell. I know that sounds strange, but even when he wasn't breathing anymore, I could tell he was still there. So I had to wait until he wasn't."

I stare at her, feeling all the muscles in my face go slack.

Oh God. Twenty-four hours. I was in the house. I argued with her about making dinner. Returned from the barn, and snuck down for Valium. Got up in the morning and made toast, while in the other room—

I moan.

"*Liebchen*, *Liebchen*, it was what he wanted. It was for the best," Mutti pleads, her eyes searching mine. Surely she doesn't think I blame her?

"I know, Mutti, I know," I say.

But do I? How can this be for the best? And yet, under the circumstances, how can it not be?

I want another option. I want the clock turned back. I want to go back to before Pappa was sick and fend it off. And if I can't have that, I want another chance. I want to go back to that day in April when Eva and I arrived, and behave differently, responsibly, compassionately.

But I can't. I've failed him again, and this time there's no putting it right.

I had every chance—months' worth of chances—and what did I do? I ran like a baby, hiding in the wash rack when he came to the stable, leaving early in the morning so I'd be gone by the time he got up, coming back late so I'd only have to face him at dinner, when we were surrounded by other people.

But what was I supposed to do? Ask his forgiveness? Give him mine? Tell him I understood why he pushed me so hard? (I don't.) Tell him I loved him?

Maybe I wouldn't have needed to say anything. Maybe just sitting with him would have been enough. Maybe we could have come to some kind of understanding simply by being together. Then I have the most hideous thought of all: maybe we already were on the same page, and I simply never took the time to find out.

I look over at Mutti, who is shrunken and pale. Suddenly, the need for the autopsy and the officer's parting words converge in my head. I sit bolt upright.

"Mutti, you didn't tell them you had anything to do with it."

"Of course I did. I have done nothing wrong."

"My God—Mutti, what if they arrest you?"

Mutti's lips press together. She straightens her spine, and pushes herself back against the chair.

"We have to call a lawyer," I say, suddenly frantic.

I leap up from my chair, scanning the room for a phone book.

"We will do no such thing."

"Mutti, for Christ's sake!" I press the heel of one hand against my forehead and breathe quickly through my open mouth.

"I did nothing wrong."

"That's actually not the point. It's against the law."

"Then the law should change."

"Yes, of course it should. But you don't need to be the one to do it!"

"It's a barbaric law and if I can help change it, then I will."

"And if you can't?" I stare at her, challenging her.

She puffs up her chest and looks away.

"Mutti?"

She stares at the wall.

"Mutti, could you go to prison for this?"

"I did what I needed to do," Mutti continues. Her voice is steady and calm. The martyr, prepared for whatever comes. "I helped my husband when he needed it and could no longer help himself. I did it out of love."

"I know that, Mutti. But why in God's name did you have to tell them about it?"

"I will not lie about it."

"No one asked you to lie. You could have just omitted a few things."

She shakes her head.

"Mutti," I say, trying desperately to sound calm. "Tell me exactly what you told them."

"I told them what I just told you."

"Oh, Jesus . . ." I swallow hard, and turn back to

her. "We have to get you a lawyer. Right now. You may be in really big trouble."

"What does it matter? Anton is gone. You are running the stable."

I feel as though a lake's worth of water was being stored in my head, and someone just yanked the tarp out. It crashes—*sloosh!*—into my lower legs. I fall to my knees in front of my mother.

"Mutti, Mutti," I cry hoarsely, clutching at her knees.

She puts her hand on my hair. She tries to run her fingers through it, but they catch in a knot. She disentangles them gently.

"I know, *Liebchen*. I know," she says. For the first time tonight, her voice cracks, and I know she's crying.

"No, Mutti," I say, burying my face in her lap. "You don't. There's something I need to tell you."

• • •

Mutti listens in silence as I tell her what I've done to the stable. Partway through, her hand disappears from my head.

I know even without looking up that I've driven the final wedge between us. And it took some doing, too. She tolerated my behavior toward Pappa and my obsession with Hurrah, absorbed Eva and me into her life when we landed on her doorstep. But this, this, she cannot accept, and I don't blame her.

My final act to my father was to destroy his life's work. It seems appropriate somehow. A different, more definitive version of what I did twenty years ago, only this time I have no excuse.

When I am finished, I keep my head on her lap. I know I'm only delaying the inevitable, but I can't look up. I'm afraid to.

Finally I do, leaving my arms on her bony thighs.

"Mutti?"

She is staring at the wall behind me, pale and fragile. Except for the rapid rise and fall of her chest, she's completely still. Then her eyelids shut dramatically.

"I'm so sorry. Mutti, I'm so sorry," I say sniffing piteously. My arms slide from her legs, aware they are no longer welcome. "Please say something. Yell at me if you want to. But please say something."

For five long seconds, nothing. Then she opens and closes the fingers of her hand, dismissing me.

• • •

As I retreat to my room, I pass by Eva's. Her door is open, and the light is off. I look at my watch and frown. It's just past six thirty.

I go back downstairs. Before I step into the living room, I pause for a moment, screwing up my courage.

Mutti is still in the winged chair, staring at the wall. She has not moved a muscle, although Harriet has laid herself across the ends of her slippered feet.

"Mutti?"

"What is it?" she says without looking at me.

"Do you know what's happening with Eva tonight?"

She closes her eyes, obviously wishing I would just go away. "What do you mean?"

"Am I supposed to pick her up or is Dan dropping her off?"

"I don't know."

"Well what did she say when you dropped her off?"

Mutti turns sharply. "I didn't drop her off this morning."

I stare into her eyes as it dawns on me. I haven't seen Eva since last night.

I stumble to the kitchen, blinded by fear. In my haste, I drop the telephone. When I finally catch the receiver, I grip it so tightly my knuckles are white.

"Hello?"

"Dan?" My voice is breathless, sharp.

"Yeah. Annemarie? Is that you?"

"Is Eva there?"

"No, she isn't."

"When did she leave?"

"She didn't come today."

I hear myself shrieking and then sink to the floor, each of my vertebrae bumping against the cabinet on my way down. A moment later, I'm vaguely aware that Mutti is kneeling beside me.

"Annemarie, what is it? What's going on?" Dan's canned voice comes through the receiver, which is dangling free again, banging unchecked against the kitchen cupboard.

• • •

For the second time today, the police are here. So is Dan, who showed up about ten minutes after the phone call. I think. I have no real memory of what happened between then and now.

Again, I am ensconced in the winged chair, although I don't know how I got here. Dan is perched protectively on the arm. Mutti sits opposite me, pale and ghostlike. The finger that hovers at her lips trembles violently.

The police have been through Eva's room, questioned me ad nauseum about our history—my marriage, her relationship with Roger, her relationship with me—have already gone to and returned from Luis's residence, called the homes of all of Dan's teenage volunteers. Eva is nowhere.

Their attitude shifts visibly when I tell them about our argument last night, an attitude that cements when they discover her backpack missing. Suddenly they are in wrap-up mode, preparing to leave. This is absurd, so clearly wrong that I'm overcome by panic.

"What are you doing? You can't just leave!" I say to the pale officer with the shark eyes. I'm standing in front of her, ready to grab her if she tries to go.

"I know this is difficult," she says gently. "But there's nothing else we can do right now."

"Like hell there isn't!" I spin around, gesturing wildly. "Tap the phone, leave someone here, put someone on surveillance at Luis's house. But Jesus Christ, do something!"

The shark, calm and steady: "We've filled out a missing person report and we've sent out an APB. They're keeping an eye out for her at nearby bus and train stations, but with runaways, that's about all we can do. It's very hard to find someone who doesn't want to be found. We just have to hope that she eventually contacts you."

"My daughter is missing—do you understand me? *My daughter is missing.*"

Dan puts an arm around my shoulders and tries to guide me to the couch. I shake him off, stumbling backward.

The officer shifts so she's standing like Colossus. She's sensed a mother out of control, is standing in a way that's protective of her gun.

"Mrs. Aldrich, I know this is very difficult, and I know how scared you are. If we had reason to believe she'd been taken against her will, then it would be a very different situation. But all evidence points to her running away."

"So what? She's fifteen years old—fifteen years old! She doesn't know a damned thing. Anything could happen to her."

Dan puts his hand on my shoulder.

"I'm sorry. I really am," continues the officer. "Keep calling her friends, keep checking the stable. And if you hear anything, let us know right away."

"Don't leave! Please don't leave!" I step forward and grab her by both arms. My face is slick with tears and mucous, my eyelids so puffy they frame my field of vision. "Please say you'll find her," I beg. "Please."

"Annemarie," says Dan, stepping forward to help the officer extricate herself from my grasp. Why isn't he backing me up? Why isn't he blocking the door?

He wraps his arms around me. I brace against his chest with the flat of both hands and try to shove him away. When that doesn't work, I pound him with my fists. "Don't leave. Please don't leave!" When the officer ignores me, I raise my face to Dan's, pleading. "Don't let them leave."

Dan holds me tighter, a human straitjacket.

"Do you have a family doctor?" I hear someone ask. Mutti mumbles in response, too low for me to hear. The other voice continues, "See if he'll come out and give her a sedative. She's going to need some help getting through the night."

"I don't need a sedative. I need my daughter!" I scream, still struggling against Dan's solid frame.

Some time later—an hour? Twenty minutes? I don't know—there's more activity. It seems the doctor has arrived. By now I'm quiet, curled up on the couch, leaning heavily against Dan.

The doctor and my mother confer, whispering in the hallway. A moment later, Dan shifts, and I look up.

The doctor is a man in his fifties, heavily jowled, multi-chinned. His flesh looks like a cadaver's, his figure ridiculous, as full-breasted as a pigeon.

"Annemarie?" He sits beside me, speaking gently. "I'm going to give you something to help you sleep. Is that okay?"

I sniff, and continue to stare at the doorframe.

Dan shifts slightly again, and I feel the sleeve of my tee shirt being rolled up and out of the way. The coldness of alcohol, the prick of a needle, and then the pressure of a thumb.

"Can you hold this?" the doctor says. Dan's hand moves down, replacing the doctor's. I hear the rip of paper, and then the release of pressure as a Band-Aid replaces Dan's thumb.

"Can you help her to bed? She's going to be lightheaded. She'll need help."

"Of course," says Dan, standing up.

As his body disappears from beside me, I slump against the arm of the couch. A hand cups my elbow. Another surrounds my upper arm.

"Come on, honey. Can you stand up?"

I'm so tired—so very, very tired. What I'd really like to do is just go to sleep here, but Dan already has me on my feet.

"Are you okay? Do you want me to carry you?"

I shake my head, leaning heavily against him. When we get to the bottom of the stairs, he starts to turn, but I stop.

"What's the matter? Do you want something?"

"Mmmm," I say, unable to articulate. He lets me drag him to just inside the kitchen, where the calendar hangs on the wall. Then, with great difficulty, I pluck the black pen off its Velcro patch. With Dan now bearing almost all my weight, I pull the cap off with my teeth and meticulously fill in the square that represents today. A black gap, a checkerboard square, a hillbilly smile, where July 23 used to be.

• • •

Soon I am swallowed by a dense, heavy blackness. It is unlike sleep, because it leaves no room for thoughts or dreams. There is just an all-encompassing void that expands outward, preventing thought and movement. Eva is there, but beyond my reach. Pappa is there, but I do not mourn. Hurrah is there, but I do not panic. They orbit my blackness like distant satellites.

Soon, though, they start to return. As the Ativan wears off, the pain, grief, and loss slide slowly closer, until finally I can ignore them no more.

My daughter is gone. My daughter—my only child—is out there somewhere, unprotected and naïve. She could be cold. She could be hungry. She could be hurt, slumped against a concrete curb in a pool of murky sludge, sobbing for her mother.

A vision of Eva hitchhiking flashes through my mind, and then a man—unshaven, leering, his hand roaming toward her thigh—and a panic wells up in me that leaves my heart pounding.

Oh Eva—Eva! The thought of my little girl out there somewhere—without help, without money, without even the protection of good sense—makes me dizzy with terror. I moan her name, and then turn my face into the pillow, pressing it against my cheek.

I lie like this for what seems like hours, although I can't say how long. The medication has dulled any real sense I have of time passing.

An eerie silence permeates the entire house, broken only by the sound of birds chirping merrily from a tree just outside the window.

Eventually, I hear the clicking of Harriet's nails as she comes up the stairs and approaches my room. There's a pause. In my mind's eye I see her lifting a chocolate brown paw to push the door open, and then there it is—the squeaking of the hinges. More clicking, and then another pause, and she leaps up, scrabbling with all four feet to gain a foothold on the quilt.

I roll over, locate her rear end, and help her onto the bed. I have the sense that my brain continues to move after my head stops. I press my hand to my eyes. When my brain stops throbbing, I peer between spread fingers at the clock.

I've been in bed for fourteen hours.

Shocked, I jump up. As the bedclothes fall away, I note with dismay that I'm wearing just underwear and the same filthy tee-shirt I had on yesterday. I remember Dan helping me up the stairs, but everything after that is a blank.

I look up and catch sight of myself in the mirror above the dresser.

I move in closer to get a better look. My hair is straggly and matted, a straw rat's nest tinted faintly pink at the front. My face is streaked with dirt, my eyes recessed in darkness. My fingernails, broken, encrusted with black. My teeth, at least, are perfect, but why wouldn't they be? They're porcelain. I chose them.

I strip, curling my nose as my tee-shirt passes over my head. I sniff in the general direction of my armpits, and then sit on the edge of my bed. I've been up for three minutes, and already need to rest.

After a moment, I rise again and move to the dresser. Slowly, I start working a brush through my hair, perversely enjoying when it catches on a tangle. I'm pondering this when a flash of movement outside the window catches my eye.

I walk over, and then lean forward until my forehead rests against the cool glass.

Dan appears from the door of the stable, pushing a wheelbarrow. Jean-Claude passes him going the other direction, hauling a bale of hay.

The horses are out, including Hurrah, and the sight of his coat startles me. It all has the feel of a dream, somehow. I've still done nothing about getting him off the property, but that will have to wait.

Even finding a lawyer for Mutti will have to wait, as will making arrangements for burying Pappa. Until I find Eva, nothing else matters.

I have to do something. I can't just wait around hoping she'll call. If we were in Minneapolis, I'd at least know where to start, but here . . . What can I do? I can't just get in the van and start driving.

I wrap myself in my dressing gown and step into the hallway, leaving my hand on the doorknob.

Eva's room is in front of me, dark and cavernous. Through the partly open door, I see her things on the dresser—bottles of nail polish in blue, green, and gold; open lipsticks in meretricious reds; a half-finished glass of stale Coke, its rim imprinted with a greasy lower lip-print. A romance novel, resting open on splayed pages, all her stopping points marked by white lines along its broken spine. A thin silk sweater, hanging by one shoulder from the back of a chair. I am drawn and repelled, wanting to immerse myself in her things, and afraid to, in case they're all I have left.

My hand is still on the doorknob of my room. I start to pull it shut, but it encounters something soft. Harriet yelps and then cowers indignantly in the doorway. I scoop her up, carrying her like a football under one arm.

The rest of the house is so silent I'm afraid to descend the stairs, afraid of the news that is waiting for me at the bottom. I'm even more afraid that there will be no news at all.

I wander through the downstairs rooms, peering into each one, but there is only the sound of the house—a tick as a wall settles into itself, the whir of the clock as its hand moves a notch, the shudder of the refrigerator as it shuts itself off.

I return to the living room and sit in the winged chair. After yesterday, this chair and I have some serious history. The information I received while sitting here is almost beyond comprehension: from how Pappa died to Mutti's outrageous act of martyrdom to learning that the police were completely uninterested in helping me recover my missing child.

Suddenly, I reach saturation point. I leap out of the chair and look accusingly at it. It stares back at me, crushed velvet innocence, smirking its open-armed welcome.

I should take the van and go looking for Eva. I should go help at the stable, since the mess they're dealing with is mine. I should find Mutti and help her make arrangements for Pappa. I should call a lawyer, even if Mutti doesn't want one. I should get Hurrah the hell out of here.

I return to bed.

• • •

Against all odds, I fall asleep. It's not the anesthetized nothingness of before, but it's certainly informed by the Ativan. I just have no will to move, or be conscious. Until there's a reason to be up, this is the only place to be.

After an indeterminate period of time, the phone trills on its little table by the window. It's a tiny fragment of a ring, which means that it was either a wrong number or else someone downstairs jumped on it immediately.

I look at the clock, and am shocked into wakefulness. It's the middle of the afternoon—almost an entire day has passed.

A few minutes later, there are footsteps on the stairs followed by a tentative knocking on the door.

"Come in," I say.

The door squeaks inward, revealing Dan. His expression is ominous. He comes in and sits on the edge of the bed. Then he takes my hand in his, and looks deep into my eyes.

"They've found Eva," he says quietly, and just as I open my mouth to scream my grief, to rage against the thing I don't want to know, he says, "She's at Roger's. She's fine. She showed up an hour ago."

I stare at him, feeling my face contort.

"She's fine, honey. Eva's just fine."

I make a noise, an unidentified yelp that's a little like a laugh but more like a sob, and then cover my face as the tears come. And then I sit upright and he's holding me, holding me, holding me, while I try to fit together the pieces of my fear and anger and relief.

• • •

Of course, now that I know she's safe, I'm going to have to kill her. She had me scared out of my head, simply beyond comprehension.

She told Roger, who told Dan, that she hitchhiked back to Minneapolis. My beautiful, blonde, nubile daughter stuck her thumb out on the side of the highway, riding with one trucker after another, switching at truck stops, until she finally found her way across the top of our great country, apparently unharmed and unmolested.

"When is he bringing her back?" I say, interrupting Dan's narrative.

"He's not going to. He said—"

"Oh yes he is," I say, straightening up. "She's still a kid. She needs her mother."

"Slow down, Annemarie. You've got hold of the wrong end of the stick. He said you were going to be in town in a couple of days anyway, and you could bring her back then. If he can convince her, that is. Apparently she's not too keen on coming back."

I stare at him, blinking my incomprehension. And then it comes to me.

The hearing. With everything going on, I've completely forgotten my divorce.

Chapter 16

Mutti won't speak to me. Not that night, nor as I pass directly behind her on my way out the door the next morning.

I've managed to beg my way onto a flight, although I'm going to pay through the nose for it. And not just because of the short notice—with fatuous logic, the airline is charging me more for a one-way trip than they would for a return one. It didn't occur to me until afterward that I could just buy a return ticket and throw away the other half.

Mutti is standing at the sink as I drag my small suitcase through the kitchen. Its wheels clatter and bang, and then fall silent as I stop and stare at her. There's no question she knows I'm here, but she remains focused steadfastly on her chore. I pause, staring helplessly at her tight coil of blonde hair. I want to say something, to force her into acknowledging me, but I can't.

I don't blame her for feeling the way she does, but it still pains me terribly. What a family we are, with one intransigent daughter giving rise to another.

When the screen door slams behind me, I breathe a sigh of relief. There's no sign of the taxi yet, but the closed door signals the beginning of my journey, or at the very least, a buffer between Mutti and me.

I push the retractable handle down into my bag, and lean against the wooden deck railing, staring grimly at the sum of my parents' life together.

The scene is pure bucolic perfection: the horses, fat and dappled, grazing in an expanse of pasture against a backdrop of indigo sky. A breeze rustles lightly through the surrounding maples, their leaves parted occasionally by the darting streak of birds. The sky, bright and blue and full of the noise of cicadas, crickets, sparrows, finches, and a single Carolina chickadee. I can relate to that chickadee. I, too, should have taken a left turn at Albuquerque.

It may look perfect, but I know the truth. Just beneath the surface, as tangible as the wood under my arms, is a pain as relentless as toothache.

I turn my head. The taxi is here, winding its way slowly down the lane, a yellow ant on a ribbon of sidewalk. I hitch my purse onto my shoulder, pull the handle out of my bag, and drag it, clacking, to the bottom of the ramp we no longer need. A family's progress, measured in redundant ramps.

A minute or so later, I climb into the backseat of the taxi. The ache climbs in beside me, taking up more than its fair share of the seat.

• • •

An hour and a half later, I'm crammed like a sardine into an airplane seat, unable even to cross my legs. I scowl at the attendant, who wants money for my gin.

It seems to me that for what I'm paying, they could pony up an ounce and a half of liquor. An hour and a half after that, I'm in another yellow taxi, traversing the familiar roads of my old neighborhood. And then, with a sick feeling of déjà vu, I am in front of my house.

I drag myself out of the backseat and set my suitcase down on the sidewalk. And then, as the taxi pulls away, I stare at the scene of my old life.

There's a wooden For Sale sign on the lawn, with the name of the realtor swinging beneath. The house, a redbrick structure that used to strike me as proud and solid, now looks neglected and forlorn. The grass is short but brown. Long weeds—ironically among the more attractive plants in the yard—reach up between the wooden stairs that lead to the porch. The parched and cracked flower beds have been overtaken by thistles, some almost three feet high. After the apocalypse, cockroaches and thistles will rule the world.

There's a lockbox on the doorknob, a clumsy thing that makes it difficult to unlock the door. By the time I do, I'm cursing under my breath.

The door opens inward with a great rush of air that swoops up a half dozen pamphlets from the hall table and sends them fluttering to the floor. They are realtor's sheets. I stoop to collect them, and replace them messily.

I step past the foyer and look around, taking in the desiccated plants and the candles sagging on the mantel. There's a picture of Roger, Eva, and me—a relic from happier times—sitting on the coffee table between a portrait of Roger's parents and a vase from his great-aunt. I'm surprised they're still here, even though I did stipulate in the agreement that everything in the house would stay with me.

I never expected him to agree to it. I was making a statement. I wanted him to know that the price for going off with Sonja was to walk away with nothing but the shirt on his back. Not for one minute did it occur to me that he'd view that as an equitable trade.

• • •

The next afternoon, I approach my dear old car with needless trepidation: it starts without protest, despite being abandoned for months. Grateful, and fond almost to the point of tears, I back out of the garage and head to Carole's office.

I'm already beginning to regret my choice of outfit. Days don't come any hotter than this, but I've chosen a business suit—a power suit, as we would have said in the eighties—in eggplant crepe with big padded shoulders. I want to impart a sense of power. I want to appear in control.

Carole's office is in an older part of town, established and heavily treed. It's mostly residential, so the parking lot is tiny, and accessible only by a narrow gravel driveway that runs beside the house.

"Hi. May I help you?" asks the receptionist when I walk through the door.

"I'm here to see Carole. I have an appointment at two forty-five."

"Your name?"

"Annemarie Zimmer. Aldrich," I add quickly. "Annemarie Aldrich." For the next hour, maybe. Then I really will be Annemarie Zimmer again.

The receptionist seems to think nothing of my name waffling. She calls Carole.

"Your two forty-five is here. Uh-huh. Uh-huh." She picks up a pen and makes a tick mark on a ledger. Then she hangs up.

"Carole's ready for you. Do you know the way?"

"Yes," I say. "I've been here before."

Despite the receptionist's call, Carole's door is closed. I knock.

"Ah, Annemarie. Come in, come in," says Carole, opening the door and smiling broadly. She takes my hand, shakes it vigorously, and then uses it to pull me into the room. She steers me toward a chair and then takes a seat behind her desk. Everything in this room is in miniature, including the woman. I think all of it was built at three-quarter scale.

"This should be pretty straightforward," she says, leaning forward in a way that's intended to put me at ease. If she were a man, she'd unbutton her cuffs and roll up her sleeves. "We've filed signed copies of the agreement with the court, so unless the judge finds something totally out of line, it should just go through."

"What do you mean, totally out of line?"

"The usual distribution is somewhere between fifty and fifty-five percent, usually in favor of the wife, so this is not wildly out of line. Besides, he makes a lot more money than you, and you're not asking for support."

"No, I'm not," I say quickly. "I want nothing more to do with him."

She glances at her watch. "I'll have Nicole call a

cab. Oh, one last thing. When the judge asks how long you've been separated, say two years."

"But we haven't been."

"Do you want to get divorced?" she asks.

"Yes, of course."

"Then say you've been separated two years."

• • •

Fifteen minutes later, Carole and I arrive at the courthouse. As she pays the driver, I look over at the building.

Roger and Sonja are standing in front of the courthouse steps. She has her back to me, but who else could it be? She's dressed in a pale yellow sundress, her tanned, trim arms and legs exposed. Her hair tumbles down her back, a mass of loose chestnut curls. Then she rises on her tiptoes, exposing the bottoms of her flat-soled shoes. Roger leans forward and envelops her in his arms. His eyes close, and he presses his face into her hair with a look of wonder.

I turn my head so violently my neck cracks. I feel as though someone has just driven a machete into my chest.

"Are you ready?" says Carole from beside me.

I turn to her. "Pardon?"

She's looking at me, her hand on the door handle.

"Uh, yeah," I say.

"Let's go then."

I close my eyes, breathe deeply, and get out.

When I look back, Roger has mounted the stairs and is passing through the revolving doors. Sonja is walking away, disappearing into the crowd with her diaphanous yellow dress swirling around her calves. She carries herself like an African queen, proud and tall, although in reality she is Caucasian and petite. She is a center of energy, a nucleus of sunshine in a sea of drab business suits. I can't help myself; I stare at the monochromatic crowd until the last flashes of yellow disappear.

When I turn back, Carole is looking at me.

"Are you okay?" she asks.

"I'm fine."

"Courage, Annemarie. It won't be long now," she says, laying a hand on my elbow. I let her guide me up the stairs.

At least Sonja won't be at the hearing. I'm not sure I could stand that. I'm not sure I can even stand Roger being at the hearing, because at this moment, I hate him more than I've ever hated anything in my entire life.

• • •

I'm both officially divorced and officially drunk.

The hearing went just as Carole said it would—the judge asked a couple of questions, including how long we've been separated, looked over the agreement, and declared us divorced.

I hot-tailed it from the courtroom before Carole even had a chance to return to her seat, a retreat that almost instantly threatened to turn ignominious. In my haste to get out of there, I had forgotten that we came over together in a cab. I tripped coming down the stairs of the courthouse, shook off the kind man who offered to catch me, and then, finding no taxis at the curb, walked three blocks away before trying to hail one. When a cab finally pulled over, I just prayed that I'd get back to my car before Carole returned to her office. I didn't want to face her, or anyone else.

On the way home, I stopped for a bottle of gewürztraminer, and then on second thought, bought two. There wasn't any point in buying food. Just the thought of Roger's delicate little flower with her slim brown calves makes me want to barf.

I'm only just starting to recover now, sitting in my sweltering living room (no energy to turn on the air-conditioning), and nursing my fourth glass of wine.

I was totally unprepared for this. It's not that I expected to be completely unaffected—after all, this life that we built, whether on love or convenience or habit—whatever, because that part simply doesn't matter anymore—was just dissolved. It hit me when I saw the piece of paper tacked up beside the courtroom door: WONG VS WONG, SCHWARZ VS SCHWARZ, LIEBERMAN VS LIEBERMAN. And, of course, ALDRICH VS ALDRICH.

It moved me to tears, and I don't know why. It's not as though I want to recreate my life with Roger, so why do I feel so empty?

It's because of what I saw today. It was the way they touched, the way their bodies inclined toward each other, bodies so familiar each anticipates how the other will move. The tenderness with which Roger cradled the back of her head in his hand, the look of wonder on his face. The way she stood on her tiptoes and pressed her body to his.

Roger and I never shared that kind of passion. I never stood on tiptoe and pressed my body to his. We just never could make it work, and I have no idea why. In fact, I didn't even know what an orgasm was until the year before I conceived Eva, and that was while Roger was away on business. That was just me, a half bottle of wine, and a good bit of determination.

I stare glumly at the bottle and then reach for it, tipping the last of the gewürztraminer into my glass. Then I hold it there, waiting in vain for more to come out.

I lean toward the coffee table. There's a watermark on the wood, and I try to set the bottle back down on it, but my vision is swimming a little. As it makes contact just shy of the watermark, the doorbell rings. I freeze.

I look down at myself. I'm still in my power suit, but am considerably rumpled. My skirt is wrinkled, my blouse untucked, and I have a large run in my stockings. I stand up and stuff the blouse back into my waistband, hitch my stockings up unceremoniously, and go through to the foyer.

I look through the window by the door, although I already know who it is.

I open the door a crack and glare at him. "What do you want?"

"May I come in?"

I pause, hoping it's long enough to make him think I'm going to refuse, and then stand aside. I wave him in.

"I'm sorry about your father," he says, standing awkwardly. After a moment, he advances and tries to give me a hug. I shake him off.

"I tried to find you after the hearing," he says.

"I left."

He nods. "Can we sit and talk for a minute?"

I say nothing, again hoping he'll think I'm about to throw him out, and then lead the way to the living room. He follows and sits on the edge of the couch opposite me. We are separated by the coffee table. His eyes light on the empty bottle.

He looks back at my face. "I would have called, but the number's been disconnected."

"Look," I say wearily. "I'm really not in the mood for a chat. Just tell me when you're going to drop Eva off."

"That's one of the things I wanted to talk about," he says. He rubs his hands together, hands that have touched Sonja. I feel my lip curl.

"When are you going back to New Hampshire?" he asks.

"I don't know. Tomorrow or the next day."

"I thought you flew."

"I did, but I'm going to drive back."

His eyes widen. "You've been without the car this whole time?"

"Yes," I say sharply. "When are you going to drop Eva off?"

"Ah, well, we have a slight problem there."

I wait.

"She doesn't want to go back with you."

"Roger, don't do this to me. I don't need this right now."

"You may not believe me, but I've tried to talk to her—"

"Just drop her off tomorrow, okay?" I say, feeling perilously close to tears. "I'll talk with her myself."

"I can't force her, Annemarie. You know how she is."

I jump to my feet and scan the room for my purse. It's on the hall table. I stumble over to it and plunge my hand into its depths, digging for my cell phone. When I don't find it, I turn the purse upside down and dump its contents. The cell phone falls to the floor with a clatter. I lean over and pick it up.

"What's your number?" I demand.

"What are you doing?"

"I'm going to talk to Eva. I assume she's at your place. What's your number?"

"Annemarie—"

"Just tell me your goddamned number."

I stare at him. He stares back. Then he recites the number.

It rings three times before someone answers.

"Hello?" It's Sonja, not Eva. Her voice is clear and high. "Hello?" There's a pause, and then she continues, sounding worried. "Hello? Is there anybody there?"

I stand with the phone clutched to my ear, not sure what to do. Finally, I pull the phone away and switch it off.

"No answer?" asks Roger.

"No," I say, my eyes fixed on the wallpaper.

Another agonizing silence fills the room.

"When is the funeral?" Roger finally says.

I close my eyes and shake my head.

"I'll talk to her," Roger says. "Why don't you head home to be with your mother, and when I get Eva sorted out, I'll fly her out to you."

I somehow manage to nod.

After a moment of silence, Roger says, "There's something else I need to tell you."

"What?"

He's quiet for a long time, and after the first few seconds, I get scared. Is he sick? Is he dying? Does he have a brain tumor? I've read that such things can make you act out of character—could this be the entire reason for his behavior, for his leaving me in the first place?

I look over at him. His dark brown eyes are staring directly into mine. "Sonja and I are expecting a baby in January," he says.

I hear him, and yet I don't. I feel like a gutted fish, as if Roger has actually held onto the back of my collar with one hand and eviscerated me with the other. There is nothing more painful he could have done than conceive a child with this woman, and he knows this better than anyone in the world, because he knows I cannot have more children. And then another, even more horrifying thought occurs to me—what if he left me because of that?

"Annemarie?"

"You bastard."

"I wanted you to hear it from me."

I stare at the top of his head, imagining how it would feel to sink a hatchet into it.

"How could you do this to me?"

He says nothing.

"Unless she trapped you. Is that it? Did she spring this on you?"

"It was planned."

"You're a bastard. Did you know that?"

"I'm sorry, Annemarie."

"Just leave, okay? Just get out."

He sits contemplating his hands for a moment,

and then gets up and walks to the door. He opens it and stands staring outside with one hand on its edge. Then he looks back at me. "I'm sorry, Annemarie. About all of this. I know you hate me, and you're entitled, but it was never my intention to hurt you. I always loved you. I always, always loved you. Maybe more than was good for me."

"What the hell is that supposed to mean?"

"It means that I always knew I loved you more. There was never any question about it. I knew it when we got married, but I guess I thought that eventually . . ." He shakes his head. "I really did try, Annemarie."

He pulls the door shut behind him, and I'm left staring at the wood. A moment later, I hear a car door slam, and then the sound of the motor.

I have an overwhelming need to get out of here, but I can't. I've already had too much to drink. Besides, there's still the other bottle to get through.

I settle on the couch for the night, not wanting anything to do with the bed. Approximately halfway through the second bottle and a rerun of *Jackass*, I have come to an astonishing conclusion: Roger is right.

I was always aware that he loved me more than I loved him, but that seemed natural. In my mind and in my heart, Roger was always just the supporting act.

Why? Why did I think that? Because I'm better than him? Because I am special and intrinsically entitled to his devotion?

As shameful as it is to admit, that's exactly what I thought. I was the colorful Annemarie, the Wunderkind, the eighteen-year-old Olympic contender.

Of course, you'd think that my attitude would readjust after I no longer had any claim to fame, but it never did. I may have been special once, but I'm not anymore. I haven't been special in a long, long time.

My attention is drawn back to the television screen. The *Jackass* guys are on a dock, using an enormous slingshot to heave a dwarf into a lake. Disgusted, I stick my hand between the couch cushions, digging for the remote control. I encounter several coins and chunks of petrified food before my fingers finally close around the cool, smooth plastic.

With the television off, the only light in the room is coming through the windows. It's the glow of streetlights, whiter and harsher than the moon. No matter, though. I can still find the bottle.

I take a swig, not even bothering to pour it into my glass. I wonder what Roger would think of that. He always accused me of being too formal, too reserved, although I suppose that was actually a euphemism for not being passionate enough.

And the horrible thing is, I now see that he was right about that, too.

Chapter 17

I wish I were dead.

I passed out somewhere close to midnight, but woke again at three, suffering from a combination of self-hatred, room spins, and insomnia. Of course, once the sun began to rise, I could have gone to sleep. But there's no time for that. For the sake of my sanity, I have to get out of here as soon as is humanly possible.

I haul my bones up the stairs, seeking Tylenol. An eerie feeling permeates the house—it's as though it's outfitted for a ghost family. There are clothes in the drawers, medicines in the bathroom, bottles of shampoo on the edge of the tub. I'll have to hire somebody to come in and do the packing, because I don't think I'm capable. It would feel too much like an autopsy.

There is no Tylenol, but at least there's aspirin. I'm so parched I drink four glasses of water, and promptly throw up in the sink. I take a couple of aspirin and sit on the edge of the bathtub, waiting for my stomach to settle.

After a while, I clean the sink and set about to make the house look like I haven't been here.

It doesn't take much. I fold up Roger's grandmother's afghan and replace it in the cedar chest, wash and dry my wineglass, and then spread the realtor's pamphlets into a pretty fan on the hall table. Then, when I'm pretty sure no one's looking, I sneak out back and drop the two empty bottles in the neighbor's recycle bin. I hope neither of them is an alcoholic. Otherwise, I might be getting someone into a heap of trouble.

I pause before leaving, because the moment feels loaded. I feel like I ought to do something ceremonial, like a farewell tour. And maybe if I weren't so hung over I would. But I am, so I grab my suitcase and Harriet's dog bed and hit the road.

The sun is merciless, beginning its assault the second I back out of the garage. When Eva was little, she used to say the sun was shouting at her. Today, it's positively screaming. I squint to the point of blindness and grope in my purse for sunglasses. I locate a pair in the glove box, but not before my brain is pounding as though it will explode. I almost wish it would.

I can't even feel sorry for myself. I drank more last night than I ever have in my life. Not that I wasn't provoked.

My God, if Roger really felt that way, why didn't he say something years ago? I'm aware that plenty of blame falls my direction, but what about him? He didn't even give me a chance to make it right. He has to take some of the blame just for staying silent, because by doing so he made it easy for me to take him for granted.

The more I think about it, the more I resent Roger's implication that he is the only one who tried. I tried extremely hard—at everything—even if I didn't always succeed.

When we first married, I had visions of being the perfect housewife. When you're nineteen, there's something romantic and appealing about the thought of being the lovely wife making a lovely home. Unfortunately, only the thought was appealing, and I grew bored instantly. Roger suggested I go to college, but I refused. It's not like he tried to force me into anything. He would have been perfectly happy for me to stay at home if I weren't so utterly miserable. But I was. I had him stumped. I didn't want to be home, and I didn't want to do anything else. He couldn't figure out what I wanted, and neither could I.

So I got pregnant.

• • •

I stop for coffee, pulling over at a service-station-cum-fast-food-outlet with a long row of trucks parked behind it.

The coffee is bad, and the pastry worse, but at least it gives my stomach something other than my hangover to think about. I sit at a sticky little table, scowling at the truckers.

It's funny how I still imagine men are leering at me. They're probably staring at me because I look like a freak. Did I even brush my hair this morning? I can't remember, so probably not.

A man comes in to refill the newspaper box, which is right next to my table.

"Morning," he says as he kneels.

Unfortunately for him, he looks like Roger. I stare fiercely until he turns away.

I can't believe they're having a baby. How could Roger do this to me? He knows how much I wanted more children. He knows what I went through with Eva.

It started out fine. I couldn't have been more delighted to find myself pregnant, and ate lots and got fat, and started to wear maternity clothes long before it was necessary. I even started to seek Roger out at night, something that surprised him at first but didn't take him long to get used to. Being pregnant gave me something to think about, a sense of purpose. It made me special again.

Then everything changed. At one prenatal visit when I was eight months pregnant, the doctor stopped me as I slid off the table. She had forgotten to listen to the heartbeat.

I lay there chatting idly as she smeared gel on my stomach, and stopped talking only when she went searching for the heartbeat. Then she found it, and the cosmos split.

Every second, third or fifth beat was missing. Kerthump, kerthump, nothing. Kerthump, kerthump, kerthump, nothing.

The doctor went pale. I started screaming.

After our fourth fetal echocardiogram, the pediatric cardiologist told Roger and me to prepare ourselves, because our baby was going to need open-heart surgery immediately after birth. Then they sent me home.

I wanted to be admitted to the hospital. I wanted to be hooked up to a fetal heart monitor. I wanted to be right there so that if anything happened they could get the baby out. I simply couldn't believe that they were going to do nothing.

I wept for two days. I even considered dismantling the nursery, just in case we came home without a baby. I walked around pressing my fingers into the side of my belly, trying to get her to kick. And if she wouldn't comply, I'd collapse into hysterics.

I went into labor at forty weeks. Everything seemed fine, or so I've been told, because I have no memory of that day. Things were progressing slowly, but that's normal for a first baby. About thirteen hours in, before the pains were bad enough to warrant it, I let loose a bloodcurdling scream and lost consciousness. Roger says that a doctor tending a woman in the other bed turned to look and immediately realized I was in trouble. My uterus had ruptured—weakened first by the accident and then stretched beyond capacity by a nine-pound, seven-ounce baby.

When a uterus ruptures, you have literally minutes to get the baby out; after two minutes, you risk death or permanent brain damage. They saved Eva, but my uterus was gone.

I was in the ICU for six days, too out of it to even know that I had a baby. But I did. Before I even regained consciousness, Eva had straightened herself out. Within twenty-four hours, her floppy valve closed on its own, and her little heart began pumping its perfect, dependable rhythm.

I attribute this to her temperament. She was simply too ornery not to be healthy. Eva has had a world-class temper from the moment she was conceived.

• • •

God, my head hurts. You'd think that by now it would start to subside, but perhaps there are different rules for a two-bottle hangover. It feels like my skull is going to split. I want to pull over to the side of the road and lie down, but I can't. With each passing mile, I'm increasingly desperate to get home.

Like a four-year-old with a scraped knee, I just want my mother. I want her so badly my chest aches. Somehow, I know that if she'd just forgive me, things would be okay.

I should have asked her for help the second things started to go wrong. I should have just swallowed my pride and gone to her, despite her doubts about my ability. Why is that so hard for me? Other people manage to admit that they're human and still remain dignified.

I can't think about it anymore. I don't want to think about it anymore. I should turn on the radio and continue raising the volume until I can no longer hear my thoughts.

• • •

I'm surrounded by trucks, and I don't like it. They block out the sun, but also the signs and my view of the road ahead. If we had to stop quickly, I'd be smashed like an accordion between them. I'd be squashed so flat, they might never even know I was there. The only hint would be a bit of rag and a splash of blood on the front of the radiator grill that swallowed me.

I turn on the radio, but there's nothing but static. Actually, there's a Christian rock station, and a Country and Western one that's already starting to crackle. Finally, I locate NPR, but the story they're playing is about depression. I switch it off again.

Immediately after the pregnancy, I fell into a depression that lasted several years. This was no normal postpartum depression—I was mourning the loss of my uterus. It was a terrible, dark period, and like the events that spawned it, it did a great job of masking the thing I didn't want to look at. And Roger was a rock: he held our family together when I was a sullen, useless lump.

Funny, that. Since, Roger did everything right, at least nominally, why is it I was never happy?

It's the same nameless thing I've been evading since Harry and I crashed into the ground. Marrying Roger, leaving New Hampshire, getting pregnant—all of it was a smoke screen. I was always searching, always seeking the next big thing, because that was the thing that was going to make everything all right again. And while I was working toward it, it gave me something to think about other than that thing I couldn't put my finger on. But it always came back.

As I started to emerge from my depression, I was even less satisfied with my life. I hated housewifery with a vengeance. I felt trapped. I used to watch the wives of Roger's colleagues with bafflement—they seemed happy, seemed to actually enjoy what they were doing. They'd go off and learn Cordon Bleu cooking, would organize playgroups and trips to the park. I didn't do anything. I didn't care. I didn't even want to get out of bed. The house was a mess. Eva was bored out of her skull because I didn't want to associate with the other neighborhood mothers, who struck me as perky and Stepford-like. I couldn't even bring myself to try to learn how to cook.

So I decided to carve out a new career—anything, so long as it got me out of the house. I wasn't particularly trying to get away from Roger. I just wanted a life of my own, and I threw myself into it with absolute vengeance. I completed a four-year degree in three years, and graduated summa cum laude with a medal from the dean. After that, I attended a year-long program on technical writing, and before I knew it, I was in the software industry, churning out manuals. A few years after that, I moved into editing, and a few years after that, I became the managing editor at InteroFlo, pulling in eighty-six big ones a year. And no one could have been prouder of me than Roger. I was once again—at least nominally—a success.

But it wasn't long before the old familiar discontent started creeping up on me. I suppose it was always there, somewhere in the background. All I've done, my whole life, is keep it temporarily at bay.

Chapter 18

By nine o'clock, it's clear that I'm going to have to stop for the night. I had wanted to make the trip in a single go, but I don't think I can. My head is only just starting to clear, and for the first time today, I feel hungry rather than sick.

I check into a Red Roof Inn near Akron, and immediately collapse on the bed. In the old days, I would have peeled the bedspread off first, because I've always suspected they don't get cleaned between guests. But that was the old Annemarie, the Annemarie who used to cover her hand with her sleeve before touching public doorknobs. The new Annemarie doesn't care about such things. She flops right down on the bedspread, shoes and all.

I stare at the crack in the ceiling, savoring the silence. My ears still ring from the vibrations of the road.

I sit upright and stare at the telephone. I should call Mutti and find out when the funeral is. In this, at least, I can't let him down. I consider my words and chew my lips. Then I go into the bathroom to freshen up for dinner.

The restaurant is drab, and full of round tables and knobby chairs that could most kindly be described as captain style. The carpet is short pile and green. There is a dark pattern on it, which is barely discernible in the dimmed light.

There is no one at any of the tables, although there are a half dozen men at the bar. They sit facing a wall-mounted television, a row of backs lined up in front of a baseball game. Occasionally they explode with manly noises, but mostly they sit silently, puffing their individual contributions to the smoky haze that fills the top third of the room.

"I'll have the French onion soup," I say when the waitress appears. My stomach is clamoring for more, but I'm afraid to push it.

"Would you like a salad with that? Maybe a sandwich?"

"No, thanks. Crackers would be nice, though."

"Do you want something to drink while you wait?"

I shudder violently.

"I'll take that as a no," says the waitress, stuffing her pad back into her waistband.

After dinner, I return to my room. When the door shuts, an unexpected feeling of peace washes over me. Within the room's impersonal confines, the world is a million miles away. Roger, Eva, Mutti—even Ian McCullough and his hateful attempted murder—are merely specks on the horizon. I turn on the television and kick off my shoes, perching on the edge of the bed while I cycle through the channels.

Before long, my eyes drift back to the telephone, and then, with a mixture of shame and relief, to the clock. It's too late to call. I'll have to do it in the morning.

I wander into the bathroom, dropping clothes behind me like Gretel's crumbs. Minutes later, I'm luxuriating in a hot, steaming shower. The water pressure is excellent, and the supply of hot water outlasts me. I come out feeling cleansed—if not in spirit, then at least of my hangover. Perhaps I could have handled a sandwich after all.

I shut the bedside lamp off, and am plunged into blackness. When I turn my head, I see the red glow of the clock, but it does almost nothing to penetrate the darkness of the room. I settle in with a sense of satisfaction. It's been almost a week since I've slept properly.

Two and a half hours later, it becomes clear that tonight is going to be no different.

• • •

I don't know what time I finally fell asleep. I do know that it was after four, because that's the last time I looked at the clock. That's not when I fell asleep. It's just when I stopped looking.

When I finally open my eyes, it's still dark. I'd like to make an early start, but there's no point in being fanatical about it. The next time I surface, it's still dark. Suspicious now, I roll over to look at the clock.

It's nearly ten o'clock. I leap up, cursing the curtains. How was I supposed to know they were completely opaque? I've got a good twelve or thirteen hours of driving in front of me.

I shove myself into jeans and a tee-shirt, and cram the rest of my stuff into my suitcase. A quick look around, and I'm out of there.

A few minutes later, I'm on the I-90, staring at the back of a truck. Actually, I'm staring at a poster that's stuck to it.

It's a picture of a girl. Stephanie Simmons, it says. Missing since May 1997. To the right of the picture is a description.

She was fourteen when she dropped off the face of the earth, a runaway. It doesn't actually say so, but I can tell from the look of her—from the heavy makeup and dangly earrings, all carefully applied to make her heartbreakingly fresh face look older. She probably fought with her parents about her curfew, her clothes, and her boyfriend—maybe even more serious things too, like smoking up or getting drunk—and in a moment of rash teenage bravado, decided that anything was better than living under their tyranny.

Four years later, what hope is there? If she's even alive, she's probably a prostitute, some street hooker who got caught up and can't get out. Needle marks in her arms, bruises from bad "dates." Teeth missing at the back, which her pimp won't pay to replace because the gaps don't show when she smiles. And her smile, flashed at an endless parade of potential johns, exposing the pain of the world.

Stephanie Simmons, born January 14, 1983. Lost to the world before she ever really joined it.

Her picture blurs as tears well up in my eyes. My God, child—why didn't you just call your mother? How could you possibly imagine that she wouldn't drop everything immediately to come and get you? How could you possibly think that she would be so mad about where you were and what you were doing that she wouldn't have done anything—anything, including killing someone with her bare hands—to get you back?

Stephanie Simmons, Stephanie Simmons, Stephanie Simmons. I repeat her name, committing it to memory.

Tears are rolling down my face now. When Eva ran away, if she hadn't decided to go to her father's . . . I can't even finish the thought.

Eva is the only worthwhile thing I've done in twenty years, and that's largely in spite of myself. That changes right here, right now. I think of Stephanie's mother, never knowing the truth and always suspecting the worst. What would she have done differently had she known where it would lead? If she'd realized that what was happening in her house was not just garden-variety teenage strife? That it would actually cause her to lose her daughter forever?

I sniff, and staunch my runny nose with the back of my wrist. I may look soft and leaky, but I've just hardened with immeasurable resolve.

There's nothing in this world I won't do to prevent Eva from ending up on the back of a truck.

• • •

The decision itself is easy. But figuring out how to effect it is not.

The first thing, obviously, is to get her home, and then to make sure she wants to stay. But how? How can I get her home when she can't stand the sight of me? And once I get her there, how can we avoid fighting like cats and dogs?

It's just like Mutti and me, and look at us—two adults, one of us heading into old age, and still unable to get along. But at least I never ran away.

I have this eerie sense of puzzle pieces floating around my head, threatening to come together. I'm not sure if I should just let them or bat them away, but it's too late.

Of course I ran away. I left my parents and avoided them for years. We spoke occasionally by telephone, but I never visited them—I couldn't stand to be anywhere near Harry's empty stall. But it wasn't just the absence of Harry that kept me away. I didn't want to see my parents. It's hard to look someone in the face when you've single-handedly destroyed their dream.

When I had all the trouble with Eva's birth, Mutti flew to Minneapolis to help. She stayed for six weeks, and I don't know what I would have done without her. She took over in typical Mutti fashion: the house was spotless, our meals served at seven, twelve, and six on the nose, the baby delivered to me for nursing every three hours, freshly changed and swaddled.

It was an uneasy peace, but peace nonetheless. We never discussed my previous life, nor the tension that had grown between us. We went on like this for some years—ten, in fact—until the scene five years ago.

I had finally gotten to the point where I could face the farm again. Eva and I were there alone because Roger was at a conference. Mutti said something about Roger that I took as derogatory, so I flew into a fury and left. It was a fake fury, a fury I had to work hard to stir up. I can't even remember what Mutti said—that's how important it was—but he was my husband. To not stick up for him would be to admit that there was something wrong, and to admit there was something wrong would mean I had to at least consider doing something about it. So I took the easy route and left in a snit.

So I guess it boils down to this: I threw over my mother to preserve my self-delusion. And now she seems to view going to prison and continuing to live with me as equally desirable.

• • •

I'm still thinking about this as I roll up to a toll plaza. I head for the manual lane even though I have the exact change because the line is shorter, and I'm in a hurry to get home.

The attendant is fiddling with the coins in her drawer. She continues to do so, ignoring my outstretched hand.

"Excuse me!" I say loudly.

She looks over at me, eyes glazed and belligerent, and then returns to her drawer. After a few more seconds, she holds her hand out the window, still not looking. I drop the coins into her palm. One of them falls to the ground. She pulls her hand back into the window, and then extends it again.

I open my door and pick up the coin. Again I place it on her hand, and again it falls off. She's still looking into her drawer, clinking coins with her right hand. The guy behind me starts to honk. The guy behind him starts in, too. Before I know it, three or four car horns are blaring at me.

"Oh, for fuck's sake," I explode. I open my car door and swipe the quarter from the concrete, breaking a nail in the process. "Would it kill you to look at me?"

I drop back into my seat and slam the door. Then I turn. The attendant is staring at me.

"Here," I say pressing the quarter into her hand. This time, her fingers close around it. I glare back, and then speed off, my squealing tires voicing my frustration.

Is this the end of the line? Is this the famous rock bottom that people hit before they straighten out? And how does it work, anyway? Is recognizing you're at rock bottom enough, or do you have to have a moment of epiphany and total surrender, like people who give themselves over to Jesus and believe they've been born again?

I envy those people. They know how to have a meltdown, or at least how to come out of it on the other side. I'm stuck flailing, facedown at the bottom of the pool.

• • •

The next six hours pass in a blur. My hands grow numb from grasping the steering wheel, and my eyes sting from the effort of keeping them open. I feel almost comatose, and at one point actually slap myself in the face to make sure I stay awake.

I'm standing in line at the service center waiting to pay for my coffee when a man approaches me. He's grizzled, with a hefty paunch and a thin dirty tee-shirt. His jeans hang low because the waist is too small and his belly has slid over top. His front teeth are missing, his fingernails dirty, his hair sticks up in odd directions. He comes to a stop in front of me. I stiffen.

"You okay?" he says.

"I beg your pardon?"

"Are you okay?"

I stare suspiciously. "I'm fine. Why?"

"You just look . . . I dunno, like maybe you've been crying. Just making sure you're okay."

I'm so shocked I can't reply right away. It's as though I've suddenly forgotten English.

"Yeah," I say finally. "Yeah, I am. Thanks, though."

"Sure," he says, and wanders off.

• • •

Back on the road, heading into darkness. I switch on my headlights and search fruitlessly for a radio station I can stand. Finally, I switch it off.

How the hell am I going to get Eva back, and what am I going to do with her when I get her?

When it comes to me, I slap the steering wheel with the heel of my right hand. Flicka! I'll adopt Flicka! I know Eva won't come back for me—there's no point in kidding myself on that score—but Flicka?

So what if it's bribery? So what, if it gets her home and gives us a chance to start again? In this case, the ends absolutely justify the means.

I form the conversation in my head, figuring out how to word it most enticingly. I'll help Eva train her. We'll arrange it so that Eva is the only person who ever gets on her back. It will bring her home, and give us something we can do together.

My heart leaps for joy, and the warm glow of victory floods me. It may be only one thing to tick off my list of worries, but still, it's a start.

Unless I really have caused Mutti to lose the farm. Up to now, I've been thinking about how it would affect Mutti, and how devastated Pappa would have been if he'd known. But suddenly, for the first time, I see what it means for the rest of us. If Mutti loses the farm, where will Eva and I go?

I press my foot closer to the floor. The engine roars as it picks up speed.

I will get Flicka. I will get a job. I will call Dan and apologize, and if he doesn't want to listen, I'll tell him that I know what I've been—I finally, really know what I've been—and beg him to give me another chance. I will give up on this ridiculous notion of hiding Hurrah, and simply talk to the insurance company. Surely there's a way I can keep him—they can't just turn him back over to Ian. They also can't possibly expect to get the amount he was insured for, not with his joint problems and missing eye. But even if they do, I can pay by installment. I'll get a job.

My stable management days are clearly over, but it's not as though I don't have other choices. Even if Kilkenny doesn't have a software industry, I can contract from home. There's no reason in the world an editor can't telecommute. Not that I particularly want to be an editor again—in fact, it's more than that, I *really*, *really*, *really* don't want to be an editor again—but desperate times call for desperate measures. I'll put money into the stable, help Mutti keep the farm. I'll pay for Hurrah. I'll tell Eva after we get Flicka that she can only keep her if she stays in school.

Yes. Yes, yes, yes.

• • •

At midnight, I pull through the gates of our farm. I pause at the crest of the hill, just inside the gates, and survey the scene before me. It looks so peaceful. The house, nestled quietly at the top of a hill's gentle swell, the fences shining white in the moonlight. The stable, looming large and sleepy in the distance. The scene is so familiar it breaks my heart.

I'm already halfway out of the car by the time I notice that the floodlights over the stable's parking lot are off. There's a bulky shadow at the end of the drive. I stare, squinting, until I see its outline.

I drop back into the car and dump the contents of my purse on the passenger's seat, scrabbling through it until I find my cell phone.

"Nine-one-one, what's your emergency?"

"This is Annemarie Zimmer from Maple Brook Farm, off Forty-one, just south of Ninety-seven. I'm calling to report a horse theft in progress."

"Okay, Annemarie. Help is on its way. Stay on the line and tell me what's going on."

"There's a truck and trailer in front of the entrance of the stable. And someone's turned off the floods."

The car is in neutral, the motor off, and I'm coasting silently down the drive toward the stable.

"Do you see anyone?" asks the dispatcher.

"No."

"Is it possible someone just parked there?"

"No. All the boarders park their trailers in the back. And besides, this one is backed up to the door. No, there's someone in there. I'm pulling up now."

I coast to a stop in front of the truck and put the car in park. I squint through the side window.

"The license plate is ess three oh five oh two," I tell the dispatcher. "I don't think it's from New Hampshire but I can't quite . . . Oh Jesus, I just saw flashlights," I say. "I'm going to see what the hell is going on."

"Annemarie, stay where you are. Help is about three minutes away. Stay where you are and don't hang up."

I obey, inasmuch as I don't hang up. I toss the phone onto the passenger seat and move to the dark shadows beside the entrance of the stable, hoping that whoever's inside won't hear the gravel crunching under my feet.

Two flashlights are moving like searchlights, from one stall to the next. I hear the sound of bolts being thrown, and doors sliding partway open.

"Where the hell is he?" says a hushed male voice.

"I don't fucking know," says another in frustration. "Are you sure this is the place?"

"Maybe it's this one."

"Maybe nothing. He's fucking striped."

I reach inside and throw on the light. The two men in the aisle are holding flashlights and lead ropes. Most of the stall doors are partially open and the horses are moving nervously. "Jean-Claude!" I scream. "Jean-Claude!"

The men bolt. The first knocks me backward into

the doorway, but the second is not so lucky. As he passes, I tackle him, throwing him out the door onto the gravel. He grunts and swears, a rumble I hear through his rib cage because my face is pressed against his shirt. My arms are wrapped around him, my hands locked in a death grip on the loose cloth at his shoulder blades. In the distance, I hear sirens wailing.

"Fuck, lady! Are you crazy? Let me go!"

We roll around in our absurd embrace. I am alternately beneath him, with gravel poking through my shirt and into the back of my head, and on top, with my knuckles bearing our combined weight. Finally, he starts swinging. Both my arms are still wrapped around him, so I cannot deflect. His fist makes contact first with my ear, and then with my chin, driving my teeth into my tongue. My mouth fills with blood.

"Jean-Claude!" I scream again, and a moment later the man's bulk is lifted off me. I roll onto my back and scootch backward with my feet, instinctively wiping the blood from my face with the back of my hand.

Behind me, the truck's engine has started and a voice shouts, "Paco, Paco! *Vamanos*!"

But Paco is not going anywhere. Paco is up against the doorframe of the stable, held there by Jean-Claude, who has one hand around his throat and is pressing the tines of a pitchfork to his chest with the other.

The man in the truck revs the engine until it's roaring.

"Paco!" he shouts one last time. Then he dumps the clutch and rams into the passenger door of my car. The two vehicles meet with a screeching moan, almost like whale-song, and then my car is moving in front of the truck, pushed along by its nose. After nearly twenty feet, it drops by the wayside and sits rocking on its shocks. I see a light come on in the house and then the flashing lights of one, two, three police cars wailing down the drive.

The man in the truck throws his door open and bails. He hits the ground hard, taking his weight on his shoulder. When he regains his feet he staggers a few strides before rolling over the fence and lurching toward the forest.

The cruisers slide to a stop in front of the truck. Behind them, I see Mutti's tiny form running down the drive.

And then I know it's all over. Really all over, and I've been hoisted on my own petard.

• • •

It takes the police an hour and a half to take everyone's statements, not to mention collecting the second man with the help of their canine unit. After they leave, I sit at the kitchen table dabbing my chin with a cloth napkin. My car is ringing like hell.

"I assume Eva is still in Minneapolis?" Mutti says, handing me a bag of frozen peas.

"Yes," I say, pressing the peas to my jaw. I pull the bag back and look at it, and then wrap it in the napkin.

"When is she coming back?"

"I'm not sure that she is."

"What?" Mutti's face blackens. "She's going to miss her Opa's funeral?"

"It's me. She doesn't want anything to do with me."

Mutti flashes me a look. Finally she says, "It's because of that boy, isn't it?"

I glare at my coffee.

"He's a good boy, you know. A nice boy."

"Yes, Mutti. I know that now, don't I? I messed everything up. It's all my fault. I know that. I admit it. And now I'm trying to fix it."

I cross the kitchen and put the peas back in the freezer. Mutti follows me with her eyes. I pause to rinse my hands, and then turn to face her.

"When is the funeral?" I ask.

"Monday."

"Monday!" I look up sharply. "But that's so . . . Isn't that late?"

"It was delayed by the autopsy."

A silence, in which we both think the same terrible thing. It reminds me of right after I learned that Harry was dead, when all I could think about was what was happening to his body.

"Monday," I repeat gloomily. I don't even have a black dress.

I look at Mutti, who is tapping one bony finger on the table.

"I'm going to try to get her back in time for Pappa's funeral. For now, that's the best I can do. Believe it or not, it means as much to me as it does to you."

My eyes fill with tears, but hers are as clear as the arctic sky. I cross the kitchen again, under her scrutiny, and am about to exit to the hallway when she calls to me.

"Annemarie, I have something to ask you."

I stop, still facing the hallway. "What is it?"

"Did you have anything to do with what happened tonight?"

"What? No, of course not. I'm the one who called the cops. You heard my statement. Why would you say something like that?"

"You know exactly why."

"No, I don't," I sputter indignantly.

"You thought I wouldn't notice that he's not striped anymore? You're up to something Annemarie, and I want to know what it is."

In fact, it never crossed my mind that she'd notice the dye job. That's how rational I've been. I have no answer for her.

"It's time for you to start telling the truth," she says, her voice rising headlong into anger.

And so I do. At the end of it, she drops her head into her hands.

"Mutti?" I take a tentative step forward.

"Just go," she says without looking up. "Go to bed, Annemarie. It's late, and I need some time to think."

• • •

Sleep is, of course, completely out of the question. At some point I give up and creep down to the living room to watch Peter Sellers movies and *Gilligan's Island* reruns.

Shortly after sunrise, I hear the dining-room door open, and then, a few minutes later, the gurgling of coffee. I wait until Mutti has gone back into the dining room before getting a cup. Then I take it up to my room.

I have no idea what I'm going to do today, but I'm too anxious to be still. I'm almost certainly not wanted at the stable—presumably Mutti has taken over as manager again, and I can see from the cars in the lot that she's persuaded the stable hands to come back. There's nothing else to do around here, and as for going into town—I don't even know if my car still runs.

By late morning, the place is crawling with cops. There's one car stationed at the end of our drive, by the road, and two more at the stable. From my bedroom window, I can see them putting up yellow tape, blocking the entrances. I run down the stairs and press my face to the kitchen window. Jean-Claude is stalking up the drive, his face like thunder.

He climbs up the porch and throws the door open, hard.

"What is it? What's going on?" I demand, searching his face.

He turns to look at me. His right eye is purple. "An 'investigation,' " he says with disgust. "They are insisting that we cancel all the lessons."

"What? For how long?" I ask, but he just grabs a file from the bookshelf and leaves, slamming the door behind him.

I slide on the gardening clogs by the back door and jog to the stable. Mutti must have seen me coming, because she exits the stable just as I arrive. She walks toward me with both hands extended, preventing my progress.

"Go back to the house," she says quickly.

"What's going on? What do they want?" I crane my neck, trying to see around her.

Mutti grabs my face in both her hands and forces

me to look into her eyes. "Annemarie," she says, each word a sentence. "Go home."

I spend the day going from one window to another, watching the goings-on at the stable and the entrance to our farm. The police stationed at the entrance turn away about a half dozen cars, presumably students that Jean-Claude didn't reach in time. In the early afternoon, a white Dodge Neon turns into the drive, and after a short window-to-window conference with the police car, makes its way to the stable. Two men and a woman emerge. The woman stretches her arms over her head and then turns to study first my sorry car, then the outdoor arenas, the house, and the trailers behind the parking lot. After she drops her arms, she leans through the open passenger window and retrieves a binder. A uniformed officer meets them and leads them into the stable.

After forty minutes, they leave again. Shortly thereafter, the hands start turning out the horses. All except Hurrah.

• • •

Just before we would normally have dinner, a cop walks up the drive toward the house.

I let the lace curtain fall, and then go to the living room to wait for his knock. Then I let a few seconds pass before I open the door.

"Annemarie Zimmer?" he says.

"Yes," I say, sticking my face in the crack of the door.

"Detective Samosa of Kilkenny PD," he says, flashing a badge. "I need you to come to the station to answer some questions."

"But I gave a statement last night."

"Yes you did. But you neglected to mention that you're housing a horse on which an insurance company has paid out a one-and-a-quarter-million-dollar mortality policy. A horse that appears to have been disguised."

I stare into his square-jawed face.

After a few seconds, he adds, "We can do this the easy way, or we can do this the hard way."

"What's the difference?" I ask.

"The easy way is you cooperate and get to drive your own car." He pauses. "The hard way is that I arrest you and you ride in the back of the cruiser."

I feel my lips tighten into a straight line.

He crosses his arms. "Well?"

"Can you wait and see if my car runs?" I ask.

Chapter 19

The room is dingy, like a conference room at a cheap hotel. The walls are plain, with white boards on two of them. There is a white laminate table with a tape recorder in the center, six quasi-office chairs, and bright fluorescent lighting that renders Detective Samosa's complexion splotchy and very nearly green.

I know how it's going to be as soon as we start, because Detectives Samosa and Freakley come in with coffee for themselves and none for me.

They sit opposite me, looking over notes and sipping their coffee. It seems calculatedly slow. Eventually the blond one—Detective Freakley, who evidently made up for daily beatings in high school by working out eighteen times a week—leans forward and presses the RECORD button with a beefy finger. I stare at the tape recorder and then at him.

"Can you please state your name," he says, leaning back in his chair.

"Annemarie Costanze Zimmer."

"Please state your address."

"I live at Maple Brook farm, off Route Forty-one, south of Ninety-seven."

"What is your place of work?"

"The same. I'm the manager of our family's riding school."

"Are you in charge of the daily care of the horses?"

"I supervise it."

"Are you in charge of the acquisition of horses?"

"I'm responsible for those owned by the stable, yes."

Throughout all this, both detectives have sat leaning back in their chairs, their notepads on the table. Now Freakley picks his pen out of his shirt pocket.

"Tell us how you came to have possession of the horse in stall thirteen," he says, looking at his notepad. His face bears the scars of deep acne, and I can't help noticing that the end of his pen has been chewed.

"I adopted him from a horse rescue center."

"Dan Garibaldi's place?"

"Yes."

Freakley pauses to write something.

"When was that?"

"Not sure of the exact date. Near the middle of May. I have the papers at home."

"And what did he look like at that time?"

"What do you mean?"

Freakley glances over at Samosa. "Did the horse have any distinguishing markings at that time?"

"Well, he had only one eye."

"Anything else?"

I don't answer. My eyes flit to the spinning reels of the tape recorder.

"What is your relationship with Dan Garibaldi?" asks Samosa, taking over for Freakley.

Again, I don't say anything, but this time it's because I don't know the answer. My face starts to burn.

"What is your connection with Ian McCullough?" Samosa continues, leaning forward and resting both elbows on the table.

I lean back instinctively. "There is no connection."

"Are you saying you don't know him?"

"No, I know him. I rode against him a lot, but that was twenty years ago. I haven't had anything to do with him since."

"Is that a fact," says Samosa, phrasing it as a statement rather than a question.

"Yes, it is," I answer.

"Are you sure?"

"Yes I'm sure."

"You don't want to revise your answer?"

"Why would I want to do that?"

"We have your phone records."

I miss a few beats, remembering Ian's tone of voice. I look from Samosa to Freakley, who is staring impassively at his notepad. "Am I being arrested?"

"Not yet."

"Yet? Oh my God." I sit upright and blink furiously. How did this become such a mess? "I think I'd better speak with a lawyer."

"That's your right, but since you haven't been charged with anything, we are not obligated to provide one."

• • •

They will, however, provide me with a phone book and point me toward a pay phone. I pick a defense lawyer pretty much at random, opening the Yellow Pages and calling the 1-800 number from the first ad to leap out at me.

Norma Blackley bustles into the conference room an hour and a half later with the odor of spaghetti still clinging to her nylon sweater. We confer for about twenty minutes, during which time I tell her everything. She leans toward me, nodding encouragingly.

"Okay," she says at the end of it. "It sounds to me like the most you're guilty of is trying to keep a horse you loved. However, you're in a delicate position here and will be until we all know exactly what happened. Don't answer anything you don't want to, and I'll let you know when I think you shouldn't. Remember, you have the right not to say anything that incriminates you. They can't hold that against you, and despite what they might have led you to believe, it won't make them lay charges where they wouldn't otherwise have done so. Are you ready?"

I nod. "I think so."

She goes out to the hall and gestures the two men back in.

"Hi, Norma," says Freakley.

"Gentlemen," replies Norma.

The detectives take their seats opposite me, and Norma sits at the narrow side of the table, effectively between us.

Freakley rustles his papers for a moment, takes a

swig from his refilled coffee, and then resumes questioning me.

"Do you know what a brindled horse is?"

"Absolutely. I used to have one."

"When was that?"

"Twenty years ago."

"The horse in stall thirteen is registered as a brindled horse. Do you have any knowledge of how he came to be a solid color rather than brindled?"

"Annemarie, don't answer—"

"Sure I do. I dyed him."

"—that," finishes Norma. She turns slowly to face me.

Samosa and Freakley freeze, their pen nibs still pressed to paper. Both pairs of eyes stare at me. "You dyed him?"

"Sure I did, and instead of giving me a hard time about it, maybe you should be thanking me. If I hadn't, those guys—and I'm assuming from what you asked me earlier that they're associated with McCullough—would have gotten away with Hurrah, and that would have been the end of it."

I look at Norma. Her face reminds me of a ripe pomegranate.

"Gentlemen," she says in a chilled voice. "May I have a moment with my client?"

• • •

An hour later, they spring me. When my crippled car gets to the back of the house, I brake for a moment, checking all the windows for lights. The house is dark, so I continue on my way. I'm no longer even pressing the gas pedal. My poor mashed car simply coasts along the same path it did last night, running out of steam where the trailer had been parked.

A minute later, I throw the latch on Hurrah's stall and slide the door open.

I stand blinking in the darkness, because it takes me a moment to figure out what's going on. Then the bare floorboards come into focus, stripped of all shavings. The upside-down bucket, my unobscured view of the back wall.

"Annemarie," says a voice behind me.

I spin around.

It's Jean-Claude, wearing boxers, a tee-shirt, and work boots pulled over bare feet. He's obviously just gotten out of bed.

"Where is he?" I say, hearing the tremor in my voice.

"He's gone," he says quietly. "They took him early this evening. Your mother, she argued with them, but they had a warrant."

"Where did they take him?"

"I don't know."

I stare at him, blinking. "Are they going to bring him back?"

"I would not think so. No."

Jean-Claude is standing with his arms slack against his sides. His palms are open toward me and his fingers extended, almost in supplication. Despite the darkness, I can see the pained expression on his face.

I feel drained, an empty brittle shell. "Were you here?" I whisper.

Jean-Claude nods.

I say nothing for a long time, picturing it. The police, perhaps even the county animal warden, leading him out of this very stall. Hurrah lifting his beautiful striped hooves over this very door track. His unshod feet clip-clopping as they led him out of the stable and toward the ramp at the back of the truck.

"How was he about getting on the trailer?" My voice cracks halfway through the sentence. I clap my hands to my face and moan into them. I feel like I'm falling, falling, and step backwards, seeking support from a wall. Instead, I trip over the door track and hit the floor. I'm momentarily shocked, and then roll onto my side. My body curls like a potato bug, knees against chest. My cheek rests against the cool, worn floorboards of his stall. I howl.

Jean-Claude kneels beside me. "Shh," he says gently. He lays a hand on my shoulder. "Come now, *cherie*. Come now."

My response is to cry louder: soul-rending, coyote-yipping wails.

His hands are on my shoulders now, pulling, and then he slides an arm behind my back. He scoops me up and presses me against him.

He holds me like this for several minutes, squeezing tighter each time my sobs begin afresh. But I don't want to stop. I don't want to get over this. I don't even know how I'm going to live through it.

Jean-Claude rocks slowly, side to side, as though I were a child. Eventually I fall silent.

I sniff, and pull my head back. He stares down at me, his face lined with concern. In the darkness, his eyes are almost buried in shadow, but the rest of his features are clear. The line of his jaw, the shape of his mouth, his forehead, creased with worry.

I reach up quite suddenly and press my lips to his.

His body stiffens. He pulls away.

"Annemarie—"

I pull him back to me, violently, drowning out his objections. I keep my lips pressed against his mouth, letting the tip of my tongue slide over his clamped lips even as I rise to my knees. I reach up and grab handfuls of his hair, pulling his face to mine. He does not push me away, but he lifts his arms up, holding them out to the side.

I don't care. I continue my assault on his closed mouth, probing and biting and enjoying the feel of his stubbly chin under my hands, the strangeness of his moustache against my lips.

A few seconds later, he is crushing me in his embrace, sliding his tongue into my mouth. He tastes of Courvoisier and Galloise. He tastes of man.

I'm on my knees, clutching his head in both my hands. Then I reach for the bottom of his shirt, surprised by the amount of hair I encounter. As I run my hand up against his skin, I savor the feeling of it, a texture so very different from mine. I pause at his nipple, rolling it slightly between my fingers, and then move on. I dig my fingers into the hard contours of his chest, curling his hair around my fingers, feeling his body respond.

He rises to his feet, lifting me with him. As soon as we're upright, I fall forward onto him, roughly, holding the back of his neck with one hand and reaching for his boxers with the other. I need him now, there is no time to waste.

He lifts me from the floor, and I wrap my legs around his waist, locking them behind. With his mouth still pressed to mine, he walks forward until I'm against the wall. Then he stops. He pulls away, searching my face with his eyes. By way of an answer, I pull him back to me by the hair.

I let myself slide down until I'm resting on his erection. It presses against me, hard and insistent.

I pull my head back so hard it thunks the wall. I'm dizzy, seeing stars.

"What? What is it?" he says. His face is raw with desire, still inches from mine.

"I can't," I say. I turn my head toward the wall, hoping I won't throw up.

He leans forward, trying to kiss me again.

"No!" I bark.

He drops me as though I were radioactive. We stand staring at each other, panting.

"I don't understand," he says.

"Neither do I," I say, my lip curling into an involuntary grimace. "But this is all wrong."

"It doesn't have to be—" he says, reaching a hand into the open space between us.

"Just—Just—" I interrupt myself, flapping my hands jerkily beside my ears. "I have to go."

We're still in the stall, and I have to pass him to leave. I head for the door, looking studiously at the floorboards.

"Annemarie—" he says. He grabs my upper arm as I pass.

I stop, but I don't look at him. His grasp is gentle but firm.

He's looking at me—I can feel it. A few seconds later, he lets me go.

I run back to the house, blubbering and watching the grass pass beneath my feet.

• • •

"You're back," says Mutti. She's sitting at the kitchen table with her hands folded in front of her.

I stand just inside the door, not sure whether I should join her. "Yes," I say, wiping my eyes hastily.

Harriet scurries out from under the table, doing a dance of joy. I scoop her up. She squirms and wiggles. I turn my head, cocking it toward my shoulder to prevent her tongue from probing my ear.

"Harriet, stop that," I say, trying to offer my chin instead. Then I catch sight of Mutti. She's staring at me, her pale eyes icy.

I set Harriet down. She stands with her front paws on my feet, stamping hopefully in case I change my mind.

"When did you get back?" says Mutti.

"I don't know. Maybe twenty minutes ago."

"I didn't see your car."

"I left it at the stable."

"So you know, then," says Mutti.

"Yes. I know."

I cross the kitchen and open the fridge. There's a bottle of Liebfraumilch in the door. I pour two large glasses and join her at the table.

"I tried to stop them, you know," she says. She

rests her hands on the base of the wineglass, staring at the top of the liquid.

"I know."

She looks up quickly. "How?"

"Jean-Claude."

"Oh," she says. "So what is going on with you?"

"They let me go."

"Obviously."

"I mean, they haven't charged me with anything, but they know I dyed Hurrah. So I don't know." I down a third of my wine in one gulp. "How about you? Have you heard from the police?"

"About what?"

"About what the coroner said?"

"No," she says, continuing to stare at her hands. Finally she looks up, and apparently takes pity. "The lawyer said that if we don't hear anything in a month or two, everything is probably okay."

"You have a lawyer?"

"Dan arranged for one."

Funny, but if I'd had to lay odds on which Zimmer woman would end up needing a criminal lawyer, I would have been wrong. Twice.

• • •

The next morning, I call Minneapolis. "Roger?"

I know it's him, but it's an alternative to hello. I'm grateful beyond expression that he is the one who answered. I don't know why the sound of Sonja's voice hurts me so much, but it does, almost physically.

"Annemarie," he says. "I've been hoping you'd call."

"You were?"

"Yes. How was the drive?"

I'm rendered mute. How do I answer that? I can't tell him that I thought I'd traveled to the depths of hell and back, only to arrive home and find that my descent had just begun.

"It was fine," I say.

"Good, good . . ." he says, and then pauses. "There are a couple of things I need to tell you."

"Oh?" I say. If he tells me they're having twins, I'm going to have to kill someone.

"Good things. Don't worry," he says quickly. "First of all, someone's made an offer on the house."

"Oh," I say again.

"It's four percent below our asking price, but I think we should take it."

"Um . . . sure," I say.

"I'll fax something for you to sign."

"Okay. Fine."

"The other is Eva. I've convinced her to return to New Hampshire."

"Oh, Roger," I say. My voice cracks.

"No, wait, Annemarie. She doesn't mean for good. Yet. But she wants to go back for the funeral."

I fall mute, which he apparently mistakes for anger.

"You know how she is," he continues quickly. "She's drawn a line in the sand, and now it's a matter of pride. She doesn't want to be seen going back on her word. But it's a step in the right direction. I'm going to buy her a return ticket—but before you say anything, it's cheaper that way. Also, it will make her feel like we're taking her seriously. Then you can work on her when she gets there."

I drop my head, supporting it with my free hand.

"Okay," I say in a tiny voice. "Thank you." And then I hear myself say something else. "Roger?"

"Yes?"

"I'm sorry."

"For what?" he says, sounding confused.

"For everything," I say.

And I am. Sorrier than he'll ever know.

• • •

The day stretches interminably before me. I don't know what to do with myself. I can't go to the stable. I don't work there anymore, and anyway, I don't think I can face it now that Hurrah's gone.

The house is no better. Everything in it reminds me of Pappa—the curtained dining-room doors, the track in the ceiling. There are other things, too, reminders of his life before his illness, and these make me even sadder.

Just shy of noon, I find myself on the back porch, standing virtually unprotected in the blazing sun.

I poke a finger experimentally into the dirt of Mutti's hanging baskets, and then go in search of a watering can.

I find one under the sink. Each basket takes a full can of water before starting to leak out the bottom.

I stand back, admiring the flowers. Mutti really does have a green thumb. I'm no gardener, but even I know that petunias are difficult. Notoriously so, in fact. If you don't deadhead and prune and basically do everything but read to them daily, you'll come out one sad day and find they've gone belly up. It's usually about halfway through the summer, and their collapse is almost instant. Their limbs wilt and shrink, and their blossoms take on the texture of old skin.

Not Mutti's, though. These babies will last until October. They're gorgeous, hanging so luxuriantly they obscure the pots completely. They also reach upward, a thick mass of magenta flowers.

I start idly pinching off finished blossoms. Eventually, I take one basket down and carry it to the edge of the porch. I slide an arm through the mass of hanging flowers and lift half of it carefully over the railing. Then I rest the pot on the edge. Now I have access to the entire basket.

I'm just starting on the second basket when I see Mutti heading down the lane toward the house. I'm secretly pleased that she's going to find me doing something useful.

"What are you doing?" she says sharply when she climbs the ramp and surveys the colorful mess at my feet.

"I'm deadheading," I say, continuing to pinch.

"Those are the buds," she says.

I freeze, and look in horror at my feet. Masses of curled trumpets, so tender, so friséed they look finished, not nascent.

"Oh God, Mutti. I'm sorry. I really thought . . . Oh God, Mutti," I say helplessly.

"Never mind," she says, reaching for the handle and yanking the basket out of my grasp.

I stare at her back as she reaches up and places it

on its hook. She walks over to the other basket and examines its denuded greenery.

"I'm so sorry."

"Never mind," she says. She wipes her hands on her hips, and then turns to look at me. "Are you wearing sunscreen?"

"No," I admit.

"You will burn. Come inside."

I follow, miserable.

She starts a pot of coffee, and sits at the table waiting. I sit on the floor in the corner, stroking my recumbent dog.

Harriet still likes me. Harriet even thinks I'm useful, since I showed up with her basket.

When the coffee gurgles to a finish, Mutti rises and pours two cups. She doctors mine with cream and sugar, and then takes them to the table. Then she pats the tabletop in front of where she wants me to sit.

"So what are your plans?" she says after I've obeyed.

"What do you mean?"

"Where are you going to go?"

"When? What are you talking about?"

"To live," she says.

"I thought I'd live here," I say weakly.

"You can't. I'm selling the farm."

"You what? What did you just say?"

"I'm selling."

"You can't! You and Pappa poured your entire lives into this farm—what would Pappa say?"

"I don't have a choice, do I?"

"What do you mean?" I say, with a sinking heart.

"I cannot make the payments. I cannot keep the horses fed—"

"But—"

"—I had to sell our stocks to pay the stable hands. I have empty stalls. I have no trainer."

"What?"

Finally, Mutti stops. She looks me square in the eye. "He didn't tell you?"

"No!" I say.

And indeed he did not. Even as he was preparing to make love to me, he did not. I'm flabbergasted. "When did this happen? Why?"

"The day you returned. Because I guess this struck him as a somewhat less than ideal work situation. Because his paycheck bounced. Because he spent most of last week mucking out rather than giving lessons."

"Oh, God."

"He gave a month's notice."

"Mutti, don't sell."

"There's no way around it," she says. Her lips are pursed, her hands wrapped around her mug. She hasn't taken a single sip.

I push my coffee away and lean forward, stretching my arms out onto the table. Then I drop my head onto them. The surface of the table feels cold against my forehead.

My whole world has suddenly come unmoored. My God, if Mutti sells the farm, every home I've ever known has just—

I lift my head, blinking. My hair flops forward over my face.

"Mutti," I say quickly. I grab for her hand across

the table and hold it tightly in both of mine. "Mutti, listen to me. You don't have to sell."

She looks at our hands. She's shocked, but doesn't pull away.

I blow the hair away from my eyes, but it falls back instantly. I don't care. I have a plan.

"I'm serious. We've had an offer on the house—the house in Minneapolis. If it goes through, I'm going to have a big wad of cash. Soon. It'll be totally liquid until I do something else with it. We can use it."

"What for?" she says. She doesn't mean it the way it sounds. What she's actually saying is, What's the point?

She has regained her icy demeanor. Her hand remains in mine, but is limp and cold. She moves not a muscle.

"Because I want to. I really want to." I'm pleading now, wheedling like a kid trying to extract money before the ice cream truck passes out of range. "Please Mutti, we can do this. I want to do this. I owe you."

"You owe me nothing."

I grow increasingly desperate. "Then for Pappa. If you won't let me do it for you, let me do it for Pappa."

Mutti stares at me for a moment. Then she withdraws her hand and goes outside.

• • •

I collect Eva from the airport the next day. When I catch sight of her coming through the gate, she stops and sets her bag on the ground. I run the final steps and hug her fiercely. Her body stiffens, her arms pinned against her sides by mine.

She's not amused when she discovers that the passenger door of my car won't open.

"You can slide through the window, like the *Dukes of Hazzard*," I joke feebly, and then realize that the show's final episode probably aired years before she was born. Eva glares at me, walks around to the driver's side, and slides gracefully across the front seat.

Dinner is excruciating. We eat in the kitchen, now that it's just four of us.

Mutti's not talking to me, I'm not talking to Jean-Claude, Eva's not talking to me, and that doesn't leave a lot of room for conversation. Eventually, we give up and finish in dreadful silence. The only sounds are of cutlery clinking and food being chewed.

"May I please be excused?" asks Eva.

"Yes—" I say at the exact moment Mutti says, "Of course."

I look quickly from Eva to Mutti. Eva is staring at Mutti. Jean-Claude is watching all of us. I glare at my plate, furious.

"Thanks, Oma," Eva says pointedly. She tucks her napkin under the edge of her plate and gets up.

As soon as she leaves the room, I set my own napkin on the table and stand up.

"Where are you going? You haven't eaten a thing," says Mutti. Her voice smacks of rebuke, not concern. I look over and find her chin jutting sharply.

"I'm not hungry," I say. I turn and go out the back door. There's a pause before the screen door slams, preceded by a tiny yelp. It appears that Harriet has decided to come with me.

I head up the lane, away from the stable.

I look down at Harriet, who is struggling to keep

up. What silly little legs she has. I slow down. I have no particular agenda.

Before I'm a hundred yards away, I hear someone running behind me. I scoop Harriet under my arm and march off.

"Annemarie," says Jean-Claude, falling into step beside me.

I look sternly ahead and walk even faster.

"Annemarie," he says again, taking hold of my arm. I stop.

Still holding my arm, he turns me so that I'm facing him. "What's this about?"

"As if you don't know," I say.

"I don't," he says.

I continue to glare.

"Annemarie," he says softly. He puts a finger under my chin and lifts my face. Finally I raise my eyes to his.

"Is this about the other night?" he continues. He looks concerned, his forehead furrowed.

I turn my head to the side. "Yes."

"Did I do something wrong?"

"Well, yeah," I say in my best *Well, duh* voice.

"What?" he says.

I look at him in surprise. He really does look baffled.

"What were you going to do," I say loudly. "Take me to bed and *then* tell me you were leaving?"

He sighs as understanding dawns on his face.

"Now let's be frank here," he says, letting go of me and crossing his arms in front of him. "Who was taking who to bed?"

"Okay, I don't need this," I say, as my face starts to burn. I set Harriet down and step around him.

He catches up to me again. We walk in silence until we reach the road.

I stand staring at it, unsure what to do. In the end, I drop Harriet over one of the whitewashed fences, and climb over it myself. Jean-Claude does too, and we head across the pasture, toward the far corner of our property.

"I'm going back to Canada," he says eventually. "To Ottawa. I thought you would understand," he says.

"Why would you think that?"

"Because you also have a daughter."

"Mutti said it was because you resented mucking out last week."

"Come now," he says harshly, once again taking my arm. Harriet snarls from the ground, a vicious Vienna sausage. He looks at her in surprise, and then lets go of me.

"You know better than that. Yes, it is a mess here," he says, gesturing at the farm in general. "I cannot deny that. But it is not the main reason for my leaving."

"It's to be with Manon, then, is it?"

I watch him carefully. His face is so expressive, his personality so—I don't know what, exactly, but I'm finding it hard to stay mad at him.

"My wife—my ex—she has been having trouble with Manon. Much like you and Eva. It is kids, you know?" he says, shrugging. "But I have been watching you and Eva this summer, and . . ." He stretches his lips into a flat line, and then moves his head from side to side as though deciding whether to continue.

Perhaps he thinks he would offend me. He

wouldn't. I know I've made a hash of it. Accepting that is part of my plan for correcting it, although I can't say I'm thrilled at having become a cautionary tale.

"Well," he says, apparently deciding to leave that part of it unexpressed. "I have accepted a position at the National Equestrian Centre. It is where she trains. Manon will not be thrilled, but *c'est la vie*. It is where I should be."

"And your ex-wife?"

"We are amicable. She is relieved for some backup. We can—what is the term? 'Gang up' on her."

I try to smile, and then shake my head. "So when are you leaving?"

"I start there in a month. I told Ursula I would stay until then, if she found it useful. We are taking students again, but . . ." He lets it trail off, and I know what he means. He means that he'll help Mutti eke the last few dollars out of this place before she tallies up her final losses.

I step forward and take his upper arms in my hands. His muscles are hard, like baseballs. Harriet whimpers, confused.

"Good luck," I say. "I mean it. With everything. Especially with Manon."

A smile plays around his eyes and lips. He leans forward and kisses me, first on my left cheek, and then on my right.

We continue walking until we've gone around the property's entire perimeter. Then Jean-Claude squeezes my arm and disappears into the stable. I start down the lane, headed for my sad, lonely room in my sad, lonely house.

• • •

The phone rings as I cross the kitchen. I lunge for it, hoping it's Dan.

"Hello?" I say, clutching the receiver with both hands.

"Annemarie?" says a female voice.

"Yes?"

"It's Norma Blackley. I have good news."

"You do?" I could use some good news.

"I just got off the phone with Detective Samosa. They're indicting McCullough and four of his employees. Apparently the two they caught at your place started singing like canaries at the thought of fifteen years inside."

"What are they charging him with?"

"A list as long as your arm. Grand theft, grand theft by deception, third degree attempted theft by deception, two counts of extreme cruelty to animals—"

"Two?"

"They killed another horse after Hurrah got away. Burned it to a crisp so the vet wouldn't know the difference."

"Oh," I say, shuddering.

"The upshot is that they have bigger fish to fry than you."

"They're not going to charge me?"

"To tell the truth, I don't think they know quite what to make of you. You don't come out of this looking very good, but Dan Garibaldi's statement and the auction house records establish that you did come by the horse in the manner you claimed. That still leaves the phone call to McCullough and the dye job, but since no one in McCullough's camp has implicated you, they'd have a hard time making anything stick. In strictly legal terms, you're allowed to dye a horse as long as you don't injure the horse and you aren't doing it to aid in the commission of a crime. It would have been quite different if you had moved the horse to another property or tried to conceal his presence."

"That's exactly what I was going to do, but then all hell broke loose."

"And that is something you are never going to repeat to anyone else, ever again," Norma says firmly. "Understand?"

"Yes. I know. I won't. Look, what's next? How do I go about getting him back?"

"What, Hurrah? That's not going to happen."

"Why not? He's my horse. I got him entirely legally."

"Ownership wasn't the center's to transfer to you in the first place, so you have no claim on him."

"That's preposterous."

"It's the law. It's the same as with any other stolen property. The party who ends up buying it is simply out of luck."

"So I'll buy him from whoever does own him. Who is that?"

"That's not clear yet. He could belong to the insurance company, but if they sue McCullough for the return of the settlement, ownership might revert to him. For now, though, the horse is being kept as state's evidence."

My mind is reeling. "I'm going to call them."

"As your legal counsel, I don't recommend it."

"Why not?"

"Because your position is still shaky. You don't want to do anything to change their minds."

"I have to call them."

She sighs. I seem to have that effect on people.

"In that case, be very, very careful. Don't push them, or our next meeting might very well be at the station."

"Okay."

"And Annemarie? For God's sake, don't mention that you were planning to move Hurrah. Just don't."

"Okay," I say, feeling small and contrite.

Chapter 20

"Hey there."

Dan is standing in the doorway of Hurrah's stall, a dark outline with light spilling in around him.

"Hi," I say miserably. I'm crouching down against the back wall.

"Your mother's been looking for you," he says.

I sniff twice, and then run a finger along the lower lashes of each eye.

Dan watches me for a moment. Then he comes in and crouches against the opposite wall. We fall silent.

"I've been trying to reach you," I say after nearly a minute has passed.

"I've been busy," he says.

He's too polite to say any more than that, and I'm too exhausted to push it.

"I called the police," I say, twisting my hands.

"You did? And?"

"Same story they gave me before. Which is to imply that even though they didn't charge me I'm obviously a criminal and don't deserve to know anything."

He stares at me, eyes unreadable, and then drops his head. He seems to be studying the floor between his feet.

"I called them too," he says finally.

"And what did they tell you?"

"They said that normally they auction off confiscated property at the end of the year, but that these were special circumstances."

"Special how?"

"Well, for one thing, he's livestock. And for another, McCullough's in New Mexico, so that's where the trial will be. They might have to take Hurrah back there."

I stare at the dark grainy planks that run vertically behind him. My eyes feel like sandpaper. I blink, trying to clear them.

"It sounds like they told you a lot more than they told me," I say.

"Well, I didn't find out much that was useful either," he says. "But I did ask them to call me if anything changed."

I examine my ringless hands. I'm out of things to say.

Dan looks at his watch, and then back at me. "It's almost time to go," he says gently. "Are you ready?"

I nod wordlessly. He gets up and approaches me with both hands extended. I take them, breathe deeply, and let him pull me to my feet.

I brush the dust from my new black dress, and head for the house.

• • •

So this is what it all comes down to, is it? A box, poised above an open grave?

I haven't been to a funeral in my entire life. I'm an anomaly, I know. I foolishly expected the coffin to be lowered into the grave by pallbearers. I expected stony-faced men, three on each side, slowly letting out strap until the coffin finally reached the bottom.

Instead, my father's coffin rests on two blue straps, held snug by a rectangular device that squats around the open grave like a scaffold.

It's hard to believe that he's in there. Harder still to believe that what made him Pappa, the essence of him, is gone. Is it, really? Does it just dissolve, like a wisp of smoke? If so, how long does it take? Or is it still there, in and around his body? Is he aware of what's going on, terrified at being shut in the darkness? Shouldn't we let him out?

The priest is singing, a low, beautiful incantation: "*In paradisum deducant te Angeli; in tuo adventu suscipiant te Martyres . . .*"

I am flanked by Mutti and Eva. Dan stands grimly on the other side. There are probably three dozen other people here, which is considerably less than at the funeral mass.

I was surprised at the turnout. Mutti and Pappa were never particularly sociable—they never had dinner parties, they didn't belong to clubs, and the only family either of them has are distant cousins in Austria, but the congregation came out in full force.

" . . . *Dominus Deus Israel: quia visitavit et fecit*

redemptionem plebis suae. Et erexit cornu salutis nobis, in domo David pueri sui. Sicut locutus est . . . "

Oh God. It's going down now. My father is actually disappearing into the earth. I catch my breath, unsure whether I'm going to be able to keep myself from crying out, Stop! Stop! You're making a terrible mistake! Instead, I hold the air inside my lungs and concentrate on staying absolutely still.

The coffin continues on its way, silently, smoothly, until its burnished lid disappears from sight.

He's gone. Just like that.

I am unable to fathom this. How can someone just be gone? You know—in theory, anyway—that life is an arc. That you start out as a child, and rise until you are at your peak, and then slowly taper off again until you die. But I can't seem to apply this to Pappa.

I've seen the silvery pictures of his childhood, the fat baby with the huge smile tearing across the lawn in a cloth diaper and white baby shoes. I've seen the newspaper clippings and photographs from his heyday as a jockey. I remember him as a father: stern, silent, impossible to please. How instead of praise, he'd give me a single kiss on the forehead if I managed to do something right. I remember him knocking on my door before dawn, clapping his hands and shouting that it was time to get started. In the middle of the day I had a three-hour break to do schoolwork with my tutor, but other than that I was on horseback all day long. I rode until I could barely walk back to the house, one horse after another. I was miserable, I was lonely. I felt like I was living under an enormous black cloud that shut out the sun.

Until Harry. Harry changed everything. For the

first time, I was passionate about what I was doing. The problem was in getting me *off* the horse, not on. But by then Pappa was no longer around to terrorize me. By then, he'd sent me off to train with Marjory.

I feel ashamed now at how happy I was that my parents sent me away. Marjory worked me hard, hard, hard, but she also heaped praise on me. I wanted to please her. I adored her. I felt like a released convict. My life at Marjory's was nothing but blue skies, rolling horizons, and one enormous striped horse. Are other kids as desperate to get away from home? Probably not, but damn it, he was really hard on me. And that's what baffles me the most as I stand here by his grave: how did Pappa the Drill Sergeant turn into the older Pappa, the man who defended me against Mutti? The man who defended Eva against me when I found her tattoo?

I stare at the gaping earth.

"*. . . misericordiam cum patribus nostris: et memorari testamenti sui sancti*," says the priest. He looks around solemnly, and then switches to English. "I am the resurrection and the life: he that believed, in Me, although he be dead, shall live: and every one that liveth and believeth in Me shall not die forever."

God, I hope so. I don't believe it, but I hope so. Maybe that thought in itself dooms me to eternal death. I can't help it, though. I don't think I have it in me to believe.

We're supposed to recite the Lord's Prayer now. Silently, but we're supposed to think it in unison. I begin, falteringly, and then find I can't continue.

Possessed by I don't know what, I reach out and take Mutti's hand. As my hand crosses the space between us, I bite my lip, afraid that she'll brush my hand away. But when she feels me groping, she grasps my hand like a leg-hold trap. Her cold bony fingers close so tightly around mine that her rings cut my flesh. I hold my breath and close my eyes.

When I open them again, the priest is leaning over and taking a handful of dirt. He swings his fist forward in an elegant arc, releasing a few grains of earth into the open grave. The sound of it hitting the top of the coffin is almost more than I can bear.

"*Memento homo quia pulvus es et in pulverem reverteris*," he says, moving his hand back and forth two more times.

I close my eyes again, feeling unsteady. Although the world stops spinning, I'm still nauseous, afraid I might faint. I've done it before. I know how it feels. If I did faint, would I fall into the grave? How would they get me out?

Mutti tightens her grip on my fingers, and the pain makes me wince. With anybody else, I'd just shift my hand, silently suggesting a new configuration. But with Mutti, I'm afraid she'll let go.

Maybe if I focus on the pain, it will help me stay conscious. I'm still pondering this when I feel Eva's warm hand slip into mine on the other side. I gasp, and suddenly hope that the service isn't over.

• • •

The mood at the reception is not nearly as mournful as I expected. It's not exactly jovial, but you hear the occasional laugh, muted out of respect. I suppose it's a stepping stone, a midpoint to help you ease away from the grief of the funeral.

The house is full of people. They stand or sit in groups of three or four, holding drinks and small plates of food. The food appeared with the guests. I don't know what it is about death that makes people cook, but casseroles and cakes and spinach dips in hollowed-out granary loaves started coming into the house, and now every surface in the kitchen is full.

Other than Mutti and Eva, the only people I know are Dan, Jean-Claude, and the stable hands.

I hold a drink and a plate, although I am neither eating nor drinking. I clutch them as protection, after having my hand grasped by strangers more times than I can stand. If I hear one more person say "I'm sorry," I might have to scream and throw my plate out a window.

I wander down the hall to the living room and stop in the doorway. Eva is sitting on the couch. Luis is beside her, holding her hand.

"Annemarie."

A woman I've never met appears in front of me. "I'm so sorry for your loss," she says, reaching out and giving my arm an encouraging squeeze.

"Thank you," I say, looking past her, or rather over the top of her head. Dan is kneeling in front of Eva, is talking earnestly. She nods, and looks up at him.

"It was a lovely service. I'm sure he would have appreciated it," says the tiny woman in front of me. "And Ursula is holding up so well, poor thing. Such a sad business."

I look down at her. She's older, her hair dyed into a stiff blonde mass. Her face is an unnatural pinky-rose color, somehow spongy and powdery at the same time. There are deep vertical lines running from her upper lip to the bottom of her nose. Her lipstick has bled into them.

I turn my head. From where I'm standing, I can see straight through the hallway to the kitchen.

"My husband has been dying to meet you," the woman continues. "Oh, I'm so sorry—" she says, clapping a jeweled hand over her mouth. "I didn't mean that. But Anton spoke of you so often. He was so proud of you. Ernie and I remember when you used to compete, and that was before we even knew your parents. We used to see pictures of you in *Sport Horse Illustrated*, on that spectacular Hanoverian. So you see, we've known of you for a long time." She takes my elbow, tugging it gently. "Come meet him. He's right over—"

I start to walk. All I can think of is getting away from this woman and her husband Ernie, of making it to the back door before I blow up. A few feet into the hallway, I ditch the plate on the telephone table. As I pass the staircase, I reach through the railing and set my drink on a stair.

My need to get out is overwhelming, all-encompassing. I have the sense that I'm walking through a tunnel, and the sides are closing in on me. People's faces keep popping in front of me, distorted, as though I'm viewing them through a fish-eye lens. I don't stop, so they all disappear, and I'm glad, because if they didn't, I think I'd just stretch my arms out and shove them aside.

As soon as I'm outside, I can breathe again, although I don't dare stop. I'm afraid someone will take that as an invitation to follow me.

Halfway to the stable, I reach down and take off

my shoes. My sheer nylons are no protection from the gravel, so I move over to the grass, watching carefully for thistles.

I have to cross a bit of crushed stone and I tiptoe gingerly, as though walking on lava. When I finally reach the stable, the cement floor feels cold and smooth.

These stockings cost a fortune—they're a shimmery black that I bought because the sample puff on the rack felt like water in my fingers. I splurged for two pairs, convinced I would put a run in the first pair just getting them on. I should remove them before they're ruined, but I don't have much use for black stockings. My colors are blues: periwinkle and indigo, robin's egg and cobalt. I've only had one other black outfit in my entire life.

I had just started at InteroFlo. I was going to my first departmental meeting, and wanted to come across as serious, no-nonsense, the consummate professional. I wore a fitted skirt and soft ribbed turtleneck, both black as night. I felt sleek and streamlined, like a cat burglar, or an artist in a loft. Later on, I went to the washroom and found a green lollipop stuck to my shoulder, planted there by Eva as she clung desperately to me in the morning. And why was Eva sucking a lollipop at eight in the morning? Because she wanted to wear her winter boots in July, and I needed to get to work. Besides, she'd had a healthy breakfast.

I stop at Hurrah's stall, and then walk past. I also stop at Harry's stall, which hardly even feels like Harry's stall anymore. It feels like Bergeron's, although soon he will be leaving, too. If Hurrah were here, I'd move him into it the second it was empty. It's the prime stall, the best real estate in the place.

I'm sitting in the lounge when Dan appears in the doorway.

"Hey," he says. "You okay?"

"I don't know," I say. I'm slouched on the faded green couch, staring blankly through the window. My bare feet are on the table in front of me, crossed at the ankles. My Italian leather shoes sit in a heap in the corner, on top of my crumpled stockings.

Dan steps forward, surveying all.

"Do me a favor, will you?" I say quickly. "Lock the door."

He stops. "Do you mean with me in or out?"

"In," I say.

He looks relieved. He shuts the door and depresses the button in the middle of the knob with a click. Then he joins me on the couch, sitting so close our hips are touching. A moment later, he reaches over and takes my hand, pulling it into his lap.

He doesn't say a word. He just sits holding my hand, and I am grateful for the silence. After a few minutes, I drop my head onto his shoulder.

"I saw you talking to Eva," I say.

"Yes, and I think you'll find what she had to say very interesting."

"What's that?" I straighten up and turn to face him.

"She asked me what courses she would need to take to get into vet school. She also asked me if she could continue helping out at the center over the winter."

I stare at him, letting this sink in.

"Oh Dan . . ." I say, suddenly overcome. My eyes

grow moist. "Oh Dan," I say again before dissolving into tears.

He pulls me forward, holds me tight. I want to melt into him, and stay like this forever. I can feel strength flowing from his body to mine.

It's not long before I find myself running a hand tentatively along his arm and shoulder—gingerly, in an exploratory fashion. After a moment, I look up at him. His blue eyes are so intense it takes my breath away.

I kiss him, and he responds instantly. His lips are warm and full, his face smooth. He puts his hands on either side of my face, kissing me so tenderly I'm afraid I might melt.

I lean back and unzip my dress. He stares at me.

"Annemarie," he says.

"Shh," I say, wiggling out of the top half of my dress.

He glances down at my breasts, pale mounds in a black lace bra, and then back at my face. He looks quickly at the window. "Can anyone see in?"

"Not unless they're on a horse," I say.

There's probably a tenth circle of hell reserved for people like me, people who make love just hours after burying their father. But nothing has ever felt so right—his naked body stretched out along mine feels like a homecoming, a final piece in the puzzle.

Afterward, we lie in a lazy tangle of limbs on the couch. He is stretched against the back of it, and I am stretched against him, my leg thrown wantonly over his. He strokes my skin with the very ends of his fingers, from shoulder to hip and then back again. He traces the scar on my abdomen, the outline of my breast, my raised nipple. Then he leans forward and plants a breathy kiss in my ear.

"You're incredibly—"

There's a noise. We both freeze, and then scramble onto our elbows, trying to see out the window.

Eva has led Bergeron into the arena and is preparing to mount. She has one foot in the stirrup, and is gathering the reins in her left hand. Then she grabs the pommel, and next thing I know, she's sitting in the saddle.

Dan wraps his arms around me and rolls us onto the floor. I land on top of him. My heart pounds wildly.

"Oh my God," I say, clapping a hand to my mouth. My fingers are trembling wildly.

"Shh," whispers Dan. His mouth is right by my ear.

I look over at our clothes. It's hopeless. There's no way to get to them.

"Jesus Christ, Dan—what are we going to do?"

Dan continues to hold me. Then he lifts his hips and scootches both of us over until we're against the wall, directly under the window.

"We can't do anything," he says, once we're there.

"Can she see us? What if—"

Dan rolls me over so that I'm wedged between him and the wall. Then he lays a finger on my lips. "She can't see us. But we're stuck here until she leaves."

I glance up at the window, still desperate.

"Don't worry. She can't see us. I promise you. It's impossible." He leans up against me, pressing me against the wall. His breath is moist and warm. "Look on the bright side," he says. "There are worse places to be trapped."

His body feels so good against mine, so warm and solid, that despite the peculiar circumstances I relax into him. Incredibly, I feel a stirring against my naked hip.

"Dan!" I say, shocked.

He moves my hair aside with his fingertips and touches his tongue to my ear.

"Mmmm," I say, shivering.

"I love you, Annemarie Zimmer."

"Oh Dan," I say.

"You don't have to say anything back," he says, still whispering. "I just wanted to tell you that."

I am choked with emotion, my eyes full of tears.

"Oh Dan," I say as he rearranges me into a position more receptive of his intentions. "I love you too. Oh, I do, I do, I do."

• • •

Later that night, Mutti and I sit facing each other in the winged armchairs. She kneels down to light the gas fire, despite the fact that it's August, and then turns out all the lights.

The guests have long since gone—even those who stayed behind to help clean up and pack the food. Eva has gone to bed, pleading exhaustion. Before she did, she stood on tiptoe and kissed me on the cheek.

Mutti and I sip Jägermeister from cut-lead crystal, neither of us speaking. After today's events, we are grateful for the silence.

I'm sitting sideways in my chair, with a leg thrown over the arm. I'm playing with my glass, holding it in front of me and trying to catch the flames in its facets.

Mutti tips hers upside down, draining the last drops into her mouth.

"Do you want another?" she says, rising.

"No thanks, Mutti," I say, continuing to rotate my glass in front of me. "You go ahead, though."

She walks over to the collection of crystal decanters that she set out for the reception and pours herself a tiny second. Then she returns to her seat.

"Mutti?"

"Yes?"

"I was serious about using the house money to bail out the farm."

"You don't need to do that."

"Well, yes, I do, actually."

Mutti stares at me for a very long time. "It's because you are feeling guilty."

"No, it's not."

"Yes it is. You don't owe him this. He loved you, and he knew that you loved him. That is all."

"He did?" I ask. Tears fill my eyes, spilling over before I have a chance to check them.

"Of course, *Liebchen*."

"Did he ever forgive me?"

"For what?" she says. "What nonsense is this?"

"For never riding again?"

Mutti stares at me in horror.

"No, I'm serious. I know I broke his heart. I know—"

Mutti shakes her head and lifts a hand, signaling

me to stop. "Pappa loved you. He was disappointed, yes, but he never blamed you."

"But all those years we barely spoke . . ."

"You could not bear to be with us."

"That's because I was ashamed of what I'd become."

Mutti is silent for a moment, weighing this. "We were hard on you. Harder than we should have been, I think. It was because you had such opportunities . . ." She shakes her head. "We thought that if we encouraged you, then you would find another horse. That you could still make it. I don't know. Perhaps we were wrong."

I can't believe I'm hearing this, am afraid to speak in case I break the spell.

"Your father," she continues. "He wanted so much for you to have a career in riding. I know he pushed, but it seemed for the best. After all, you advanced so quickly . . ." Mutti pauses, tapping a finger repeatedly on her lips. "If we were wrong, then may God forgive us, but we thought we were doing the right thing. You were so good. It seemed a waste of God-given talent. And we thought you would be happy."

"I could have been, I think."

"You found your own way in the end," she says.

"No, I never did. I mean, I've done things, one after another, my whole life. But I've never exactly found my way. I've never found anything that made me feel the way I did when I was riding Harry. That's why I think I went a little bit nuts when Hurrah turned up. It seemed like a second chance. I don't know. It does sound crazy, doesn't it?"

I stop for a moment, afraid that if I don't, I'll cry. Mutti sips her drink and waits.

"I still want to use the money for the farm." Another pause, as I grope for words. I'm not sure how to make her understand. "It's not because of Pappa. It's because of us. All of us. You, me, and Eva. Listen," I shift to the edge of my seat, gathering steam. "I don't want to leave here. What am I supposed to do? Go back to Minneapolis? I'd rather move to Iqualuit. And anyway, there's a horse I want to get for Eva. She's talking about going back to school and working at the center. The last thing she needs is more upheaval. Me either. Or you. No, the only sensible thing is to stay here. You can manage the stable, I'll teach."

"You can't teach," she says dismissively.

"Why not?" I can't keep the hurt out of my voice. "I was riding at the FEI four-star level at—"

"I know all that," says Mutti, cutting me off with an irritated wave. "I was there, remember? But how can you teach if you don't ride?"

"So I'll ride."

She turns quickly, staring at me as though I've completely lost my mind.

"What? What are you looking at me like that for?"

Mutti's forehead twitches, but she doesn't say a thing.

"What's so crazy about that? I'm not offering to compete again."

"All these years, you've gotten angry at the mere suggestion—"

"Yeah, but it's different now. Things are different." I pause, wondering how to explain to her that my entire world has shifted, that staying here now means everything to me. That I see my future here, and Eva's, and I'm willing to fight for it. That I can't stand the thought of losing Dan. That I really do want to start riding again, have been itching for it, dreaming about it at night.

In the end, I decide I can't explain it. The only thing I can do is show her.

Chapter 21

"Keep your heels down, Malcolm."

The microphone isn't working, and I've shouted my way through the last three lessons. By the end of the day, I'll have no voice at all. "More. Still more. Try bringing your toes up instead."

Razzmatazz is incredibly patient. This kid's hands and legs are flapping about impossibly, and Tazz still gives it to him on a platter. No wonder Pappa loved him so much.

"That's it. Much better. Now think about your arms. Bring your elbows back. I want a straight line from your elbow to the bit . . . Good . . . Good . . . Okay, now cross at the diagonal. Give me a half-halt at the corner, and then start the canter. And watch your lead."

Halfway across the arena, Malcolm's arms start bouncing again, and his legs shoot forward, toes down.

"Come on, Malcolm. You're riding a horse, not a Harley."

The kid shoots me an appreciative grin.

"Face forward!" I bark.

Teaching is much more fun than I ever anticipated. I feel like an actor, slipping into persona. I am demanding yet patient, strict yet forgiving, inspiring and entertaining—or so I like to think. I push my students to give me their best, and tell them when I think I'm not getting it. I also make damn sure to tell them when I am.

My approach seems to be working, because we have a full retinue of students again. Under Mutti's management, our stalls are full, and I'm teaching eight, sometimes nine lessons a day.

Malcolm faces forward and adjusts his arms and legs, temporarily, into the correct form. He reaches the corner, and tightens the reins. After a tiny pause, Tazz starts off at an easy canter on the correct lead.

Which would all be very well if Malcolm had gotten around to asking for it. All he did was shorten his reins, and Tazz predicted what was coming next. Next time I'll put him on Malachite. No one ever accused Malachite of being accommodating.

"Door!" someone shouts.

I swing around, checking to see where Tazz is. He's in the far corner, cantering with glazed eyes. Malcolm is bouncing out of the saddle with every stride.

"Come on in," I yell.

Eva enters, leading Flicka on a looped purple lunge line. Everything she has for Flicka is purple: halter, fly sheet, lead rope—even a show sheet, which I suppose is her way of telling me that she plans to start showing Flicka in halter classes. I imagine they'll do other shows too, later, and I have mixed feelings about that. I want to be careful not to push her, but I also don't want to hold her back. It's a tricky business, parenting.

"Hey, babe," I call. "You done your homework?"

"Yes, Mom. Of course, Mom," she intones in a God-you're-tiresome voice. She leads Flicka toward me.

Flicka is a fine little horse, a grand little horse, and as pretty as they come. A typical Arab, spirited and playful, but without a mean bone in her body. There's no question that when the time comes she'll be fun under the saddle.

Dan brought her over on Eva's first day of school, which was nearly two months ago. When Eva came home and saw Flicka in the paddock, she burst into tears and hugged me so violently I fell backward onto the gravel. I smelled smoke in her hair, but there was no way in hell I was going to ruin that moment. They've made enormous progress together, and I'm so proud of Eva my heart could burst.

"Can I lunge her in this end?" Eva asks as she trudges past.

"Yes, just keep your circle small enough that you don't get in Tazz's way."

"You got it," she says. She keeps walking, dragging the long whip on the ground behind her. Then she stops and turns back to me. "Hey, Ma, did you see the magazine that came today?"

How could I not? Mutti left it on the kitchen table. She didn't need to leave it open at the article. Ian McCullough and Hurrah were splashed all over the cover, stretched out in descent from an enormous water jump. The picture was taken in Atlanta, during the 1996 Summer Olympics.

"Yes," I say, turning away. "Malcolm! Bring him to a walk now. Once around the arena, and then halt and cross your stirrups in front of you."

Malcolm knows what's coming, and looks at me in horror. Posting without stirrups is something none of my students enjoys. I don't admit to them that I was never any good at it either. In fact, I don't know anyone who is good at it, but I don't see any reason to tell the students that. It's a rite of passage. They can learn the truth once they're in the fold.

"So did you read it?"

Eva is still standing behind me, so I turn to face her. Flicka swings her black head around, nuzzling Eva's belly.

"No, I didn't have time," I say.

"Ian McCullough made a deal. Four years. There isn't even going to be a trial."

I blink two or three times. Four years? The prosecutor had been going for fifteen, and that's the least the bastard deserves. Four years is nothing. He'll probably be out in three. If it were a perfect world, someone would strap him into his car by his head and then set it on fire, like he did to Hurrah.

I turn around. "Okay, Malcolm. Start trotting now. Sit once around, and then start posting."

Malcolm's heels lift a couple of inches from Tazz's sides, and then drop against them.

Oh dear. We're a long way from *descente de main, et descente de jambe*.

I peer over my shoulder, checking to see where

Eva is. I see with relief that she has taken Flicka to the far end of the arena.

I can't bear to talk about Hurrah, and Eva knows it. Usually she respects it, but I guess this news was big enough that she couldn't help herself.

I had planned to fly out for the trial, despite Norma's protestations. Throughout all of this, she has urged me to keep a low profile, which I find hard to balance with my need to find Hurrah. I can't simply let him go, and Lord knows I've tried not to—I called twice a week religiously for eight weeks, but not once would anyone tell me anything useful. Dan continued to call after I gave up—and I think still does, although he's stopped mentioning it. Hurrah is lost, trapped inside some bureaucratic labyrinth. We don't even know what state he's in, although maybe that will change now that there won't be a trial.

I jump, surprised by the vibration against my left buttock. It's my cell phone, which is set to vibrate so that if I'm riding, it won't spook the horse. At least, that's the theory. I still haven't been able to bring myself to ride. I pull the phone from my pocket and press it to my ear.

"Yeah?" I say.

" 'Yeah?' " says Mutti. "What kind of greeting is 'yeah'?"

"Sorry, Mutti. I'm in the middle of a lesson."

"Fine. I'll be quick. I just got back to the office. Dan left a message. He thinks he'll probably make it home today and wants to come over."

"Cool. Do you know when?"

"He hopes around dinnertime, but it will depend on traffic. He's got at least five more hours of driving."

"Great. Thanks for letting me know. Oh, Mutti?"

"Yes?"

"Um, could you do me a favor?"

"What?"

"Could you make your gâteau des crêpes?"

"Oh, Annemarie." She makes a great show of sounding irritated, but she's not. It's important to her that we all love her food. Otherwise, why would she have branched out into French cooking?

"Please?" I say.

She sighs, a long and protracted exhalation. "Yes, all right," she says. She sounds stern, but I'll bet you any money she's smiling.

• • •

Dan's timing couldn't be better. For one thing, maybe Eva will finally shut up, and for another, he manages to arrive just as I'm tossing the salad.

I look like a vision in my blue silk dress, and the salad provides just a soupçon of domesticity. The dress is wildly inappropriate for the season, silk and sleeveless, but he's been gone for four days, and I want to look nice.

Dan sweeps into the room, leaving the door wide open. "How are all my favorite ladies?" he booms. I'm about to tell him to close the door—it is early November, and I have bare arms—but it's too late. He's already making his rounds. He goes first to Mutti and stops beside her. She smiles and cocks her head. He kisses her cheek.

"Hi Dan," says Eva, closing her magazine. She's been torturing me for nearly ten minutes, reading the article on Bastard McCullough aloud.

Dan comes up behind me and plants a kiss on the base of my neck. Just before he pulls away, he takes a tiny piece of my flesh between his teeth. I gasp as all my hair stands on end.

I wiggle sideways and look quickly at Eva, wondering if she saw. It's hard to tell. She's smiling broadly, but staring at the table.

"How was the conference?" I say, safely beyond Dan's reach.

"What conference?" he says.

I balance the salad tongs against the side of the bowl and carry it to the table. "The one you were just at," I say.

"I wasn't at a conference," he says.

I set the bowl on the table, and turn to face him. He is staring at me, trying to look normal. It's not working. He's blinking too much.

"What are you talking about?" I say.

"I wasn't at a conference."

"You said you were."

"I lied."

I stare at him. "Dan, tell me what's going on."

Nobody moves, not a muscle. Mutti has turned from the sink and is watching me closely. Eva is staring as though at a train wreck.

"So where were you then?"

"Santa Fe," he says.

I'm frowning, shaking my head. I don't understand.

Dan steps behind me, takes hold of my shoulders, and steers me toward the door.

I know before we even get there. I know the second Dan takes hold of me, although I don't believe it until I'm actually looking at him through the screen.

He's fat, he's sleek, and he's striped again. He's in the pasture, ripping up grass as though he's never been gone, swishing his long tail from side to side.

I clap a hand to my mouth, unsure whether I'm going to scream or cry. "Oh, Dan," I say. "Oh, Dan."

I spin around. Eva shrieks happily, and claps her hands. Mutti brings her hands to her face, almost in a gesture of prayer. They all knew. Every one of them.

I look through the screen again. He's beautiful. He's gorgeous. He's shiny, sleek, and groomed.

Dan comes up behind me. "So do you forgive me?"

"Forgive you?"

"I mean for losing him for you in the first place."

I choke back a sob and turn to him, throwing my arms around his neck. After a moment, I let go, wiping my eyes and nose on my arm.

"How did you do it? How did you get him?"

"Police auction."

"How did you find out? I mean, I've been trying for months . . ."

I lean my forehead against the glass, staring in disbelief. "He looks great. I mean, really, really wonderful."

"They were boarding him at a local stable. I understand he was something of a favorite."

"How much did you get him for?"

"You don't want to know."

"Yes, I do."

"Almost nothing."

I'm offended. "Why?"

"Perhaps because he has degenerative joint disease and only one eye?"

Dan looks into my eyes, and realizes I don't see

the humor in this. "Because the only other person bidding was a dealer, and he couldn't bid above what he would have gotten from a slaughterhouse."

"Oh, Dan," I say, horrified. "What if you'd been outbid? You should have told me about it." The idea of Hurrah ending up in the kill pen again is inconceivable.

"I didn't want to tell you in case it didn't work out. And being outbid was not going to be a problem. Your mother authorized an obscene amount."

I look from Mutti to Dan, and then back again, speechless with gratitude. I feel physically overwrought, as though someone were wringing out my heart.

"So here he is, and he's yours. Legally this time. Well, actually, he's mine legally, but if you're nice to me, maybe I'll transfer ownership to you."

I stand blinking, unable to speak.

"So, you going to ride him?" asks Dan.

"Of course."

Dan laughs. "Go on, then."

"Not now. He just got here. He needs a day or two to get settled."

"Yup. Because you can see he's all emaciated and stressed," says Dan.

Mutti goes to the oven and peers in the door. "Eva, set the table please."

I pull on one of my paddock boots. "You guys get started. I'll be along in a minute."

I expect Mutti to argue with me, but when I turn to grab my other boot, she's coming toward me. "Here," she says, holding out an apple.

I trip twice on my way to the pasture, because I

can't take my eyes off Hurrah. I'm afraid he'll disappear, like a vision of water on a hot road. When I get to the fence, I hitch my blue silk up with one hand and climb over. I must be the picture of elegance, tromping through the long grass in my rubber boots and bare legs.

Hurrah raises his head, staring at me as I approach. Then he snorts, swinging his head up and down.

I laugh, and reach for him, grateful when my hand meets cool, smooth coat. I try to run my hand across his shoulder, but he's seen what's in my other hand, and turns to reach for it. He takes the apple in his teeth, spraying droplets of juice over both of us.

When he finishes, I lean forward, sliding my arms around his neck. I close my eyes and press my face against his muscled neck, running my hands along both sides of it and then down his chest, seeking the cowlick. I know this body. I know it frontward and backward and with my eyes shut.

When I open my eyes, Hurrah is looking at me quizzically. He swivels his ears, and then presses his muzzle against my hips, unaware that dresses don't have pockets.

I cup his muzzle in both hands, feeling the cool velvet of his lips, and the firm, fluted curves of his nostrils, the in and out of hot breath on my open palms.

I look back at the house. Mutti, Dan, and Eva are standing at the door, looking through the screen.

"They want me to ride you, you know," I say to Hurrah. I reach up and grab one of his ears in my hand, and then let it slide slowly through my fist.

Then I straighten his forelock, smoothing it neatly down the center of his forehead. "How would you like that? You want me to ride you?"

Hurrah turns and snorts wetly. I look down at my dress, which is now completely destroyed.

"Yeah, you're right," I say softly. "There's time for that later."

Hurrah is losing interest now that it seems I'm out of apples. He checks once more and rubs his head up and down my front, further desecrating the silk. Then he drops his head and starts to graze.

I lean against him, resting my arms and chin on his back. I stand like this until the last bit of sun disappears beneath the horizon, casting floss-pink streaks across the sky.

When I head back to the house, there's a hiccup in my heart, a peculiar feeling I cannot identify. My hands are freezing and I'm trembling with the cold, but it's more than that. There's something running through my veins, welling up from the core of me.

It's as though the ground has shifted, and the chasm closed. This horse is not Harry and I am not the girl who rode him. There are no Olympics in our future, but I don't care. At this moment, I am all I want to be.

I stop, perplexed. I examine it a little, and toss it about in my head, testing its consistency. I poke it, and it pokes back. Is this what it feels like? Yes, by God, it is. It's contentment, and I'm so full of it I almost don't know what to do.

• • •

It's night, and I'm standing at the entrance of the stable, illuminated only by what spills around the corner from the parking lot floods.

I unlatch the main door and slide it open. There's a fluttering in my chest, and my breath is coming fast. I am giddy and excited, and filled with a sense of purpose. I've been working toward this moment for twenty years.

I step into the stable, pausing to breathe the fragrant horsy air. I'm tempted to go see him first, just to say hello, but am afraid I might lose my nerve. Instead I slip into the narrow hall that separates the aisles.

I flick on the light, suppressing a cough. The air is sharp with hay dust from the loft above. Particles float lazily among the saddles.

There are probably twenty burnished tack chests lined up against the walls, some covered with quilted, monogrammed covers. Above them are rows of saddle racks, sporting English saddles of all shapes and sizes—dressage, jumping, general purpose, even saddleseat. There are shelves stacked with freshly laundered saddle pads, fly sheets, and leg wraps. Round rubber bell boots shoved up against the wall. Grooming kits, set on top of boxes. Pastern boots spread open to dry. Bridles, halters, and chaps hanging from hooks.

I start to walk, slowly, looking from side to side. About halfway down the hall, I find a pair of schooling chaps that looks about right. I pull them from their hook and hold them against me, checking for size.

I step into them and lean over to gather the open flaps around my legs. One zip, and then another, and my legs are encased in leather. I press the snaps shut and straighten up.

I take a deep breath because my heart is pounding, and then continue walking.

I stop to scrutinize a saddle. I picture the slope of his back, and move on. A few steps later, I see a Passier dressage saddle, black, with a sixteen-and-a-half-inch seat and an extra-wide tree.

I crouch down and peer through the gullet. Then I straighten up and curl my fingers around the cool leather of the pommel. It's nice and high, and will clear his withers easily. I take the stirrup in my fingers and run the iron down, savoring the slapping sound as I pull the leather through it. Then I pull it into my armpit. With my other arm, I reach for the saddle. My fingertips just reach—I may not even have to adjust the length of the stirrups.

There's a bridle on the hook above the saddle. I finger the bit. It's a slow twist snaffle—I'd have preferred an egg-butt, but this will do.

My heart is pounding so hard I can hear it in my ears, a great whooshing machine. I hang the bridle over my left shoulder, and then lift the saddle so that it's resting along my right forearm. With my free hand, I grab a saddle pad and head for the aisle.

I hang the bridle on the door of the opposite stall. The horse inside shifts, and I see a flash of gray face through the bars. Then I swallow my breath and turn.

I cross the aisle like a cadet, in three long strides. As I lay my hand on the latch, I pause, frozen by doubt. Then I throw the bolt and slide the door along its track.

I stand in the doorway, watching my breath in the cold night air. The saddle is heavy on my jutting hip, and as Hurrah comes into focus I wonder if I'm ready for this. Twenty years. Twenty years, and I just don't know.

"Are you ready?" I ask Hurrah.

He turns and snorts, and I burst out laughing, because it's suddenly clear that I've never been so ready in all my life.